The Dead

Months

Steve Chambers

Zymurgy Publishing

First published in Great Britain in 2024 by Zymurgy
Publishing, Newcastle upon Tyne UK

ISBN 978-1-903506 52-3

Printed and bound by Ashford Press, Hampshire, UK
10 9 8 7 6 5 4 3 2 1

Author details

STEVE CHAMBERS was born and brought up in Nottingham. He read mathematics at Imperial College, London and now divides his time between North-East England and the South-West where he writes and walks. An award-winning dramatist, Steve has written for all the dramatic media. For TV, he has written for 'Casualty' and 'Byker Grove' and his feature film 'Hold Back the Night' starring Sheila Hancock opened Critics Week at the Cannes Film Festival. He adapted 'Robinson Crusoe', 'The Grapes of Wrath' and Graham Swift's 'Waterland' for BBC Radio 4. His successful BBC Radio 4 sitcom 'Highlites' (co-written with 'Shameless writer Phill Nodding) ran to six series as well as a theatre spin-off. His first novel, 'GLADIO – We Can Neither Confirm Nor Deny' - was also published by Zymurgy Publishing.

Acknowledgements

I am grateful to the following for their support and encouragement.

I'd like to thank Richard Thomas for relating his experiences as a Royal Marine in Northern Ireland as well as his technical expertise in all things military.

Thanks are due to Dr Chris Russell talking to me about electronic detection devices for biological markers and for showing me a dust-free 'clean room' at Leeds University.

Thanks are also due to Greg King for his invaluable assistance with the cover image.

I am indebted to all those who responded to manuscript drafts, in particular Ross Irvine for his important strategic suggestions and to my partner, Lesley Brooks, for her detailed notes and suggestions.

I would like to thank my fellow ramblers for walking in isolated locations in all weathers. Without them, the idea would not have arisen.

Finally, I am indebted to my publisher, Martin Ellis, for his hard work, persistence and determination.

Stars, hide your fires;

Let not light see

My black and deep desires

William Shakespeare

November 1986
Ulster

Observation Post (OP)

Bobby Evans put down his binoculars, grabbed his backside through his combat pants and rubbed vigorously. 'Jesus, I've got something seriously wrong with my rear entrance.'

'Most blokes would call it their exit,' Tony grinned.

'Piss off, Tony,' Evans barked.

'Keep your voices down!' Matt whispered angrily.

'Sorry Corp. but it's driving me crazy,' Evans said, rubbing again.

'I don't want to hear any more about your piles,' Matt hissed.

'Maybe it isn't piles. Maybe it's something else, something worse. They won't stop itching, and there are swellings. What d'you think, Tony?'

'How would he know?' Matt asked.

'I could always give you a physical examination,' Tony offered deadpan.

'Do you think that might help?'

'Sure. I might have to use my bayonet, though. Wouldn't want to get too close to your naked arse.'

Matt chuckled; Evans winced.

'I just need a decent crap; those k-rations are doing me in.'

'Shut up, will you?' Matt whispered.

'How much longer is this going on, Corp?'

'I don't know. Now get back to your bleeding job.'

Evans scowled and settled back down to look through his binoculars.

Six bloody days they'd been there, in November for God's sake, shivering in the sodden grass, peeing into a bottle, shitting

1

in a bag, going without hot food or drink just in case something important happened. Nobody ever volunteered for OP duty, but it didn't matter; this was why they were there, according to the lieutenant in charge, some red-cheeked public school Jeremy not much older than Tony. There were three troopers and a corporal in their brick, each rotating the duties. That morning, Tony was on guard, Corporal Matt Hardwick and Evans were gathering intel and Terry Roberts was asleep. They were cold, filthy, hungry, and bored out of their skulls. The other two bricks in their multiple were presumably watching the farm from a different POV or watching something else, somewhere else. It didn't matter. Their world had shrunk to this wet hollow in a grove of stunted oaks overlooking a suspect farm in bandit country. Situated at the end of a blind, upland valley reached by a rutted track, the farm was about as isolated as it was possible to be. Surrounded by hills and trackless moorland, there was nothing except heather, bog, and the wind. In the time they'd been there, they'd seen the farmer and his two dogs come and go, but that was about it. The dogs were a worry, but the four soldiers were well hidden, high above in a fold in the valley side.

'I mean, what's so special about this farm?' Evans said as he adjusted his position.

'Not many sheep,' Tony said, scanning the hillside behind.

'Eh?'

'A farm with no animals is suspicious, so it is,' Matt said gruffly.

'Maybe they're all inside the barn,' Evans said, settling down again. 'Wish I bloody was.'

Evans was the grumbler, Terry the joker, Matt was a bear, an Ulsterman who said little, and Tony was the clever one, which in his unit meant he liked reading. At twenty-four, he still enjoyed soldiering, but he'd begun to tire of the endless blind obedience. Nobody ever asked why, and that had started to bother him. Books were his escape, and he devoured them voraciously whenever he got the opportunity. That was another thing he hated about OP duty. They had to hump everything in on foot, and that meant minimum kit and no books. After six days and nights, they could cheerfully have killed each other. If it wasn't Evans going on about his arse, it was Terry whistling that damn tune. They hated the song, yet they all found themselves humming it because of Terry and his awful 'Hits of the Seventies' cassette that he'd played incessantly before their current deployment. There was a lot of decent music, so why did he have to fixate on that? Terry blamed Billy, the Jack Russell stray, who had adopted the patrol and followed them around for a few weeks as summer waned into autumn. Billy was first into the Lynx helicopter when the patrol left and first out when they landed. The lads enjoyed having him around, and Billy clearly liked them until the patrol swapped their Lynx for a Sea King. It was a hot, late September day, and everyone was sweating like pigs in their kit, so the flight engineer opened the side door to let in some fresh air. Thinking they'd landed, Billy jumped out of the hatch and fell two thousand feet. There was a hushed silence as everyone took in what had just happened, and then Terry started humming, 'Billy Don't Be a Hero', and they'd all joined in and pissed themselves laughing. How that song had ever got to number one was anyone's guess, but it had become their constant companion. Tony grinned like always, but the joke had worn very thin.

The things he'd loved about army life—the physicality and the craic—weren't enough anymore, not since he'd met Kate in a Liverpool bar when he was on leave. A lapsed Catholic nurse with an Irish mother, Kate was full of energy and despite having trenchant views about the British Army in Ulster, she hadn't dumped him when he'd owned up to being a squaddie. The surprise to Tony was that it wasn't just about sex; Kate was fun, and she was a great listener and full of ideas. He loved being with her, but more than that, he wanted a different kind of existence where he solved problems with his brains instead of a gun. Tony hadn't mentioned Kate or his frustration to the others, but his thoughts had crystallised during this comfortless November sojourn. He wanted out.

'Hold up,' Evans muttered,'something's happening. Vehicle.'

3

Matt looked through his binoculars as Tony peered through his sniper sight to see a filthy blue transit nosing into the farm complex. A big man wearing a donkey jacket got out, followed by a second, smaller guy who nodded to the driver and slammed the door. The two men walked across the farmyard to the barn. The transit reversed out of the yard and drove away. Matt looked up and caught Tony's eye.

'Is that them?'

Matt nodded. 'Yes, Batman and Robin. Better let them know.' Tony picked up the radio mic.

'This is alpha two-zero; dinner's on the table; repeat, dinner is on the table; over.' They kept the radio messages short in case anyone else was listening, which they usually were. In the event, they could have just said straight out that the IRA's top bomb-maker and his quartermaster had arrived; it wouldn't have made any difference. It stopped them from being bored, though.

About an hour later, four men appeared out of nowhere and scared the shit out of them.

'Jesus, where did you come from?' Evans grinned, but the smile faded when he saw the look on the faces of the newcomers.

'Like in the panto,' replied the one in charge, a short, stocky man with close-cropped ginger hair and small, delicate hands. Evans' mouth puckered in an unspoken query.

'Behind you,' explained another. 'Who's on guard?'

'That'll be me,' Tony muttered.

'If you'd been doing your job properly, you might have seen us. Probably not, though.'

The four newcomers had beards, uniforms without insignia, and lots of non-standard kit, including silencers for their firearms. SAS execution squad was Tony's guess. They began setting up, ignoring Tony and the others. They must have crept over the ridge and down to their eerie, but Tony hadn't seen them. He hadn't heard a helicopter either, so how come they'd got there so quickly? Typical SAS; they loved making you feel small. It wasn't surprising Tony hadn't seen them; he'd been watching the farm with the others after the arrival of transit.

'What happens now?' Matt asked.

'You piss off,' the ginger SAS said, looking down his rifle sight. The other three SAS blokes started checking their equipment.

Tony ignored the tone of the SAS leader and started to organise his gear; he was looking forward to getting back to civilisation. But Matt had his awkward head on. He got to his feet and towered over the SAS trooper. 'We've been freezing our bollocks off for six days and nights.'

'Then you'll be ready for some R and bastard R, won't you?' the ginger SAS snapped.

'You wouldn't be here if we hadn't been here.'

'Is he always this sharp?' The SAS leader chuckled.

Matt faced him. 'You're right, we are ready for some R and R, but I think we've earned the right to see what happens next, so we have.' He could be stubborn when he wanted to be and not someone you'd mess with. Bigger and broader than everyone else, his tone caused the ginger SAS to regard him. He paused for a moment, then spoke quietly.

'You haven't earned anything corporal. Now do as you're told and piss off unless you want to be directing traffic in South Antrim.'

But Matt wasn't about to move. He'd been there for six days, and he didn't like being spoken to as if he were the village idiot.

'Make me, you ginger twat.'

'Easy, Corp,' Evans said uneasily.

'Piss off,' Matt said. The other SAS troopers stopped checking their equipment and watched. Terry went and stood next to Matt.

'I haven't got time for this,' said the SAS leader.

'You'll have to make time then, won't you?' Matt said.

'What do you reckon?' said the SAS leader, 'Seems like these lads have just grown some balls, eh Billy?' The nearest SAS trooper smiled.

'Is he really called Billy?' Terry asked. Evans sniggered, and Matt smiled grimly. The SAS leader was momentarily confused, and that made him angry. He took a step towards Matt.

'Leave it, Matt; it's not worth it,' Tony said, stepping between Matt and the SAS leader. Tony looked into Matt's eyes, and as he did so, someone punched him hard in the back, throwing him to the ground, which seemed to heave up and down. A deep-throated bass note followed by a roar that went on and on threatened to shake Tony's insides loose, and then it went black. He came round to find everyone lying on the ground in various poses. The ginger SAS leader was unconscious, blood coming from the back of his head and being tended by the one called Billy, also bleeding from a face wound. Matt was sitting on the ground, looking dazed. Evans and Terry got to their feet and started jumping up and down.

'Fuck me for Christmas; did you see that?' said Evans. Terry did a jig and shouted,

'Take that, you IRA twats.'

Tony looked down at the farm. Where the barn had been, there was a blackened, smoking crater. The stone farmhouse was now just a foot high at ground level, with some of the chimney standing but leaning at a crazy angle. The rest was gone. SAS Billy looked up at Tony.

'Get on the blower. Tell them somebody just lit the blue touch paper.'

They were having a pint in the mess after debrief and medical checks when SAS Billy appeared. Matt was on his fifth pint, having been told he was concussed and ordered not to drink. Terry alerted them by humming 'Paper Lace'. SAS Billy had a bandage around his head and a whisky in his hand. He sat down next to Matt.

'Everyone OK?' They nodded. He frowned. 'There were four of you, weren't there?'

'Yeah, we had one casualty,' Terry nodded solemnly.

'Bad?'

'Not good; he's been hospitalised,' Terry replied.

'What happened? Shrapnel?'

'Worse,' Terry had Billy's attention now. 'Anal warts. Won't be able to sit down for months.' Terry, Tony, and Matt barked with laughter. SAS Billy grinned.

'Seriously?'

'Yep, he's being operated on as we speak,' Terry grinned, shuffling in his seat to demonstrate.

'How about your lot?' Tony asked Billy. 'Your boss OK?'

'Not sure. They're keeping him in overnight, concussion or a fractured skull.' He sipped his whisky and looked at Matt. 'No hard feelings?'

Matt regarded his pint. 'I wouldn't go that far. Did yous want something?'

Billy shook his head. 'You heard what happened?'

'The silly bastards blew themselves up?' Terry said, smiling.

Billy nodded. 'That's not the interesting bit, though.'

Matt looked at him. 'Don't start talking in bastard riddles.'

'What is the interesting bit?' Tony asked.

'The body parts,' Billy said, pausing. He had their attention now. 'No heads, but they found six legs and six arms.'

Terry grinned. 'So there were three of them then?'

'Maybe.'

'What do you mean, maybe?' Matt slurred. It was beginning to sound like he was concussed.

'Here's the thing: they found five livers.' The three soldiers paused, their glasses halted in mid-air, as they absorbed this information.

'Five livers?' Tony asked. 'How's that possible without any other remains?'

'Good question,' replied Billy.

'So what does it mean?' Tony asked.

'It means it's your bloody round, squaddie,' Matt interjected, obviously bored with the discussion.

SAS Billy grinned and stood up. 'Oh, that stuff about the livers; keep it to yourselves. It's classified.' He winked, turned on his heel, and walked away. Tony watched him go.

'That's what I like about the SAS,' slurred Matt, his Belfast accent stronger now that he was drunk.

'What?' Terry asked.

'Nothing,' Matt replied and downed his beer. 'Where's my bloody pint?' He stood up, swayed for a moment, and keeled over, taking the table and the remaining drinks with him.

December 2018
Northumberland

1. The Church

The stranger sat in one of the pews in the small chapel behind the second choir screen, gulped some water from a bottle in his bag, and tried to catch his breath. A notice explained that the chapel was reserved for people who wanted peace and time to think; well, he fitted the bill. The church was deserted and very still. Weak winter sun slanted through the stained glass and picked out the large sandstone blocks the church had been built from. Dust hung in the air, settling on the tombs at the side where men in Elizabethan ruffs knelt in stone supplication. He wiped the mud from his trousers and boots as best he could and chomped on an energy bar as he scanned the two-page leaflet about the building, just in case anyone asked what he was doing there. There had been a church on the site since Saxon times. The west gate and north wall were Norman, but the vast majority of the structure was mediaeval, built in the fourteenth and fifteenth centuries. The exquisite rood screen had been constructed around 1500, but the second choir screen was what marked the building out. There'd been a dispute between parishioners and some Benedictine monks about who could sit where. The monks had obviously won because the second choir screen had been purpose-built so they could sit apart from everyone else, but their triumph had been short-lived. Within thirty years, their order had disappeared, leaving their chapel within the church a forgotten footnote of the Reformation.

An ancient oak strongbox bound with iron and possessing five separate loops for padlocks sat below a window. A poster explained that the box was over nine hundred years old and was where the monks had kept their most precious items. The five padlocks had five separate key holders drawn from the prior and the other monks so that the box could only be opened if all five were present. Security was always a problem.

They would find him. There was no escape and no possibility of redemption, but instinct had driven him. He'd hidden in plain sight, just as he'd been taught. Don't hide; be discreet. His tiny converted barn in the middle of Northumberland was attached to an ancient farmhouse that appeared occupied but wasn't. Charlton, the farmer, had moved his family to Bellingham to make it easier for his kids to get to school and his wife to get to work. He still worked the land but the sheep were low-maintenance, and there wasn't that much to do in the depths of winter. Some of the hedges and ditches needed attention, but Charlton's building job was what kept the wolf from the door. As he explained to his mates in the pub, it suited him having someone there keeping an eye on things. And when Charlton revealed that the well-spoken tenant was a semi-retired academic writing a history of church architecture and that the university was paying the generous rent, they'd all laughed and shaken their heads. What a lucky beggar Fred Charlton was; if he fell in the Tyne, he'd come up holding a tin of salmon.

He'd always hated December, but it was a good time of year to lie low. The early dark and increasing cold discouraged snooping and sent people home to family and hearth. The car had been his downfall, well, that and his cat, but he couldn't have left her behind. He should definitely have got rid of his top-of-the range Mercedes and traded down, but the vehicle comforted him. He'd left the fake plates and parked it around the back, out of sight. The farm complex was a hundred metres back from the tiny lane that ran east/west. Apart from the postman, there was precious little traffic, and he hadn't worried. If he needed a quick getaway, he still had one. He'd avoided driving the Merc, preferring to walk to the main road and catch a bus on the few days he ventured out. Charlton had mentioned the car admiringly; he'd explained it was something he'd held back after a messy and acrimonious divorce settlement, and he'd appreciate it if the farmer kept

11

it to himself. Valuing the rent he was being paid, the farmer readily agreed. Everything was hunky-dory until the bloody Ramblers

It was a dreadful grey day, rain driving against the windows. He was lying on the sofa listening to Eroica when they appeared, coming down off the moor—a bunch of walkers, some with sticks, clad in a variety of multi-coloured rain gear. The back of his converted barn opened onto a small square of garden, surrounded by a dry stone wall. Beyond lay the moor, heather, and peat stretching away into the gloom. To one side was a paved area where the car was parked. He switched off the music, withdrew into the shadows, and watched the walkers as they came closer. They stopped, consulting their maps and arguing about which way to go. One of the Ramblers spied the Mercedes and wandered over, pointing it out to a fellow walker. Some of the others gathered around the vehicle while the car enthusiast took a photograph of them all. The route decided, the leader turned, waved his stick imperiously, and led the way past the rear of the property and down the muddy track to the road, where, one by one, the walkers turned left and disappeared from view. All the time, he'd watched helplessly from inside the barn, his pulse racing. Why hadn't he covered the vehicle with a tarpaulin? Yes, he'd fitted false plates, but if the walker was a real enthusiast, he might make enquiries about the car. If the leader posted the photograph on a website, someone might find it. Then again, they might do nothing. Three days later, they found him.

He hadn't slept well, not for more than a few minutes at a time. He'd moved the car into the ruined piggery and covered it with a sheet. Then, he'd rigged up an early warning of sorts—a few empty tin cans threaded together and laid across the end of the track. He was in hiding, incognito, and he didn't have any of the usual tech support to call on. Besides, Charlton had a habit of turning up before six in the morning to pick something up, and he couldn't afford to alienate him. He'd asked Charlton to let him know if anyone started asking about him in Bellingham, explaining that his wife's solicitor was on the warpath again.

Charlton agreed, but a questioning look had appeared in his eyes that hadn't been there before.

It was just after five in the morning when he heard the tins clattering. He'd been asleep and was momentarily disoriented when he came awake. Already dressed, he grabbed his coat and rucksack and slipped out of the rear door, making his way onto the moor. He wondered briefly about his cat, but she was off hunting somewhere; she loved the wild. He stopped in the gully afforded by the beck that ran behind the farm buildings and waited, hoping it was Charlton making an early call, but when lights clicked on in his hideaway, he turned and headed up, across the moor. It was difficult walking in the dark, but at least it wasn't raining. If it had been, he might not have heard them. He couldn't see much in the moonless night, and the heather and bog were treacherous, but he couldn't risk using a torch. As a result, he fell often, but he managed to keep going. His boots were sodden, his clothes spattered with mud, and by first light, he was exhausted. He had one idea in his head, and he held onto it, pushing other thoughts away. A small road provided him with some relief, and he followed it downhill into a small valley. The sight of the church tower poking up through the dawn mist energised him. Under the pretext of conducting research, he'd visited some of the local churches on his few excursions from his hideaway, but in reality, he'd been surveying the locality just in case. Old habits again.

Pauline Atkinson opened the door to the church and wandered in. She put down the two bouquets of fresh flowers and shook her head in frustration. Christmas was imminent, and she was no further forward despite the fact she'd missed practically all of the first semester's teaching. She'd thought that she would enjoy the tranquility of the countryside, but she had begun to feel like an object in a still-life painting. The ancient church usually reassured her, but she was bored. She'd only started volunteering at St. Leonard's for something to do; she'd intended to look for bits of teaching work, but her heart hadn't been in it. When people asked her what she was doing

13

with herself, she told them she was busy with other things, which mainly involved taking long walks in the countryside and attending a couple of pilates classes in Hexham. It simply wasn't enough. At fifty-three, she hadn't lost her energy; she was still trim, fit, and presentable, and she bitterly resented the fact that she'd been 'let go' as the child from HR had put it before adding helpfully that she no longer fitted the university's demographic mission statement. She was too old and too resistant to modern technology, although what modern technology had to do with teaching history was beyond her. In fact, in her opinion, the youngsters could benefit from reading some books instead of snippets from Google.

So here she was, organising the flowers for St. Leonard's every Monday and Thursday, and she wasn't even a Christian. She loved the church and the services because they reminded her of her childhood. Most of the Christians she knew were good people who tried to help those less fortunate than themselves and the ceremony offered a comforting, if illusory, reassurance. She would have liked to believe, but she knew she never would. Apart from anything else, she'd always rebelled against male authority, a habit she blamed on her authoritarian father. Actually, she hated being told what to do, especially by people who didn't know what they were talking about. That's what led to her leaving the university. She'd been listening to the fresh-faced, energetic new Dean of Faculty blathering on about KPIs, SSRs, NDAs, and a host of other acronyms. High heels, an Armani suit, too much make-up, and a winning smile—Pauline had seen it all before. So when the Dean opened it out for questions, Pauline asked if it was possible for her to speak in plain English instead of jargon. Her line manager had hauled her over the coals and criticised her for being oppositional and negative again. Pauline had a record of saying what she thought and thinking about the consequences later.

Shortly afterwards, the email from HR offering voluntary severance appeared. Reading between the lines, it was non-negotiable. History was being absorbed into Humanities and her role was being redefined; if she chose to remain, she would have to reapply for her job. In other words, take the offer or have a horrid time, and the offer wasn't ungenerous. Her parents had left her enough to live on until her pension, if she were careful. The three-month notice had stripped away roles and responsibilities, and she'd felt as if she were gradually becoming invisible. Her leaving 'do' had been pleasant enough; nice things were said, and they'd bought her a wonderful crystal vase, but she couldn't shake the feeling that she had been attending her own funeral. Afterwards, she'd kept in touch with her closest friends and some colleagues, but when the conversation turned to university politics, she had less and less to contribute, and she grew tired of lying about her work prospects. In the end, she'd stopped making the effort to contact people, and they'd all but stopped contacting her. She had been put out to grass, reduced to arranging the flowers in church.

She walked up the aisle to the small chapel, and that's when she saw him. She gave a cry of surprise. He was tall, rather gaunt-looking, and greying at the temples. In his mid-fifties, she'd have said, but it was so difficult to tell as people got older. He was sitting straight-backed in one of the pews in the quiet section, but there was something furtive about him. He smiled apologetically.

'My car broke down, and I had to walk,' he explained.

'Don't you have a phone?'

He shrugged. 'I must have left it behind. I'm always forgetting things.'

'How did you get in? The door was locked.'

'The side door was open.'

'It shouldn't have been,' she frowned.

'Oh dear,' he replied.

'Well, you can't stay here,' Pauline said sharply. She didn't want him there; it was an imposition. She wanted to get on with the flowers and go for a walk.

'I thought this chapel was reserved for people who needed some space?'

'Where did you break down?'

'On the moors somewhere, I'm not sure exactly.' He stood up, and she saw that his clothes were mud-spattered. 'I'd better leave you to it then.'

'Are you in trouble?' she asked.

'My car broke down.'

'You said you needed some space.'

'Did I?'

Pauline examined him. He looked exhausted.

'Was it an emergency?' she asked.

'Why do you say that?' He replied, his eyes animated.

'Driving in the middle of the night without your phone. You look all in.'

'I could do with a shave,' he smiled, rubbing his chin. At that moment, there was a bang, and the church door opened. A female voice called out confidently, 'I say, is anyone there?'

Pauline was about to reply when the man grabbed her wrist. 'Don't give me away, please?' He shrank backwards, as if trying to hide in the shadows. Pauline looked at the man. He looked beaten, and she found herself feeling sorry for him before pushing the thought away.

'Excuse me!' The female voice came again.

'Coming.' Pauline went forward, towards the door and the rear of the church, to be confronted by a couple. The woman was about forty with dyed red hair to match her lipstick, high heels, and a black cashmere coat. A step behind the woman, the man was younger and lean; his eyes watchful, ranging over the church.

'Sorry, I'm Pauline. I do the flowers on Mondays and Thursdays.' They weren't interested. The woman smiled, but her eyes were blank, and Pauline felt herself taking against her. The man gave her a quick once-over and disregarded her. It was a look she was getting used to. Students, staff members, shop assistants, and her own GP—they all dismissed her as invisible and unimportant.

'Can I help you?' Pauline asked.

'We're looking for a friend of ours,' the woman said with a smile.

'Oh?'

16

'Yes, he's been unwell with his nerves. When we went to see him this morning, he wasn't there.'

'What do you think's happened to him?'

'We're not sure,' the woman smiled again, but she seemed uncertain.

'Has he done this kind of thing before?' Pauline asked.

'You haven't seen him?' The man interjected. He spoke with a slight accent.

'No,' replied Pauline. 'And you are?'

'Actually, we're his brother and sister-in-law,' said the man, taking a step towards Pauline.

'Well, I haven't seen him. Besides, he wouldn't be here. The church is locked overnight, and I'm the first key holder,' she replied, standing her ground.

'For the flowers?' said the woman.

'That's right,' replied Pauline. 'Now, if you don't mind, I must get on.'

'We'll just have a quick look around,' the man said, moving towards the front of the church. There was something about his manner that really irritated Pauline, another bossy man telling her what to do.

'Actually, it's a bit difficult,' Pauline replied, stepping in front of him. 'I have to lock up. I've got a hospital appointment that I've waited months for; I can't miss it. Jonathan will be here at midday. You could look around then.' The man's mouth tightened, and he looked at his companion.

'Jonathan?' The woman asked.

'He's the vicar. I could leave a note for him if you like,' Pauline breezed.

'We can't have a look now?' the man asked.

'Well, you can, but I've got to go. I'm late as it is, and I do have to lock the church,' Pauline smiled again. There was a moment when it seemed that the man was considering what to do, but the woman took control.

'And you haven't seen any strangers?'

'Not this morning,' Pauline smiled. 'Strange men are something of a rarity at my age.'

The woman nodded and whispered something to the man. He was annoyed and whispered something back. The woman shook her head, and they turned to go.

'Does he have a name?' Pauline asked. The woman stopped and turned back, frowning. 'Your brother in law?'

'Anthony,' the woman replied, 'Anthony Brooks.'

'Alright,' Pauline said cheerfully. 'I'll leave a note for the vicar.' The woman forced a half-smile and turned to go again. 'What about a phone number? In case he turns up?'

'No,' the woman replied and left. The door slammed shut. Pauline held her breath and wondered what she'd done. But they weren't from the police, so how serious could it be? If she had known how much danger she was in, she might have thought twice, but, as her line manager used to say, she had a bolshy streak. After a moment, she went back to the small chapel.

'You can come out now. They've gone.'

He appeared from behind a tomb. 'Thank you.'

'Come on,' Pauline announced. 'You're coming with me.'

'Where to?'

'My cottage,' Pauline explained. 'You can't stay here.'

He nodded, then shook his head and frowned. 'Have you got any paper?'

'Why?' asked Pauline

'That note for the vicar.'

'I just said that to get rid of them,' Pauline smiled, but he was deadly serious.

'Then lock the church and drive to Newcastle.'

'It's forty miles!'

He sighed and spoke quietly. 'If they're pros, they'll be watching to check.'

'I don't want to drive to Newcastle; I've got things to do,' Pauline complained.

He smiled ruefully. 'It's just a precaution to keep you safe.'

'You mean both of us?'

He nodded. 'Yes. Look, surely there are things you could do in Newcastle?'

'I don't want to go today.'

He leaned close, looked her in the eye, and lowered his voice. 'These people could be dangerous. Please?'

His seriousness reminded Pauline of the surgeon explaining her mother's final operation. Pauline shrugged. As usual, she had left her Christmas shopping until the last minute; it wouldn't do any harm to make a start.

'What about you, Anthony?' He looked confused. 'That's what they called you. Isn't it your real name?'

'My friends call me Tony.'

'Alright, Tony, what will you do when I've gone?'

'I'll slip out the side door before the vicar appears,' he explained. 'Give me your address, and I'll find it.' He stared at her.

'How do I know they aren't your brother and sister-in-law?' Pauline asked, but she did know.

He touched her hand. 'The less you know, the better for you. Please?' The tenderness of the gesture ambushed Pauline, and she felt a flush of emotion, and while it was not unpleasant, it was unsettling.

2. Newcastle

As Pauline drove along the A69 towards Newcastle, she tried to rationalise what had happened without success. Why had she helped him? The truth was, she was bored, and she'd always been a sucker for a sob story. Her musings were interrupted by an insistent car horn behind her, and she realised that her ageing Nissan Micra was straddling both lanes of the dual carriageway. She pulled into the slow lane, allowing the angry SUV driver to speed past.

Half an hour later, she was sitting in the Costa Coffee concession pod in the gleaming new foyer of the Royal Victoria Infirmary, sipping a cappuccino, and growing more and more irritated by the insistent Christmas musak. Although Christmas was only days away, the huge Christmas tree in the foyer and the ubiquitous decorations felt like overkill. Pauline had always disliked Christmas, at least the contemporary consumption-obsessed Anglo-Saxon version. However, surrounded by patients and visitors all animated and engrossed in their own lives, her mood abated. The events in the church began to seem fantastic, and she determined to find out what was going on when she got back to the cottage. The whole thing was ridiculous. Now that she was in Newcastle, she may as well enjoy herself, have lunch later in Fenwick's, browse a bit, and maybe get herself a new coat and some presents. She was just pondering what she might buy when she glimpsed him riding the escalator to the first floor. Relaxed, the athletic man from the church was looking around as if interested in the building, but Pauline knew what he was doing. Her pulse quickened, and her insides clenched. She forced herself to sip her coffee, and when she looked again, he was gone. Had he seen her? Had she imagined it?

'Pauline? I thought it was you.' The voice made her jump and spill her coffee. She looked up to see a florid-faced woman smiling beatifically at her. 'Sorry, I didn't mean to startle you.'

'Mary, what are you doing here?'

'Same as you I imagine.' Mary paused. 'Are you alright? You're very pale.'

'I was miles away,' Pauline blustered, mopping up the spilt coffee with a napkin.

'I could see that. Not bad news, I hope?'

'No.'

It was a relief to see a familiar face, even if it was Mary Campion. In her mid-sixties, Mary was an erstwhile colleague who had retired from the English department the year before Pauline. Although not close, Mary and Pauline shared similar views of the university hierarchy, often giggling at the back of faculty meetings like naughty schoolgirls. The problem with Mary was that, once started, she could talk for England. Unloading her winter coat, bags, scarf, and hat, Mary sat down at Pauline's table. 'You don't mind me sitting here. I was just going to treat myself to an almond croissant because I thought I deserved one after all the prodding and poking. Of course, they're not nearly as good as the ones you get in France, but I needed something familiar and comforting. Don't you find that as you get older?' Pauline nodded and smiled, but as she did so, she scanned the foyer. For once, Mary's wittering didn't get on her nerves. 'What's wrong with you then?'

'Me?' Pauline asked stupidly.

'Well, you are in the RVI, dear.'

'Oh, nothing's wrong; I'm fine,' Pauline managed.

'Visiting someone?'

'No, no, I had to come about some tests,' Pauline lied.

'Serious?'

Pauline shook her head. 'No, they're all negative, thankfully.'

'Lucky you,' Mary leant close and pointed to her midriff, 'Gallstones. Got to be atomised or removed, apparently. Hence all the prodding and poking.' Mary bit into her almond croissant.

'Should you be eating that?' Pauline asked. Mary shook her head.

'No, but since Jack, I can't see the point. May as well enjoy what I can.' Mary's husband, Jack, had died from cancer a few months after Mary's retirement. They lived in an old farmhouse in the middle of nowhere.

'Are you still in the same place?' Pauline asked.

'Greenstone?' Mary nodded. 'I know I should be nearer civilisation—a hospital or a shop—that's what Oliver keeps telling me.'

Pauline was puzzled for a moment, then remembered that Oliver was Mary's son. Mary hadn't finished.

'I love it up there, and it's got all mod-cons. If I drop dead, so be it. At least I'll be somewhere I like. You should come and visit.' Pauline smiled. Before today, the idea of being trapped with Mary prattling on in the middle of nowhere hadn't appealed. 'Hey, I've just remembered; you're in the country now, aren't you?'

'Yes, bought a cottage in Bridgford.'

'Don't you just love the peace and quiet?' Mary asked. Pauline nodded, wondering when she would be able to enjoy them again. 'Give me your mobile number, and I'll text you my details.'

'I haven't got one.' Mary frowned, but Pauline explained. 'I hate the damn things. Students unable to do anything without being clamped to them.'

'I know what you mean,' Mary smiled. 'Landline number?'

Pauline grinned ruefully. 'I can't remember what it is. I've only had it in a month.'

Mary shook her head. 'Never mind; you know where I am. We should get together, you know. We're practically neighbours.'

Pauline frowned. 'Bridgford's miles from Greenstone.'

'It's sixteen as the crow flies. Come and stay over; we can have a drink and gossip about everyone. By the way, did you hear about David Thingy, the sociology Prof? He's been having an affair with the new Dean—you know, Mrs. Lah-di-dah lipstick! He left his wife and kids, apparently.'

As Mary talked, Pauline continued scoping the foyer, but she didn't see him again. After a few minutes, she made her excuses and left, but not before promising Mary she'd keep in touch.

On her way to the car park and on the drive back, Pauline didn't see anyone else, but she couldn't shake off the feeling that she was being watched.

3. The Cottage

Tony was upstairs, asleep on Pauline's bed. At first, she thought the cottage was empty, but there were some muddy footprints in the kitchen and a broken pane in the back door.

'I thought you might have gone,' Pauline said as he came awake.

'I came upstairs in case anyone looked in the windows. I must have dozed off.' He stood up and swayed unsteadily.

'Why don't you have a bath while I make something to eat? There's plenty of hot water.' He nodded, then hesitated. 'Don't worry, I've locked the doors and drawn the curtains. No one will see you.' Pauline was angry, which was hardly surprising, and for the first time, he looked closely at her. She was attractive, slim, medium-height, and wearing close-fitting trousers and a red jumper. Her eyes were brown and intense, while her lustrous grey hair looked as if it had been recently cut.

'I'm sorry,' he said. 'I broke some glass in the back door.'

'And left muddy footprints everywhere.' He nodded and pursed his lips apologetically. 'What about the key under the plant pot?'

'It was raining; I couldn't find it. I heard a noise, and I...' he trailed off.

She stood with one hand on her hip, looking at him, her eyes blazing. 'If you have another pee, leave the seat down.' Then she turned on her heel and stomped back downstairs.

He'd given Pauline half an hour before he slipped out of the church. He stood in between two hawthorns in the graveyard and listened. It was quiet, apart from the distant sound of a chainsaw, and she'd said the village was deserted on weekdays. The trouble was that a stranger stuck out like a sore thumb.

She had drawn a map for him, so he knew roughly where her cottage was, but he still had to figure out the best way to get there. It was in a row of two-up, two-down, stone-built workers' cottages that had been updated and extended by the owners. Most of them were holiday lets and empty at this time of year. At the end of the row and close to a small wood, Pauline's home was slightly bigger than the others. He'd found his way to the woods and then to the back of her cottage without anyone seeing him, or so he hoped. It had started to rain heavily, which was good cover if uncomfortable. Rain muffled sound and kept people indoors. As he stood hidden in the wood, watching the back of the cottage, a plan had formed. Involving Pauline had been unfortunate, but he hadn't had a choice, and she was a clean skin. Of course, she might be a loose cannon, but if he was lucky, he'd leave without putting her in any more danger. But he needed Pauline to do something for him first.

'So what's going on, Tony?' Pauline asked as they ate some pasta. 'Oh, I know, you can't tell me for my own good.'

'Look, I'm sorry,' he began, but she overrode him.

'You were right. I was followed.' That got his attention.

'Are you sure?'

'Aren't you!?' She poured herself some wine and drank it down. 'I saw him at the hospital for Christ's sake, the man from the church. Who are these people? Why are you so scared of them?'

'The less you know, the better it is for you, Pauline.'

'You don't look like a gangster.'

He grimaced, 'I'm not.'

'Then why can't you go to the police?'

'It's complicated.'

'What's to stop me from dialling 999?'

'What would you tell them? That a strange man appeared in the church this morning, and another strange man followed you to Newcastle when you had no reason to go there?'

It was infuriating, but he was right. 'You don't work for the government?'

'No.'

'Do they?'

25

He shook his head. 'No. Well, not ours.' He sipped some wine. 'You put yourself out for me, Pauline, and I'm grateful.'

'So grateful, you broke the glass in the back door.'

'Look, this time tomorrow, I'll be gone.'

'What if they question me?'

'You don't know anything. They followed you because you wouldn't let them look around the church, but it's me they're after.'

'And you're definitely going tomorrow?' He nodded, but there was something in the nod that gave him away. 'What?'

'I just need to borrow your car.'

'What for?'

'To get my cat.' She began to protest, but he overrode her. 'I had to leave her behind when I left the barn. She'll be hungry.'

'She'll find something. For God's sake, she's a cat.'

He sighed. 'She's a townie, used to roads and people and central heating.'

Pauline laughed. 'I thought you were in danger?'

'I know it sounds foolish,' he said, 'but she's all I've got. I like her, and she doesn't know why I've vanished.'

She drank some more wine while he picked at his food. 'Who are you, Tony? Who's after you?' she asked quietly. 'Come on, you're in my cottage, eating food off my table.'

He sighed. 'I wrote a dossier.'

'What kind of dossier?'

'One that contains uncomfortable facts.'

'Why do it if it's dangerous?'

'I was paid to.'

'Who by?'

He looked at her in that way again. He wasn't going to tell her. He changed the subject. 'What about you?' he asked. 'Who's in your life?'

Pauline sighed. 'No-one.'

'I'm surprised,' he smiled.

'I was married. We had a son, Robert. He was killed in a motorbike accident.'

'I'm sorry,' he said.

She shrugged. 'It was a long time ago.'

A look of concern crinkled his eyes. 'Even so.'

'It never goes away,' she sighed. 'But life goes on.'

'And your husband?'

'Ralph?' She looked away. 'We couldn't get past it.'

'You blamed each other?'

She shook her head. 'We blamed ourselves. That's when Ralph started drinking. The marriage fell apart after that.'

'That must have been hard.'

'Everyone has their troubles.'

Tony nodded, satisfied with her story. It was the truth, but not the whole truth. For the past two months, she'd engaged in some personal research on something important to her, but that was her secret, and she didn't feel like telling a complete stranger.

He sipped his wine and looked around. 'I wondered why there weren't any photographs or pictures.'

Pauline chuckled. 'The reason there aren't any photographs is because I'm a lazy sod.' He frowned. 'I moved in in August when I retired and immediately went on holiday for three weeks. When I got back, I unpacked what I needed. The rest is still in boxes and cases in the garage and the attic.'

He frowned. 'Why?'

'Unpacking everything feels like it's permanent.'

'You've got a few Christmas cards up?'

Pauline smiled. 'That's about not feeling lonely.'

'So what's wrong with things being permanent?'

'I don't want to be another retired person looking for something to fill my time.'

He considered this for a moment. 'There must be lots of things you could do.' She smiled, and then she had an idea.

'I could go,' she said quietly. He looked up. 'I could go to the barn and pick up your cat.' He shook his head, but she overrode him. 'If they are watching and you take my car, I will definitely be implicated. But if I go in my car, who's going to think there's anything odd about it?'

'I don't like it.'

'Neither do I, but at least this way, I might get rid of you and get my life back.' He shrugged. 'I'm right, aren't I?'

27

'What will you say if you meet someone?'

'On the moor, I'm a walker. I walk a lot, and I'll look the part, boots rucksack, you know?'

'And if someone comes when you're at the barn?'

'I'll say I'm your cousin and that I'm there for your cat.'

'How will you get her to come to you?'

Pauline grinned. 'Open a tin of cat food and bang it with a fork. That always used to work when we had cats. And you did say she'd be hungry?'

'You seem to have worked it all out.'

'Well, not all.'

She gave him the spare room. It served as her office with a desk and shelves bulging with books. It was comfortable and homely but he couldn't settle. Finding Pauline had been fortuitous, but the next step was critical. Damn it, every step had been critical but this could mean putting her in jeopardy, and he liked her. She was sharp and funny and didn't deserve to be part of it, but she was or at would be if things didn't go well. He lay in bed, listening to the sounds of the cottage as it cooled, but he couldn't maintain his concentration. Sleep claimed him.

Getting undressed in her room, Pauline felt distant and dislocated, as if she were watching herself. She unlocked the catch on the bedroom window and left a pile of clothes on a chair next to it in case she needed to dress in a hurry. She was scared but alert, as if a long-dormant instinct had been awakened. In bed with the light out, she replayed the events of the day as she too listened to the familiar sounds of the cottage. It had been a long time since she'd had a man in her house, especially one who was attractive and interesting, and she couldn't help wondering at the turn of events. Nothing had happened for weeks, and then this cloak and dagger stuff in Bridgford, of all places. It was unreal—a series of small things, nothing she could tell anyone about without sounding silly. Was she just being a foolish middle-aged woman? A bang downstairs sent her heart racing, and she lay still, listening intently for more sounds, but none came.

4. The Barn

Pauline left her car on a rough verge and walked the three miles across the moor to the converted barn. It was a bright, glorious December day, the low sun illuminating the muted colours of heather and tussock grass. Pauline felt alive and purposeful as she walked along. He'd told her there was a ladder stile half a mile from the old farm, and she took her time climbing over it to scrutinise the barn and the outbuildings. Everything appeared tranquil in the sunshine and there didn't seem to be anyone around. Tony had told her to observe the buildings as she approached and to go straight in if it was quiet. That way, she wouldn't look furtive. Despite herself, she found it difficult not to slow down, which was just as well. As she approached the small burn close to the wall behind the barn, she heard a terrible scream. She threw herself into the gully that the burn flowed through and lay there, breathing heavily. Eventually, she lifted her head and peered over the wall in time to see the athletic-looking man from the church leave the building. After a moment, she heard an engine start and a vehicle drive away. She waited for another minute and stood up, shaking the excess water from her clothes. She was about to head back to her car when a cat coiled itself around her legs, meowing insistently. She tried to pick it up, but it ran off towards the back of the barn. Pauline tried to coax it back, but it wouldn't come so she followed it.

The door of the barn was open. She went in and found herself in a small vestibule furnished with a boot rack, coat hooks, and a washing machine. A shelf covered with tins of cat food overhung the washing machine. She emptied one of the tins of cat food into a bowl, and when the cat began to eat, she unzipped her rucksack, grasped the animal by the back of the neck, swept her up, and stuffed her inside. She stepped into the room to see a mess of upturned furniture and scattered papers, but what caught her attention was the man sitting on a chair in the middle of the room. His head was thrown back while his face was a mixture of ashen grey and crimson. She let out an involuntary cry and turned around, then turned back. The man's arms were hanging loose, and he was wearing work trousers tucked into Wellington boots. An ancient waxed jacket was on the floor. She checked the man's pulse but detected nothing; he was dead. Her heart raced as she wondered again about Tony. Why was this man dead in his living room? She didn't know the answer, but she knew she hadn't been told the truth. She had to call the police. Tony had said there was a landline in the barn. She found the handset and was about to dial 999 when she noticed the telephone wire had been cut. For once in her life, she wished she had a mobile. Then she heard a noise outside and held her breath, sure that the man was coming back, but all she could hear was the drumbeat of her heart racing. The cat began to complain, but Pauline ignored it and moved into the vestibule.

She waited for another moment, then hoisted the rucksack onto her shoulders and walked back onto the moor without a backward look. She kept on going, half-expecting a shout or a shot, but nothing came. The cat fought and scratched in the rucksack, but Pauline didn't stop until she reached the ladder stile. As she climbed over, she looked back, but the barn was quiet and peaceful in the winter sunshine. The peak of the day had passed, and the declining sun left lengthening shadows and pockets of gloom.

Her elderly Micra was still there, parked on the verge. She took off her rucksack and put it on the back seat. The cat was going crazy inside, but she ignored it and sat in the driving seat. She grasped the wheel and breathed deeply in an attempt to control herself. The world had changed; she had crossed over and there would be no going back. She started the engine and drove slowly towards the darkening sky.

She stopped at the T-junction and sat there, her hands gripping the wheel, struggling to function normally. Turning left led to Bridgford, while turning right would take her to Hexham and the police station. She nosed forward, intending to turn right and caught sight of a large, shiny black 4x4 with tinted windows facing towards her. She thought she could make out the figure of a woman in the driving seat, but she couldn't be certain. The vehicle bothered her. A farmer might possibly have a new 4x4, but a clean one with tinted windows seemed unlikely. Besides, Tony hadn't killed the man in the barn. She sat there for a moment, knowing that, if they were watching, her hesitation signalled guilt. Abruptly, she floored the accelerator and screeched away down the lane towards Bridgford. After a few hundred yards, she regained control and slowed to a more sedate pace.

5. The Cottage

Pauline parked in her usual place outside her garage, grabbed the rucksack and walked towards the back door. Conscious that someone might be watching, she tried to do everything calmly, as if nothing was wrong. By now, the cat was yowling loudly inside the rucksack, but Pauline ignored its struggles and went into the cottage. Tony was out of sight upstairs, hiding in the study bedroom. Pauline locked the back door and drew the curtains. She poured herself a large whisky and took a gulp before calling quietly upstairs. 'You can come down now.'

He appeared in the main room and began to smile. 'Everything alright? I was beginning to worry... ' He saw her face and the whisky in her hand.

'You lied to me, Tony!' He began to respond. 'Don't shake your head as if you don't know what I'm on about.' She opened the rucksack and the cat sprang out, hurtled round the room still yowling before hiding under a dresser. 'There's your damn cat. I hope she's worth it!'

Tony looked at Pauline. 'What happened?'

'Nothing much; I didn't need the key. The back door was open, and the place deserted.'

'There was no one there?' he asked.

'Apart from a dead man sitting on a chair, the place was empty.'

Tony's eyes widened, and he swore to himself. 'You're sure?'

'He wasn't breathing, so yes, I'd say he was dead. Good god, Tony! Who was he?'

Tony took a glass from the dresser, poured himself a scotch, and drank it down. 'How old?'

'Forty, fifty, middle-aged.'

'How was he dressed?'

'Dirty trousers, wellingtons, and an old Barbour. Like a farmer.'

'Shit.'

'You know who it is, then?'

Tony poured himself another scotch and nodded. 'Sounds like Fred Charlton, my landlord.'

'It looked like he'd had a heart attack or something.'

Tony shook his head. 'Did you see anyone else?'

'The man from the church again.' Tony looked at her, and she explained how she'd heard a scream and seen the athletic man leaving the barn.

'Did he see you?'

'No. Who are these people?'

'Did you touch anything?'

'I don't think so. You think Charlton was murdered?'

Tony nodded. 'Was it a mess or tidy?'

'What!?' Pauline asked.

'What state did they leave the place in?'

'What does it matter?'

'It might tell us who they are?'

'You don't know?'

'Not for certain. The room?'

'It was a mess—papers everywhere, furniture upturned.' He nodded, considering. 'So who are they?'

'British and Israelis tend to leave places tidy. Russians and Americans leave a mess.'

'What if it isn't any of them?' Pauline asked. Tony shrugged, deep in thought. 'Those two people in the church didn't sound American,' Pauline said, remembering the athletic-looking man's accent.

'No,' Tony replied.

'So they're Russian?'

'Or some arms' length freelancers.'

'Like you?'

'I don't go around killing people, Pauline.'

'How do I know? Everything you've told me is a lie.' She

turned and went to open the back door, but he put his hand on the handle and stopped her.

'What are you doing?' he asked quietly.

'What I should have done straight away, go to the police.'

'If you report it, you'll put yourself in the frame. You'll be a target forever.'

'What do you suggest, Tony?'

'I'll go to the authorities myself, tell them everything, but keep you out of it. You'll be able to go back to your life.'

Pauline stood away from the door. 'Go on then. You'll have to walk mind. You can't use my car.'

He nodded. 'Before I leave, I just need to use your computer.'

Pauline frowned. He beckoned her back into the living room and shut the doors. She felt a tremor of fear, but he bent down by the dresser, murmuring quietly to the cat as he did so.

'Have you got anything tempting she could eat?' Tony asked. Pauline went into the kitchen and returned with some cold chicken on a plate. Tony put the plate on the floor in front of the dresser and whispered encouragingly to his cat. After a few minutes, the animal appeared and began to eat the chicken. Tony waited until she had finished, then put his hand around her neck and removed something from her collar.

'What's that?' Pauline asked. He held it up.

'A flash drive.'

'So that's why you wanted the cat?' Pauline said.

'I am fond of her,' Tony replied, stroking the creature gently.

'That's not what they killed Charlton for?'

Tony shrugged. 'He didn't know anything, poor sod.'

'So what's on the drive?'

'Documents, an audit trail, a couple of photographs.'

'What of?' Pauline asked. She saw that he was still wary of telling her, but she wasn't having that. 'For Christ's sake! It's a bit late to be coy about it.'

Tony pulled a chair out and sat down at the small table. 'A privatised poisons laboratory.'

Pauline frowned. 'Like Porton Down?'

'Yes, but Porton Down is reactive, whereas Argentina has an

offensive capability.'

'Argentina?'

Tony nodded. 'Argentina Farm. It's a facility—not far from here, actually. The NSDD relocated to it about ten years ago.'

'NSDD?'

'Noxious Substances Development and Delivery is its official title.'

Pauline frowned. 'Argentina?'

Tony nodded. 'It was set up during the 'troubles' in Northern Ireland to attack the IRA.'

'And the problem is?'

Tony leant close and began to whisper. 'We think they've gone rogue, selling their services to the highest bidder.'

'Who's in charge?'

'We're not sure. They were sold off to a hedge fund during the coalition. In theory, the government has a controlling share, but...' He trailed off.

'Can't you tell someone?'

'We tried, but because the NSDD is classified and deals with cutting-edge science, the number of people with clearance is extremely small.'

'What about the press?'

'It's tricky.'

'Is that why Fred Charlton was killed?'

Tony shrugged, 'Maybe.'

'So what's in the dossier?'

'I'm not sure.'

'It was important enough to get Charlton killed,' Pauline snapped.

Tony nodded. 'I know, but I really don't get why it's kicked up so much dust.' He was about to say more but stopped himself. 'Look, I've said too much already.' Pauline began to protest, but he overrode her. 'Up to now, everything I've told you is in the public domain, if you know where to look.'

'Right.'

'I'll do one more thing and get out of your life. Now, where's your computer?'

Pauline realised what he wanted to do. 'It won't do you any good.'

'What do you mean?'

'I'm not connected to the internet.'

For a moment, Tony looked desperate. 'Why not!?'

'I didn't know how long I was going to stay here and I wasn't going to saddle myself with some lengthy and expensive contract. Besides, I hate the fact that everyone's always connected. I like my privacy.'

'Mobile?'

She shook her head slowly. 'Can't stand them either.'

'Bugger.' Tony thought for a moment. 'What do you do when you want to book a flight or send an email?'

'Go to the library in Hexham or a café somewhere. Most have free Wi-Fi these days.'

He regarded her with something like respect. 'You're off the grid.'

'Is that good?'

'It can be.'

'So what now?' she asked.

'You're going to phone the police and tell them that you've got a strange man in your cottage. A man who wants to report a murder. They will come and get me, and I'll tell them everything.'

'I'll have to make a statement?'

He nodded. 'You say that you came home from a walk to find that I'd broken in. I was cold and hungry and I asked you to call the police.'

'And that's it? I've never seen you before?'

He shook his head. 'No. But there is one more thing I want you to do. After I've gone, I want you to go to one of your cafes in Hexham and publish what's on this drive on a website. I'll write down the web address.'

He wrote the address down and handed it to her along with the flash drive. She pocketed them and picked up the handset from her landline.

'What about the cat?' she asked.

'I'll come and get her when it's safe,' he replied. 'You'll have to do the honours till then?'

Pauline shrugged and began to dial. 'That's odd.'

'What?'

'There's no dialling tone.' Tony came over to her.

'Are you sure?' He listened, then examined the connection socket in the wall before listening again. 'It's dead alright.' A banging on the back door caused them both to stiffen.

'Are you expecting anyone?' he whispered.

She shook her head. The knocking came again. 'I'll have to answer it.'

'No,' he whispered.

'The lights are on. They can see I'm in. It'll look suspicious if I don't.' He nodded and scrabbled in a drawer in the dresser until his hands located a pair of scissors. Then he retreated to the stairs, listening as she went to the door.

Breathlessly, Pauline opened the door to be confronted by the vicar. 'Oh, Jonathan, it's you?'

Diffident, mid-forties, easily embarrassed with a wispy beard, Jonathan Williams was the vicar of several churches in the diocese, but he lived in Bridgford. He had this irritating habit of nodding encouragingly when speaking.

'Sorry to bother you at this hour, Pauline,' he said, nodding furiously. It was a cold night and the fact that she didn't invite him in hung between them, unacknowledged.

'Is it about the flowers?'

He shook his head and half-smiled, his features trapped between the youth he had been and the old man he would become.

'You left a note in the church? About the hospital and some strangers?'

'Oh yes,' Pauline replied, relieved. 'I think that's all sorted, thanks.'

'And you? Are you OK?'

'Me?' Again, she was momentarily confused before she recovered. 'Oh, fine, thanks, false alarm,' she smiled unconvincingly. 'I'd invite you in, Jonathan, but I've just run a bath.'

'Oh well, as long as you're alright?'

'I am thanks,' she began to close the door.

'There's something else.' She paused at the door. 'The lines are down for the whole village. No one's got a landline or internet access.'

'I wondered why the phone was dead.'

Jonathan shrugged. 'It's probably the wind. The lines over Black Hill are always blowing down.'

'Right. Well, thanks for letting me know.'

'I'll let you get back to your bath,' he nodded.

Pauline smiled and closed the door before leaning against it, exhausted. Tony appeared, the scissors still grasped in his hand. 'Well?'

'It was the vicar about the note I left.' She noticed the scissors. 'Thinking of doing some needlework?'

Tony grinned and put them down. 'I half expected a squad to come barreling in.'

Pauline warmed herself on a radiator. 'Oh and he came to tell me that the lines are down for the whole village. No one's got landline or internet access.'

Tony switched the downstairs lights out. 'We haven't got much time.'

'It's probably just the wind. The telegraph poles go over a high spot.'

'It's not weather-related, Pauline.' He slid a bolt across the top of the back door.

'You think it's them?' He nodded. 'Can I drive you somewhere?'

'They'll be waiting for us.'

Pauline remembered the black 4x4. 'Then we're trapped?' Tony nodded grimly.

6. The Path

They left from the back door just after six, an hour before first light and two hours before dawn. The village was quiet they hurried in single file into the trees where Tony had hidden two days before. Pauline led the way through the wood to the back of the church, where they stopped again, shivering. There was no moon; it was pitch-black and bitingly cold. At least the frost made the going firmer underfoot after the rain. They listened for a moment, then hurried out of the churchyard and up a small lane running out of the village. This was the dangerous part. They had to pass two cottages to reach the start of the footpath; if they were seen, they were lost. They passed the first cottage and were almost past the second when a dog started barking. Pauline made to run, but Tony dragged her down below the level of the garden wall. A light came on; they heard a door open, followed by footsteps and a man's voice.

'What the bloody hell's the matter with you, Prince?' The dog calmed down. 'Fox again? Well, I haven't got any bleeding chickens, so pipe down.' The man was going to say more but was overtaken by a violent fit of coughing which ended in him hawking a gobbet of phlegm, followed by more swearing. The footsteps receded, a door closed and the light went out. Tony grabbed Pauline and they hurried away; this time the dog stayed silent. They found the fingerpost for the footpath, squeezed through a gap in a hedge, climbed over a wooden stile and started walking upwards, away from the village and into the darkness. The pace was steady and they began to warm up. Pauline stopped after a few minutes to catch her breath.

'Are you OK?' Tony asked quietly.

'Fine. At least I'm not cold anymore.' They looked back at the village; lights were starting to appear in cottage windows. The first faint streaks of light stained the eastern sky.

'You sure we're on the right track?' Tony asked.

'Yes, I've walked up here loads of times.'

'Come on,' Tony said. 'We want to be over the ridgeline before dawn.'

They turned and carried on walking uphill.

They'd had the idea during the night. At first, they'd sat in darkness, spooked by every strange noise. They'd tried sleeping in two-hour shifts with one of them on guard, but neither of them got much rest. The notion had come over a cup of tea.

'I should go,' Tony said after checking the doors and windows for the umpteenth time.

'Where to?'

'Anywhere. It doesn't matter as long as it's away from here.'

Pauline shook her head. 'Where though?'

'I don't know. I could walk to Hexham.'

'You said they'd be waiting.'

'I'll go cross-country then.'

'Twenty-five miles in the dark; at this time of year?'

He shrugged. 'Have you got a map of the area?' She went and got one from the dresser. 'Maybe something will come to me.' He spread it out on the table and examined it using a small torch. He turned the map this way and that. 'You really are in the wilds, aren't you?'

'That's why I came here,' Pauline whispered. 'Thought I'd enjoy the seclusion.'

He looked up from the map. 'Is there no one who could help us?'

Pauline shook her head. 'I've only been here a couple of months. My friends are all on Tyneside or down south.'

'And you don't know anyone around here?'

'The only person I know is Mary and she's in Greenstone, but that's no good; it's miles away.'

'Show me,' he said, offering the map.

'There.'

Tony examined the map closely and traced a rough route. 'About fifteen miles cross country.'

'Closer to seventeen,' Pauline muttered.

Tony considered. 'Has your friend got internet access?'

'I think so.'

He frowned and re-examined the map. 'It might just be possible, but it's not worth trying if she can't help.'

'She's got a fancy mobile phone and a car.' He looked at Pauline. 'She could always drive us somewhere.'

'I suppose so.'

'There is one thing, though,' she added. He looked up from the map. 'I'll have to come with you.'

'No.'

'I know the paths around here and I know Mary. She won't let you in on your own.'

'How far do you normally walk Pauline?'

'Five to six miles, sometimes a little more.' She saw the doubt on his face. His attitude was starting to annoy her. 'I went on a week's walking holiday to Crete last summer. We did twelve miles a day.'

'Bit different to Northumberland in December,' he murmured.

'Don't patronise me!'

'I wasn't... I...'

She overrode him. 'What's the alternative? Sit here and wait for them?'

'Alright, but it won't be easy. There's a path part of the way, but some of it is over rough ground.'

'Less chance of being spotted.'

Tony considered then nodded. 'If we can make two miles an hour, we'll need at least eight hours, probably more.'

Pauline went into the kitchen and filled a kettle. They checked their gear, made some sandwiches and a flask and left two hours before dawn. This way, they would be out of the village and away before they were seen but still have daylight for most of their trek.

41

After an hour, the steep gradient eased and the walking became easier. The village had disappeared from view and they walked in silence on a narrow path in a gloomy dawn half-light. Apart from a cold breeze, the day was overcast and still. Pauline felt dreamy and dislocated, as if she were walking underwater. She wondered if it was the lack of sleep, but the whole situation was surreal. Two days ago, she'd been a bored volunteer at St. Leonard's, longing for something to fill her time. Well, she wasn't bored anymore. Tony was trying to focus on the task at hand and not think too far ahead—a lesson from his army days. Despite that, he found himself planning his next move and fell over. Pauline came back to him.

'Alright?' she asked. He nodded. 'How do you feel?'

'Embarrassed,' he said, picking himself up. The path had degenerated into a series of grassy tussocks interspersed with bogs, it was easy to miss one's footing. 'Are you sure this is the path?' he asked.

'Yes. It disappears for a while, then firms up again at Dead Woman's Ditch. You'll see.'

'This is supposed to be the easy bit,' he grinned. 'The green dotted line on the map.'

Pauline nodded. 'We'd better get on,' and she started walking again. He followed behind. She was warm enough with boots, a walking coat, a scarf, a hat and gloves. Tony's outfit was more makeshift. He had the waxed jacket and boots he'd worn in the church and he'd borrowed a bright red bobble hat and scarf. In addition, he had some of Pauline's old tights with the feet cut off under his trousers, a misshapen jumper and some fingerless gloves. He carried a flask of coffee and their supplies in his rucksack. Pauline had packed some make-up, underwear and a toothbrush in a small rucksack of her own.

Dead Woman's Ditch was so called because a murderer had left the body of his mistress up on the moor at the beginning of the nineteenth century. He was hanged and forgotten, but his victim lived on, naming the place where he'd abandoned her. Dead Woman's Ditch also marked the furthest extent of Pauline's previous excursions; after that point, they had to consult the map more often. The path was clear enough and for three more hours, they made good progress. They stopped for half a cup of coffee and an energy bar.

'How're we doing?' Pauline asked.

'Alright; I reckon we've done at least six miles, possibly seven.'

'That's great.' He nodded uncertainly. 'Isn't it?'

'I don't like the look of that weather,' he nodded northward. The sky was an intense purple-blue, the wind was getting stronger. Pauline watched as he took another compass bearing.

'Know where we are?'

He showed her the map. 'That small wood is that stand of trees over there.' They looked at a bleak cluster of pines on the skyline.

'When do we have to leave the path?'

'Half a mile or so; the path veers off and we carry on northwest,' he pointed across the moor. Pauline looked and shivered. Tony hoisted the rucksack onto his shoulders. 'Come on.'

After ten minutes, the path turned sharply to the left. Tony glanced back at Pauline and took off across the heather on the same heading as before. Pauline followed. The vegetation was a mixture of dead bracken, heather and peat bogs, progress was much harder. The heather looked even, but concealed rocks and occasional deep holes could snap a carelessly placed leg. The bracken was easier, but underneath everything, the bog squelched and sucked. A wrongly placed footstep and they sank up to their knees. The wind in their faces began to grow in intensity, forcing them to bend into it. They struggled on and after two more exhausting hours, they chanced upon a vehicle track and stopped. The temperature was plunging; they turned their backs against the wind as they consulted the map.

'Problem?' she asked.

'We should be here,' he said, pointing at a featureless part of the map. 'Red Nab.'

'Charming.'

'But there's no trace of this track.' In the wind, the loose part of the map flapped like a trapped eagle. Pauline bent down to examine the track.

'It looks new. Someone's put down hardcore.'

Tony nodded. 'Probably a shooters' road.' It was approaching midday, six hours since they'd left the cottage. Pauline was tired; her thighs were aching and the base of her spine throbbed. Tony was cold and had a burning sensation in his right heel that felt like a blister. His exposed fingers were beginning to worry him. They made a brief, uncomfortable stop to eat a sandwich and share another cup of coffee. The first snowflake fell as they were repacking the rucksack.

Tony swore to himself, stood up and rechecked the compass bearing. More flakes followed, swirling in the strong wind. 'We must keep moving,' he said, turning to go. 'The going should be easier on the track.'

It wasn't. The snow fell thickly, obscuring the track until they were engulfed in a whiteout. They tried to carry on, bent double against the roaring, howling tempest that stung their cheeks and threatened to blow them off their feet. They had to look where they were going, but the needle-sharp snow on their faces felt as if they were being sandblasted. Pauline discovered that planting her feet in Tony's footprints made the going a little easier, but his stride was longer and she struggled to keep up. Then she missed her footing altogether and fell heavily. The snow was soft and comforting; she realised how very tired she was. She lay for a moment before pulling herself to her feet. She looked around, but Tony had vanished. She called out his name but her voice was lost in the wind. A rising panic threatened to overwhelm her. She could see what she thought were his footprints, although the blizzard covered them as she watched. She began to follow them, pushing away the thought of what would happen if she didn't find him, but she was in trouble. The walk had taken more out of her than she'd anticipated and she was struggling to keep warm. The wind tunnelled in through every gap and her walking jacket felt as thin as pyjamas. After a few more yards, she tripped again; this time she didn't get up.

Tony wasn't finding it easy. His fingers were in danger of being frostbitten. His waxed jacket was sodden, as was his woolly hat and he was close to exhaustion. They needed to find shelter, but where? In the army, he had been taught to dig a snow hole, but he didn't think the snow was deep enough for that and by the time it was, it would be too late. He looked around for Pauline, but she wasn't there. How long had she been gone? Where was she? He began to retrace his steps. He knew there was a chance he wouldn't find her, but he had to try; otherwise, they were both lost. After a couple of minutes, he saw something and then it was gone. He carried on, the shape gained definition. She was lying down, already half-covered in snow. He grabbed hold of her and tried to pull her up, but she didn't want to.

'Let me sleep.'

'No, you've got to stand. Come on!' He lifted her to her feet, looped one of her arms around his shoulder and began to walk. Progress was agonisingly slow, but they carried on for another half hour. He was just about to start digging a snow hole in a drift against a bank when he spotted a dark shape off to the right. He wondered if it was a mirage but as they staggered forward he could see it was a hut. The door was padlocked, but he broke the hasp with a boulder and helped Pauline into a small, square shed made of corrugated iron. He pulled the door shut and stood inside, breathing heavily, his breath combining with the steam of the snow on their boots and clothes. Outside, the wind roared, moaned and howled, the building shook. Inside, there was a wooden floor with two wooden benches on either side of a trestle table. Pauline had half-collapsed over the table.

'You can't sleep yet,' he told her, 'got to get out of your wet things.' He removed her hat, gloves and jacket and helped her lie on the table. Then he upended one of the benches against the corner and hung his jacket and her anorak off it, together with hats and gloves, so that they had a chance of drying out. Pauline moaned, but he ignored her and unpacked his rucksack onto the table. They had some coffee left, a sandwich and a couple of energy bars. He helped her drink some coffee and watched as she ate an energy bar.

'You seem to know what you're doing,' she slurred.

'Misspent youth,' he grinned. Pauline began to shiver. Tony took her hands and rubbed them between his.

'What time is it?'

'Tea-time.' She looked at him, confused. 'Just after four p.m.,' he explained. She tried to say something, then vomited over the end of the bench before slumping forward with a moan.

'Pauline!' Tony shouted. 'Pauline!' She moaned and tried to lift her head before falling back onto the table. Her skin was deathly pale and clammy. Tony cleared the rucksack and supplies onto the bench and his face lit up.

'Eureka!'

'What're you doing?' She slurred.

'Survival bag. You've got a survival bag. Now lie back.'

Pauline lay back on the trestle. Tony put the rucksack under her head and slid the plastic bag underneath her. Then he climbed onto the table and slithered inside the bag with her. 'Hold me,' he commanded. She looked quizzically. 'Hold me and I'll hold you,' he whispered. They lay on the table and held each other while the storm raged outside.

It wasn't comfortable, but it was dry. The table was hard and narrow, but their mutual warmth somehow sustained them inside the plastic. Pauline was unconscious or sleeping. Tony fervently hoped it was the latter as he listened to the wind.

Sometime after midnight, she came awake, alone in the survival bag with the hut door open. An eerie luminescence illuminated the inside of the hut. She called out in alarm.

'Tony!?'

He appeared in the doorway. 'Sorry, I was desperate for a pee.'

She fell back onto the rucksack pillow. 'I thought you'd gone.'

He approached her. 'You're feeling better then?'

'Mmm. Sorry about before.'

46

'I was worried.' She nodded. He turned to the door and then back to her. 'Can you hear it?'

'I can't hear anything.'

'Exactly; the wind's dropped.' The howling, battering gale had been replaced by stillness. She struggled out of the orange plastic and tried to walk to the doorway. Her right leg almost gave way, her thighs and back ached. He came to her and held her.

'Easy now.'

Straightening, she hobbled to the door and looked outside. The sky was clear, there was a full moon that made the new snow glow like silver.

'It's so bright.'

'Enough to walk by.'

'How deep is it?'

'About fifteen to twenty centimetres.'

'What's that in old money?'

'Six to eight inches. Can you manage it?'

'I feel better than I did,' she grinned.

'Maybe we should wait till first light?'

'How far is it?'

'Five, six miles; we don't want to arrive too early.'

Pauline nodded and turned back into his chest. He grasped her shoulders, leaned in close and whispered, 'Why were you so uptight about me leaving the toilet seat up?'

Pauline smiled. 'It's something men do.'

He nodded and let go. 'What do you want for breakfast?'

'What's on the menu?'

'Two energy bars, my half of the sandwich, and a shared cup of cold coffee.'

She nodded unenthusiastically. 'Fantastic.'

'And this,' he said, producing a small plastic bottle and offering it to her.

'What is it?'

'Rum. Go on, have a swallow. It will help.' Pauline had a mouthful and swallowed it down. The taste was acrid in her mouth, but she could feel the warmth permeating her insides as it went down. She felt better.

'It works,' she said, surprised. He nodded. 'Where did you learn that?'

'Army basic training; four of us left to fend for ourselves in driving rain and a howling gale. After three days, we were cold, wet, ravenous, but they gave us rum. The effect was miraculous.'

'How old were you?' Pauline asked.

'Nineteen,' he smiled. 'Breakfast?'

They ate slowly. At first light, they donned their damp clothes, repacked their rucksacks and set off. The snow was hardening in the cold air and the going, although slow, was much easier than it had been in the storm. Their aches and pains eased as they warmed up. Dawn broke, the brilliant winter sun reflected off the snowfields, so they had to shield their eyes. They began following a streambed downhill.

'We're going down,' Pauline observed.

'Yes, I think this is Swinhope Gill. See?' He pointed to the map.

Pauline peered. 'What if it isn't?'

He shrugged. A couple of hours later, they spied a group of buildings a mile distant.

'Is that it?' She asked.

'Should be. It's certainly off the beaten track.' Surrounded by snow-covered hills and moorland, the farm complex looked like a Christmas card fantasy. Smoke curled from a chimney, grey against the white.

'Looks like someone's home,' Tony said as they began to walk towards it.

7. Argentina Farm

It was a silly name for an upland farm in the foothills of the Cheviot Hills, but the name had been given in 1920 by Frank Robinson, who returned to take over the family business when his father died suddenly. Frank had spent fifteen years in the pampas with the gauchos and always intended to return to Argentina but never did. He remained in Northumberland and so did the name. By 2008, Frank's grandson's attempt to trade in rare birds had failed to take off and he'd been relieved when a hedge fund made a generous offer for the farm and the business. Surprisingly, the new owners invested and expanded the rare bird business until the place looked more like a secure storage complex than a farm. They retained a few sheep on the rougher pastures together with a few pigs near the main complex, but according to Google, the core business was rearing and exporting rare birds of prey, principally peregrine falcons to the Middle East. According to their records, it was a lucrative enterprise, which was why they needed so much security. The birds were kept in dark green wooden sheds with locked doors, shuttered metal windows and state-of-the art heating and ventilating systems with their own power supplies. There were a couple of three-metre-high circular metal pens with wire mesh over the top where the young birds were flown. Next to the road, hungry dogs prowled back and forth in a large, fenced enclosure and set up a fearful racket if strangers chanced by. An aggressive mixture of pedigree and mongrel, they would hurl themselves at the chainlink fence. Hill walkers might catch sight of birds of prey tethered on perches in front of the farmhouse but heaven help them if they strayed off the designated footpath to get a closer look. To accommodate the new buildings, the footpaths had been re-routed with council approval, but the signposting wasn't that clear. A walker with an ageing OS map might well walk on the line of the old path until sirens, angry voices and ferocious dogs alerted them to their mistake. As the farm manager explained, security was necessary because the birds were valuable and there were plenty of ne'er-do-wells about.

The birds were exported with special livestock licenses which meant that after a cursory inspection, they were fast-tracked through ports and airports to their destinations. And lots of people wanted them, it seemed, not just in the Middle East but Eastern Europe and the Far East. Argentina was quiet and profitable; they paid their taxes and were left alone by the County Council and the authorities. They had no neighbours— well, none close by; they had bought out the adjacent smallholdings with generous offers; only a few delivery people had cause to interact with them. It was the North Country; life was hard, people kept themselves to themselves.

As Pauline and Tony walked down towards what they hoped was Mary's place, there was unusual activity at Argentina. The roads in and out had been recently snow-ploughed; two shiny four-by-fours with tinted windows had come roaring in through the gates and disappeared into a gated compound behind the farmhouse. Once out of sight of external surveillance, a body bag was unloaded onto a barrow and wheeled to a storage facility by one of the guards. Few in number and ex-military, they had been hand-picked for their tight-lipped toughness. Physical security was paramount but so was electronic safety which is where Brian came in. A teenage hacker, he'd been arrested, prosecuted and endured community service. Now, he was getting paid to spy on others and keep Argentina Farm safe. His duties were strictly delineated and did not involve snooping into things that did not concern him but Brian had never felt constrained by rules. Following the CCTV pictures on his laptop, he watched the woman get out of the first vehicle, shake her lustrous red hair and march across the farmyard to the farmhouse. He focused on her glorious rear-end as she sashayed away and sighed; there were no cameras inside the building. By disposition, Brian was a watcher, an observer who spent a lot of time in his head but if he appeared in control on the surface, he was far from relaxed underneath. He had hacked the redhead's file, discovered her name, Tina and enjoyed her photographs. She was preoccupied and didn't notice Brian, but she would. He switched off the camera feed and went back to preparing the drones and checking the metadata.

Inside the boardroom, voices were raised and maps pored over, but they couldn't resolve what was upsetting them. They ran through their options and shook their heads. Tina was annoyed by the situation. It was messy and inconvenient but there was little they could do except keep watch and wait for their prey to break cover. When it did, they would be ready.

8. Greenstone

The farmhouse was an ancient, rambling, low building that had been added to at different periods. Most of the windows looked Georgian but some of the stonework was Tudor or earlier. The snow was three feet deep and it was clear that no one had been outside yet. Pauline and Tony approached the front door and rang the bell, but there was no answer. They tried again with the same result and then trudged around the side. There was another door that Tony tried, but it was locked.

'Is this the right place?' he asked quietly.

'Think so.' Pauline pointed at a faded sign high up on the wall that said, Greenstone.

'What do you want?' a disembodied voice shouted. They looked around but couldn't see anyone. The voice came again. 'Who is it?' Pauline nudged Tony and pointed upward. She stepped back a few feet and looked up at an open Velux roof window. Mary Campion was framed in the opening.

'Mary, it's me,' Pauline shouted. 'Pauline.'

'Hang on, let me get my glasses.' Mary's head and shoulders disappeared and then reappeared wearing glasses. 'Pauline? What are you doing here?'

'Our car broke down in the storm nearby. We had to spend the night in it. This morning, we decided to try and reach you.' They'd come up with the story as they walked. Obviously, they couldn't tell Mary the real reason they were there. It was Tony's idea. They were an item, newly met via the internet, a first date gone disastrously wrong. Pauline thought it was incredible but Tony insisted it was plausible.

Mary leaned further out and peered, 'Who's we?'

Tony stepped into view and waved up at Mary. 'Hello. I'm Tony.'

Mary looked down at them. 'Hang on, I'll be down in a minute.' She disappeared, shutting the window behind her. A few moments later, the side door opened and they were ushered into a long, untidy kitchen. Every available surface seemed to be covered with dirty pans and half-eaten food; damp washing hung from a frame over the Aga while piles of clothes sat on chairs and the table. An ancient labrador struggled to its feet from a battered basket and then flopped down again, exhausted. Mary was flustered. Clad in a dressing gown and slippers, her hair awry, she covered her embarrassment by noisily clearing some space, putting on the kettle, ushering them into a small sitting room.

'Sit yourselves down while I go and try and make myself presentable. I won't be long.' On her way out, she pulled Pauline to one side and whispered, 'I wish you'd let me know you were coming.'

'We didn't know Mary. I'm sorry.'

'Put some coal on the stove, will you? You'd better rake it first. I haven't seen to it yet.'

The stove sat under a stone inglenook. Two ancient sofas and an equally venerable armchair faced it in a semi-circle. Newspapers and books covered every surface. Pauline raked the ashes and emptied some coal into the stove. As she stood up, she caught sight of herself in the mirror. Never mind Mary; she was in need of some care and attention herself. Her hair was a mess, her face was dirty, she looked knackered, which wasn't surprising. She tried to clean some of the dirt off her cheeks and straighten her hair. Tony was busy examining the back of the large flat-screen TV in a corner of the room.

'What are you doing?'

'I'm looking for the router.'

'What?'

'Wi-Fi?' Pauline nodded, still looking at herself in the mirror. 'Or the phone. I can't see one, can you?'

'There will be one.'

Tony turned and looked at her. 'What were you saying?'

'Nothing,' she said flopping down on a sofa only to have to move because of a pile of unopened Christmas cards. She put them to one side and forgot about them. Now that she could relax, the aches and pains of the trek came rushing in. 'God, I'm tired.'

Tony sat next to her. 'But we made it, Pauline. We bloody did it.'

Pauline nodded, then frowned. 'Something's wrong.'

'What?'

'This house, the mess in the kitchen—it's not like her. Her office was clean and obsessively tidy. And then there's all these unopened Christmas cards.' Tony shrugged and went back to following the wires along the skirting board.

Further conversation was cut short by Mary's reappearance. She bustled through the room and into the kitchen and after five minutes of banging and swearing, she reappeared with a pot of hot coffee, croissants and jam. The smell of the coffee and the warm croissants was intoxicating.

'My God, Mary, this is amazing. Croissants up here,' Pauline gushed, her mouth full. Tony didn't speak but contented himself with filling his mouth. Mary watched them with a mixture of amusement and satisfaction.

'Well, it's not quite the dark ages. Anyway, it's tradition. Jack and I always had them on Saturdays.'

'Is it Saturday?' Pauline asked, realising that she had lost track of time.

'You've got the internet then?' Tony interrupted. 'And a landline?'

'I've got everything.'

It happened by accident. Neither of them had been thinking about it. Mary had believed their story and, seeing that they were all in, she offered them a bath and a double room while she washed their clothes. Tony went first; he was asleep by the time Pauline joined him. Mary had quizzed her while she waited.

'Where on earth did you find him?' she asked.

Pauline flushed uneasily. 'By accident, really.'

'He's gorgeous.'

Keen to get off the subject, Pauline changed it. 'Is everything alright, Mary?'

Mary's face clouded and she turned away. 'Why shouldn't it be?'

'You were always so tidy at the university...'

'I've let myself go a bit since Jack died.' Mary fussed over a cushion in a way that discouraged further investigation. The exchange stayed with Pauline as she soaked in a hot bath.

She struggled as she climbed into bed beside Tony; the voluminous nightie she'd borrowed from Mary caught on something and she tumbled into him. The firmness of his skin and the outline of his shoulders was a surprise. She had a moment to enjoy the feel of him beside her—the clean sheets, the softness of the bed—and she was gone.

She came awake to find him looking out of the window.

'What is it?' She asked.

'Thought I heard something.'

'Probably an owl; it's dark outside. What time is it anyway?'

'Just after six.'

'Morning or afternoon?'

'Morning.'

'We've slept all day and all night?'

He nodded. 'Pretty much.' The noise came again—a distant shrill call.

'There it is again,' he said.

'I think it's Mary,' Pauline said, sitting up.

She got out of bed, wrapped a blanket around her and went to investigate. The bedroom opened onto a long corridor. Pauline followed it, trying every door as she went. The last one was Mary's bedroom; Pauline found her sprawled on the floor at the end of her bed, whimpering. She was wearing a thin nightie that was up above her waist, she was very cold. Pauline wrapped the blanket around her and tried to help her back into bed, but Mary couldn't stand. In the end, Pauline had to half lift and half drag Mary to the side of the bed and then lever her back. Mary kept apologising.

When she was back in bed with the duvet covering her, she looked at Pauline.

'I'm sorry. I'm ill.'

'I know you are; gallstones. You told me at the hospital.'

Mary shook her head. 'It's terminal.'

'Are you sure?'

Mary nodded. 'They told me this would happen.'

'Haven't you got any medication?'

'I refused it. I've been a pigheaded old fool. I didn't want to prolong things with endless painful treatments like Jack. I was going to finish myself off.'

'What happened?'

'You turned up,' she grinned, then began to shiver violently.

'Don't worry, Mary; we'll get an ambulance. Where's the phone?'

'In my handbag.'

'Your landline?'

'I haven't got one. The line's forever blowing down, so I got a super-duper smartphone. The phone tower's only a mile away.'

'Where's your handbag?'

'In the kitchen.'

'OK, I'll go and phone and make you a cup of tea.'

'Hold me.' Pauline put her arms around her old colleague. Mary sobbed. 'I'm scared.'

'That's alright.'

'I wish Jack was here.' Pauline held her close and then rested her back on the pillow.

'I'll be as quick as I can, Mary.'

Tony was in the kitchen with the kettle boiling when Pauline appeared. She made Mary's tea and explained the situation.

'Her illness is terminal. She was planning to take hemlock until we turned up.' Tony stared at her. 'That's why she hadn't opened her Christmas cards.' Pauline took Mary's handbag and the tea intending to go back upstairs. Tony blocked her way.

'Let me get this straight. Pauline. Are you telling me Mary hasn't got internet access?'

'No. She has the internet; she's got a state-of-the art smart phone.'

'That's no good,' he said angrily.

'Let me pass Tony.'

He didn't move. 'You can't phone an ambulance.'

'We've got to. She's in a lot of pain.'

'A call from a mobile phone can be tracked.'

'She took us in, gave us shelter. Are you planning to let her suffer?'

'I haven't published the info. A mobile's no use; it hasn't got a USB connection.'

'Mary is frightened and ill, she needs help. At least one person has died because of your bloody dossier. I'm not going to add another, not if I can help it. Now get out of my way.' Tony looked at her for a moment, then stepped aside. They were both angry now. Pauline tramped up the stairs and gave Mary the tea. Then she dialled the emergency services.

Two hours later, Pauline watched for the air ambulance out of the window while Mary lay on the sofa in front of the stove under an old duvet. Tony brought Pauline another mug of tea.

'How is she?'

'Sleeping, I hope,' she said, taking the mug.

'When will the helicopter get here?'

'Shouldn't be long now.'

'Look, sorry for being awkward before...' he trailed off before adding, 'about the flash drive.' Pauline nodded and continued to scan the sky. 'The thing is, I'm in a bit of a hole,' he said. 'Publishing the dossier's my last chance.'

Pauline snorted. 'So you keep saying.'

Tony took her hand. 'Lives will be saved.'

'That'll even up the ones lost,' she snapped, shaking her hand free.

'Please, Pauline?'

'You do it if it's that important.'

He shook his head. 'I can't. I'm staying here.'

'More games?'

'Look, if I go with you, you'll definitely be implicated, but if I lie low here for a couple of days, you'll be fine. We both will.'

Pauline shook her head. 'I'm sorry, Tony...' she began, but he overrode her.

'You did bloody well on that trek, Pauline. It was your idea; I couldn't have made it without you. And you did brilliantly at the barn when you fetched the cat.'

'I panicked.'

'You completed your task and didn't get caught.' Pauline looked at him; he grinned in that eager, boyish way, just as he had in the cottage. 'You're a natural.'

She found herself smiling back. 'Don't be silly.'

'You can post the information in a way that they won't know it's you.'

Pauline was about to reply when a relentless industrial clatter overhead signalled the arrival of the helicopter. Tony had time to brief Pauline before he made himself scarce. Half an hour later, Pauline was strapped in, given a thumbs up by a paramedic and watched Greenstone disappear below as the helicopter lifted off into the leaden sky. Ordinarily, they wouldn't have given her a ride, but because the roads were blocked, they took her as well as Mary.

Tony watched them go from a bedroom. When he was satisfied that he was alone, he recovered three items secreted in his clothing. The SIM card was stitched into his shirt collar, the mobile phone battery and the small phone were hidden in the lining of his waxed jacket. He assembled the phone and switched it on. With a signal established, he sent a short, three-word text message: 'Dinner on table.' As soon as it confirmed delivery, he switched off the phone, removed the battery and the SIM card and checked his watch. Then, he made a tour of every room of the farmhouse, noting their contents before checking outside from every window. His inspection complete, he returned to the warmth of the kitchen, checked his watch again and settled down to wait.

9. The Clean Room

The entrance was through the old piggery that flanked the back of the courtyard to the rear of the Argentina farmhouse, where the vehicles were parked. To a casual observer, the building looked disused, but despite being covered in moss, close inspection revealed the roof to be intact and well maintained. Once inside the piggery, entrance to the clean room was via an old wooden shed door, which gave onto a small lift that carried staff down to the cellar below. Apparently flimsy, the door only opened in response to an electronic pulse from the handprints of security-cleared staff. Below ground, the lift opened onto an anteroom where the operatives removed their shoes and donned paper overalls, paper shoes and elasticated paper hats before entering the first of the clean areas through an airlock. The air was filtered to reduce the density of dust particles to one hundredth of normal, which facilitated the construction and testing of microscopic electrical probes. There were highly specialised machines that coated prepared surfaces with a layer one-molecule deep. Below this first level was a biologically clean area, reached by another airlock. Operatives who entered that room donned biohazard suits despite the fact that they did most of their important work via robots in a third completely sterile containment area. The work went on calmly and without fuss, even though they were dismembering a corpse. After processing, what was left was collected remotely before the remnants were hoovered up. The residue was then ferried upstairs and fed to the pigs.

Above ground in the farmhouse, there was rather more excitement. Several drones had been launched to range over the snowfields, beaming back pictures of the ground below. Reformed hacker, Brian, watched the infrared video pictures from the drones he'd sent out but they just revealed a featureless grey landscape, delineated by the craggy tops of dry-stone walls and small numbers of sheep huddling together. The blizzard had left man and beast isolated in their fastnesses; few chose to venture far. Tina nodded to Brian with a hint of a smile as she and the athletic-looking man scanned the monitors impatiently. Brian's pulse quickened at this nuanced acknowledgement, but she did nothing else; she was preoccupied. They had wasted too much time, but she didn't have a way to speed things up.

10. Hinterland

Exactly seventy-four minutes after sending the text message, Tony retrieved a second SIM card from his shirt collar and reassembled the mobile. A minute later, the phone rang. A gruff voice with a Belfast accent spoke.

'What's going on?'

'We said text messages only,' Tony replied.

'Your bloody car's all over the internet.'

'Bloody ramblers,' Tony muttered. He must have posted the snap of the car and that was enough.

'Poor brains keeping it, not to mention the false plates.'

'I know, alright,' Tony replied tartly.

'And, you haven't posted the information.'

'Someone else is doing it. A clean skin.'

'That wasn't the plan.'

'They killed Charlton. That wasn't the plan either.'

'Tell me about this clean skin of your,' asked the Belfast voice.

'She helped me and I trust her,' Tony answered.'

'She?'

'She's a fifty-year-old retired lecturer.'

Tony heard a throaty chuckle. 'Jesus.'

'So what now?'

'Sit tight and wait.'

'My cover's blown. I'm on the run.'

'You've done that before.'

'There's been a blizzard here, the roads are all blocked.'

'Weather's lovely in London.'

'Piss off.'

'Just follow procedure. The plan hasn't changed.'

Tony was about to say something, but the call had been ended. He swore to himself as he dismantled the phone again. The plan had been to lie low for a few weeks and then post the dossier, but the ramblers had seen his car and bolloxed all that. If he'd posted when he'd planned to, he would have texted 'Dinner on the table.' Missing out a word was a warning that things hadn't gone smoothly, hence the phone call. If someone was listening, they couldn't have listened to the call, but the text and the call would have lit up the mobile phone mast. Tony didn't like that. He didn't know how many houses and farms there were round about, but sooner or later, someone would come here and check it out. He needed to get away. It was after two in the afternoon, two hours until he could make a move. But even if he did get away, where would he go and for how long. He decided to cross that bridge when he came to it. In the meantime, he raided Mary's kitchen and began to plan. Outside, it started to snow again. That would deter snoopers, but it wouldn't help his getaway much either. He didn't want to spend another night at Greenstone.

At the hospital, Pauline waited in a corridor for news of Mary. After the events of the last twenty-four hours, the normality of the institution was surreal. Patients were wheeled past with relatives in tow; orderlies, nurses and the occasional doctor hurried back and forth. Occasionally a tannoy rendered an incomprehensible announcement followed by a discordant, tinny rendition of 'Good King Wenceslas'. Bunting had been hung on the wall above a cut-out of a smiling Santa in his sleigh pulled by a laughing reindeer. Both the sleigh and the reindeer had seen better days. Pauline stood up and looked out of a window down to a courtyard, three floors below. A square of grass, a border and three small cherry trees had been provided in the gap between the buildings, but in the bitter cold, the trees looked as if they had given up. Paths had been cleared leaving the snow piled into greying heaps. A few devoted smokers huddled under an ugly plastic shelter, a couple of them in hospital gowns attached to drips. There was something intensely human about the activity; they were ill, possibly terminal but they still clung grimly to the life they had had. Pauline understood that only too well. In fact, she felt like running down and sharing a cigarette with them, even though she didn't smoke.

'Excusez-moi?' A voice interrupted her. Pauline turned and was confronted by a ridiculously young female doctor. 'You are a member of Mary's family?' The doctor was French.

Pauline smiled. 'No, I'm an old friend from work. I was staying with her when she collapsed.'

The young doctor absorbed this before adding, 'Your friend is very ill.' She half-smiled nervously.

Pauline nodded. She had no desire to be Mary's significant other, but fate had apparently anointed her. Then, she felt mean.

'How long has she got?' The younger woman's eyes widened in alarm. She made as if to speak but emitted no sound. Pauline helped her out. 'A year?' The doctor shook her head quickly. 'Months?' The same response came, only less vigorously. 'Weeks?' The doctor took a deep breath and dipped her head in a half nod. 'How many?'

'One, maybe two.'

'Right.' Pauline hadn't bargained for this.

'You aren't related?'

'She has a son, I think.'

'You must contact him.' It was Pauline's turn to shake her head.

'I don't know him; I've never met him.'

'You know his name?'

'Er, Oliver, I think. Yes, that's it.'

'He will be on her phone, no?'

'I don't know,' Pauline replied.

'You can look, then you contact him.'

'Can't you do it?' Pauline asked.

'I am not allowed,' the doctor said, adding, 'data protection.'

'But you want me to do it?'

The young woman smiled. 'You are her friend?' She moved down the corridor, inviting Pauline to follow her.

63

Mary was in a small ante-room off a larger ward. Hooked up to a series of monitors and a drip, she had a view of the city looking west, or she would have done if she hadn't been unconscious. The doctor scanned the monitors and then led Pauline to the bedside table and nodded towards it. As Pauline began to search the contents, Mary opened her eyes and smiled.

'Not sure you should be rummaging through my drawers, dear.'

'How are you feeling, Mary?'

'Better, thanks to you.'

'I was looking for Oliver's contact details. Someone needs to tell him.'

Mary frowned. 'I'm sorry about all this fuss, Pauline.'

'Don't be silly.'

Mary looked round anxiously. 'Where's my handbag? Did I bring it with me?'

Pauline nodded. 'It's in the bottom drawer. The doctor put it there.' Pauline opened the cabinet and retrieved Mary's bag.

'Don't let him go, Pauline,' Mary said abruptly. 'Tony, I mean.'

Pauline smiled ruefully at her erstwhile colleague. 'It's not that simple, Mary. I've got myself into a bit of a fix.'

'Embrace it,' Mary replied, grabbing Pauline's hand. 'Embrace the adventure, whatever happens.' She paused, breathing hard, but she hadn't finished. 'You know what Jack and I had?' Pauline shook her head. 'Fun. We laughed together.'

'We're not really in a relationship.'

'I saw you two.' Mary gasped for breath, 'there's something there.' She fell back onto her pillow, exhausted and smiled weakly.

'I'll call Oliver and tell him what's happening,' Pauline whispered.

'He lives in Thailand. You should probably email him; it's cheaper than calling. Also, check my emails will you, he might have been in touch.'

'I don't know your details.'

'They're in my purse,' Mary whispered.

'I'm not sure if I should...' Pauline began.

'Don't be silly,' Mary mouthed.

Pauline took Mary's purse, then bent down and kissed Mary on her cheek. Her skin was clammy and had a waxy, unhealthy colour. 'Silent Night' was playing as Pauline left the small anteroom. As she walked down the pristine hospital corridors, past endless injunctions to be merry, she began to cry. Outside, the wind blew the falling snow into swirling eddies.

11. Communications

Pauline caught a train to Hexham and sat watching the snow-covered fields disappear into the winter gloom while she tried to calm down. As the light went, the world dwindled until it felt as if it were just her and the train. The carriage was full of school kids shouting and laughing. One of them had carried a snowball onto the train and dashed up and down while the others squealed and laughed. Ordinarily, the noise would have irritated her, but after what had happened, their innocence was reassuring.

Wanting to get it over with, she'd chosen to send the emails from the university next door to the hospital, but it had been a mistake. She'd turned a corner and immediately been engulfed by a throng of students and staff clamouring and shouting. Despite the weather, smiling staff members in multi-coloured fur-trimmed gowns and Henry VIII hats mixed with students from the Pacific Rim, wearing gowns and mortarboards.

'Winter Graduation Day,' Pauline muttered. The last thing she wanted was to meet a former colleague, so she ducked into the nearest building, which happened to be the library. Open 24/7 so that students with evening jobs could study after they'd finished their shifts, the library had a lot of computer terminals. It also possessed blanket CCTV coverage. Pauline walked downstairs and scanned the place. It was empty, apart from five male students lounging on bin bags, getting noisily drunk from bottles. One of the drunken retinue, a round-faced youth with an incipient beard and wearing a Russian hat, sniggered as she passed, but she ignored him and headed to a terminal in the corner as far away from the drinkers as possible. She logged on successfully and was confronted by the familiar university desktop. Departing staff members retained email access for a few months in case students wanted contact and support with a tutor they knew. She took a deep breath and attempted to insert the flash drive into the computer, but the first two slots she tried didn't fit. She swore to herself and tried again and this time she was successful. When prompted, she instructed it to upload the contents onto the desktop so she could post them onto the website, but the university firewall refused to upload the data. She tried again with the same result and found her hands shaking on the keyboard. Maybe the tension of the last few days finally got to her, but whatever the reason, at that moment she had to get out of there. Gathering up her stuff, she hurried up the stairs and was at the front door when she realised someone was following her. In a panic, she pushed at the heavy door, but it wouldn't open. A hand grabbed the handle and pulled it towards her.

'You have to pull it,' a voice said. She turned to see the student with the Russian hat. 'It's a bit counter-intuitive,' he grinned, the ear flaps of his hat flapped like a toy rabbit, 'like the terminal you were battling with downstairs.'

'You were watching me?'

He shook his head. 'I'm a technophobe myself. My brother sends me films to watch. I can never get them to work.' He opened his hand to reveal the flash drive. 'You left it behind?'

'Oh yes, thanks. Thanks a lot.' She took the flash drive and hurried out into the snow. Sitting on the train later, she cursed her foolishness.

At Hexham, Pauline found a 4x4 cab and, despite the falling snow, persuaded the driver to take her to Bridgford. Had it only been a day and a half? At the cottage, she opened the back door cautiously and entered carefully, as if the place were radioactive, but it was just as they'd left it. She turned on the heating, drew the curtains, locked the doors and set about making herself something to eat. After the last two days, doing something ordinary raised her spirits. The cottage, which she'd so despised, now felt like a haven from the storm. She poured herself a whisky and took it with her as she checked every room. She wanted a bath and some clean clothes. She undressed, put on a towelling robe and went into the bathroom. She smiled; the loo seat was up. She ran a hot bath and luxuriated in it. Then she dressed again and had something to eat when she was disturbed by a scratching at the back door. Pulse racing, she took a kitchen knife from a drawer and held it behind her back as she unlocked and opened the door. Tony's cat hurried in and coiled around her legs, meowing and purring. The creature was wet through, but she gave it some food and watched as it gobbled it down. Afterwards, she stroked the animal and, while crouching over it, reattached the flash drive to its collar.

She went to bed early but spent a largely sleepless night replaying the events of the last two days, jumping at every noise in the old cottage. The trek through the blizzard felt remote and surreal, but they had made it to Mary's place. Tony had probably saved her life when she'd collapsed and there'd been that moment in bed together at Greenstone. There'd been something between them before they heard Mary calling. Helping someone in distress—that's what she thought she was doing, but here she was in the midst of something terrifying. 'Be careful what you wish for,' her mother used to say when Pauline was a teenager when all she'd wanted was to get away and see the world. She'd been bored and wanted more in her life; she'd regretted it before. She felt slight and vulnerable and returning to the cottage had confirmed something for her. She wanted her old life of flower-arranging, pilates and boredom back. There was just one more thing to do, then it would be over.

Next morning, at twenty-nine minutes past eight a.m., Tony stopped Mary's car by the side of the lane and checked his rearview mirror. He had taken the car the previous evening and managed to drive down the valley by following the rutted tracks of a tractor. The tracks were too wide for the car, which now had a few dents it hadn't had before, but he had escaped. He had driven to an isolated car park on the Roman Wall, where he'd spent an uncomfortable night before an early breakfast in a

68

small cafe on the military road. Then he headed north again and waited until it was time.

Satisfied that he was alone, Tony reassembled his mobile phone and switched it on. At exactly ten thirty, the phone rang. The Belfast accent was unmistakable.

'So much for your clean skin.'

'What's happened?' Tony asked.

'Nothing. She hasn't posted.'

'Shit.'

'That's bloody right, so it is.'

'How are things at your end?'

'They're conducting a level four sweep.'

'Jesus.' Four was the most extreme sweep. 'What now, Matt?'

'Find your bloody, clean skin and post that info.' Matt cut the call. Tony swore to himself and switched the phone off. He shouldn't have used Matt's name aloud but he was rattled. In the silence of Mary's car, he removed the SIM card and the battery and reflected. He was in a bit of a spot.

Pauline woke up early and drove to Hexham, where she parked in her usual place. The day was clear and bright, the winter sun shone with a cold nordic intensity out of a sky that was all stratosphere. She walked to one of her favourite cafes, ordered a cappuccino, went upstairs, and logged on as a guest to one of the cafe's terminals. She emailed Mary's son and told him that his mother was very ill and that he should come home soon if he wanted to see her. Afterwards, she lingered over her coffee and remembered the radio messages they used to put on the end of the radio news before the days of the internet. Pauline shook herself out of her lethargy and looked forward to the rest of the day. She'd decided not to post anything because she was sick of the whole business. She'd emailed Mary's son, and now she intended to return to the normal world of Christmas shopping and boredom.

She finished her coffee, paid the bill, and sauntered downstairs and out into the sunshine. A few yards down the street, Pauline bent down to tie a shoelace and dropped the flash drive into a drain. Then she went into the Oxfam shop to buy Christmas cards and browse.

Hexham Abbey was founded by St. Wilfrid in AD 674, only to be burned down several times by marauding Scots in succeeding centuries. To a visitor's eye, it's a quiet, prosperous place where nothing much happens. Certainly, on that quiet morning, nobody noticed the two men sauntering along on different sides of the street or the white van parked with its engine running. Pauline certainly didn't see anything as she left the Oxfam shop and headed up the main street towards the SCOPE store. She didn't spot the white van as it drew alongside or until one of the men grabbed her arm. She struggled and began to yell, but the second man put his hand over her mouth.

'Don't struggle. Pauline Jennifer Atkinson, we're arresting you under Section 7 of the 'Prevention of Terrorism Act'. You do not have to say anything, but anything you do say will be taken down and may be given in evidence.'

Even if she'd had the wit to react, she didn't have time. She was picked up bodily and thrown onto a mattress in the van. The two men jumped in after her; the sliding door slammed shut, and the vehicle accelerated away. Inside the vehicle, Pauline was hooded, and her arms were pinioned behind her. She couldn't move or see anything. On the main street, an elderly dog-walker observed the whole episode while his aged spaniel sniffed and peed at a drainpipe beside the SCOPE window. The dog-walker watched the van disappear up the street and frowned. He looked around to see if anyone else had witnessed it, but no one seemed bothered. His first thought was to call for help, but he hadn't had the presence of mind to take the van's number, and he didn't think he would recognise the two men involved, or was it three? And if he did report it to the police, they would probably keep him hanging about for hours; it was steak and kidney pie at the Plough on Thursdays. It was probably a stunt for charity or a film. Anyway, it was too late now.

12. Consequences

The floor was tiled in pale blue and white and sloped upward to a low white wall some twenty metres away. Pauline was handcuffed to a chair facing the distant wall. A voice spoke.

'What have you done, Pauline?'

The space echoed with the voice in a familiar way, but she couldn't work out why. Male with a cut-glass English accent, it was the first thing she'd heard since she'd been arrested. It had been a few hours, but it felt like days. Locked in a windowless room with an unshaded light bulb that never went out. The walls were a mottled brown, as if a hundred smokers had been trapped inside, and there was a stink of dampness and decay. She'd slept intermittently, eaten some of the food provided, but hadn't yet managed to use the bucket in the corner. She was by turns scared and indignant. She hadn't done anything wrong, so why had she been arrested? She still hadn't seen anyone in uniform.

'Answer the question, Pauline.'

'Where am I? Why have I been kidnapped?'

'Kidnapped?'

'I was snatched from the street and brought here against my will.'

The unseen voice chuckled. 'You were arrested.'

'This isn't a police station.'

'It's a facility.' He enunciated each syllable carefully so that it sounded alien.

'What do you mean?' Pauline asked. She was sitting on a wooden dining chair, and her hands were cuffed to the arms. She could have stood, but not without lifting the chair with her. Besides, she felt weak. She rephrased her question.

'What kind of facility?'

Footsteps approached behind. The voice whispered in her ear. 'The kind we reserve for suicide bombers and terrorists.' Her mind struggled to comprehend. 'It's a swimming pool. Well, it was, until the council amenity budget became overstretched.'

'I'm a retired history lecturer.'

'Perfect cover.'

'It's true!'

'Ferreting about in the files, unearthing secrets, disturbing the equilibrium—isn't that what historians do?'

'Since I left the university, I've spent my time arranging the flowers in St. Leonard's and doing pilates twice a week in Hexham. I'm just an ordinary person.'

'With very few friends.'

'What?'

'You don't appear to have had much contact with anyone.'

'I lost a good friend last year to breast cancer! We met in hospital when I had Robert.'

'Still not many.'

'My best friend Jenny's in Australia for four months while her daughter has her first baby. We were at university together.'

'Have you had any contact with her?'

Pauline shook her head; he raised his eyebrows in mock surprise. 'We both hate telephones and emails. We've agreed to write to each other and save everything up until she gets back.'

'So that's two?'

'There were some colleagues I used to see when I was lecturing, but that fell away when I moved to the country. The man stared at her. 'Is that why I've been arrested? For not having enough friends?'

He smiled. 'Academics are like actors and spies. You never retire...'

'When do I get to see a lawyer?'

The question seemed to antagonise him. 'When I say you can,'

'I haven't done anything.'

'The name's Buchan, by the way.' He walked in front of her,

and she saw a tall, sleek man in his fifties with short greying hair. He was wearing an expensive dark blue suit with a white shirt open at the neck and running shoes. He approached her.

'Where were you the night before last?'

'I went to visit a friend of mine, Mary. She's not been well.'

'You didn't take your car?'

'It doesn't start well in bad weather. The forecast wasn't great, so I got a lift to Hexham, and she picked me up.'

Buchan considered her answer. 'You're lying.'

'I'm not!'

He grimaced at her answer and stood up to his full height. 'Why did you use the university computer?'

'I wanted to email Mary's son, Oliver. She's in the RVI. She wants to see her son before...'

'Before what?'

'There isn't much time. Her illness is terminal.'

'Why didn't she call him?'

'I don't know. He lives in Thailand.'

'Don't lie to me, Pauline,' he said smoothly.

'I'm not lying.'

'What was the file you tried to upload?'

'Mary had some photographs of her and her dog at the farmhouse, Greenstone. She wanted Oliver to see them. He's her son.' Pauline had no idea where the lie had come from or where it might lead.

'What did you do with it?'

'What?'

'The flash drive. The one you used in the university.'

'I threw it away.'

Buchan chuckled. 'Of course you did.'

'It didn't work.'

'Why throw it away? Why not try it somewhere else?'

'Mary said it was ancient. She's got the originals on her phone, and Oliver can see them when he visits. The important thing was to email him.'

'Which you didn't do?'

'I was exhausted. I didn't like being back at the university, especially on graduation day.'

'Guilty conscience?'

'No.'

'Then why didn't you like being back?'

'I didn't belong anymore.' She could see he wasn't following. 'I didn't want to bump into former colleagues and have to lie about what I was doing with myself.'

'Are you an accomplished liar?'

'No!'

'What did you do after?'

'Went home. I decided to sleep on it.' Buchan looked at her before turning and walking in a figure of eight deep in thought. When he was close again, he leaned in.

'Where is he?'

'I beg your pardon?'

'Anthony Brooks? Where is he?'

'I don't know any Anthony Brooks.' Mary was the only person who'd seen Pauline with Tony. Pauline thought it unlikely that Mary would be able to say much, even if they questioned her.

'He is a very dangerous man, Pauline.'

'Could I have a drink of water?'

'What?'

'I'm thirsty. I'd like a drink.' Buchan looked to one side and beckoned urgently. High heels on a hard floor clacked towards them.

A well-spoken female voice said quietly, 'Colonel?'

He walked to the side, took a glass of water, and helped Pauline drink it.

'Anthony Brooks has placed the security of this country in extreme jeopardy.'

'How?'

'Sold secrets to foreign powers. Killed people.'

'Killed people?'

'What do you know about Fred Charlton?' The memory of the dead farmer detonated in her brain. She struggled to remain in control.

'Fred who?'

'Charlton. He's a local farmer. Brooks rented a barn from him.'

'What about him?'

'He's disappeared.'

'Disappeared?' Pauline repeated, confused.

'His wife and children haven't seen him for several days. We think he could be with Brooks.'

'I've never met Charlton or Brooks.'

'I don't believe you.'

'...but even if I had, I'm no Judas,' Pauline said quietly.

Buchan laughed and shook his head. 'We don't want you to be a Judas.'

'What?'

'Judas betrayed an honest man.' He paused, leant in even closer, and whispered in a sibilant hiss. 'We aren't asking you to betray Jesus. We want you to give us Barabbas.'

Terrified, Pauline said nothing. What the hell was going on? She hadn't done anything. She hadn't posted the dossier, and she'd got rid of the flash drive. If she could just make them understand that it was all a mistake, they'd let her go and she could return to her old life. But Buchan wasn't finished. With a casualness that belied his intention, he regarded her knowingly and raised his eyebrows. Pauline shook her head angrily. 'I haven't done anything!'

'What about your own illicit investigations?'

'What do you mean?' But as soon as he said it, she knew.

He smiled thinly. 'A visit to Nottingham? An address in Wollaton?' Pauline shook her head hopelessly; terror gripped her. Buchan looked at her and sighed. 'Pretty name, Lavinia; the wife of Aeneas apparently.'

Thirty-two years before; that's how long it was. She had been in her first year at university in Nottingham, her first time away from home, and she'd fallen for a local West Indian lad called Leroy. He was a little older than her and when she'd told him she was pregnant, he'd done a runner. Her father had called her a bloody fool and her mother had cried, but the child was gorgeous. Pauline had named her Lavinia; she'd wanted to keep her, but her parents had gone on and on. Pauline had her whole life in front of her. Why sacrifice her education to bring up a half-caste kid who would be better off with her own kind? Pauline had tried to argue with them, but she'd been numb in the face of Leroy's desertion and her parents' certainty. She loved Lavinia with all her being, but she just didn't feel like enough of an adult to be a mother, and it was at least partly true that she didn't want to exchange university for a life of drudgery. In the end, she'd signed the piece of paper, and Lavinia had disappeared.

At first, Pauline had managed to excuse herself. She'd been very young; she hadn't been ready, but, as time passed, she discovered that memory could ambush and overwhelm her. Consequently, she'd learned to be circumspect about the books she read or the films she watched. Robert's birth had helped; she'd been able to focus on his needs rather than worrying about somebody she didn't know. But in the time since Robert's death, she'd found herself wondering about her daughter, and this had come to a head since her retirement. Maybe it was the church atmosphere at St. Leonard's, the inscriptions on the tombs and the sense of her own mortality, but she'd started to investigate.

It had begun in Hexham library. Every Wednesday morning Pauline travelled in for her pilates class, and afterwards, she'd gone to the library and undertaken some historical research, only this time about herself. After a week, she'd tracked down the adoption agency that had handled Lavinia's case, and after another week, she'd identified the appropriate contact person and emailed the woman. Five days later, she'd travelled to Nottingham to see the case worker and, by sheer good fortune, they'd hit it off. Pauline had been honest about the adoption and her reasons for wanting to know about her daughter now. The case worker was ten years younger than Pauline but she'd been sympathetic, explaining the official legal position with a twinkle in her eye. If, and it was a big if, if Lavinia wanted to see Pauline, she could write to Pauline, and Pauline would have the right to refuse, but that was all. As the birth mother, Pauline had no rights of access or anything else. Afterwards, the case worker had gone to the loo and left Lavinia's file open on her desk. Pauline had had time to read the relevant details; Lavinia was divorced with two children and living in Nottingham. As well as Lavinia, Pauline had two granddaughters called Luna and Miriam and this had both excited and terrified her. She'd thought about writing to Lavinia, but the fear of her refusing any request had paralysed her, and she had done nothing. Now, this stranger was threatening to destroy any chance Pauline might have of making contact with her daughter and her grandchildren. More than that, there was the possibility that he might place them in some sort of jeopardy. Pauline felt her courage drain away as he bent towards her.

'Losing your son, Robert, must have been hard. It cost you your marriage. Be tough to go through it again.' There was a brief pause before he stood up straight and walked behind her. 'Alright,' he ordered.

She heard a loud rushing sound, which she couldn't make sense of until she felt the cold water on her feet and gasped. She tried to stand, only to discover that the chair was bolted to the floor. The water was ice-cold and rising.

Two Weeks
Earlier

13. The Meet

To the west of the M5 and a few miles north of Exmoor, the Quantock Hills rise a thousand feet above the Bristol Channel. Just sixteen miles by nine, the hilltops are a mixture of heather moorland and lush grass, while the flanks are densely populated with stunted oaks in mysterious steep-sided valleys, which the locals call combes. Deer hide in the more isolated spots to avoid stag-hunters. In the winter months, frost pockets and mist are common in these combes, as are the occasional secluded country house reached by narrow, unsigned lanes. Porlock Lodge was an oblong, sandstone blockhouse nestling in a slim combe shaped like a boat. Steep wooded slopes rose on both sides while mist hung like a pall and mixed with the woodsmoke curling from the chimney. Leaves carpeted the floor, and thick green moss coated every west-facing surface.

Tony arrived just before midnight on a bitterly cold evening. He parked up, walked to the front door, and went inside. A large wooden staircase dominated the hall. Ancient portraits hung above the stairs while a suit of armour stood guard on the half-landing where the stairs turned back on themselves. He put his bag down, looked around, and shivered as Matt Hardwick appeared from a doorway.

'Yeah, sorry about the temperature. I've lit the stove and turned up the boiler, but it will take another Ice Age for this place to warm up.' Tony stamped his feet; the stone flags didn't help. 'Takes your breath away though, doesn't it, squaddie?' Matt's Ulster accent was still strong, and he knew it irritated Tony to be called 'squaddie'.Tony followed Matt into a large, oak-panelled dining room.

'Why all the cloak and dagger stuff?' Tony asked.

'It's Hilary's idea. She wanted us to meet somewhere private.'

'It's certainly that.'

'Apparently, it's been in her family for two hundred years.'

Tony raised his eyebrows. 'In her file?'

Matt shook his head. 'You'd have to dig. It belongs to a distant maiden aunt. She's in sheltered accommodation in Taunton, which she thinks is a five-star hotel with indifferent service. She complains like the devil, but nobody listens; she's got dementia.'

The day before, Tony had collected a parcel from Hammersmith sorting office. He'd been confused because he hadn't ordered anything. The parcel was stuffed with newsprint, but a cigarette paper fell onto the floor of the car. Picking it up, he read '1603551920' and, despite himself, his pulse quickened. He knew what it meant. The last four numbers were two pairs and indicated the nineteenth and twentieth letters of the alphabet, ST. The other six numbers were two groups of three and, placed after the letters ST, created a map reference. He burned the cigarette paper and drove home, where he established that the map reference was in Somerset. The communication was off-grid, and that meant no cars, no electronic devices and no bank cards. When darkness came, he put some food out for his cat, donned black jogging bottoms, a black hoodie and black trainers, and stuffed a large wad of cash into his pockets. With the hood up, he left his flat and slipped into the back alley, checking up and down before hurrying away. The lamppost that was supposed to light the alley was broken again; he'd made sure of that. He caught a bus to Hammersmith, then walked the remaining distance to Paddington, where he boarded a Bristol train just as it was leaving. He bought a ticket on board with cash after telling the conductor a sob story about rushing to see his brother, who had just had a heart attack. At Bristol Temple Meads, he walked away from the station and stole a ten-year-old VW Polo parked in a back street. It was standard training for agents off-grid: steal an old car because they don't stand out and they're easier to break into. Reliability was important and Polos were recommended. Once on the road, he headed down the M5 before taking the Bridgwater turn-off. Finding his destination with a map and a torch hadn't been easy, hence the lateness of his arrival.

'Were you followed?'

Tony ignored the question. 'Why am I here?'

'All in good time. How about a livener first?' Tony nodded and watched as Matt poured two large whiskies from a decanter. They had both filled out since their army days. Always a big man, Matt had added more than a few kilos, but he was fit for his age. Tony was, too. They had joined 'the business' by different routes. Tony had wanted to know the truth about the 'livers' when the bomb factory blew up. He had taken a journalism degree and become an investigative reporter before being headhunted. Matt had been recruited from the army. He'd gone undercover and joined the loyalist paramilitaries, working for Force Seven in Belfast on some very dirty operations. After the Good Friday agreement, he had been retained for his specialist knowledge.

Tony sipped his scotch and enjoyed the warmth coming back into his limbs. 'So when does Hilary get here?' he asked.

Matt frowned. 'She should have been here by now.' Tony felt the first twinges of alarm.

'She's not coming?'

'We'll give her an hour. Have another drink; tell me what you've been up to.'

Hilary de Pear was the MD. Mid-forties, blonde, ruthlessly ambitious, and divorced, she was a career spook who didn't suffer fools gladly. She never repeated herself and never apologised, but she was loyal to her 'people' and always did what she said she was going to do. Her absence was worrying. Tony suppressed his misgivings; after all, this was an unsanctioned meeting so maybe she'd had trouble getting away.

Tony and Matt had a couple of more drinks and tried some small talk, but that soon dried up. Off-grid was dangerous; they were on their own, unsanctioned and it could so easily be misconstrued. After forty-five minutes, Matt checked his phone, looked out the window, and shrugged.

'Alright, I'll have to brief you. I'll make it quick because you need to be back home by first light.'

'That's not long.'

'Long enough. Hilary wants you to go OG again, up north, near Argentina Farm.'

'How long for?'

Matt grimaced. 'As long as it takes.'

'I'm not a field agent,' Tony protested.

'You've done the training, and more to the point, you did the bloody research. You found the anomaly.'

Tony frowned. 'It wasn't much. I still don't get why Hilary shut me down.'

Matt shook his head impatiently. 'The word came from upstairs. She had no choice.'

Tony absorbed this. 'Why now?'

'Hilary thinks the lab is running unsanctioned freelance operations.'

'Who for?'

'We're not sure.' Matt looked around furtively and leaned in closer. 'You remember that ECO conference in Venice? You know where Hodiak died?'

Tony nodded. 'That never made sense to me.'

'Well, what if he wasn't the target? '

'How do you mean?'

'What if it was another delegate?'

'Who?'

Matt grimaced. 'Don't know, yet.'

'There were hundreds of delegates!'

Matt nodded and shrugged. Tony stood up and walked around the oak table. 'I don't get it, Matt. What difference does it make if I go OG?'

'We might flush something into the open.'

'How?'

'Post your results on an open-source intelligence website—the sort that the press routinely monitors.'

'I haven't got anything.'

'There must be something. Otherwise, they wouldn't have shut you down. And remember, they don't know how much you know.'

Tony sighed. 'I'm the bait then?'

Matt nodded. 'If you like? The story will be that you came to us with your research, and we told you it was circumstantial bollocks and to keep quiet about it. You were annoyed at being ignored and decided to publish anyway.'

'And when do you want me to leave?'

'Tomorrow afternoon.' Matt looked at his watch and smiled. 'Today actually.'

'And if I get caught?'

'You're on your own.'

Tony shook his head. 'Hilary's not here; we've got nothing in writing and we don't know anything. If anything happens, I'm toast.'

'Better make sure it doesn't then.'

'Piss off.' Tony pushed back his chair and made for the door.

'Hold on, Tony. Where are you going?'

'Back to my flat and my day job.'

'Look, you did the research, Tony. You know what's happening...'

'I'm not going solo, Matt,' Tony said firmly. 'This job has cost me enough already. I'm not risking anything else.'

Matt nodded sympathetically. 'We've got to do something,' but Tony wasn't listening. He was out of the front door and striding towards his stolen Polo.

Tony and Matt worked for 'Wharfedale Solutions', a private security agency that operated out of a side street in Putney. Their primary function was intelligence-gathering for specific overseas locations, usually to inform a company's deal-making. Intelligence was mostly gathered from sources in the public domain: newspapers, press releases, court records and personal testimony. Occasionally they got a nudge from a classified area: Wharfedale Solutions was staffed by young nerds and ex-spooks from various agencies and was given tasks that the government didn't want to own up to. Tony had become an 'analyst', deployed to comb through the public record and other less accessible sources for information on whatever mission he was engaged in. That was when he first became aware of Argentina Farm.

He had been told to investigate Tweedsmuir Holdings, the Jersey-based hedge fund that had bought a controlling interest in Argentina Farm. Despite trawling through various records, Tony had come up with little apart from a few dead-end shell companies registered in offshore tax havens. Then he'd found R7 Securities. It was based in Vienna, and John had been examining records and photographs of the fund manager when he'd been alerted to a suspicious sudden death in the Austrian capital. John Hodiak, a Russian climate activist and virulent critic of the Putin regime, collapsed while attending an environmental symposium. A Latvian open-source activist claimed that Hodiak had been poisoned by the Russians and posted a grainy CCTV photo of Hodiak talking to someone in the conference bar a few moments before he collapsed. According to the Latvian source, Hodiak's companion wasn't an accredited attendee or a member of staff; was this Hodiak's assassin? Tony had stared at the image, compared it to the photo of R7 Securities' fund manager, and concluded it was the same man.

During the time of the Cameron-Clegg coalition, a newly appointed defence minister had privatised some highly secret research departments with the stated aim of reducing employment costs and overheads. It had the added benefit of enabling certain unpleasant activities to continue without telling the general public, and if it made a profit, the department budget would benefit. When Tony discovered that Argentina Farm was connected to the sudden death of Hodiak, he'd become excited. Was it possible that a British lab was selling its 'state-of-the-art' toxins on the open market? Hilary's first reaction had been to share his excitement, so he'd been mystified when she'd come back and ordered him to cease and desist his investigations. It was a sixth sense that made him copy his investigations onto a flash drive. It was just as well because, a week later, he'd been ordered to delete everything concerned with his research. In fact, security staff had taken his laptop and his phone and deleted his files.

Tony took the M5 north and then the M4 towards London. He filled up at a motorway service station, but he kept his hood up and his head down. He left the car near Acton and caught an early bus to Hammersmith, where he caught another bus. At six forty-four, he slipped into the back alley, entered his flat, and fed his cat, who was, as ever, ravenous. After a shower, he put on a shirt and suit and ate some cereal. The events of the previous night seemed unreal but he knew their import. He suppressed any doubts he felt about his decision and prepared to leave, which is when he received a FaceTime call on his phone from Matt.

'Get out of there now,' Matt hissed.

'What?'

'Hilary's dead. You're in the frame.'

'I don't understand.'

'Her body was in one of the bedrooms.'

'Why didn't you check?' Tony asked, remembering the whisky glass he'd handled, not to mention the door knobs.

'Her car was in the garage round the back. The house was freezing and in darkness. I just assumed I was the first.'

'How did she die?'

Matt shook his head. 'Looks like a heart attack.'

'Natural causes?'

'What do you think?'

'Why am I in the frame then?'

'That bloody report, Tony. They want rid of you.'

'What can I do?'

'Carry on as planned. Hope to flush something out.' Tony considered his options. Matt seemed to read his mind. 'Don't wait, go now!'

Tony stuffed his cat and some CDs into a rucksack, collected his 'shit' bag from the back of the wardrobe, and called a mini-cab. When it arrived, he told it to go to Shepherd's Bush, but halfway there, he changed his mind and directed the driver to a flyover in Ealing. Under the flyover, away from the gaze of any CCTV cameras, Tony left the cab and walked to a tower block via an underpass. In the underpass, he changed from his suit into a hoodie and trainers and jogged to the garage below the tower block, where he kept his Mercedes. Before he left, he attached false plates front and back, threw his bag into the boot, and headed north. He called it his 'shit' bag because it was full of things he would need if the shit hit the fan. There was five grand in cash, three changes of clothes, two second-hand phones with SIMs and batteries removed, a couple of false passports, a gun and two clips of ammunition, rations for a night, and two bottles of water. As he drove, he considered his situation. There'd been nothing on the news about Hilary, but that wasn't surprising. Spook deaths were hushed up, especially if they were suspicious. Only if the body had been discovered by a member of the public were the police involved. Of course, there was always the possibility that Hilary wasn't dead; he only had Matt's word for it, but he'd known Matt a long time, and the fear on his face and in his voice seemed authentic enough.

For the first forty miles, he avoided the big roads and chose an apparently endless sequence of suburbs, through which he carefully observed the speed limit. Past Luton, he headed onto the A1 and drove at a more appropriate pace. Taking the Mercedes was dangerous, but he loved the vehicle and, foolishly, didn't want to leave it behind. Besides, any other method of travel would expose him to CCTV cameras. At least this way, he got away from the capital quickly. He made Newcastle just after three; the rush hour was gearing up. Once past the city, he continued north, taking the A696 to Otterburn and up towards Kielder Forest and the Scottish border. He'd done a three-day field-training course in Kielder a couple of years earlier, and he knew how isolated it was. He pulled off onto a Forestry Commission track and drove far enough to be out of sight of the road. He ate some of his rations and settled down to a fitful slumber in the car. First light found him heading back down the A68. He stopped for fuel in Bellingham, and that's when he saw the faded advert for Fred Charlton's barn conversion holiday let. Tony asked the attendant, who, by good fortune, was a mate of Charlton's. Two nights later, Tony was settled in Charlton's barn with his Mercedes parked out of sight. Charlton had been worried because, although the barn had a land line, there was no internet, which most customers demanded. Tony had assured him that it was fine; he wanted to escape the internet for a month or two. Ten days passed. There was no news about Hilary, and Tony had begun to wonder if she really was dead. He'd had no contact with Matt or anyone else but he knew he would have to act soon. He'd explored the surrounding area, made discreet enquiries about Argentina and was about to publish his dossier when the bloody ramblers appeared.

14. Christmas

Pauline lay still for a moment. Something had woken her. She lay there, trying to suppress her own breathing, and heard something creak. Someone was climbing the cottage stairs.

When she'd looked around the cottage, Pauline had been put off by the stripped pine everywhere. Stripped floorboards were the flavour of the month but the old cottage was draughty and the varnished floors hadn't been sealed properly. She would have preferred carpets but by then, she'd looked at so many properties and made an offer that had been accepted. Stripped pine was easy to clean, and luckily for her, it was damn noisy.

She reached down the side of the bed, closed her hand around the thick end of the poker, and carefully eased herself out until she was upright. She was still dressed, and this reassured her. Standing behind the bedroom door, she held her breath and waited as the steps drew nearer. Another board creaked, and she felt a movement under her feet. He was outside, on the landing. The bedroom door moved aside and Pauline could just make out a dark silhouette. She swung the poker overhead and brought it down on the intruder, but at the last moment, the figure jumped to one side and turned to face her. The follow-through caused Pauline to fall against the wall, but she recovered herself and faced the intruder, breathing like a panther.

'Get out of my house!' She hissed, brandishing the poker.

The intruder whispered. 'Pauline? It's me, Tony.'

Pauline flipped the light switch to reveal Tony looking tired and dishevelled. 'Tony?' She whispered, letting go of the poker, which clattered to the floor.

He took hold of her and whispered. 'What were you doing with that?'

'I thought you were a burglar.' She enjoyed his embrace, but he was cold and shaking. 'You're shivering,' she observed. He nodded, grinning. 'When was the last time you had a decent night's sleep?'

He shrugged. 'Don't know.'

She ushered him towards her bedroom. 'Come on, get into bed.'

He grinned. 'Are we sleeping together?'

Seeing that familiar boyish look, she felt herself blushing, but she pushed the feelings away. 'I'll be in the spare room. Now, take your shoes off; I'll bring you a cup of tea and a hot water bottle.'

'Thank you,' he groaned as he flopped onto her bed.

'And tomorrow, we'll get you checked over.'

He shook his head. 'No doctors.'

He was in bed when she took him a cup of tea and the hot water bottle.

As he sipped the tea and enjoyed the hot water bottle, he looked at her. 'Where've you been, anyway?'

'What do you mean?'

'I've been waiting for you.'

'Have you?' He nodded. 'Where? You weren't in the cottage when I got back?'

'No.'

'So? Where've you been?'

'I had stuff to do. How did you get in?'

'I found the key. It was still under the plant pot.'

'But you stayed outside?' He nodded. 'Why?'

'Old habits,' he slurred.

'You must have been frozen.'

'I was in the outhouse,' he grinned. 'You were in bed?' She nodded. 'So, why aren't you undressed?'

'I couldn't be bothered. I was knackered.'

He closed his eyes, then opened them again. 'You still haven't told me where...,' but by then he was asleep.

'I'll tell you in the morning,' she whispered, turning out the light.

They had let her go. One minute, she'd been in the pool with the freezing water rising, and then the water had been turned off and strong hands were lifting her out. A couple of hours later, after coffee and a sandwich and with her clothes dried, she'd been placed in the back of a van with a blindfold over her eyes and driven somewhere. The people who ministered to her wore ski masks and said nothing until they stopped and helped her from the vehicle. They ordered her not to look around while the blindfold was removed and then drove away. Dazed and disoriented by the cold air, Pauline stood still, unable to process what had happened, until an icy blast jolted her. She was standing by her Micra in the Waitrose car park in Hexham which was unusually quiet for a weekday. An ice-cream van went past playing a tinny, reverb version of 'Rudolf the Red-Nosed Reindeer' but Pauline barely registered the sound. Hexham was cold and she was in shock. Nobody paid her any attention.

She didn't know why she had been released and right then, she didn't care. She removed two parking tickets from her windscreen and got into the car. The familiar smell and the feel of the steering wheel were surreal. What had happened to her? Why had she been arrested, and why had they let her go? She considered reporting the incident to the police but Buchan knew everything about her. He had threatened Lavinia and the girls. She was on their radar and there was no going back to her old life.

She drove home on autopilot, feeling blank and empty of everything except apprehension. She entered the cottage, poured herself a generous scotch, munched on a sandwich, and went back over everything that had happened. Just before they'd taken her from the pool, she thought she'd heard a woman's voice whispering urgently, 'Buchan!'

Something must have changed, but what? She didn't know where Tony was, and as she'd kept telling herself, she hadn't actually done anything wrong. As the effect of the scotch waned, exhaustion overtook her. She'd made her way upstairs and collapsed onto her bed, where she'd fallen asleep until she heard the intruder.

She awoke early and was momentarily surprised to find herself in her spare room. She scanned the shelves of books and smiled at the pile of 'must-read' books on her desk. She'd intended to revisit the feminist classics of her youth, Mary Wollstonecraft, Simone de Beauvoir, Betty Frieden, and Germaine Greer, not to mention literary classics like 'The Bell Jar' and 'The Yellow Wall-Paper', but the truth was that away from her university job, her motivation had waned. Isolation had weighed on her, and instead of completing a paper on the role of northern women in nineteenth-century British political life, she'd begun to excavate her own emotional history. The bedroom door opened, and Tony appeared holding two mugs.

'I thought you might like some tea?' he grinned.

Pauline sat up in bed and took the mug gratefully. 'Thanks.'

He leaned over and kissed her on the cheek. 'Oh, and merry Christmas, Pauline.'

She rubbed her cheek. 'Are you sure?'

'Think so.'

'Same to you, then.' She grinned and shook her head. 'Christ, what must I look like?'

'You look fine.'

'Before all this happened, I would have died if a strange man had seen me first thing in the morning, especially on Christmas Day.'

'I'm not strange, am I?' Tony smiled and parked himself on the chair by her desk. He was barefoot but wearing jeans and a t-shirt.

'Are you OK?' She asked.

'Better than I would have been if you'd connected with that poker.'

'Sorry about that.'

He shook his head. 'My fault. You didn't know I was here.'

'Not true.'

'No?'

'You left the seat up.'

'When?'

'When I got back from the hospital two days ago, the loo seat was up. I knew you must be around.'

Tony sprang up, went to the bedroom window, and peered out.

'Have you got a radio somewhere? I haven't heard the news for a while.'

'It'll just be more rubbish about Christmas,' Pauline began, but something in his stance alerted her. She pointed to a radio at the back of her desk. Tony switched it on and turned up the volume. He then scribbled on a piece of paper and passed it to her. 'Someone else has been here. Assume they're listening!'

'Right,' Pauline said. 'I'm hungry. Fancy some breakfast?'

The fridge was almost empty, and the freezer wasn't much better. Breakfast was beans on toast, accompanied by carols played at full volume.

'Sorry, I haven't got anything more interesting. I haven't had time to shop.'

'It's delicious,' Tony replied, but he ate hurriedly, twitching like a weasel. 'Why haven't you time to shop?'

Pauline was about to tell him, but then she shrugged. 'With everything that's happened, I forgot.'

Tony stood up. 'I need to show you where I slept, in the outhouse.'

At some point in the past, the outhouse had been the outside loo. Three steps from the back door, the walls and floor were still tiled, if cracked and discoloured, and the tiny room was as cold as a mortuary. The toilet had been removed, but a small corner sink still worked. A couple of Pauline's unpacked tea chests were stacked against the wall. She stood facing Tony and shivered.

'How do you know someone else has been here?'

'After you told me off, I made a point of leaving the loo seat down.'

'Right.'

'Tell me what's happened since we last saw each other.' Pauline told him about Mary and the ward and trying to post the dossier at the university but failing because of the firewall.

She told him about going back to the cottage and finding the loo seat up. Tony looked at her.

'That was two days ago. What have you done since then?'

She wanted to tell him the truth, but as she began to speak, the sound of Buchan's sibilant threat in her ear filled her mind, and she choked.

'I got a call from the hospital asking me to go back. They said she hadn't got long.'

'What about her son?'

'Apparently, he can't get here until the day after Boxing Day.'

'And is she dead? Mary?'

Pauline shook her head slowly. 'No. She's rallied.'

'Really?'

'It happens sometimes,' Pauline replied, amazed at her capacity to lie. She'd had no thought of dissembling, but then again, she had never been in a situation like this.

'What is it you aren't telling me?' Tony asked.

'Nothing.'

'You're lying. Why?'

'Alright,' she said, taking a deep breath. 'I haven't posted the dossier?'

'Why not?'

'I was scared for God's sake.'

Tony took her hands in his and looked her in the eye. 'I'm really sorry about everything, Pauline. I'm sorry about dragging you into this when it had nothing to do with you, but you have to post that dossier. Please?'

'I threw it away.'

'What?'

'The flash drive, I got rid of it.'

'Why!?'

'Tony, it's Christmas Day, and I'm standing in the freezing outhouse having a whispered conversation because I'm scared to death.'

Tony sighed. 'Alright, alright.'

'Who do you think is listening?'

'I told you, I don't know. Look, after Christmas, when

94

everything's open again, do me a favour and post the dossier, will you?'

'Haven't you been listening? I got rid of the flash drive.'

Tony pursed his lips and glanced to his right. 'There's a spare.'

'Where?'

'On the cat collar, sewn in.'

'Why didn't you tell me?'

'Belt and braces; another old habit.'

'You don't trust me after everything that's happened?'

'I know the kind of people we're dealing with. If they'd got hold of you, you might have been persuaded to tell them.'

'But if I don't know, I can't tell?'

'Something like that.' He began to shiver violently. 'Can we go back inside? It's freezing out here.' She nodded. She was annoyed at his lack of trust, even though she hadn't vouchsafed her own secret. She opened the outhouse door, but he pulled her back and kissed her hard on the lips. She pulled away.

'What was that for?'

He shrugged and glanced up towards the cobwebbed ceiling.

'I thought I saw some mistletoe.'

Despite herself, she looked up and grinned. 'I think I've got some inside.'

He nodded. 'Put the kettle on, will you?'

She was still smiling as she crossed the path and opened the back door. A noise behind her caused her to turn, but a hand gripped her by the throat and pushed her hard against the back wall. It was the athletic man from the church. The smell of his powerful aftershave competed with the garlic on his breath. She tried to resist, but he tightened his grip.

'I hurt you.' He said it simply—a statement of fact. Behind him, two more men pinioned Tony's arms. The athletic man looked at Tony. 'Go quiet, or I break bone.'

Tony nodded and looked at the man. Something about him was familiar, and then it came to him. He was the man from the bar in Vienna talking to Hodiak. The brief pause caused the man's crony to yank Tony's arm even more. Tony gasped in pain.

'Alright, alright. I'll come with you. Sorry about this, Pauline,' he said, looking at her, his eyes wide and intense. 'Don't forget to feed the cat,' and then he was hustled away.

The man held Pauline's throat in his powerful grip and waited until a shout came from out front. He leant in close to her. 'Do nothing. If you talk, you and your man will die.' An extra squeeze left her bent double and gasping for breath. She heard a vehicle hurrying away up the lane, and then it was quiet again. In the distance, the bells of St. Leonard's began to peal in festive celebration.

15. Short Days

The day Tony was taken was bleak. There was little light and little to eat in the cottage, but, unlike Tony's cat, food was the last thing on her mind. During the short, grey day and long night, Pauline ate sparingly, drank scotch, and listened to Bach, but she couldn't settle. She went back and forth over everything and wrote down what she knew. Buchan had threatened her with Lavinia and then let her go, but she didn't know why. If Pauline never made contact with Lavinia, then Buchan would have no reason to respond. Mary Campion was close to death; Tony had saved her in the blizzard and didn't seem like a bad person, unlike the people who'd come for him. Tony had helped her and begged her to post the dossier. Pauline wondered if there was a way of doing it that avoided attracting attention to herself. She didn't sleep; fear kept her alert even when she was exhausted, but beneath the fear, she felt a growing anger. In bed in the small hours, she raged at the injustice of it all until an unexpected noise downstairs sent her quivering beneath the duvet in terror again. And she spent too long thinking about Lavinia, wondering what she and her children were like, scaring herself by imagining them being taken into care.

The next day, she resolved to try and be more productive, but the resolution disintegrated in the face of her persistent fearfulness. Lunch was a slice of toast and a large whisky, which was followed by another. Afterwards, she sat in the armchair and promptly fell asleep.

'Is anyone there?' Pauline came awake in darkness, not knowing where she was for a moment. She wasn't expecting anyone. They had come back, and she was helpless. She closed her hand around the old poker that nestled against the chair. She wasn't going quietly. The light was switched on, blinding her momentarily.

'Oh, you are in. Good.'

She knew the voice. 'Jonathan?'

'Yes, it's me.' I hope you don't mind me popping round?'

'What do you want?' Pauline managed, releasing the poker from her grasp. As she looked at him, nodding, she could see that he was blushing, the colour spreading under his beard and into his cheeks. 'Is it about the flowers, Jonathan?'

He shook his head. 'We were worried about you. No one had seen you.' Who was the 'we' he referred to, Pauline wondered? Was he involved? 'You're not ill, are you?'

'No. Do I look ill?'

'A little tired, perhaps.' Not surprising given that she'd hardly slept for a week and hadn't done her hair or make-up. 'And you did have that hospital visit just before Christmas.'

She stood up and faced him, smoothing her hair with a hand. 'I must have fallen asleep in the chair.'

'It's allowed,' he said with a slight smile.

'Can I get you anything, Jonathan? Tea, coffee, or something stronger? I've got whisky, sherry.'

'A small sherry perhaps?' The nodding went into overdrive.

Pauline poured two sherries and handed one to him. 'Merry Christmas.'

'Indeed, Merry Christmas.' He drank appreciatively. 'I thought we might have seen you at one of our services?'

'I've er been a bit busy,' Pauline struggled.

'I mean, I know you're not a believer, but you have done such a lovely job with the flowers.' He left the sentence hanging.

'You thought I might be tempted?'

'I'm not sure that's the right word, but we would be pleased to see you there. After all, you are a parishioner.'

She nodded. 'Yes, I suppose I am.'

'And the church is for everyone.'

'Jesus loves us all,' Pauline murmured.

'Well, quite.' He finished his sherry and put the glass down carefully. 'I must be going, but please do come along. You're always very welcome.' He smiled hesitantly and turned to go, still nodding to himself. Something about his behaviour got to Pauline.

'Why do you do this, Jonathan?' She snapped. He turned back and stared. 'Why visit me?'

'It's my job,' he smiled. 'You do the flowers for St. Leonard's, and we haven't seen you.'

'Is it just me, or does everyone get your personal attention?' She snapped, wondering momentarily if he was coming onto her. He didn't answer, but a vivid flush of colour began to rise in his cheeks. Pauline wasn't finished. 'You're an intelligent man. Why waste your life being a vicar?'

He pushed his head back so that he was standing erect. 'I don't think it is a waste.'

'You're right I'm not a believer, but what confuses me is how anyone can be. I mean, life after death is a fairy tale isn't it?'

'That's not the main thing that motivates me,' he said. For once, the nodding had stopped.

'What is it then?'

'I suppose it's the notion of redemption.' He thought for a moment. 'Yes, that's it, I think.'

'What? That we can be saved if we repent of our sins and do good works?'

'Yes, but put like that, it sounds archaic.'

'How would you put it then?'

'Well, it seems to me that the hardest thing to do is forgive ourselves. But I do think that it is possible if we try and do the right thing. I mean, it takes time. It's not an instant fix. Our feelings change slowly, but we can affect them.'

'And find peace?'

'Well, less discomfort anyway.'

'But how do we know what the right thing is, Jonathan?'

He looked at her calmly. 'I think we do. There's something ineffable about it.'

'Because Jesus tells us?'

'Something does.'

'How do we find out? By praying? By standing in the graveyard and yelling at the sky?'

He took a step towards her. 'What's happened, Pauline?'

'What do you mean?'

'Something's upset you.'

Despite herself, she began welling up. She was close to losing control and telling all. Seeing her distress, Jonathan put his arm around her but she pushed him away roughly, retreating into a lie..

'I've had some bad news.'

'I'm sorry to her that,' he stuttered, still unclear about what had happened. The nodding was back. Driven by whisky and stress, she'd had to pull back before she placed him in real jeopardy

'Sorry about giving you the third degree,' she said.

'Not at all. Arguments about theology are rare these days.'

'It wasn't very fair.'

'Nonsense. That's what I'm here for,' he replied, attempting a smile.

When Pauline had moved to the village, his diffident uncertainty had driven her mad. She'd wanted to grab hold of him and shake him, but after all the skullduggery, his tentative mannerisms were gently reassuring. But she wanted to keep him safe, and to do that, he had to be at arm's length.

'Sometimes it helps to talk.' Jonathan offered.

Pauline nodded. 'I don't think I'm ready yet.'

'Well, when you are, you know where to find me.'

'That's kind of you.'

'Right, see you later.'

Pauline shut the door behind him, and when she was sure he was out of earshot, she turned the key and pulled the bolt across. She sat in the chair again, but she didn't drink any more whisky. A plan had begun to form.

On the Friday morning before New Year's Eve, Pauline drove to Newcastle and parked in one of the university car parks. She then entered one of the newer buildings and began to walk quickly down long, deserted corridors. Like all universities, Newcastle had expanded enormously over the previous quarter century, but the original, red-brick campus remained at its core. Departments had expanded to cope with increasing student numbers, creating an unlovely Legoland of buildings in different materials and styles. The haphazard nature of these additions meant that it was possible for students and staff to walk a considerable distance without ever venturing outdoors. Pauline's university pass had not been cancelled, and she selected her parking place well. If anyone was following her, they would have trouble entering the university. She emerged close to Percy Street and made her way to the central library, where she sat down at one of the communal terminals and began to type. Open until lunchtime, the library was deserted apart from a skeleton staff. The streets were filling up; the first cohort of determined drinkers was already in its stride but after two winter months, the Christmas decorations were beginning to look careworn. Pauline was the only person using the computer terminals, and she realised she was both visible and memorable. She tried to ignore her misgivings and settled down to her task.

Pauline logged on using Mary's email details. Heart racing, she took the tiny flash drive that she'd recovered from the cat's collar and inserted it into the USB slot. Unlike the university, there was no rejection as she loaded the data onto the allotted website. Afterwards, she withdrew the flash drive, logged off, and walked out into the town. She sauntered back to her car, pausing now and then to look in shop windows, but in reality, she was looking to see if anyone were following her. She didn't see anything, but that didn't mean much. She drove back via Hexham where she bought food and whisky for herself and a few tins of cat food. Then she drove back to Bridgford and settled down to wait.

January 2019
Northumberland

16. Stranger

It was New Year's Day, and Pauline had been sorting out the flowers at St. Leonard's, binning some and changing the water in others. The activity and the building had a calming effect and helped place her feelings and fears in some kind of perspective. In the days immediately after Tony was snatched, the realisation that she might never meet Lavinia or her grandchildren had become an ache that threatened to unhinge her. Despite her lack of faith, she couldn't deny that Jonathan's visit had made a difference. After the brutality and drama of recent experience, his hesitant, humane decency touched her. Perhaps for the first time, Pauline had begun to feel that she might stay in Bridgford. That's what prompted her to attend Evensong on the last Sunday of the year. It was the first time she'd been in St. Leonard's since finding Tony in the quiet chapel. She approached the place hesitantly but the atmosphere in the crowded church overtook her. The congregation, clad in winter coats beneath the guttering candles, gave the building an ethereal quality and she enjoyed the service. They sang 'In the Deep Mid-Winter', a childhood favourite that she had always regarded as pagan. Perhaps that's why she liked it. Afterwards, Jonathan buttonholed her at the door.

'Good to see you, Pauline,' he smiled.

'I enjoyed it. Sorry about giving you the third degree the other night.'

'That's alright,' he replied, nodding furiously. 'How are you feeling?'.

'Better, thank you,' she smiled.

'In that case, can we prevail upon you to look after the flowers over the New Year?'

It was neatly done. He had backed her into a corner, and she hadn't the heart to say no. And so on New Year's Day, she returned to do the flowers. Four nights had passed since she'd posted the dossier and nothing had happened. The church was empty and cold and she pottered quietly until the bells began chiming in celebration of the new year. The noise was deafening and drove her out. As she locked up, she decided she would tell Jonathan that celebrating the end of the holiday was pointless. Instead of church bells, they should have something mournful to herald the dank, grey days of January. She was arguing with herself about this as she approached the cottage when she noticed that the back door was wide open and the kitchen light was on. Her pulse went off the scale, she slowed down. She'd left the place locked and in darkness. So much for Christian virtue; reality had returned. She retrieved the poker, which she'd left in the outhouse, and tiptoed inside.

A figure was sprawled across her sofa, listening to earphones. The creature was wearing a combat jacket, walking trousers, and muddy boots, which were perched nonchalantly on the arm of her settee. At first, Pauline thought it was a youth, but as she looked closer, a female form began to appear. Pauline slammed the back door, walked up to the supine figure, and knocked her feet off the sofa with the poker. The girl sprang up with a cry.

'What's your fucking problem?' She asked in a cockney accent.

'Get your filthy boots off my sofa.'

'Jesus Christ!'

'And my carpet, for that matter,' Pauline added. 'Would you mind taking them off?'

The girl pulled out her EarPods and mimicked Pauline's accent. 'Would you mind taking your fucking boots off?'

'Now please.'

The girl sighed theatrically and began to unlace her boots. Then she took off her coat and threw it across the room. She had short blonde hair with dark roots and appeared to be covered in tattoos. Pauline put her age at mid-twenties.

'Got anything to drink?' the girl asked.

'I'll put the kettle on.'

'It's New Year's Day. I want a proper drink and put that bloody thing down.'

Pauline put down the poker and poured two large whiskies.

'How did you get in?' She asked as she passed over a glass.

'I picked the lock, didn't I?'

'I don't know. That's why I asked.'

The girl gulped her whisky and nodded. 'I'm Lissa.'

'Well, Lisa, I'm Pauline.'

'Not Lisa, fucking Lissa.' Lissa yelled. 'And I know who you are, don't I?'

'I don't know. What are you doing in my house?'

'What do you think? I'm the bleeding cavalry. I've come to fucking help you, haven't I?'

Pauline stared at the dishevelled, foul-mouthed young woman. 'Help me with what?' She asked quietly.

'Getting Tony back. Beating the bad guys.'

Pauline felt a stab of alarm. She picked up a pad and wrote a message in capital letters, 'THEY ARE LISTENING' and showed it to Lissa, who grinned.

'Don't worry; I've scrambled it.'

'Won't they be suspicious when they can't hear us?'

Lissa shook her head. 'They'll think it's their equipment shorting.' She went to the bottle of whisky and poured herself another one. She stopped with her glass in mid-air and looked at Pauline quizzically.

Pauline smiled. 'Help yourself.'

'You want one?' Lissa asked.

'No, I'm going to make some food.'

She made the same simple pasta dish she had previously made for Tony. Lissa picked at it with her fork as if it might be dangerous.

'What's in it?'

'Tomatoes, onions, garlic, and a bit of dried basil. I'm sorry, I don't have much in.'

106

'No, it's OK. It's just food, you know, but we never know where it's from.'

'Don't we?' Pauline asked, puzzled.

'Unless we produce it ourselves, we don't know who grew it or what their lives are like.'

'And that's important to you, Lissa?'

Lissa nodded. 'Should be important to everyone, or it should have been. Doesn't matter now.'

Pauline put down her fork and chewed for a moment. 'Lissa, is it short for Melissa?'

'It's not short for anything, alright? It's just Lissa!'

'Why are you so angry?'

Lissa sighed. 'Because everything's so shit.'

'How come you want to help Tony?'

'He's an old mate of my dad's.'

'And who's your father?'

'Matt Hardwick. He works with Tony, or he did.'

'I don't follow,' Pauline said quietly.

Lissa sighed. 'Tony's been shafted. He went off-grid to help my dad's boss, but then she died, and they're both knackered unless I can help.'

Pauline ate some food and considered. 'You're young Lissa. Shouldn't you be off enjoying yourself?'

Lissa laughed loudly. 'How?'

'Travelling, falling in love, the usual.'

Lissa snorted. 'I can't do that, can I?'

'Why not?' Pauline asked.

'The planet's dying. The world's had it.'

'That's very bleak.'

'Climate change is melting the glaciers, changing weather patterns, raising sea levels, and increasing the acidity of the oceans. We're in the middle of a mass extinction event that we've caused. In a hundred years, there won't be many humans left, and their lives will be brutal. How can I go on holiday knowing that? Knowing that everything I do is making it worse.'

'There must be something we can do,' Pauline said quietly.

Lissa pointed her fork angrily in Pauline's direction. 'What, like cleaning plastic off beaches or shopping with a Hessian bag? Piss off!'

Pauline nodded. 'I see.'

'You think I'm mad, don't you?' Lissa snapped.

Pauline shook her head. 'No. I used to feel the same when I was your age.'

'What happened then?'

Pauline grinned apologetically. 'I fell pregnant with Robert.'

Lissa continued chewing for a moment, then she had a thought.

'There is one thing humans can do that will make a difference,'

Pauline looked up. 'What's that?'

'Die.'

'What?'

'You heard!' Pauline shook her head. Lissa went on. 'It took a hundred thousand years for the human population to reach a billion, but just another fifty years to reach two. We're approaching eight billion, and in forty years there'll be thirty-two billion. There are too many people on the planet, and we all want everything. So we cut down forests, build cities, fly around the globe, drive everywhere, cover everything with plastic, fish out the oceans, and eat meat, and it won't stop until we're stopped.'

'You think we will be?'

Lissa nodded. 'Eventually, but by then, it will be too late. It'll start with shortages—food, water, and stuff—so then there'll be wars and disease.'

'The four horsemen,' Pauline muttered. Lissa frowned. 'War, famine, pestilence—the Four Horsemen of the Apocalypse? From the book of Revelation?' Pauline offered, 'I was brought up in a religious family. Most people were back in the day.'

Lissa considered it for a moment. 'That's only three. What's the fourth?'

'Death.' Lissa nodded and went back to her pasta. 'And that's why you don't do holidays?'

Lissa looked up. 'I tried getting away from it all, you know, doing what everyone else does—sun, sea, sangria, and all that—but I had to stop.'

'Why?'

'Wherever I was, I couldn't stop thinking about what the place would be like after the apocalypse.'

'Coastal cities inundated?'

Lissa nodded. 'Settlements filled with burnt-out, deserted houses Villages and leafy suburbs deserted, windows gone, doors smashed, gardens full of weeds, and huge packs of wild dogs.'

'Dogs?'

Lissa nodded. 'After people, they're the most successful mammal on the planet. There are eight billion people and a billion dogs. Four hundred generations ago, they were wolves. Go figure.'

'You don't like them then?'

'It doesn't matter. I don't mind them on their own, but now there are so many of them. People have gone nuts. Go to any beach and you'll see more dogs than people.'

Pauline nodded. 'I know what you mean.'

'Imagine them hungry, aggressive, and working together.'

'It's happened before.'

'Has it?' Lissa was interested now.

'There were packs of ravenous dogs in Madrid during the Spanish Civil War.'

'There you go then,' Lissa finished her pasta and pushed her plate away. 'How do you know that?'

Pauline smiled. 'I'm a history lecturer, or I used to be.'

'Yeah?' Lissa grinned, then stopped. 'Dad thinks you must be a pro.'

Pauline felt a pulse of fear in her gut. That's what Buchan had said. She tried to recover herself. 'Why?'

Lissa shrugged. 'You posted the dossier.'

Pauline nodded. 'Yes?'

'Why?'

'Tony asked me to.'

Lissa leant towards Pauline. 'But if you're just Miss Joanna Normal, why take the risk?'

Pauline sighed. 'I thought it was the right thing to do.'

'Yeah?' Lissa shook her head sceptically. 'Whose email did you use when you logged on?'

'My friend, Mary's. She's dying. I thought it might throw them off my track.'

'But they weren't Mary's email details,' Lissa said.

'Whose were they then?'

'Some dead bloke called Karl.'

Pauline was momentarily confused, then she remembered. 'Mary's husband, Jack, a few years ago, he fancied himself as a novelist. Karl was his pen name; it was a private joke because he was a lifelong Marxist. That's why he used Karl as his email address. Mary never got around to setting up her own email details.' Lissa shook her head, smiling. Pauline protested. 'It's true! I don't understand digital technology. Mary's the same. That's why she uses Jack's email.'

Lissa grinned, unconvinced. Pauline tried again. 'Lissa, I'm a middle-aged woman living alone who took pity on a stranger when he asked me for help.'

'Why did you do that?' Lissa asked.

'He looked interesting, and I felt sorry for him; more fool me. Next thing I know, I'm a fugitive in the middle of a murderous conspiracy I know nothing about, and everyone thinks I'm a spy.'

Lissa thought for a moment and nodded. 'Yep. That's right.'

'And the only person who can help me, apparently, is a profane, eco-nihilist.'

Lissa looked at Pauline for a moment, then shook her head. 'I'm not a fucking nihilist; I'm a realist, a fucking eco-realist.'

Pauline sighed. Then she stood up and made sure the doors and windows were locked and bolted. She came back, sat down again, and sipped her drink.

'If everything in the world is so hopeless, Lissa, why do you want to help?'

'I can't just sit around and do nothing while I wait for Armageddon, can I?' Pauline shrugged. 'Besides, my dad asked me. At least this way, I can try and take down some bad people.'

'You're doing this for your father?'

Lissa shook her head. 'Not really. We don't get on; we clash all the time, but every so often, we help each other, don't we?'

'What makes him think you can help?'

'I was in the business, wasn't I?'

'The business?'

'Cloak and dagger bollocks, security.'

'That's where you learned to scramble listening devices?'

Lissa nodded. 'Five years in the army, the last two seconded to some hush-hush unit. Dad pulled a few strings.'

'So what happened?'

'I looked around and saw what was happening. So I got out, didn't I?'

Pauline considered for a moment. 'Would you mind not doing that?'

Lissa was nonplussed. 'Doing what?'

'Putting a rhetorical question at the end of everything you say and using 'fuck' all the time.'

'What?'

'It's driving me mad, isn't it? I don't understand fucking digital technology, do I?' Pauline blurted in a mock cockney accent.

Lissa looked at Pauline and then burst out laughing. 'Piss off! I'm the fucking cavalry,' she paused before adding, 'aren't I?' Despite herself, Pauline couldn't help laughing.

As the light faded, Pauline drew the curtains and cleared the plates into the kitchen. Then she went upstairs and checked the spare room. Lissa appeared.

'What are you doing?'

'I presume you want to stay?' Pauline replied.

Lissa shook her head. 'We've got to go.'

'When?'

'Now. Tonight!'

Pauline sighed and sat down on the bed. 'I'm not going.'

'They'll come looking to see why their equipment isn't working.'

'I'm sick of all this nonsense, Lissa.'

'They'll question you.'

'So? I'll say I don't know or I'll just tell them about you. The truth is so much easier than lying.'

For a moment, a look resembling confusion passed over Lissa's face. 'Don't be a bastard, Pauline. I can't do it without you.'

'Do what?'

'Rescue Tony.'

'How are we going to do that, Lissa?'

'I have a plan.'

'What possible use am I?'

'You saved him before, didn't you? Walking over the moor?'

'You know about that?'

'You made a big impression on him.'

Pauline considered this. 'Is he seeing anyone?'

'Interested, are we?' Lissa said, raising her eyebrows archly. 'That's why you helped him.'

'No!'

'Methinks she doth protest too fucking much,' Lissa grinned.

'Well, is he in a relationship?'

Lissa shook her head. 'Not since Kate, and that was years ago.'

'What happened?'

Lissa shrugged. 'Nasal sex.' Pauline looked confused. 'Fuck knows. He doesn't confide in me.'

'I see.'

'He's a spook. He doesn't tell anyone anything. Right, come on then; we need to move.'

Pauline stayed where she was. 'No, I'm not doing it.'

Lissa swore softly and fished something out of her pocket. When Pauline looked up, she saw that Lissa was pointing a gun at her. 'You've got to.'

'You're going to shoot me?'

Lissa shook her head. 'No, because you're coming with me.'

"Why?' Pauline didn't understand.

'If you're an amateur, you're a bloody good one, and you may be able to help.'

'And if I'm not?' Pauline said.

'Well, then you'll be warning them as soon as I've gone, and I can't have that, can I?'

'For Christ's sake! What if I try and run away?'

'I'm thirty years younger than you; I'm fitter, and I'm trained in martial arts.'

'And you've got a gun,' Pauline added. 'Don't forget that.'

Lissa grinned. 'Yeah,'

Pauline took a deep breath. 'What is so bloody important that makes all these people run about killing each other?'

Lissa regarded her and shrugged. 'There are two kinds of poison attacks: very public ones like Litvinenko and the Skripals designed to scare anyone else who might be tempted to fight back. But they've always wanted the other sort, the kind that leaves no trace.'

'That's not new,' Pauline said. 'They killed Beresovsky with something similar, didn't they?'

Lissa shook her head. 'No. They found traces of a plant extract when they looked. This leaves no trace. Extremely useful for high-value targets.'

'Like who?'

'Powerful people with lots of security. If their genome is known, and it usually is, then all Argentina needs is an emissary.'

'I don't follow.'

'The emissary carries a molecular trigger in their bloodstream. It's harmless to them, but if they get into the same room as the target, that's it.'

'What happens?' Pauline asked.

'The target absorbs a virus and dies of a heart attack. It looks natural because it is.'

'And you think they're going to use this on someone?'

'We know they are, but we don't know who and we don't know when. Now come on.'

'Where are we going?' Pauline asked.

'You'll find out soon enough, but go and put an extra layer on top and bottom and get some gloves, will you?' Pauline began to move but Lissa hadn't finished. 'Have you got any boots?'

'Yes.'

'Well, put them on.'

'Are we walking?'

'Sod that, I'll call a cab.'

'Right,' Pauline said, confused. Then she remembered something. 'I must leave a note for Jonathan.'

'Who!?'

'The vicar. I promised I'd do the flowers for him on Friday.'

Lissa stared at her and frowned. 'You're mad, you are.'

'You think it's a bad idea?'

Lissa nodded, then stopped. 'No, go ahead. It's bloody clever.'

'Is it?'

Lissa nodded. 'No wonder Dad thinks you're a pro.'

17. Argentina Farm

They had shackled Tony's hands and feet with plastic ties so tightly that he was losing the feeling in them. In addition, they'd shoved a gag in his mouth, but, surprisingly, they hadn't bothered to blindfold him. In the gathering gloom of the end-of-year dusk, he had watched the countryside passing by through the tinted windows of the black four by four. They drove quickly—too quickly for the twisting lanes as they climbed up the narrow river valley. The reckless speed showed that they thought themselves untouchable, a dangerous assumption.

They hurtled into the Argentina complex and skidded to a halt in the farmyard. Tony was hustled from the vehicle and straight into the lift in the piggery. His final destination was an ante-chamber off the biological clean room, some seventy feet below. There, he was stripped naked, his clothes were burned, and his orifices were inspected. Then he was placed in an all-in-one paper suit with a plastic zip from the crotch. Finally, he was placed on a gurney, clamped by his hands and feet and left. The room was high-tech, all stainless steel and plastic moulding. In one corner was a sealed inspection chamber with a glass front, which could be reached by two rubber gauntlets attached to the glass. Behind the window was what appeared to be a cage. Small cables and filaments hung from the ceiling, apparently for use as required. Tony couldn't see what they were for, and he had to strain against his shackles to see the chamber. After a short while, he gave up, exhausted.

Brian was watching the monitors alone when Tina entered the room. For once, she was smiling and in a good mood and nodded to Brian as she leant forward on the desk to peer at his checker-board screen with its four views of the surrounding area. With Tina right next to him, Brian was rattled. Her secret smile a few days earlier had become his nightly obsession, and here she was leaning in so that he could smell her perfume and see the line of her jaw and neck. Breathing heavily, he stroked her hand on the desk, turning his face upwards towards her as he did.

'Tina?' he whispered, but she stiffened and pulled her hand away.

'You?' She looked at him wide-eyed, incredulous, and shook her head. Brian felt himself going red. He tried to speak, but nothing came. Tina grimaced and left the room, slamming the door behind her. Brian watched on the monitor as she strode across the yard and into the piggery.

Tina was surprised and irritated by Brian, but she had important business below ground with Tony Brooks. This operation would be over soon and Argentina Farm would be a fading memory. Brian didn't respond well to rejection and he bore grudges.

They must have left Tony for several hours because he was very thirsty by the time they came for him. There were two of them, the same pair, who had come to the church. The redhead's face came into view.

'Why did you investigate Ivan Hodiak?'

She was talking about the Ukrainian eco-activist who had died suddenly while attending a conference in Venice.

'Who?' Tony whispered and got a blow to his jaw that caused his head to jump up and down off the gurney.

'Why you interested?' The man asked.

'We had a tip-off, saying someone had been targeted.' Tony knew he had to give them something while trying to keep the important stuff back. 'Hodiak was found dead in his hotel room. Everyone else went home.'

'Hodiak die of natural causes,' the man smiled.

Tony nodded. 'Certainly looked like it.'

'Where did tip-off come from?'

'We weren't told,' Tony lied. The information had come from a Russian source.

'What were you told?' The red-headed woman asked.

'That a female eco-journalist had been targeted.'

'Hodiak not female,' the man sneered.

'No shit, Sherlock,' Tony whispered, receiving another blow to his temple.

'Why you investigate him?'

Tony shrugged. 'He was an eco-activist. Maybe the tip-off was wrong about the gender? Nobody could work out why he died.'

The redhead's face reappeared above him. 'Tell us about your woman, Tony?' Tony frowned, confused.

'Woman from church,' the man said.

'Oh,' Tony said, 'she's not my woman,' he struggled. 'Look, is there any chance of a glass of water?'

'Tell us what you know, and we give you water.'

'Don't know what you mean,' Tony replied, but he felt himself sinking. They were pros; they knew how it worked. They weren't going to let him go, whatever he told them. The longer he could hold out, the better, but in the back of his mind, doubts were beginning to assert themselves. He was on his own. Hilary was dead, and Matt was stymied. So what if he held out? The end would be the same. He was worried about Pauline; he'd used her, and she had been decent. Lying there on the gurney, he realised he liked Pauline and now she was in jeopardy. He pushed the guilt away and tried to remember his training, but his days on the run had taken their toll, not least the shivering in Pauline's outhouse. The only way to hold out was to make them believe he had something important he hadn't told them.

'The woman who help you in church. Who is she?'

'Pauline? As far as I know, she's a retired history lecturer,' Tony replied.

The man hit him hard across his cheek with the flat of his hand. catching him off-guard. The noise of the blow was deafening and reverberated inside his skull. Then the pain began. 'Answer question.'

'I don't know anything,' Tony protested. 'I asked her not to give me away in the church and she didn't.'

'Why she help you?' The man asked.

'I think she felt sorry for me.' Tony flinched, anticipating a blow, but none came.

'Why?' The woman asked.

'I don't know. Really, I don't.' That was true. When it came down to it, Tony had no idea why Pauline had helped him.

Tina peered down at him. Looking up at her face, Tony could see her make-up needed a retread; there were bags under her eyes. 'You go back to cottage after church?'

Tony nodded. 'I had nowhere else to go.' Tina shook her head in disbelief. Tony pushed on. 'You were after me; my lot are after me, not to mention the police. I didn't have many options. Still don't.'

Tina lent back and muttered something to the man. Tony couldn't make out what they were saying, but it wasn't English. He heard a couple of words. They were arguing, and it sounded like Italian. Tina was berating the man for leaving Pauline behind; the man replied in an angry gabble. Tina shook her head, told him to be quiet, and turned back to Tony.

'This woman, Pauline, she help you for no reason?'

'I don't know.'

'Is she Christian?' The man asked.

'She was in church,' Tony replied. This time, the blow was on the other side. As before, the roar of the blow seemed to echo inside his head.

'Why she post file?'

Tony feigned exhaustion as he realised the import of the question. She'd done it; she'd posted the dossier. The man hovered over him.

'Why post file?'

'What file?' Tony asked, trying to remain deadpan. He didn't hear their answer. This time, the blow knocked him out.

18. In The Deep Mid-Winter

Pauline grabbed Lissa's leather-clad body and clasped her hands around the young girl's midriff as the motorbike hurtled through the winter night. After Robert's accident, Pauline had sworn never to go near a motorbike again, yet here she was, frozen and clinging on for dear life. She didn't know where they were going, and Lissa wasn't saying.

Lissa had called a cab to the vicarage in the name of Williams, but because it was New Year's Day, the fare was double the normal rate, and they'd had to wait two hours. Half an hour before it was due, they'd walked to the church, left the note about the flowers, and caught the cab as it arrived outside Jonathan's house. It drove them to Hexham, where they spent the next two hours moving from pub to pub up the high street. Despite it being the arse-end of the holiday, the pubs were full of die-hard revellers determined to wring out every last moment of pleasure. In each bar, Pauline and Lissa bought a drink and sat or stood opposite each other while the drunken party swirled around them. Despite being bumped and jostled, no one bothered them. Something about Lissa's demeanour deterred familiarity. Once, when Lissa was at the bar, Pauline considered dodging out of the front door and running, but where could she go? After her arrest by Buchan, she couldn't go to the police, and everyone knew where she lived. She resolved to stay with Lissa for the moment.

Despite the noise, Pauline had told Lissa everything that had happened since meeting Tony, but she left out her arrest and interrogation by Buchan because of Lavinia. She didn't know if it would make a difference, but she wasn't willing to take the chance. At one point, the pub door had been blown open by an icy blast before slamming back; Pauline had longed to be back in her cottage. She decided that if she ever got her life back, she would have a wood burner installed. She allowed herself to imagine Lavinia and the grandchildren staying there, then she panicked over where everyone would sleep. She didn't have enough room.

'A penny for them?'

Pauline looked up. 'What?'

'You were miles away,' Lissa said, swallowing the last of her drink. 'What were you thinking about?'

Pauline shook her head. 'My son, Robert. He was killed in a motorbike accident when he was nineteen.'

Lissa frowned, shook her head, and said, 'Sorry.' It sounded like she meant it.

'It was a long time ago.' Once again, Pauline was amazed at the alacrity with which she was able to lie. Lissa went to the bar and bought another two halves of lager. 'What's going on, Lissa?'

'What do you mean?'

'Pub-crawling in Hexham?'

Lissa shrugged. 'We need to wait.'

'What for?' Pauline was getting annoyed. 'We could have waited at the cottage.'

'Couldn't risk it.' Lissa looked around and leaned forward. 'You haven't asked me, have you?'

'Asked you what?' Pauline replied.

'How I ended up in your cottage; how I knew to go there?'

Pauline sipped her drink. 'I assumed it was something to do with Tony. After all, you knew about our trek through the blizzard.'

Lissa nodded ironically. 'Yeah. He had this routine. He checked in with my dad every 24 hours.'

'Your Dad?' Pauline asked, confused.

'Matt,' Lissa explained. 'I told you. He worked with Tony.'

Pauline nodded. 'So how did Tony check in then?'

'Basic Nokia phone, no internet shit. Put the battery and the SIM in at the right time and make a call—never longer than a minute. Ring off and pull it apart.'

Pauline nodded. 'So you knew he was here?' Lissa nodded. 'And when he didn't check in?'

'We knew something had happened to him.'

'That was a week ago.'

Lissa nodded. 'Dad's worried about him.'

'But he didn't do anything?'

Lissa shook her head. 'No point until the dossier was posted, was there?'

'No?'

'Tony was off-grid. His job was to scare some shit into the open.' She took a sip of her drink. 'At least that was the plan.'

'What? Hasn't it worked?'

Lissa shook her head. 'It got swamped by other shit.'

'What shit?'

Lissa shrugged. 'Brexit, Christmas, Twiggy becoming a bleeding dame.'

Pauline was outraged. 'I risked my neck for nothing?'

Lissa shook her head. 'There has been some reaction to the post, but the mainstream media haven't picked up on it yet.'

'So what was in the dossier then?'

Lissa frowned to herself. 'Evidence.'

'Of what?'

'We're not sure. There's an audit trail. Monies are being paid by a circuitous route from a company or companies in Serbia to Argentina.'

'South America?' Pauline asked, confused.

'No!' Lissa hissed. 'It's a farm in the middle of nowhere.'

'Called Argentina?'

'Yeah.'

'Where is it?'

'Near here. Why do you think Tony ended up in this god-forsaken county?'

'Right.'

'And you think that's where Tony is?'

Lissa nodded. 'If he's alive.'

Pauline remembered something Tony had said. 'Is that the poisons lab?'

A sudden roar of laughter from a group of drinkers covered Lissa's shock. She leaned in closer and whispered. 'He told you?'

'Not in so many words.'

'Jesus,' she said, taking a large mouthful of beer.

'What's so important about it?'

'Did he tell you they'd gone freelance? Selling to the highest bidder?'

'No.'

'He thinks they've developed something new and deadly, but we don't know what it is. And we don't know what's in the dossier that's upset them.'

'Is it the photograph?'

Lissa looked at Pauline sharply. 'Why do you say that?'

'If you can identify the man in the picture, that might explain something.'

One of the revellers lumbered towards them. Clad in an unflattering, figure hugging England rugby shirt, he leered towards Lissa. 'Doing anything later, gorgeous?'

'Piss off,' Lissa hissed, but that just emboldened the would-be Romeo.

'Don't be like that,' the rugby-shirted reveller said, grinning back at his mates.

Lissa was about to respond, but Pauline intervened. She stood up and faced the drunk. 'If you don't mind, we'd like a little privacy.'

'A pair of lezzas, are you?'

'No, Sharon is my daughter, and we buried her father today.' Pauline spoke quietly but with some force. The reveller took a step back.

'Right, sorry. Her dad?'

Pauline nodded. 'My ex-husband. Anyway, we were just going, weren't we?'

Lissa necked her drink and nodded. They gathered their things and left the bar. In the street, Lissa looked at Pauline angrily. 'Sharon?'

'All I could think of; you didn't want me to tell him your real name?'

'Sodding Sharon. Jesus.' Lissa muttered as they walked up the street.

'So what happens now?' Pauline asked.

'We go there, to Argentina Farm.'

'How? We can't just turn up at the front door, can we?'

Lissa grinned. 'There's a back way.'

They left the pub and walked a half-mile or so to a covered passage between two houses, where Lissa unlocked the motorbike. Pauline was horrified, but Lissa explained that the Kawasaki was quicker and harder to track. Pauline had put on extra layers, but, given the ferocity of the arctic blast, they were not enough. Lissa hadn't said where they were going. Instead, she had pointed delphically towards the River Tyne. They went slowly at first, but once past the Roman Wall, they travelled much faster, swooping along tiny lanes and diving around bends. Despite her fear and discomfort, Pauline realised that it wasn't the river Lissa had pointed to but the north, because that was the way they were headed.

Just after one a.m., the bike turned off a paved road and nosed slowly along a rutted track uphill before coming to a halt in a small stand of trees. To Pauline, it seemed as if they had ridden at speed down every tiny road in Northumberland. She had glimpsed the odd signpost in the headlight and seen signs to Rothbury and Wooler, as well as lots of other places she'd never heard of. Finally, they had turned into a steep-sided valley of snow-capped hills. Pauline suspected they were in the Cheviots, but she didn't know where. Lissa turned the engine off and removed her crash helmet, encouraging Pauline to follow suit. The still, silent darkness was disorienting after the noise and movement of the motorbike. Hoarfrost enveloped every leaf and branch while, underfoot, the ground crunched.

'Where are we?' Pauline asked quietly.

'Why are you whispering?' Lissa asked. 'There's no one within five miles of here, and if there is, they'll have heard the bike. Besides, it's New Year's Day; they'll all be sleeping it off. There's nothing else to do up here.'

Pauline looked around. There was no chance of escaping. Besides, she had no idea where she was. Lissa produced a flask, poured hot liquid into a plastic cup, and offered it to Pauline. Pauline gagged as she swallowed, causing Lissa to laugh as she grabbed the cup.

'Don't drink it all.'

'What is it?' Pauline asked.

'White man's magic.' Pauline was nonplussed. 'Black coffee and rum. I've got some supplies too.'

'When do we get those?'

Lissa shouldered a rucksack. 'Later. Come on, we're walking from here.'

'How far?'

'A mile, two maybe. Now, shut up and let me use my GPS.' Lissa lit up the dial of her watch, which she used to guide them. They went uphill for a while, then had to backtrack when they came to a cliff edge. Finally, they arrived at an outcrop of rock on the hillside.

'Right, I think this must be it,' Lissa said. 'You ever done any abseiling, Pauline?'

'Yes, but it was years ago.'

'Like riding a bike. It never leaves you.' Lissa pulled back some bracken and revealed an opening with a warning sign. 'Mine Workings: Keep Out.'

'We're not going down there?' Pauline asked, incredulous.

'It's fake. It's a secret shaft. According to my information, you can drop down and hook up with a series of tunnels that run south-west.'

'How far down?'

'Not far, maybe forty feet. Don't worry, there's a metal ladder after ten feet. I've got a rope and harness in case it's not up to it.'

'Is that likely?'

'Well, the rungs are cast iron, and they've been there for ninety years. Might have rusted a bit.'

Dropping forty feet into the darkness wasn't on Pauline's agenda. 'No way, Lissa.'

'Am I going to have to get my gun out again?'

Pauline could see that Lissa was grinning in the darkness. 'You're enjoying this?'

'Too right. We're about to abseil into the darkness and fight the bad guys. We're doing something worthwhile.' She attached Pauline's harness to the metal grill and then dropped the line into the darkness.

'How come I have to go first?' Pauline asked.

'Well, you wouldn't do it second now, would you?' Lissa said checking the equipment again. 'Right, here's a torch. Try not to drop it.'

Lissa grabbed hold of Pauline's line and positioned her at the edge of the shaft. 'Take your time. Pull on the rope and shout when you get to the bottom.'

'What if something goes wrong?'

'We'll improvise, won't we?'

Pauline got ready to go, and then something occurred to her. 'Your information. Who told you?'

What?'

'You said 'according to your information'. Who told you?'

'Who do you think? Mr. Google.'

'So you don't even know if this is the right shaft?'

'I found it, didn't I? Now are you going, or would you rather I shoot you?' Pauline stayed where she was. 'Well?'

'I'm thinking about it.' At which point, Lissa pushed her backwards into the void.

19. Operating Theatre

The executioner wears a black hood. Two executioners wear two black hoods. Tony was trying to recall something from his training about black body radiation, or was it from school? His brain wasn't working properly. He knew the answer, but it kept slipping away. Something wasn't quite right, but he didn't care because he was as happy as Larry. One of the executioners hovered overhead, but he couldn't quite make it out. He began to hum a tune from his childhood, but as soon as he remembered a couple of words, the tune went belly-up. Something uncomfortable pressed into his back, causing him to grunt in pain. Then he faded away again.

When he came to, he had been moved. The room was more like a hospital room than a torture chamber; the walls were pale green under muted light. He had been dressed in a soft fabric. He looked down and laughed; he was wearing striped pyjamas. He hadn't worn anything like them since childhood. It didn't make sense. Why had they stopped the third degree? He was still pinioned by metal ties on his wrists and ankles, but at least he was alive. Why hadn't he been dispatched and fed to the dogs? He wondered idly what day it was.

Then he thought about the questions they'd asked. They'd been very interested in Pauline, and it seemed from what they'd said that she had managed to post the dossier. Tony had to admit that she was extremely effective. Could she really be what she seemed? But if she wasn't, that would mean she'd been waiting for him in the church. No, it was the ramblers who'd bolloxed everything. She couldn't have known he'd end up at St. Leonard's. Hell, he hadn't known until they came for him. A loud click was followed by a disembodied, velvety voice. 'Feeling better now?' Tony looked around and then spotted a recessed speaker in the ceiling. He nodded and lay back. 'That's good because we will want to ask you some more questions.'

'You said yourself; I don't know anything,' Tony said quietly.

'There are other things you haven't told us.'

'If I haven't talked up to now, what makes you think I will in the future?'

'I'll leave you to think about that,' the voice chuckled. There was a click as the speaker switched off. Tony lay back. Apart from a low hiss, the room was quiet. As he listened, the hissing became louder, and a misty vapour began to fill the chamber. Tony struggled against his ties until the vapour overwhelmed him and he lapsed into unconsciousness.

20. The Tunnel

Plummeting into the black shaft, Pauline had a brief sensation of falling before the rope caught her and pulled at her feet, banging her against the sides of the shaft and knocking the wind out of her. She felt a stab of pain in her left side, and the shock caused her to gasp and drop the torch at the same time. She swore to herself and struggled on the rope, but she appeared to be stuck fast.

'Stop wriggling, will you?' Lissa's voice rasped.

'I can't breathe,' Pauline gasped as she heard Lissa's feet coming down the ladder.

'Your own bloody fault, isn't it? Why didn't you just go down the ladder like I asked?'

'You pushed me!'

'Stop bellyaching and hold still then.' Pauline heard Lissa behind her and then felt the rope slacken as her body weight was taken up from below. With a few grunts, Lissa climbed back up the ladder, lifting Pauline up and unhooking the rope, which was snagged around one side of her neck and under her left arm.

'Right,' Lissa's voice came again, taking her right hand and placing it on a rung. 'Grab that and hold on while I climb down, holding your legs.' Pauline did as she was told, grabbing onto a narrow rung that was pitted with rust. It creaked alarmingly as she pulled on it and felt herself begin to turn upright. At last, the rope around her ankles was released, and one of her feet was placed on a rung below.

'Now follow me down to the bottom of the ladder. I'll switch my head torch on to help.' The shaft was illuminated with an incandescent light which cast long shadows against the dark wall. The rock behind the rungs twinkled in the penumbra, displaying thousands of shimmering crystals. Momentarily, Pauline felt impelled to touch it, only to pull her hand back when she discovered it was slimy. A tug on her foot from below disturbed her reverie.

'Come on, we haven't got all night.' Pauline began to climb down the metal ladder. The rungs ended before the bottom of the shaft. Below, Lissa's head torch danced back and forth.

'The rungs?'

'What about them?'

'They stop. They don't go to the bottom.'

'I know,' Lissa replied, clearly distracted.

'What are you doing?'

I'm looking for your bleeding torch, aren't I?' The torch stopped momentarily and illuminated the shaft as Lissa looked up. 'Just sodding jump.'

'How far is it?'

'About two metres. Look, climb down and dangle from the bottom rung, and then just let go.'

Once again, Pauline did as she was told, but as soon as she put weight on her left arm, the pain from her side made her cry and lose her grip, and she fell into a heap onto an unexpectedly soft, sandy floor. Pauline got to her feet, brushing her clothes down and rubbing her sore shoulder. Lissa thrust the torch into her hand.

'Don't drop it, alright!' Pauline held it for a moment. 'Turn it on then.'

Pauline did as she was told and saw that there were two tunnels in front of them, apparently side by side but going off at different angles.

'Which one is it?'

Lissa turned back to Pauline, nearly blinding her with her head torch beam, which caused Pauline to cry out. 'Jesus!'

'Sorry,' Lissa said, turning back to the tunnels. 'It should be due west.'

'What's that smell?' Pauline asked, wrinkling her nose at a damp, musty odour.

Lissa grimaced. 'How should I know? Don't think it's dangerous.'

'It's not firedamp anyway; that doesn't smell,' Pauline said. 'That's why they took canaries down mines.'

'We haven't got a canary.' Lissa was preoccupied with her compass.

'Is there a problem?' Pauline asked.

'Not sure how well it works down here,' Lissa said, peering up one tunnel and then the other. 'Oh, sod it; we'll try this one.' Lissa stepped into the right-hand tunnel, and they began to walk. Pauline became aware of a slight breeze blowing in their faces.

'There's a draught.'

Lissa nodded. 'Hopefully that means there's a hole at the other end.'

'Why wouldn't the compass work down here?' She asked

'A lump of iron in the rock or a big steel structure up top can skew it.'

'So we could still be in the wrong tunnel?' Pauline asked.

'Better not be,' Lissa said, and put on a spurt causing Pauline to struggle behind her.

The tunnel was just under five feet high and this caused them to walk in a crouching position, which became increasingly uncomfortable. The roof was supported by a series of wooden props and ceiling ties, some of which had disintegrated. Dust powdered from the roof onto the floor, and Pauline realised that it was this debris that had cushioned her fall. She wondered again how secure the roof was.

Despite the slight breeze, it was much warmer underground, and both of them were soon sweating under their layers. After some forty minutes, they stopped and both had a drink from their flasks.

'What are these tunnels?' Pauline asked. 'Lead workings?'

'Government site. Sunk during World War Two in case of invasion.'

'What for?'

130

'Resistance dumps. In the sixties, they considered storing nuclear waste down here.'

'It's hot,' Pauline said. 'Can't we leave some of our clothes here?'

'We might not come back this way,' Lissa replied.

'I thought there was a plan,' Pauline rasped.

'We have to be there by two forty-four am, alright?' Lissa was getting annoyed.

'What happens then?'

'Not sure.'

'So, we're making it up as we go along?'

'Look, get moving!' Lissa snapped.

'Or what? You'll shoot me?'

'If I have to.'

They set off again, but with greater urgency than before. The crouching, shuffling position made Pauline's back, knees, and thighs ache at various points. It was just after two a.m.

After twenty minutes or so, they rounded a bend to find their way blocked by a roof fall.

'Christ's sake!' Lissa hissed, examining the debris. Pauline took out her flask and offered Lissa a drink. They both had a swig. 'What now?' Pauline asked.

Lissa looked at her watch. 'I don't know.'

Then Pauline had an idea. 'Turn off your head-torch.'

'What?'

'Just turn it off,' Pauline said, extinguishing her torch at the same time. Lissa did as she was told, and they were plunged into total darkness.

'What the hell?' Lissa began, but Pauline cut her off.

'Watch!' And as they watched, small pinpricks of light began to appear in the roof fall—pinpricks that grew brighter, and as they stood there, they realised they could hear the bass rumble of machinery.

Pauline was about to turn her torch on, but Lissa stopped her. 'Wait,' she said, creeping forward and peering through one of the holes in the debris.

'What can you see?' Pauline asked.

'It is the right tunnel. Look.'

Pauline peered through the gap. On the other side of the roof, she saw a large chamber with man-made, vertical walls illuminated by industrial lighting. In the middle of the chamber was a large, gunmetal-grey cube, standing about seven feet high and emitting a base humming sound. Several heavy metal cables were attached to the cube and ran across the floor to the wall beyond.

'We need to get in there,' Lissa said, switching her head-torch back on.

Pauline stood back. 'What is that thing?'

'Generator.' Lissa checked her watch and began pulling away small boulders and debris. After a moment, she stopped and turned to Pauline. 'Give me a hand, will you?'

Pauline did what she could. They pulled away at the debris, creating a storm of dust that made it difficult to see, but it quickly became clear that the blockage was minor. After a couple of minutes, they had made a hole big enough to get through. Lissa went first and surveyed the imposing grey metal box. She scrabbled in her rucksack and produced something soft and malleable, which she split into two pieces and packed at the point where two of the cables mated with the box. She then took out two pieces of wire, inserted them into the material, and lit them with her cigarette lighter. She turned back and saw Pauline watching.

'Get back behind the barrier!'

Pauline hurried; Lissa followed and threw Pauline to the floor and waited.

'Will it work?'

'We're knackered if it doesn't. Probably are anyway.'

'You sure it's a generator?'

'It's big and hums, and it's got wires coming in and out.'

Pauline was about to reply when a loud bang caused the earth to shake and the lights to go out.

21. Night Exercise

At the same time, Matt Hardwick was lying prone inside his camo sleeping bag some five hundred metres from the Argentina compound and trying to control his shivering. It was a long time since he'd done a night-time OP, never mind in the depths of winter. He was getting too old for this. For the umpteenth time, he checked his watch and swore to himself, wondering if he'd launched the drone too soon. It was two forty-three a.m.

Two days ago, he'd driven north to Carlisle in a stolen white van with false plates and a BT Openreach logo on the side. He'd driven along the A69 and then north up the A68 before turning off. Via a series of small lanes and tracks, he drove until he was some five miles south of Argentina Farm. Clad in a high-viz jacket, equipment belt, and safety helmet, he had shinned up two of the telegraph poles that carried the land line to Argentina and left small explosive charges with a state-of-the art timer set to go off at exactly two forty-four a.m. He had done the same to two of the small pylons carrying the power to Argentina. Being so far away was a problem. It would kill the power and telecommunications to three other small farms, but it couldn't be helped. Afterwards, he had driven in a large circle until he was just over the Scottish border before turning south into the Cheviots. Then he'd driven down a secluded forest track and parked up. He'd cat-napped for a couple of hours before beginning the second part of his improvised mission.

Exchanging his BT uniform for that of a hiker with a rucksack, he had hiked the five miles over rough ground to his observation point. He'd walked in daylight because it was easier to hide in plain sight. With the advent of night vision glasses, it was almost impossible to move in the landscape at night if people were watching for incomers. Nevertheless, his age told. He was heavier and unused to walking over rough ground, and his left knee, which had been injured long ago in an ambush, began to click painfully with each step. Again, it couldn't be helped.

He checked the camera on the drone, which, according to the controls, was two hundred feet high and within a hundred and fifty metres of the target. He wished he could have had a more original idea than explosives, but as Lissa maintained, at least you knew if they'd worked. He'd decided to use some older C4 explosive he'd hoarded because he didn't want anything to be traced back to him or Lissa. The trouble was, he'd forgotten to check on its longevity and wasn't sure if it was even serviceable. The plan was minimal: create a diversion, add to the chaos, and hope that Lissa could do the rest. It was a long shot, but they were on their own and running out of options. As the digital clock on his phone turned to two forty-four, he tensed, waiting for the explosion, but nothing happened. He counted ten seconds, then twenty, and still nothing happened.

'For God's sake!' He checked the drone camera again, but everything looked tranquil and dark.

A door opened, causing a flare of light as a figure emerged with a flashlight and crossed the farmyard to the dog compound. Matt could hear dogs barking, growing excited. At that moment, two flashes of light appeared in the distance, followed by the faint sound of explosions. As he watched, the light from the doorway was extinguished, and from the drone, he saw figures piling out of the building into the farmyard. There appeared to be plenty of chaos.

Matt counted three of the four charges detonating, and that meant two problems. If the undetonated charge had been one of the power lines, they might still have power, and the second problem was that, although they couldn't trace him through the explosive, they could narrow it down from the timer. At least Lissa had insisted on old-fashioned fuse caps. The only problem with them was getting out of the way in time. He tidied his gear, packed it into his rucksack, and began his yomp back to his vehicle. He wanted to make as much time as he could, but the ground was uneven, and he had to take care. If he could do the return trip in two hours, they might have a chance. Then he heard a sound that set his pulse racing. Dogs barking and handlers shouting; they had opened the compound and were conducting a sweep. If the dogs were on leads, he might be OK, but if they let them loose, he was done.

22. Alarms and Excursions

Tony came awake in darkness. Something was different. He could hear shouting and banging and there was an acrid smell that burned his throat and caused him to cough violently. He struggled and found his shackles were open. He wriggled off the gurney but his legs gave way, throwing him to the floor and winding him. He hadn't realised he was so weak. The air was better down on the floor, so he crawled to the side of the room and the sliding door which was also open. Outside in the corridor, the smoke was worse. There was a sound of excited shouting and running feet from above. He turned back towards the chamber, but the door had shut, and he didn't have the strength to open it. He pushed hard, but the smoke overwhelmed him, and he subsided into oblivion again.

Lissa's explosive charges had disabled the generator, but the chemical smoke had been an unintended consequence. As the dust cleared, she and Pauline scrambled back through the roof-fall and immediately began to cough. Fortunately, Lissa had a pair of primitive face masks, and she shoved one into Pauline's hands and told her to put it on. Pauline struggled with it, but it was at this moment that panic overcame her. She had always hated confined spaces, and now, a hundred feet underground, trapped in a narrow tunnel being choked to death, she lost it. It was as if the enormity of what had happened to her and how much everything had changed crystallised in that moment. What on earth was she doing? She was a single, fifty-three-year-old, retired academic who did the flowers twice a week for St. Leonard's, and yet here she was taking on some ruthless killers who had killed at least two people, possibly more. She wanted her old life back; she longed for the boredom and routine of changing the flowers in the draughty church, of the nuanced greetings of the parishioners, of Jonathan's nodding embarrassment. The coughing became so violent that she leant against the tunnel wall, bent double. Even so, she felt remote from her physical self, as if observing her difficulties. She longed to see Lavinia and the children but pushed the thought away; it wasn't helping.

Lissa saw Pauline's difficulty and shouted at her, but it had no effect. She bent down, fixed the face mask over Pauline's nose and mouth, and slapped her hard on her cheek twice, causing Pauline to gasp. Lissa took hold of Pauline's head and bent her forward.

'That's it, Pauline; breathe deeply. Again, that's it.' Pauline did as she was told and gradually came round. 'Can you hear me?' Lissa shouted. Pauline nodded. 'Say yes if you can,' Lissa ordered.

'Yes,' Pauline said.

'Louder!' Lissa shouted.

'Fucking yes!' Pauline shouted, causing Lissa to chuckle.

'Right, we haven't got much time. Stay here.' She produced a hip flask. 'Have a nip of this if you feel rough, but not too much mind.'

Pauline nodded again. 'Where are you going?'

'Where do you think? To get Tony, aren't I?' And with that, she was gone. Pauline unscrewed the hip flask, pulled down her mask, and had some of the liquid. It was whisky, and she enjoyed the familiar sensation. She shone her torch. The gas that the explosion had vented from the generator had dissipated, and the air was clearing. Pauline got to her feet and looked around. There was a chance she might have to get out of this tunnel on her own. She decided that the way back was her only option, even though the thought of climbing the shaft was daunting. She had to hope that Lissa made it.

Tony's chamber was on the deepest level, but it was ten metres above the shaft where the generator sat. As the acrid smoke cleared, he came around again. It was still dark, but he could see points of lights dancing above and footsteps on the steel staircase. He wanted to escape, and his instinct was to head upwards, towards the light and the surface. Then again, the footsteps were coming towards him, so he tottered the other way and struggled down the stairs where he met Lissa.

'Tony?' Lissa hissed, her head-torch almost blinding him. He put a hand up against the glare.

'Who's that?'

'Who the fuck do you think it is? It's me, Lissa.'

'Oh right; sorry,' Tony gasped.

'What are you wearing?'

'Pyjamas, I think,' he grinned.

'What about your shoes?'

'Nasal sex,' Tony grunted. 'Good to see you, Lissa.'

'Yeah,' Lissa grunted. The footsteps were getting closer. 'Can you walk?'

'If I have to,' he replied.

'You have to! Come on!' She led Tony down the steps, but he couldn't hurry.

'We must go faster,' she hissed. Tony tried, but he wasn't used to walking in bare feet, and his legs kept collapsing. He tottered down the stairs as the clattering footsteps above drew nearer. Lissa fired a couple of shots back up the stairwell, which caused a flurry of shouting, but the pursuing footsteps halted. They arrived at the bottom of the stairs as the pursuit from above resumed. Pauline appeared and grimaced when she saw Tony. He managed a weak smile.

'Pauline?'

'How are you?' Pauline asked.

'Don't ask stupid questions,' Lissa snapped. 'Give him some of that rocket coffee, then get him through the barricade tout-de-suite.'

'What are you going to do?'

'Hold them off. Give me a shout when you're through, then get as far down the tunnel as possible!'

Lissa disappeared up the stairwell as Pauline grabbed Tony

138

and guided him around the generator and through the small hole in the barricade. She shouted back to Lissa. 'OK, we're through!' Then she and Tony started walking. Thankfully, it was warm in the tunnel and relatively soft underfoot, so he could shuffle along without too much trouble. After twenty metres, the tunnel turned to the left. Pauline gave Tony another drink of coffee and left him sitting on a ledge while she returned to the barricade. Lissa climbed through and fired a volley of shots through the aperture towards the generator. She saw Pauline and thrust the gun into her hand.

'Keep an eye on the gap, and if you see anything moving, shoot at it.'

'I've never fired a gun before.'

'Just point it and pull the trigger,' Lissa hissed as she searched her rucksack. 'You've seen it in the films, haven't you?'

'What are you doing?' Pauline asked, peering through the hole.

'We need to buy some time. I'm going to bring the roof down.'

'Isn't that a bit risky?'

'You're telling me,' Lissa chuckled. She took her explosive and packed it at the junction of the roof and the side of the tunnel where the original fall had come from. 'Where's Tony? I told you to look after him.' Pauline was about to reply when she glimpsed movement near the generator. Without thinking, she fired and heard a cry of pain, followed by a yell from Lissa.

'Bleeding bullseye!' She grabbed Pauline by the sleeve and pulled. 'Hurry, I've lit the fuse!'

They hurried down the tunnel and found Tony slumped at the side of the crook of the bend. Lissa pushed Pauline and Tony into the tunnel wall and folded herself over them.

'Close your eyes and your mouths!' she ordered as the charge detonated. The floor shook, and the explosion sent a pulse of rubble and dust down the tunnel, which rebounded at the bend and swirled around them. They coughed and spluttered, but after a few seconds, the dust began to settle. They stood up and wiped the dust from their faces.

'Come on,' Lissa said. 'We have to get going.'

'Has it worked?' Tony asked as he stood up.

'It'll work for a bit, but...' Lissa trailed off. 'Shit.'

'What is it?' Pauline asked. Lissa was flexing her right arm and grimacing.

'I've bolloxed my bleeding shoulder, haven't I?'

'Will you be OK?'

'I'll have to be. We'd better get moving.' She saw the gun in Pauline's hand. 'I'll take that if you don't mind.' Pauline handed over the gun, and they set off.

'I hope he's OK,' Pauline muttered.

'Who?' Lissa asked.

'The man I shot.'

Lissa laughed. 'How d'you know it wasn't a woman?'

'I hadn't thought of that,' Pauline said.

'You've got to be a pro,' Lissa grinned.

'Don't start that again.'

'Never fired a gun before, my arse.'

'I haven't!'

Tony struggled on ahead. 'Come on, you two. I thought we were in a hurry.' Lissa and Pauline looked at each other and set off after him.

They shuffled and crouched as fast as they could, but, as before, the bent locomotion was exhausting. After ten minutes, Tony sank to the floor with a moan. Lissa gave him an energy bar and some more of the liqueur coffee.

'Eat and drink,' she ordered, but she kept looking back down the tunnel. After a minute, Tony got to his feet, and they were about to go on when Lissa put her finger to her lips and told them to shush. They listened for a moment, but Pauline couldn't hear anything.

'Well? Are they coming?' She asked.

Lissa shook her head. 'Can't hear anything, but this floor deadens sound anyway.'

They continued at the best pace they could, and after an hour or so, they arrived at the bottom of the shaft. Looking up towards the surface, Pauline thought she could see the stars, but she wasn't sure if it was real or just the elation at the prospect of getting out of the tunnel. Then she remembered that the first rung was two metres above the ground. Lissa had obviously had the same thought because she was kicking the wall and swearing.

'Quiet!' Tony said from the floor. He had dropped to his knees exhausted when they stopped, but he was alert now. Pauline and Lissa listened and heard nothing. They had almost begun to relax when they heard a shout.

'Shit,' Lissa muttered.

'Sit on my shoulders,' Pauline suggested.

Lissa looked at her, considering, and shook her head. 'No, you're not tall enough.'

'Sit on mine then,' Tony said.

'It'll have to be Pauline,' Lissa said angrily.

'What?' Pauline exclaimed.

'I've bolloxed my shoulder, haven't I? I need the rope as well.'

'You'll have to sit on my shoulders, Pauline,' Tony whispered, kneeling down as he did so.

Pauline was about to argue, but the sound of shouts from the tunnel made up her mind. 'Can you hold me?' she asked, but then gingerly climbed onto Tony's shoulders.

'Alright?' Lissa asked. Tony grunted in assent. 'Here,' Lissa said, putting the rucksack around Pauline's shoulders.

'I can't stand up,' Tony said.

'Use the tunnel wall,' Lissa ordered. 'Lean against it. I'll help you.'

With Lissa's help, Tony struggled to his feet. Pauline got hold of the rung and tried to swing herself up. It took a couple of tries to get the hang of it, but then she found that bracing her feet against the tunnel wall helped, and she made it to the bottom rung. She unhooked the rucksack and found the rope. She attached it to one of the rungs and threw the other end down.

'Think you can pull yourself up, Tony?'

He sighed. 'I'll have a go,' he grinned. 'But I think Lissa should go first.'

'I've got the gun. I'll hold them off, then come up last.'

The sounds of the pursuers were more distinct now. Pauline threw down the rope and began to climb up as Tony struggled to follow. From below, Lissa ordered Pauline to wait on the surface. Pauline did as she was told and emerged into the black, cold night. She heard shots and some shouting but had no idea what was happening. She was trying to remember the way they had come and considering what she would do if Lissa and Tony didn't appear when she heard a low shout.

'Pauline? Pauline? Where are you?'

'Here.'

'Give me a hand, will you?' Lissa offered the end of the rope and hauled herself out of the shaft. 'Right, heave after three, one, two, three... heave.'

Pauline pulled on the rope. 'What happened?' She gasped.

'He ran out of juice. I had to rope him up and leave him.'

'I heard shooting.'

'Yeah, I just wanted them to stay away from the bottom of the shaft. Don't ease up; we have to get him out.' Finally, Tony's head and shoulders appeared as he pulled himself free to collapse on his back, gasping like a landed salmon on the rime of the frosted grass. Lissa fiddled at the top of the shaft and then stepped back. There was a muted boom, and she turned with a look of triumph.

'Right, let's get him to the motorbike.'

They struggled the mile or so over rough ground with Tony between them. Pauline gave him her socks and a thick fleece, and Lissa donated a woolly hat and gloves. It was hard going at first, but at least it was downhill. From time to time, Lissa grunted with pain, presumably because her shoulder was hurting, but she didn't complain until, finally, they reached the motorbike. Lissa checked her watch and swore.

'Bollocks, we're late,' she said, putting her helmet on.

'Can you take all of us?' Pauline asked. Lissa looked at her. 'On the bike?'

Lissa shook her head. 'No,' Lissa said. 'You're staying behind.'

'Just a minute, Lissa,' Tony argued.

'Shut up, will you? You're the reason we're bloody well here, aren't you? I need to get you somewhere warm and safe.'

'We can't leave her,' Tony protested.

'I'll be fine,' Pauline said gently.

'I'll drop you off and then come back for her.' Lissa snapped. 'Now put that bloody helmet on and get on the bike.'

Tony stood his ground until Pauline put her hand on his and kissed him gently. 'Please Tony.'

He looked at her and shook his head. 'I'll make it up to you, I promise.' Pauline nodded. Then he got on the bike and put his arms around Lissa's waist. Lissa turned to Pauline.

'Follow the track down to the lane and then turn right. Keep going. Wooler's about six miles. If I don't make it, you can get a bus from there.'

Pauline nodded and watched as Lissa gunned the motorbike engine and drove away. She watched until the red tail lights winked out of sight, leaving her and the silence of the cold, black night.

23. Dawn Chorus

Matt was not in great shape by the time he made it back to the BT Openreach van. His lack of sleep and match-fitness had made for a very uncomfortable yomp back to his vehicle. His knee was stiffening, and he knew it would be all but useless in twelve hours. Despite pushing hard, it had taken nearly three hours to do the five miles. At least he'd lost the dogs, or, to put it more accurately, they'd lost him. He knew how searches with dogs worked. Start doing sweeps with one hundred metre radius, then two hundred, then three hundred, but you had to stay coordinated; otherwise, it was pointless. He'd been on the hounds' side many times in Northern Ireland, and the hare almost always got away. The only time they ever caught someone was because they surrendered. Anyway, he'd managed to make the vehicle, but so what? Tony Brooks, the man who'd produced the dossier, had disappeared with a price on his head, and now Matt Hardwick, his colleague and old army mate, had gone AWOL too. He might as well pin a target on his forehead and send up a flare.

He got into the cab, got the engine running, and turned the heater up high. He put on the high-viz jacket and laid his helmet and tool belt on the passenger seat. Then he had some coffee from a flask, chewed on an elderly meat pie, and drove off. The rendezvous was between five thirty and six thirty; it was just before six a.m. He went as fast as he could on the forest track, but just before dawn, with a hard frost and icy, puddle-filled ruts, he had to be careful. If he could get back to London by this afternoon, he might be okay. The trouble was, he was going to be late. Lissa had been on the same tradecraft courses that he had. Protocol said if the contact wasn't there, you didn't wait, ever. He hoped she ignored her training.

Pauline felt as if she were the last person left alive. It was the coldest part of a bitter winter night. Her bare feet in her boots were frozen, and without the fleece she had given to Tony, she had to keep moving to stave off the cold. Exhausted, she found it difficult to concentrate, and her mind wandered. She hated the idea of not being able to see Lavinia and the children, but that wasn't her doing, and she would fight it. She knew that she wanted to stay in Bridgford and that she had found something important there. She missed her friends, but apart from Sally, her other friends had mostly become preoccupied with grandchildren, while contact with those from the university had faded since her retirement. She was alone, but she wasn't as desperate as she had been when Robert had died. That had been the worst time in her life, and it did at least provide a yardstick against which other difficulties could be measured. And then there was Tony. There could be something between them, although she might just be imagining it. She struggled on and came to the lane. What was it that Lissa had said? Turn right; it's six miles to Wooler. She wondered how frequent the buses were on January 2nd.

The meeting place was a lay-by on the B6351 overlooking the field where the Saxon palace of Gefrin had stood for four centuries before the advent of the Vikings and where the missionary Paulinus had baptised King Edwin and his wife. Thirteen hundred years later, on a gloomy January morning, it was where Matt decided to remove the BT Openreach transfers from the side of the white van. The transfer on the near side of the van came away easily, but the one on the off side proved more difficult. The Openreach part tore as he tried to unpeel it. Despite using the gallon of water he'd brought for the purposes, it remained stuck fast. He tried with his ice scraper and improved it a bit, but someone looking for a BT Openreach vehicle would notice it. Indeed, it was like a flashing warning light. On the other side of the road, the hill of Yeavering Bell brooded over the landscape, watching as a white van sped past, coming up the road from Wooler. Matt had been over ten minutes late. It was still dark, but the faint streaks of first light were in the eastern sky. Matt heard the sound of a motorcycle engine. He got out of the van and went around the back as Lissa pulled up behind him.

'OK?' He asked.

'Open the van, Dad. Tony's not great.'

Matt opened the back doors, and together they helped Tony from the bike and into the back. They laid him down on an old camping mat.

'Come on, squaddie,' Matt said gently, his Ulster accent appearing with the display of tenderness. Tony groaned. Matt looked at Lissa, 'What's the matter with him?

'Exposure, exhaustion, you name it,' Lissa shrugged. 'Christ, what are you wearing?'

Matt looked at himself. He had changed into a charcoal-grey business suit, shirt, and tie. I thought I'd catch the train. Get back to London by mid-afternoon.'

Lissa nodded. 'That'll have to wait.' She turned to go.

'Where are you off to?' Matt asked.

'To get Pauline, I left her in the forest.'

Matt frowned. 'Do you have to? I mean, if she's an amateur, she's a liability.'

Lissa nodded. 'I know... and if she's a pro, she's a danger. I'm going to get her.'

Tony moaned. 'Can't leave her behind, Matt.'

'I can't sit in this layby much longer,' Matt replied.

'Put some clothes on Tony, give him a drink, and I'll meet you in the Copper Kettle in Hexham.'

'Where?'

'It's a greasy spoon. We can talk tactics over a full English.' With that, she got back on the bike and drove off. Matt bent down to Tony and lifted him up gently. '

'Easy, squaddie, let me wrap this around you.'

He wrapped his friend in a blanket and put a woolly hat on his head before getting into the driver's seat, turning the heating up to full, and shaving with an electric razor as he drove away.

24. Wolf's Lair

Argentina Farm was awash with activity. A FedEx delivery vehicle was stopped at the gate, and the driver was interrogated about his origins. The driver wasn't in the mood for game-playing; he was already well behind on his schedule, having been delayed by two telegraph poles that had come down across the road. It hadn't been much, but it had managed to cause a minor traffic jam, made much worse by a pedantic local plod who'd imposed chaos on the disorder. The driver was fed up and told his questioners he hadn't got time to play silly beggars, and if they didn't want the damn parcel, he'd take it back to the depot.

Brian watched on the monitors and waited for his chance. Tina had avoided him since his clumsy advance, and now the athletic man with the mid-European accent gave the orders. His left arm was cradled in a sling, and he had difficulty controlling the computer mouse. He barked at Brian, who did as he was told and pretended to be cowed. He wasn't bothered; he'd made his own plans, and chaos at the farm was in his favour.

Argentina was being shut down. Its security had been compromised, and, after the attack on the telephone lines, it was well and truly on the map despite their earlier determination to keep it unnoticeable. As dawn broke, the final shipment of rare birds of prey had been packed in secure transport cages and driven to Newcastle Airport for onward shipment to destinations in Europe and the East. As the delivery driver backed up and sped back down the road, computers and files were packed into Range Rovers inside the complex. Below ground, the labs and clean rooms were dismantled and stripped before the lift shaft was sealed and access to the underground complex secured. Little evidence of their high-tech presence would be left for potential buyers to discover. They did not welcome scrutiny, but fortunately, this phase of their work was complete, and they would relocate to a new site.

Tina appeared and had a brief, hushed exchange with the athletic-looking man. She appeared relieved, while he was impatient. The deadline was the third week of February; if their target wasn't hit in the time window, all bets were off.

25. Full Monty

Matt stopped on a double yellow with the hazard flashers going and helped Tony into the 'Copper Kettle'. The cafe was long and narrow; the counter and serving area were on one side, close to the front door, with four-seater booths set along the wall at the rear. A few early customers, builders and contractors, were standing at the counter munching bacon sandwiches. Matt helped Tony past them and settled him in the last booth next to a door, which led out into a narrow, unkempt yard. Matt had given Tony his hiking trousers and boots, despite both being too big for him. Tony's pyjama jacket could be seen poking out of Pauline's green fleece. Tony wasn't in great shape, but at least it was warm. Matt leaned towards him.

'Stay here; I've got to go and lose the van.' Matt put a ten-pound note in Tony's hand. 'If they come and ask, get yourself a coffee or something.' Tony nodded wearily. Matt knew he was all-in and badly in need of some R&R. He glanced towards the front of the cafe and caught sight of a policeman.

'I won't be long,' he said, patting Tony on the shoulder. He hurried outside, prepared to soft-soap the plod, but the officer just waved him away. Matt wasn't bothered about getting a ticket, but he didn't want the van on anyone's radar for a while. He drove around Hexham until he found a small council car park near the abbey, surrounded on three sides by an old stone wall. He parked the van in a space by the wall and paid for a day's parking. He parked close against the wall so that the offside with the BT logo still attached couldn't be seen. From the road, it looked like any other white van. He hurried back to the 'Copper Kettle' and found Tony fast asleep.

The girl on the counter smiled sympathetically. 'Your friend?'

'Heavy night,' Matt smiled. 'Two teas and two breakfasts, please?'

'What kind?' The girl asked.

'Oh, the full Monty, definitely.'

Ten minutes later, Matt had swallowed the last of his breakfast and was wiping his plate down with his bread while Tony picked unenthusiastically at his. He'd managed the fried eggs and chewed some of the toast, but the bacon and sausage had overfaced him.

'Why did they let me go?' He asked, pushing his plate away.

'Because the cavalry arrived?'

Tony shook his head. 'Why dress me in Wincyette pyjamas and make me comfortable? Why didn't they just feed me to the dogs?'

Matt thought about this for a moment. 'Don't know.'

Tony was very pale and sweating. 'Was it worth it?'

Matt shrugged. 'We know that they're the bad guys,' he paused for a moment. 'But we still don't know anymore about the poison or the target.'

'We might do,' Tony said quietly, pushing his plate away.

'Yeah?' Matt said, interested.

'Hilary and Fred Charlton both appeared to have had heart attacks, as did Ivan Hodiak.'

'The eco-warrior?'

Tony nodded. 'They asked me about him. Suggested he wasn't the target.'

'Really?' Matt frowned. 'They let something slip?' Tony nodded again. Matt wasn't convinced. 'It's possible that the eco-warrior did die of a heart attack.'

Tony shook his head. 'I looked into Hodiak's background. He was a fitness fanatic and a health food nut; he exercised all the time.'

Matt nodded. 'The autopsy found no abnormalities.'

Tony scanned the cafe and whispered. 'Maybe something went wrong? Maybe Hodiak wasn't the target?'

'Or he was, and the female journalist is still on the list?'

At that point, Lissa appeared, armed with a bacon sandwich and a mug of black coffee.

'What took you so long?' Matt asked.

Lissa was about to reply, but she was interrupted by Tony, struggling to stand. 'Where is she?'

'Who?' At that moment, Pauline appeared, carrying a cup and a sandwich. Tony relaxed. Lissa punched him lightly. 'You do like her,' Lissa grinned, taking a huge bite of her sandwich. 'She likes you too. Told me last night.'

Matt stood up as Pauline arrived. He smiled and held out his hand. 'I'm Matt. You must be Pauline?' Pauline nodded. 'I've heard a lot about you.'

Pauline ignored him and squeezed in next to Tony. 'Well, I know very little about any of you,' she replied. Matt was a surprise; he and Tony were physical opposites. Where Tony was slim and aquiline, Matt was a bear with a thick neck, barrel chest, and thighs to match.

'Thanks for helping last night,' Tony whispered.

Pauline scowled. 'Lissa press-ganged me. I didn't have much choice.'

Lissa nodded. 'True.'

'So what's the plan?' Pauline asked.

'What do you mean?' Matt said, looking up.

'I posted the dossier, and we've rescued Tony. What happens now?'

'I get the train this morning; be back in the office this afternoon.' Matt replied cheerfully. 'See what's been flushed.'

'How will you explain your absence this morning?' Lissa asked.

'Hospital appointment,' Matt smiled. 'First day back after New Year, no one's up to speed.'

Pauline shook her head wearily. 'You haven't got a plan, have you?'

Tony put a hand on her arm. 'I'm sorry, Pauline.'

Pauline shook his hand away. 'You don't know why the dossier's important. You don't even know who's in the photograph.'

'We've got a name,' Tony whispered.

'Which is almost certainly false,' Matt muttered.

'She's right, nobody knows anything,' Tony gasped.

'Hang on squaddie,' Matt began but Tony roused himself.

'It's true Matt. Yes, we know things but they're after the fact. Most of the time, we're working off conjecture and assumption.'

'This is where I get off,' Pauline said, standing.

'What?' Matt asked.

'I want a hot bath, a good sleep, and then I'm going to see if I can get some of my life back,' she paused. 'I'm going home.'

'It's the first place they'll look for you,' Matt said.

Lissa swallowed the last of her sandwich. 'Not necessarily. Argentina's packing up.'

Matt frowned. 'Really?'

Lissa nodded. 'We came back over the tops. Took the opportunity to stop above Winston Crags. Lots of activity. Trucks leaving.'

'You're sure?' Matt asked.

'I used those state-of-the art bins you gave me. The explosions must have really rattled their cages.'

'Or just moved them onto another phase,' Tony said quietly.

'Well, if you don't mind,' Pauline said as she got to her feet.

'How will you get home?' Tony asked.

'Taxi,' Pauline said, 'I took some money with me last night. I thought it might come in useful.' She slid out of the booth. 'Good luck, and in the nicest possible way, I hope I never see any of you again.' With that, she turned and walked out of the cafe.

She'd come to a decision while riding on the back of Lissa's bike. She'd had enough of things happening to her.

There was a hiatus in the cafe after Pauline left. Lissa broke the silence. 'What do you think, Matt?'

Matt cleared his throat. 'Good cover.' Tony shook his head. 'You're soft on her, Squaddie, so you are,' Matt sneered.

'My mission went wrong because the bloody ramblers saw the car. And the car was my stupidity.'

'She was waiting for you in the church,' Matt said.

'She couldn't have known,' Tony insisted.

'If she is with them, she's played you like a grand piano,' Matt observed.

Tony became irritated. 'You don't know her.'

'Which makes me objective?'

'It felt like she was telling the truth,' Lissa said.

'No one tells the truth, not all of it,' Matt said evenly.

'Lissa's right, we don't know enough,' Tony muttered before collapsing, moaning, and sliding sideways onto the bench. Lissa took hold of him.

'He's fainted,' she said as she helped Tony back into a sitting position.

'Shit.'

She felt Tony's brow. 'He needs to go to A&E.'

Matt shook his head. 'No.'

'He's dripping with sweat. We've no idea what they did to him.'

Matt leant forward. 'Tony's in the frame for two murders and breaching the Official Secrets Act. If they arrest him now, we'll never see him again, or at least for as long as makes no difference. If we can keep him in play, we've still got a chance. What about your billet?'

'That'll blow my cover, won't it?'

Lissa had booked a static caravan on a tiny site on the Northumberland coast. The site was deserted; the vans were supposed to be empty at this time of year, but the owner couldn't resist the three hundred pounds in cash she'd offered. Her story was that her boyfriend had been killed in a high-speed collision on the M1, and she needed a bit of space to smoke something and get off her head.

'What's Phil gonna think when I turn up with a sick old man?'

Matt grinned. 'Tell him you picked him up on a bender. Didn't realise how old he was until you saw him in daylight.'

'Piss off.'

'Get him in the van and comfortable. Give him some antibiotics and hope for the best.'

Lissa nodded. She always carried a course of powerful antibiotics and painkillers when she was on an operation, but she wasn't happy. 'I don't like it.'

'Neither do I. Look, play up to Phil; just keep him away from the van.' Matt looked at his watch. 'I'm on the clock; I need to go if I'm going to be in the office by this afternoon.'

'You're Tony's mate, and Argentina Farm went up in smoke last night,' Lissa said. 'They're bound to check where you were.'

Matt grinned. 'I've got an alibi, a hospital appointment this morning.' Lissa frowned but Matt hadn't finished. 'I paid a mate to do it in my place. Same age and health issues; he owes me.' Lissa regarded Matt for a moment, then leaned across the table and kissed him on the cheek.

Matt rubbed his face, surprised. 'What was that for?'

'Just because,' she grinned, momentarily looking much younger. 'What health issues?'

Matt shrugged. 'That's just it; he's A1. Don't worry, we go back years.' Matt left the booth, then turned back with a smile. 'Oh, get the bill, will you? I gave Tony some money.'

Lissa stared after him and swore to herself.

26. The Campsite

Greenfield Caravan site should have been called Brownfield Rubbish Dump because everything was rusty, neglected, and long past its best. Even the grass on top of the dunes that stood between the site and the sea was brown and forlorn. Thirty static vans were arranged in three rows of ten, and sometime back in the Jurassic, they'd been painted green and cream to match the clubhouse livery. Now they were discoloured and water stained; rust peppered their sides, and the skylights were all corroded shut, not that that was a problem in January. The site was overlooked by a dilapidated conservatory/bar that doubled as the site office and backed onto the bungalow where Phil lived. Greenfield had been popular in the eighties, but after they'd built the marina in Amble, business declined, and the owner hadn't done much to fight it. Phil Biddles was lazy, lonely, overweight, and over sixty. His mother had been the driving force, but she'd been in the ground for fourteen years, and he'd pretty much given up. Receding hair at the front with a beard that needed trimming, he wore his thinning, mousey mop in a limp ponytail. His grey tracksuit bottoms needed a wash, as did his ACDC tee-shirt, but Phil wasn't big on washing stuff. Winter days were spent watching daytime TV, eating junk food, and drinking too much; summer days were much the same.

He was dozing and didn't stir as Lissa rode into the site. The caravan doors were on the far side and couldn't be seen from the office, so he didn't see them as she helped Tony into the van. She locked the door behind her and drew the curtains. Phil was a nosey bastard as well as being a bit of a perv, so she would have done that anyway. Despite looking rough from the outside, inside the static van wasn't too bad. The stainless steel frame helped, although closer inspection revealed dents in the walls, bodged plumbing repairs, and water stains. Nevertheless, the van had two bedrooms, a minuscule bathroom, a kitchenette with a rickety table, and some electric heating. Lissa decided to put Tony in her room; it was a double and bigger than the other bedroom, which sported bunk beds. She removed his boots and trousers, gave him a double dose of antibiotics, and left him shivering under two duvets. She wondered when Phil would make an appearance. If her bike was there, he often called in for a chat, and if it wasn't, he'd use his master key to snoop. So, from now on, if Tony was there, so was she.

She went into the kitchenette and put the kettle on. While she waited for it to boil, she checked her phone. She had two SIMs, one that she didn't care about and a second one. She swapped SIM cards and powered the phone up. There were no messages, which was good. That meant there weren't any emergencies for now.

27. The Cottage

After arriving at the cottage, Pauline couldn't decide whether to sleep first and then eat, or the other way round. In the end, she opted for a long soak in a hot bath. Lying in the water, she struggled to believe that what had happened was real. The events of the night seemed conjured from an adventure story, but the bruises around her wrist and waist where the rope had caught her were real enough. She had the feeling of floating as if she were stoned, although it had been a long time since she had smoked any dope. Three weeks ago, she had been a bored, single, retired lecturer with time on her hands, wondering what she was going to do with herself. She had considered learning a foreign language, perhaps Gaelic or Arabic, but the best courses were in Newcastle, and that had put her off. She realised she hadn't been serious about it. And then there was Tony, the man she had taken pity on in St. Leonard's. Had she been doing what Jonathan called 'the right thing', or had her motives been more Joanna Trollope? Would she have helped him if she hadn't found him attractive?

On the other hand, she had no regrets about walking away. In another universe, maybe they might have got to know each other, but his world had no stability and no future. She'd had enough adventures. Now it was normality she craved. She was dog-tired and desperate for sleep but she decided to put on a clean jumper and trousers and make herself look presentable. Bridgford was prim, and she didn't want anyone calling round to find her half-undressed in the middle of the day; it was the sort of thing people remembered.

She was pottering about the kitchen when a noise from the front door made her freeze, head on one side as she listened intently. Silently, she took a carving knife from the drawer, tip-toeing towards the front door. Flattening herself against the wall, she eased into the hall, where she saw two letters on the mat. She laughed out loud; it was just the bloody postman. She bent down to pick up the post but it was difficult because of the knife in her hand. So much for living a quiet life in Bridgford. She replaced the knife in the kitchen drawer and examined the letters.

One was an official-typed envelope, probably a circular trying to sell her broadband again. The other was an invitation from Oliver Campion but she had no idea who he was or why he was writing to her. She was about to tear it up when an invitation fell out of the envelope. It was for Wednesday, January 3rd, at eleven o'clock at the Church of St. Peter and St. Paul, Belsington, to celebrate the life of Mary Campion. Of course, Oliver was Mary's son. Pauline reread the letter; Oliver said that thanks to her efforts, he had made it from Thailand and been with his mother at the end. He thanked Pauline for the kindness and support she'd shown, especially for getting Mary to hospital. Finally, he said that it would mean a great deal to him if she could attend the funeral. His mother would have wanted her to be there and Oliver wondered if Pauline might say a few words. Pauline put the letter down and shook her head. She would have loved to go, but it was impossible. Yes, she wanted her old life back, but the trauma of recent events felt too raw, and anyway, she hated funerals.

28. Blackstock Road

At seven forty-five that evening, Matt Hardwick exited Finsbury Park tube, limped up Seven Sisters Road and turned right into Blackstock Road where he stopped and bent down to tie his shoelace. Hawkish commuters hurried back and forth, absorbed in their earpods and mobiles. Those carrying on up Seven Sisters Road had to manoeuvre past a man who stood immobile at the pedestrian crossing as if frozen in time. Staring intently into the middle distance, he was still, except for the insistent jigging of his right leg. North African class A drug user, Matt guessed, but in the streetlight, it was difficult to tell. Surely he was too obvious to be a watcher? Matt stood up and staggered slightly before walking on. His knee was banjaxed from his night exercise. He hadn't seen anyone but if they were any good, he wouldn't. You didn't spend thirty years in the security business and not get an instinct. He'd trained for this; Christ, he'd given courses on it to spotty young tyros, but it was different when you were the one in the crosshairs, especially if you were knackered and limping.

After leaving Lissa and Tony, Matt had arrived back in the office by three-fifteen. No one was bothered or interested apart from Joyce, the tiny Ugandan cleaner with the big grin.

'You happy, Mr. Matt?' She'd asked with mock concern as she manoeuvred her vacuum around the office.

'Fine thanks, Joyce. How are you?'

'I'm not the one who's just had a hospital appointment.' A generous trill of laughter accompanied this reply.

'I'm still waiting for the results,' he'd replied, but even then, he'd wondered how innocent her question was. Could Joyce be someone's asset? He stayed late at the office, catching up on work and trying to see if there was anything about Argentina on the wires. There was nothing but that didn't mean much. It was the first day after the Christmas break. Notionally, it was an ordinary day but half the office had taken it off and the other half had a hangover. Just before six, he received an unexpected text from Bobby Evans and swore to himself.

Half an hour later, he left the office and walked up Putney High Street and made a phone call.

'Bobby?'

'Yeah. Seems you might have a dodgy ticker, Matt.'

'You said you were A-one!' Matt was annoyed.

'I thought I was!'

'You wouldn't be winding me up?'

'Why would I bother?'

'I can think of reasons.'

'Look, you Irish twat, you came to me, remember?' Bobby hissed.

'You swore blind you were fine.'

'It came as a shock to me,' Bobby paused breathlessly. Matt wondered if he was putting it on for effect. Bobby carried on. 'I'm sorry, Matt, really I am. You might need an operation. Well, I might.'

'Christ's sake!' Matt said, ending the call. Despite himself, he looked around. It was stupid; it looked guilty because it was but he couldn't help that. Bobby's news had unsettled him—another loose end to catch him out—but was it more than that? Up to now, everyone who had died suddenly had looked as if they'd had a heart attack. But who knew about him and Bobby Evans? It was ancient history. He pocketed the phone, walked to East Putney station and took the district line to Earls Court. At the last minute, he stepped off the train and rode the escalator down to the Piccadilly Line and headed north. At Kings Cross, he jumped off as the doors were closing. Then he walked to the Victoria Line and waited before taking the third tube to Finsbury Park.

Joyce quizzing him about the hospital and then Evans

having a bad heart felt like a giant coincidence and he didn't believe in coincidences. He had to do something. The idea was straight out of the training manual. If you think you're under surveillance, mix things up, do something different. Instead of going home to his flat in Wandsworth, he headed north to a small Islamic hotel on Seven Sisters Road. It had rooms for single men and two clocks behind reception, one set to UK time and the other to Mecca. Matt had booked a room for the night as he walked to East Putney tube station. He'd used them before; the establishment was quiet and discreet, especially during UK bank holidays and the Asian staff and clientele made it easier to spot a tail. That was the plan, anyway. But, as usual, he forgot the second law of thermodynamics; everything goes tits up in the end.

29. The Caravan Site

Lissa needed some rest. Her shoulder hurt like hell and was not likely to improve any time soon. Tony was sleeping fitfully; she checked his brow, and he was still hot and sweating. She decided that rest was what they both needed. She'd checked on the caravan door and made sure it was locked, then braced some plastic kitchen steps against it and went to bed.

It was dark when she woke. She still felt tired, but that wasn't necessarily a bad thing. Then she heard something, switched on the light, and saw Phil Biddles at the end of the bunk. They both screamed. Lissa jumped out of bed.

'What are you doing, Phil?'

'I thought I heard something,' he muttered, staring lasciviously at her bra and panties.

'Fuck off,' Lissa said, pulling on some clothes and pushing him into the kitchenette. 'You were snooping, weren't you?' Phil shook his head and backed away. 'You wanted to see my underwear; well, you've seen it. Now piss off.'

Phil nodded, then shook his head. 'I found your friend.'

'What?'

'I saw a light. He's in the clubhouse.'

'The clubhouse?'

'It was locked. How the fuck did he get in?'

'Is he OK?'

Phil nodded. 'Helped himself to a bottle of beer. I gave him a cup of tea, and...'

'I see.' Lissa nodded, wondering what to do. 'Well, we'd better go and get him then.' They walked across the site. It was another cold night, and the frost on the grass crunched under their feet. She really needed to say something to calm Phil down but for once, she couldn't think of anything.

Some time before the last Ice Age, the clubhouse had been licenced; the tables and chairs arranged as if it were about to open. Tony was sitting in the corner, nursing a mug. Lissa bent down towards him.

'What do you think you're doing?' She asked gently.

Tony's eyes came back from somewhere, and he looked at her. He smiled. 'Lissa?'

She felt his brow; he was burning. 'You're not well. You need to sleep.' He nodded. The room was unheated and bitterly cold, and it wouldn't do him any good to linger.

'Give me a hand, Phil?' Unused to being useful in any way, Phil just nodded dumbly. Lissa turned back to Tony. 'Come on, hero , we're going to take you back to bed.' She bent down and lifted him to his feet. She motioned to Phil to go the other side and together they half-carried, half-hobbled Tony back to the van and his bed. Lissa gave him another antibiotic and shut the door.

Phil was waiting in the kitchenette. Emboldened by their shared experience, he smiled slyly at Lissa. 'Who is he then?'

'Do you care?' Lissa asked.

'Got into the clubhouse, helped himself to a beer, without a key?'

Lissa shrugged. 'He's off his head.'

Phil pressed his advantage. 'You only paid for one; it's more for multi-occupancy.'

Lissa sighed. 'He's a friend of my dad's, he's had a hard time.'

'Not keen on having sickness in a van and there's the damage to the clubhouse.'

'You just said there wasn't any.'

'Might be. He helped himself to a beer. Could be expensive.'

'Would you feel better if I gave you another three hundred now plus a bonus if you keep your mouth shut?' Phil's eyes were out on stalks as she counted out the three hundred. This was his biggest pay day in years.

'What kind of bonus?' he asked, pocketing the cash. The capacity for greed hadn't left him.

'Well, that depends if you can keep quiet.' Phil waited expectantly. 'How about another four hundred when we leave? Make it up to a thousand?'

Phil thought for a moment. 'If he's important, maybe it's worth more than that? Maybe it's worth double?'

Lissa looked at him for a moment, then nodded. 'Wait there a moment, will you?' Phil nodded as she went back to her room. She came back with the automatic in her hand. Phil looked at it and grinned.

'That's not real.'

'No?'

'It's just a toy, that is.' He grinned lasciviously and took a step towards her. Lissa fired a shot through the door. In the enclosed space, the noise was deafening. Phil turned, looked at the hole, and shrank back with his hands over his ears.

'Still think it's a toy?' Phil shook his head. 'Well?'

'No,' he whimpered.

'Do as I say, and you'll get another four hundred.' Phil cowered, nodding. 'But if you open that gob of yours, I will show you what kind of hole this toy will make in your fat gut. Comprende?' Phil nodded. Lissa opened the van door and held it there for him. 'Well, piss off then.'

Phil looked at her, then ducked out of the door and scuttled away. Lissa locked the van door and swore to herself. Phil was the worst kind of uncontrolled variable. She hadn't seen any visitors during the time she'd been there, but that didn't mean much. Lissa hadn't had time to do any prep on the site before her arrival. She looked at her watch; it was ten minutes past six, an hour before dawn, and the third day of the new year. Lissa needed rest but she had to be sure. She took another painkiller and settled down to wait.

Just before eight o'clock, she rode out of the site, revving the bike extra loudly so that Phil would get the message. She rode two miles south, turned off the main road, and left the bike at a visitor centre. She walked to the sea, then walked north, up the beach, until she came abreast of the site. She found a hollow on top of the dunes where she could watch the vans and settled herself down to wait. After four hours, she was cold and stiff. Phil didn't snoop around the van; he didn't appear on the site at all. At ten-fourteen, he emerged from the bungalow clad in a high-viz jacket and drove off in a cloud of diesel exhaust. About an hour later, he returned with some shopping.

Lissa walked back to her bike and drove back to the site. She parked up and checked on Tony; his fever seemed to be abating, and he was sleeping more comfortably. She checked her automatic, then put the gun on the kitchen table and made herself another sandwich.

30. The Ceremony

The decision to go had been last-minute. Pauline had gone to bed early with no thought of attending. Robert's death had destroyed her capacity for the ersatz sentiment prevalent at funerals. Over breakfast, she opened the typed envelope, still untouched from the day before. Inside was another envelope, along with a short, scrawled note from someone called Lizzie, who said the Christmas card would explain. Puzzled, Pauline stopped reading and tore open the second envelope. Inside was an Oxfam Christmas card showing a snowy festive scene. Gingerly, Pauline opened the greetings card; on the blank page opposite the greeting were a few lines written in a neat, generous hand.

> *'Hello Pauline,*
> *Lizzie the social worker told me your name.*
> *I always hoped that you might look for me. Of course, I have tried to imagine you and wondered why you gave me up.*
> *If you would like to write to me, I would very much like to get to know you.*
> *You have two lovely granddaughters, Luna (7) and Miriam (5) (both well and happy). I haven't told them about you yet; I thought it best to wait until we know each other better.*
> *I hope all is well with you and that you have a happy Christmas.*
> *Love*
> *Lavinia x*

Pauline stood immobile as she tried to comprehend the moment. She had dreamt of hearing from her daughter for years, but that had been a fantasy. This was different; this was real and she was happy, excited, angry, scared. What if it didn't work out? She had to reply, but what should she say? She read and reread the note, examining it for hidden meaning as if it were the Dead Sea Scrolls. The line that kept bringing her to tears was 'You have two lovely granddaughters'. The phrasing was generous; otherwise, she would have said, 'I have two lovely daughters', but she hadn't. Luna and Miriam; Pauline practised saying the names to herself.

She put the card down and read the social worker, Lizzie's scrawl carefully. Lizzie explained that Lavinia had recently qualified as a teaching assistant and had asked Lizzie if she would write a reference for her. Lizzie had agreed and when they'd met, she'd asked Lavinia if she ever thought about her birth mother. Lavinia had guessed that Lizzie knew something and had demanded to know all. Lizzie had told her about Pauline's visit to Nottingham and her desire to make contact with her. The Christmas card was Lizzie's suggestion, a possible first step for informal connection; it had the advantage of allowing both Pauline and Lavinia to back out at any time.

As Pauline stood there, holding the card and Lizzie's note, the radio played Bing Crosby's 'Accentuate the Positive'. Pauline began humming along, then joined in boisterously until she found herself dancing around the room, singing at the top of her voice. She felt happy and hopeful, with an intensity that she'd forgotten was possible. At the end of the song, she swayed breathlessly and laughed. A weight had been lifted; she was getting a second chance, a chance to make up for the pain she had inflicted.

It was then that she decided to attend Mary's funeral. The idea of doing something decent and normal was too tempting. The terrible events of the last few weeks were banished; the poor timing would not defeat her newfound hope. Her aches and pains seemed to recede and she decided to make an effort, selecting a favourite, dark woollen suit with a matching coat. Driving there through the snowfields, she hummed the song again and fantasised about meeting Lavinia and the girls. So what if she was going to a funeral?

It was a good day for it—cold and sunless with lying snow. Despite her newfound cheerfulness, the bruising to her side made driving uncomfortable. The road snaked up and down, past remote farmsteads populated by a few forlorn sheep or the occasional belted galloway cow. Under low clouds, the bleak cheviot foothills offered little in the way of comfort as the valleys narrowed and the hills closed in. Occasionally, the wind got up and blew snow against the windscreen. The eight-mile trip seemed endless, but then she negotiated a bend and the village came into view.

Surrounded on three sides by steep, snow-covered hills, the cluster of houses that comprised Belsington was not much more than a hamlet, yet, by some quirk of geography, it warranted a working church. A fast-flowing beck in an open drain hurried down the main street past the small limestone church of St. Peter and St. Paul, which stood at the bottom of the village like a sentinel. The tower and part of the nave dated from the fourteenth century, but the mechanical digger by the newly dug grave was state-of-the art. The hole was a black scar against the lying snow, Pauline shivered as she caught sight of it.

She arrived late deliberately, slipping into the church and taking a seat near the back, keen to be alone with her optimism. A few red-faced, tweedy locals chatted to each other quietly in the pews near the front, their breath visible in the cold air. In front of the altar, a tall man with longish, fair hair in his thirties stood by the coffin. He had a look of Mary, Pauline assumed he must be Oliver. She was going to introduce herself, but the sight of the coffin derailed her.

'Pauline? I thought it was you.' She turned to see Jonathan wearing a cassock and surplus.

'What are you doing here?' She barked; she hadn't expected to see him.

'Officiating,' he smiled. Was it just a coincidence?

'Belsington is miles from Bridgford.'

He nodded. 'The usual celebrant is ill. I'm doing it as a favour. They would have done it in Greenstone, but the roads are still blocked.'

Even as he spoke, the fear that he might be involved undermined her hope. She nodded and replied, 'Poor you.'

Jonathan grinned. 'I don't mind. People generally behave well at funerals. I didn't know you and Mary were friends?'

Pauline shrugged. 'We were colleagues.'

'Oliver said you put yourself out for her.'

'I did what anyone would have done.' Pauline replied. She had regained control of herself but wondered if her decision to attend was a mistake. The funeral was supposed to ease her paranoia, not stoke it.

The fair-haired man approached, smiling. 'I'm Oliver, but my friends call me Ollie; you must be Pauline. Thanks for coming.'

Jonathan made his excuses and headed towards the coffin and the altar.

Pauline smiled at Oliver. 'It's good you managed to get here in time.'

Oliver smiled back. 'It was a long flight, but we had a couple of days together.'

'You live in Thailand?'

Oliver nodded. 'I import vintage clothes.'

'Sounds very jet-set.'

'Not really. It's just buying and selling, only over longer distances.'

'Where do the vintage clothes come from?' Pauline asked.

'Most of the stuff is sourced in China. They're brilliant at manufacturing fakes,' he grinned boyishly.

Pauline nodded, but her mind was starting to wander. Oliver took her hand in his.

'You will come back to the house afterwards?'

She nodded. 'Yes, I'd like that.' She was saved from further conversation when Jonathan called Oliver to the front.

After singing 'Abide With Me' and reciting 'The Lord's

Prayer', Jonathan said something sweet about Mary. Even though he hadn't known her, he'd managed, with some humour, to convey something of her generosity and capacity for fun that was rather effective. Pauline was still wondering about his presence when Oliver waved her to the front. The pulpit was set to the side and above the congregation. Pauline climbed the steps, turned, faced the empty pews and began.

'Mary Campion was a colleague in the Humanities department at the university, but she was also a friend. I lectured in history while she taught English. I'm going to read one of her favourite poems by Yeats. It's called 'Cloths of Heaven,' Pauline paused. She didn't know if Mary liked it or not, but it was a favourite of hers; it was also mercifully short. As she surveyed the congregation, a man took a seat near the back. There was something familiar about him. She took a breath and began.

'Had I the heaven's embroidered cloths, Enwrought with golden and silver light...' and then she recognised him, the man who'd interrogated her in the disused swimming pool. Buchan dipped his head towards her in recognition, a thin smile playing on his lips. Her voice faltered and she gulped, unable to speak. Everybody tensed, interpreting her difficulty as grief. A look of concern creased Jonathan's features and he took a half-step towards her. Shaking her head, she forced herself to regain control and read to the end of the poem.

'Sorry,' she muttered, hurrying from the pulpit, her mind racing. She wanted to flee but tried to behave normally—so much for doing something ordinary. Was it possible that Jonathan and Buchan were in it together? But then, after everything that had happened, who could know? The sound of 'The Red Flag' blasting out from the sound system jerked Pauline back to the service; she'd missed Oliver's explanation that it had been his Mum and Dad's favourite. Jonathan said a final prayer and then invited everyone to follow the coffin to the graveside.

The wind had intensified, lifting loose bits of snow, stinging face and hands, making everybody turn away from the blast. At the back, Pauline scanned the graveyard as Jonathan intoned the familiar prayers. Buchan had disappeared, but after seeing him, Pauline couldn't face going back to Greenstone. She took the opportunity to hurry away while Jonathan and Oliver were busy talking to mourners.

She'd parked up the lane and around a corner, out of sight. She turned the corner there he was, leaning against her car in a black woollen coat and drinking from a silver hip flask looking for all the world as if he were at the races. Buchan offered the flask to her, but she ignored him and unlocked the car with her key fob. He didn't move.

'Cold day. Sure, you won't have a nip?' She shook her head. 'Wrote well for a Fenian, Yeats,' he smiled unpleasantly. 'But what's wrong with an English poet?'

'Whatever it is, the answer's no,' Pauline said evenly.

He grinned. 'Know how sheepdog trials work?' Pauline stared at him. 'They work because the sheep are more afraid of the dog than the consequences.'

Ignoring him, Pauline went to open the car door, but Buchan pushed it shut. She was trying to pull his hand away when Jonathan appeared.

'Is everything OK, Pauline?' He asked breathlessly.

Buchan smiled and let go of the door. 'It's all tickety-boo Vicar. Why don't you go and do some praying?'

Pauline looked at Jonathan's earnest features. If he was in league with Buchan, it was a brilliant act. Buchan spoke again.

'If you don't mind?'

Jonathan looked at Buchan and then at Pauline. 'Pauline?'

She forced herself to smile. 'Everything's fine, Jonathan; it's a personal matter.'

He glanced at Buchan, then back at her. 'If you're sure?'

'I am,' she said.

Jonathan nodded and backed away. Buchan watched him go and sneered. 'Loser.'

'Is he?'

Buchan put his face close to hers and gripped her left wrist, causing her to gasp. She could smell the whisky on his breath.

'One day I'm going to ask you to do something and you're going to do it,' he hissed. His grip was like a vice, but after a moment, he let go and smiled again. 'Cheerio then.' And with that, he turned and walked away.

Back home after the funeral, Pauline locked the doors and drew the curtains. She had just poured herself a scotch when there was a knock at the door. She opened it to find Jonathan standing there, nodding apologetically.

'Sorry to bother you,' he nodded. 'I thought I'd make sure you were er good.'

'Why?' She replied coldly. The inference wasn't lost on Jonathan, who stepped from foot to foot nervously.

'After the funeral? The man?'

Pauline considered, then opened the door wide.

'You'd better come in.'

Jonathan entered. Pauline closed the door and led him into the tiny parlour, where she picked up her drink.

'Can I get you anything? I'm having a scotch.'

Jonathan smiled diffidently. 'No, thank you.'

'You want to know about the man at the car?'

The coldness of her tone made Jonathan take a small step in retreat. 'I don't want to pry Pauline.'

'Don't you?'

'I was worried about you, but if you want me to go, that's fine.'

Pauline didn't think Jonathan was on their side, but she couldn't be sure. Paranoia was the currency of her brave new world. 'Sure you won't have a whisky, Jonathan?'

He nodded. 'Why not? It's a cold night.'

Pauline fixed him his drink and topped up her own. She tidied away Lavinia's card and Lizzie's note, but the mere act of touching them buoyed her up. Jonathan began to speak.

'I saw him come into the church during the service. Funny how you can sense things. He looked out of place. I knew he wasn't a mourner; there was a lack of er?'

'Respect?' She prompted.

'Empathy. And then, when you didn't go back to the house afterwards, I was concerned.'

'And came looking for me?' Jonathan nodded. Pauline sighed and then continued. 'I saw him arriving, but I didn't twig who he was until the poem. That's why I stumbled over it.'

'The poem was fine.'

If Jonathan was with 'the opposition', he was bloody good at it. She decided to behave as if he were dangerous until she could be sure that he wasn't.

'Colonel Buchan is the name he gave me,' Pauline explained. 'He said he was a policeman.'

'What did he want?'

'To frighten me.' Jonathan took a sip of his whisky as she stood there. 'He succeeded.'

'Do you want to talk about it?' Jonathan asked.

'I don't think I should involve you, Jonathan.'

'Don't you think that's a decision for me to make?'

Pauline sighed. 'These people are dangerous.'

Jonathan nodded cheerfully. 'It makes a change from Harvest Festival and coffee mornings.'

Pauline smiled as a wave of nausea and exhaustion washed over her. She swayed and sat down.

'I'm going to have to go to bed.'

Jonathan nodded, leant towards her and said quietly. 'If you want to talk, I'm available. It's my job.'

Pauline nodded. 'Let me sleep on it?'

'Right you are. Thanks for the whisky,' he grinned, draining his glass. 'I might have to get a bottle.'

After he had gone, Pauline locked and bolted the front door, then took a large carving knife from the kitchen drawer and placed it under her pillow together with Lavinia's Christmas card. For the first time in a while, she fell asleep easily.

In fact, that night afforded a brief hiatus for the press-ganged crusaders, time to regroup for Pauline, Matt in his tiny hotel room and Lissa in the rusting caravan as she smoked cigarette after cigarette, hoping that Tony was on the mend.

31. Central Line

Matt woke after an uncomfortable night squeezed under the eaves, sleeping in his underwear because it was a spur-of-the moment decision. He'd watched the minuscule TV and ordered a takeaway pizza. After a winter night in the open and a second night in which every noise and creak had spooked him, he'd been exhausted. That was the thing about being a spook; there was a 'sell-by' date after which you began to miss things. Approaching sixty and overweight, it all added to the pressure, not to mention the fact he was running an illegal operation with no funds. Nevertheless, he felt much better after a night's sleep. He ate a little breakfast and then took the tube to Wandsworth.

It was the morning rush hour and, close to his flat, he felt safe. Maybe that's why he didn't notice the white van parked at the end of his street. Nonetheless, at eight minutes past eight, he had the presence of mind to send Lissa a check text—a line from Macbeth: 'Stars hide your fires.' The idea was that at nine minutes past nine, he'd send the second part, 'Let not light see your black and deep desires.' He'd chosen it to wind up Lissa, who'd have preferred something from a 'Bond' movie. Not that it mattered because he never sent the second part.

He'd lived alone for almost ten years. The flat was nice enough—two bedrooms on the eighth floor of an anonymous executive block that had replaced ten Victorian villas obliterated by a stick of bombs from a Heinkel 111 in 1941. The site had remained derelict until the 1960s, when the confident, modernist lines of Belton House spoke of the value of drip-dry shirts, sliced bread and non-stick frying pans. You didn't have to be special to live in Belton House; you had to have money

Matt had been paid well for his stint in uniform. He'd bought the place because it was anonymous, handy for work and was built like a bomb-shelter. The soundproofing was top-notch, he'd wanted that.

Lissa had sort of moved in when she was twelve, after her mother died of breast cancer. He'd done his best to be a father to her, but the anger over her mother's death had never subsided. She was placed in several foster homes, from which she absconded, usually finding her way to his flat. She had a key, but he was often away on operations and, consequently, she spent a lot of time alone. Matt and Julie, Lissa's mother, had never married and he had not been named on Lissa's birth certificate. As far as the authorities were concerned, he didn't exist. When he'd suggested informing the authorities and making their relationship official, Lissa had gone apeshit. At some level, she'd blamed Matt's absence for her mother's death. Matt had tried to explain that he'd split from Julie to keep her safe after he'd found out about the pregnancy, but it cut no ice with Lissa.

He'd come back from the Maritime Alps to find an enormous party in full swing and the flat being trashed by some blow-hard rugby hooray who'd attacked a local drug dealer, all taking place to the stadium sound of Rhianna's 'Good Girl Gone Bad'. Matt pulled the plug on the sound system and told them all to piss off. The hooray attacked Matt, who side-stepped and threw him down the stairs. The sight of the blow-hard rugby-player groaning in a heap in the stairwell encouraged the rest to follow. They filed out of the flat; Lissa went with them and didn't return. She was twenty-one; she could do as she pleased and she did.

They'd remained in contact, off and on, her occasionally shouting, sometimes soft but always angry. Matt thought she should have had professional help, but she was so headstrong. She'd joined up and then, with his help, gone into some hush-hush stuff. Since then, they'd behaved as if they were workmates or colleagues and Matt never referred to her as his daughter, even though, when she felt like it, she sometimes called him Dad. He hadn't been able to tell that there was a party in the flat and that had stayed with him. There wasn't much noise on the stairs and absolutely nothing out on the street. The soundproofing was brilliant, but then, as Confucius used to say, 'you get what you pay for'.

About the time Lissa had moved out, a labrador had moved in up the street. In the early days, it had been excitable, curious and manically friendly but as the years passed and the mercury settled, it spent its days with its backside on the path and its front paws on the pavement, watching the world go by. Matt felt some sympathy for the animal because he too was feeling his age. He understood the dog's need to stay close to home, refuge and safety. But for a spook, refuge and safety meant danger; lowering your guard can get you killed.

They were waiting for him in his bedroom, which was professional. They'd gained entry, found his tell-tales and reset them so he wouldn't suspect. That was the problem. His tell-tales were old-school; he'd been using the same ones since he'd worked for Force Seven. A piece of thread across the door jamb at the top and another one on the kitchen door. If someone already knew his security routine, that would make it so much easier.

Anyway, he'd come in, checked his tells, then unloaded his phone and his shoes and started to unwind, so when he went into the bedroom, he didn't see it coming. Matt came round stripped to his Y-fronts and tied to one of his dining chairs. There were three of them: a woman of around forty, well dressed and manicured, a bit of a looker, a man with his arm in a sling and a third person who stayed behind him. Despite the training, his heart was pounding and his mouth was dry. Why hadn't he been more careful? He'd got sloppy. But hindsight is a marvellous thing. He didn't like the fact that he could see their faces. That meant they didn't care if he knew what they looked like.

'We know about your trip to Northumberland,' the man with the sling said. The accent was eastern European, maybe Serbian or Polish.

'Think you must have the wrong man,' Matt replied. Someone kicked him in the kidneys, knocking him and the chair

176

over. The pain was excruciating, and he struggled to breathe. They righted him.

'Don't waste time with fairytale,' the woman said quietly. Her accent was very good, but some of the vowels weren't closed enough. That was the thing with English; it was tough to speak it flawlessly; he should know, he'd grown up in Ulster. The same origin as the man, he guessed, but not definitely. They were angry but what did they want?

'We know you blew up the pylons,' came a third voice, upper-crust, English and familiar. 'Not a bad job, in the circumstances. Mind, you are getting a bit long in the tooth for lying out on the moors at night in January.'

Matt didn't reply. He didn't want to get kicked again. Besides, the speaker was right; he was getting too old for bollocks like that.

'We know it was you.'

'I had a hospital appointment,' Matt began. The woman laughed unpleasantly.

Cut-glass spoke again. 'The BT Openreach transfers were out of date. They've changed their logo.'

'I don't know what you're on about,' Matt said as calmly as he could muster.

'They're the same transfers that were used on an operation you ran six years ago in Leeds.'

The logo was out of date. Well, of course, it was. It was a low-rent, off-grid operation and he'd had to beg, steal, and borrow everything.

'Clever of you to put them to one side, just in case, but then again, thrift is a Presbyterian virtue, wouldn't you agree, Matthew?' Only two people called him Matthew. One was his mother, the other was...

'Buchan? What in hell's name are you doing here?'

'My job, Matthew, which is more than I can say for you.'

'With these two jokers? Come off it.'

'I'm kosher, Matthew, but you've been off the reservation, haven't you?' As he said this, Buchan moved into view. Matt stared at him and scowled. He was beginning to have a very bad feeling about the situation.

32. Flowers

After a strong black coffee, Pauline did pilates for an hour. She felt refreshed and cheerful as she searched for an old book of cake recipes of her mother's. Feeling better than she had for a while, Pauline wrote a short letter to Lavinia, which she signed, placed in an envelope and stuck down the flap. She had spent a lot of time thinking about what to say and refused to agonise over the wording.

She thanked Lavinia for the Christmas card and apologised for giving her up for adoption. Despite accepting that this was no excuse, Pauline explained that she had been young, alone and scared; her parents had put a lot of pressure on her. Not a day had passed when Pauline had not regretted her decision. She told Lavinia about Robert and his accident and she mentioned something about her work at the university. Pauline finished by hoping they could meet soon and talk at greater length. She was keen to get to know her daughter and very excited at the thought of meeting Luna and Miriam.

After the letter, Pauline made a list of ingredients for Bakewell Tart. Seeing the words 'ground rice' and 'ground almonds' was like returning to a country she had left long ago. Bakewell tart had been Robert's favourite and if Lavinia and the girls were going to come and stay, as she hoped they might, then they would need cakes and treats.

She decided to go to St. Leonard's and change the flowers. She needed to talk to Jonathan again and try to convince herself that he was harmless. Stuffing the letter to her daughter and the list of ingredients into her handbag, Pauline wondered if she dare tell Jonathan about Lavinia. After changing the flowers, she would go to Hexham; she could get the stuff for the Bakewell there and post the letter.

She hummed to herself as she went through the graveyard with the iron key to the 'Devil's door', the ancient door in the north wall that had once been bricked up. Before the reformation, the door had been left open during baptism ceremonies to allow the devil to escape. To prevent this from happening, the door had been bricked up until the enlightenment, when it was opened again, this time to combat the superstition. Even in winter, there was an air of tranquillity and timelessness about the doorway, but she was surprised to find it slightly ajar. Maybe Violet was here. She cleaned the church every Monday, but things were out of sync because of the New Year.

She stepped inside and called out, 'Is anyone there?'

There was no answer and she began to shiver. The ancient stone structure sucked any heat out of the air. The Elizabethan figures knelt in prayer by the tombs, and dust motes hung in the air as always. The stillness was palpable and Pauline found herself holding her breath. Then she spied the Christmas flowers wilting in their vase and hurried forward. Pauline took the vessel into the vestry and washed it out with cold water, but she couldn't find any fresh flowers. She searched the changing room and the area by the pulpit, but there didn't seem to be any, which wasn't like Jonathan. Every Thursday, he led holy communion at the abbey in Hexham and took the opportunity to buy fresh flowers for St.Leonard's afterwards. Pauline shrugged and used the paper peonies she kept for when fresh flowers weren't available.

She went to the little private chapel, intending to check the vase there and that was when she saw Jonathan. Her first thought was that he was prostrating himself in penance, but as she drew near, she knew the penitence was permanent. She knelt and felt for a pulse in his neck but couldn't find one. He wasn't cold; his skin had an unhealthy, lardy sheen. She turned him onto his back, unbuttoned his cassock and began doing CPR on him.

'Thirty fast compressions at one hundred beats per minute, then two breaths,' she said to herself as she pumped.

Pauline didn't know if this was the right thing to do, but she knew that if she did nothing, he definitely wouldn't survive. But, as she pummelled his chest and realised that it wasn't having any effect, another possibility occurred to her. He had been targeted because of her. The idea was monstrous, and yet, the more she considered it, the more credible it became. She finally had the proof she'd wanted: Jonathan was an innocent and they'd killed him. She stopped CPR and rechecked his pulse, and this time she felt something. She put her ear to his mouth and listened but she couldn't make out what he was saying.

'Hang on, Jonathan; I'm going to get help,' she whispered, then replaced his head on the stone floor.

She stood up and hurried away, through the graveyard and back to her cottage, where she called the emergency services. Then she went back to St. Leonard's to wait. On the way back, she knocked on several doors and by the time the ambulance arrived half an hour later, there was a group of eight or nine older women waiting in the graveyard or inside St. Leonard's itself. The police arrived shortly afterwards and cordoned off the church. After about twenty minutes, the paramedics hurried past with Jonathan on a gurney, an oxygen mask clamped to his face. Pauline tried to find out how he was, but they shooed her away, slamming doors and screeching away, siren and lights going. A uniformed constable remained standing guard over the scene.

Three hours later, Pauline was interviewed at home by the policeman she'd seen guarding the church. To Pauline's eye, he looked as young as the 'freshers' she used to teach at the university, but he was tall with weathered cheeks.

'Can I get you anything, Constable?' He shook his head, uncertain of the protocol. Pauline wondered if it was his first assignment. 'Is there any news?' she asked.

'No, I'm sorry, Mrs.'

'Atkinson and its Ms.,' Pauline said firmly. He nodded. 'Why are you here?'

'To clear up some details,' he smiled. 'You're the one who found the reverend?'

'Yes, I called the ambulance. I came straight here and phoned.'

The constable frowned. 'You used your landline?' Pauline nodded. 'You don't have a mobile?'

Pauline shook her head. 'No, the signal's terrible here.'

'I see. And you found him in front of the altar?'

Pauline nodded. 'I change the flowers at St. Leonard's.' The policeman wrote something down in a tiny notebook. 'Is he dead? The paramedics didn't say.'

The young plod nodded. 'I'm sorry. Didn't you know? Death was pronounced when he arrived at the hospital. They think it was a heart attack.'

'Right.'

'That's the preliminary report. We'll know more after the postmortem.'

'You think it could be something else?' Pauline asked.

The constable shook his head. 'It'd be above my pay grade if it were.'

'Why are you standing guard at the church then?'

'Standard procedure. Unexplained death. '

'I see.' He was still writing. Pauline felt as if she were having an out-of-body experience. Grief and fury threatened to overwhelm her and yet part of her brain still had the space to meander. Why didn't the young man use some kind of digital recording instead of paper and pencil?

'So what details do you want clarified?'

He stopped writing and looked up. 'When you called the emergency services, can you remember what you said?'

She shrugged. 'That it was urgent and he was unconscious?'

The constable nodded. 'You did say that, but you said something else.'

Pauline was confused. 'Oh? I was upset and shocked. I still am.' She felt the sobs beginning to erupt. She fought to keep hold of herself.

'You claimed he'd been attacked.' She nodded. The young plod cleared his throat. 'Do you recall saying that, Ms. Atkinson?'

Pauline stared at him. 'Yes.'

'Why did you say it?'

'I happen to think it's true.' He looked at her, his eyebrows raised in anticipation. 'You wouldn't believe me if I told you.'

'Try me,' he said. The feeling of being humoured by a younger person had become increasingly familiar of late. She decided to play it straight.

'Jonathan was probably killed with a new untraceable toxin developed at a lab in Northumberland, a place called Argentina Farm.'

The constable puckered his brow. 'I've heard of it. There was an incident a couple of nights ago.'

Pauline nodded. 'That's right.'

'How do you know this, Ms. Atkinson?'

'I broke in.'

'Alone, or did you have help?' Pauline didn't reply. 'How old are you, Ms. Atkinson?'

She attempted a smile. 'Don't you know never to ask a woman's age?' The constable didn't respond. 'I'm fifty-three.' He noted it down on his pad. Pauline carried on. 'They're dangerous people. Protected at the highest level.'

The constable frowned. 'If this toxin is untraceable, the postmortem won't find anything?'

Pauline shook her head. 'Probably not.'

'But why? Why would they kill the Reverend Williams?'

'Pour encourager les autres,' Pauline murmured. 'It means to...'

'...encourage the others?' The young copper said, 'I know. My grandmother's French. I spent a lot of summers there.'

'Lucky you,' Pauline murmured.

'You didn't answer my question.' Pauline looked. 'Why kill him?'

'I don't know,' Pauline replied helplessly. The constable pocketed his notebook, pushed his chair back and stood up. 'You don't believe me, do you? I don't blame you.'

He shrugged. 'There's no evidence. I can't do anything without evidence.'

After the policeman left, Pauline was at a loss. The recipe book was still open at Bakewell tart, but that seemed a lifetime away. She put the book back in the rack in the kitchen; then she took Lavinia's letter from her bag and held it. After Jonathan, she wondered if replying would place Lavinia and the girls in danger. Perhaps she shouldn't post the letter after all. It was just after six when there was another knock at the door. Pauline opened it to be confronted by a tall, galleon of a woman dressed in a green woollen beret, waxed jacket, tweed skirt and brogues. Pauline guessed her age at about fifty. The woman smiled like an official; she spoke like a toff.

'My name's Jane Percival. I wondered if I might come in for a moment.'

Pauline nodded and opened the door wider. Jane Percival bustled in and removed her hat and coat, offering them to Pauline as if she were a servant. Pauline hung them up and led the way into her living room. Jane Percival looked around.

'Charming place,' she murmured and sat down at the dining table.

'Can I get you anything? A cup of tea, coffee, something stronger, perhaps?'

Jane Percival shook her head, then stopped, 'A dry sherry if you have one?'

Pauline filled two large schooners and sat opposite her visitor, who sipped the sherry appreciatively. 'You've had a horrid time, my dear. I know you liked Dr. Williams.'

Pauline was lost for a moment, then realised that she meant Jonathan.

'Who are you?' Pauline asked. 'You're not the police?'

Jane shook her head. 'No.'

'What do you want?'

'It's a delicate matter,' Jane replied. 'You've done terribly well up to now, given the circumstances.'

'I don't follow,' Pauline said.

'No, you wouldn't. I'm a boffin, really,' Jane announced. 'Chemistry, microbiology, medicine, physics—a bit of everything. My job is to keep an eye on things. Make sure they stay on an even keel, so to speak.'

'Who are you?' Pauline asked. Jane began to reply, but Pauline interrupted. 'You told me your name. Who do you work for?'

Jane frowned. 'Should be whom, really. Never mind. I'm attached to the Royal household.'

Pauline became irritated. 'My friend was killed today. If this is a joke, it's in very poor taste.'

Jane shook her head. 'Look, here's my bona fides.' Jane proffered a laminated card containing her name, 'Dr. Jane Percival FRS', her photograph, royal title and a small red waxed seal under the laminate. Pauline studied it for a moment.

'It's the royal seal,' Jane explained. 'A miniature version.'

'What do you want?' Pauline asked.

'We want you to carry on.' Pauline frowned. Jane leant across the table. 'We've had our eye on Colonel Buchan for some time.'

Pauline's stomach churned at the mention of his name. She remembered the smell of whisky on his breath, his sneering at Jonathan and his threats. Jane Percival sipped her sherry and continued.

'He's sailed close to the wind throughout his career but we think he's crossed over.'

'You work for the Royal Household. Why don't you arrest him?'

'He has powerful friends and I don't have any power,' Jane said. 'There's the protection of the Royal Warrant, of course, and I have access to files and so forth, but I am constrained. My job is essentially behind the scenes, prodding and poking.'

'What job is that?' Pauline asked.

'Defence of the Realm,' Jane said, nodding to herself. 'Yes, that's it. They've developed a poison that is completely undetectable. Have you any idea how dangerous that is? How useful it would be to enemies of this country and our allies?'

'I'm a retired lecturer. What on earth do you think I can do?'

'You're a clean skin with no antecedents. That is extremely

rare. Colonel Buchan has you in his sights. We'd like you to stay there.'

Pauline sighed. 'Isn't there anyone else? '

Jane put down her sherry and leant. 'We know about Tony and Matt, they've done well. Tony, in particular, is very able but he's tainted because of his association with Matt and his daughter.'

'You know Lissa?' Pauline asked.

Jane nodded and smiled thinly. 'Like her father, two peas in a pod. They're good at what they do, but they are soldiers, and their first thought is always force. Whereas you, my dear, have a brain and you aren't afraid to use it.'

Pauline had a thought. 'You believe Jonathan was murdered?'

Jane nodded. 'Yes.'

'Thank heavens.'

'We can't prove it, unfortunately. You told the constable the poison was untraceable.'

Pauline looked at the well-spoken stranger sipping sherry and discussing murder at her dining table.

'We know that Buchan's scheme is coming to fruition. We know the attack will take place in the north of England in February and that the target is a female foreign national.'

'Have you got a name?' Pauline asked.

Jane Percival sighed. 'A first name only, Sandra.'

'Sandra?' Pauline asked. 'Doesn't sound foreign to me.'

'Our source was quite definite about that.'

'How good is your source?'

Jane sniffed irritably. 'Credible.'

Pauline shook her head and got to her feet. 'I'm sorry, Jane. The answer's no.'

Jane regarded Pauline for a moment. 'You're sure I can't persuade you?'

'Quite sure.'

Jane Percival finished her sherry. 'If you change your mind, here's my card.' She handed Pauline a cheaply produced business card. Written in simple type was 'J. Percival' and a telephone number; the royal seal was absent.

Jane Percival put on her coat and hat and made to go. At the doorway, she turned back.

'Call, any time.' She paused for a moment, then leant closer. 'It's probably better if you don't tell Tony and the others about me.'

Pauline did not respond. Jane smiled, dipped her head and bustled from the cottage. Pauline closed the door but held onto the handle for several minutes.

33. Matt

If the intruders were going to kill him, they'd have done it immediately. They had grilled him for over eighteen hours; he was running on empty but so were they and he was still breathing. Matt had discovered that the man with his arm in a sling was called Milo and the woman was Tina. They'd gone on and on about his movements on New Year's Day and the day after, but the question they kept coming back to was Tony. Why had he gone to Northumberland, what did he want? They also wanted to know where he was, which confused Matt. At first, they'd gone at him full-pelt for a couple of hours, hitting him in the midriff and the kidneys, which hurt like hell. Milo was the tough guy, Buchan the velvet glove. Tina was hard to read; sometimes she was pleasant and occasionally focused but she often appeared preoccupied and worried about Milo's injury. A couple of times, he'd told her to forget his pain and do her job. Later on, they'd rigged up some kind of electrical device to his genitals and turned on the current. It was excruciating, but Matt survived because he thought they didn't want to kill him. There were times when he was tempted to give up, but he knew he had to get through the hours. It was when he was tired that Buchan asked about Pauline.

'Is there such a thing as a clean skin?'

'That's what I thought,' Matt replied. The fundamental rule when being subject to questioning was to tell the truth as much as possible and hide the lies inside it. The truth was easier to remember. Lies had a habit of becoming entangled.

'Don't think she's one of yours, Matthew?'

'She isn't. Maybe she was just in the wrong place at the wrong time?'

'That's her story. I'm not sure I buy it.'

'Right,' Matt answered.

'What about Lissa?'

Matt shook his head, but he couldn't disguise the alarm the question caused. It was great technique. Soften him up for a few hours, keep asking the same questions and then surprise him when his defences were down.

'Bull in a china shop, but effective. You don't know where she is?'

Matt shook his head. 'We aren't close.'

'And you've no idea where Anthony is?'

'No. I've told you that.'

At which point, they turned the current on, which made his back arc upwards in an attempt to escape the pain. Afterwards, they took a break and he used the time to regroup. He was the one in the chair, the one they kept assaulting, but he had something that kept him focused; he had an edge.

When they'd broken in, they hadn't been that smart or professional; Buchan had told them what to look for because he knew Matt's security routines. Like internet passwords, agents were taught to keep changing their security checks, but, in practice, most carried on with the checks that had always kept them safe. But in the years since Force Seven, Matt had learned some new tricks.

Back in the day, Matt had been the link with a loyalist death squad that'd abducted and interrogated a Provo informant in Belfast. Force Seven suspected that he was passing tainted information and after a particularly destructive IRA attack, they ordered a stage four interrogation. The scale was from one to four, with one being a chat and four being something that often ended in the death of the suspect. The loyalists broke into the Provo's flat and waited until he came home. After ransacking the place, they tortured him for thirty hours, but he never wavered from his story. He was Force Seven's man and his information had not been tainted; he swore on his mother's life that he knew nothing of the IRA attack.

The asset was exhausted, but then so were the interrogators and they started to doubt themselves. So, when he asked to go to the loo, only one of them went with him. They heard a shot and the informer reappeared, gun in hand, the body of the dead loyalist behind him. He herded everyone into a bedroom and got them to tie each other up. Matt was the last to have his hands tied by the guy. Before the bedroom door was locked, the Provo winked at Matt and said you could never have too much insurance. The hidden weapon was his first piece of insurance; the other was the heavy oak bedroom door with a good, secure lock. The asset escaped, but when he asked his mates in the Provisionals to come and eliminate his loyalist kidnappers, they'd accused him of treachery. There'd been a spate of dawn arrests while he'd been 'incarcerated' and the Provisionals knew he'd been talking to Force Seven, so they put two and two together and made five. The Provo asset's naked body was found near the Silent Valley Reservoir; he'd been shot in the back of the head and his tongue cut out.

The lesson had not been lost on Matt. Yes, Buchan knew his old service security checks, but Matt doubted that he'd noticed the weight of the bedroom door or checked the cleaning materials in the loo. They'd searched the flat and checked the cistern for a gun; after 'The Godfather', everyone looked there. Matt had left the weapon hiding in plain sight in a plastic bag at the bottom of the airing cupboard with the bleach, cloths, cleaning fluids and loo rolls.

Timing was everything. Working army convoys at night, he'd discovered that dawn was the worst time to be driving because that was when everyone fell asleep—something to do with blood sugar, the MO had said. They'd taken his watch, but he'd had glimpses of Milo's wrist sticking out of the sling holding his left arm. The wound was bothering him because he kept grimacing and moving his elbow back and forth.

'Any chance of letting me use the loo?' Matt slurred. It was five-fifty-two. 'I need to take a shit.'

Buchan shrugged. 'I don't care.'

Milo looked at Tina and held up his arm. 'I not go.'

Tina grimaced and shook her head. 'No.'

'If I do it in here, it's not going to be nice,' Matt struggled.

'Milo!' Buchan ordered. Milo swore to himself in his own language. Matt was unshackled and Milo led him to the bathroom. Matt made for the toilet, dropped his pants and sighed with relief. Milo was preoccupied with his sore elbow and didn't see Matt launch himself from the loo and headbutt his sore arm. He screamed as Matt dived into the airing cupboard, found the gun and pointed it at Buchan and Tina.

'I kill you,' Milo hissed as he got up from the floor.

'Missed the boat, so you have. Wouldn't you agree, Buchan?'

Buchan scowled. 'You've got nowhere to go, Matthew. You're done.'

'I think you'll find I'm holding the gun,' he grinned. He herded them into his bedroom, then ordered Tina to handcuff herself to Buchan. Then he told Milo to handcuff himself to Tina. Finally, Matt handcuffed Milo and Buchan to the radiator. He removed their mobiles and watches, then checked them for concealed weapons. He found a stiletto in a sheath above Milo's ankle and tested the blade.

'Razor-sharp, so it is. Do yourself a nasty injury with that.' Milo scowled, so Matt kicked him hard on his wounded arm, causing him to scream again. 'Payback, old son.'

Buchan looked at him. 'Always did underestimate you, Matthew.'

Matt nodded. 'You used to say that was my greatest asset— that people thought I was thick.'

Buchan nodded. 'Not too late to trade?'

Matt shook his head. 'It's far, far too late.' Matt said and double-locked them in the bedroom.

He had a quick shower, changed into jogging pants and trainers and took a bag from his spare room. He had enough money for a few days and a gun, but he was on the run. What now?

34. Trailer Trash

It was just after six in the morning; Lissa was dozing on the kitchenette table when a movement brought her awake, gun in hand and pointing at Tony.

'Easy, Tiger,' he said quietly.

'Sorry,' Lissa said, putting the gun down. 'I'm a bit jumpy.'

'So I see.' Tony ambled into the space and sat on the settee seat.

'How are you feeling?' She yawned.

'Starving,' he grinned.

'That's good.'

He nodded. 'Those antibiotics seem to be working. How long have I been asleep?'

'Thirty-six hours give or take an hour.'

'No wonder I'm hungry.'

'What would you like to eat?'

'Steak and chips?'

'Not a problem apart from no steak and no chips,' she said.

'So what can you offer?'

'Pilchards on toast, beans on toast, Welsh rarebit?'

'That'd be cheese on toast?' Tony said. Lissa nodded. 'Mmm, the agony of choice. Go on then; I'll go for the cheese option.' Lissa began to busy herself with the bread. 'Are you going to tell me about it?'

'What?'

'Why you're jumpy?'

Lissa sighed. 'Well, the site owner Phil's a pervy twat and he knows you're here and that I've got a gun.'

'How does he know that?'

'Because I threatened to shoot him with it if he didn't keep his mouth shut.'

'Interesting negotiating ploy.'

'It's your fault, Tony. You got into the shithole he calls a clubhouse.' Tony shook his head in surprise. 'How the fuck did you get in? You didn't leave any trace.'

Tony shrugged. 'Didn't I?'

'You must have picked the lock.'

'I haven't done that in a while.'

'You were off your head with fever,' Lissa explained. 'He helped me get you back here, then put the bite on me.'

'So you introduced some leverage?' Tony grinned.

Lissa nodded. 'He thought the gun was a toy. I showed him it wasn't.' She pointed at the hole in the door.

'Christ,' Tony said. 'When was this?'

'Crack of dawn, day before yesterday.'

'Has he done anything since then?'

'He went out in his car yesterday morning. Came back with a bag of shopping.'

'I see.'

'He does have to shop,' Lissa said, giving Tony his cheese on toast.

'Yes,' he nodded, munching. 'Thanks; this is great.'

Lissa watched him eating for a moment. 'That's not all.'

'What?'

'Dad sent a part one security text yesterday morning.' Tony stopped chewing and looked at her. 'He didn't send part two.'

'Oh shit.'

'Yeah. Oh shit, it is.'

'So Matt's missing in action and we're stuck here with a greedy site owner who knows about me and your gun?'

Lissa nodded. 'We've got two choices.'

'Yes?'

Lissa was about to enlighten him when they heard banging from outside. Lissa stood up and sneaked a look out of the window. The banging was getting closer.

Phil was standing some twenty feet away, holding a cricket bat, accompanied by two lads in balaclava face masks. Each lad had a baseball bat and a dustbin lid, which they banged rhythmically.

'Scumbag,' Lissa muttered.

'Why's he standing over there?' Tony asked, joining her.

'Probably scared I'll shoot him,' Lissa said, watching. The drumming stopped; Phil called out.

'Come out of the van! We need to talk.'

Lissa looked at Tony. 'Get our stuff and be ready to jump on the bike.' Tony nodded as Lissa opened the van door and shouted from the doorway. 'What do you want?'

'The fee's gone up.'

'Since when?'

'I don't like being shot at.'

'Shouldn't behave like a pervy prick then, should you?'

'Do you want us to burn you out?'

'How much do you want?' Lissa asked.

Phil had a brief conversation with one of his companions. 'Five grand.'

Lissa laughed. 'Piss off. Cricket-bat, Phil? I didn't know you played.'

One of the lads spoke up. 'We want your gun.'

'You can speak. Blimey, I thought you were the walking dead.' Lissa shook her head. 'I haven't got anything like five grand.'

'We'll take what you have got then,' Phil shouted.

'You and the zombies will have to come and get it,' Lissa grinned. The lads with Phil were getting fed up with her piss-taking.

'We can take her,' one of them said. Phil shook his head.

Lissa looked around at Tony. 'Ready?' Tony nodded. Lissa gave him the gun. 'Use it if you need to.' Lissa looked back out of the van door. 'Alright, Phil, I can see we've got off on the wrong foot. I can't do five grand, but I can make three and a half. How does that sound?'

Phil stopped. Three and a half grand was still a lot more than he'd thought. He and his lads went into a huddle as they argued about what to do.

Lissa turned to Tony and shouted, 'Now!' She ran to the bike, jumped on and started it all in one movement. Tony jumped on behind her as Phil grabbed his cricket bat and the lads hefted their clubs. As Lissa accelerated away, Tony fired a shot in the air, causing Phil to duck, but one of the lads aimed a blow at them; Tony shot him in the leg, which made him squeal and fall back into one of his mates. Phil took his phone out and was about to photograph them when the caravan exploded into a sheet of flame behind him. By then, Lissa and Tony were out of the gate and on their way. Two hundred yards down the road, Lissa stopped and turned around.

'You alright?'

Tony nodded. 'Fine. You never told me?'

'What?'

'You said we had two options.'

Lissa nodded. 'We haven't got any now. What was that with the van?'

'Thought I'd create a diversion,' he smiled. 'Turned the gas hobs on and left something burning.'

Lissa grinned, pocketed the gun and revved the engine. They rode on into the winter dawn; the distant flare of the caravan burned for a long time.

35. Complications

Pauline had had a bad night; sleep was elusive and morning found her exhausted, angry and scared. Jonathan's death and Jane Percival's visit were, by turns, terrifying and fantastic. Jane Percival was real enough, as was Lavinia's card. A worrying thought occurred to her and she examined the postmark on Lizzie's letter. It was dated December 23, almost two weeks earlier. How long before that had Lavinia sent the card to Lizzie? Lavinia could have been waiting for a reply for three weeks or more. Pauline decided to go to Hexham and post the letter immediately, but as she put on her coat, she was assailed by doubts again. What if contacting Lavinia placed her in danger? She was still trying to decide when there was a knock at the front door.

She eased open the door only to have it flung back as Lissa barged in with Tony. Tony had his arm around Lissa's neck and appeared exhausted.

'Sorry about this, Pauline,' he said quietly as Lissa unloaded him onto the sofa.

'And before you ask, we've got nowhere else to go,' Lissa rasped.

Pauline shut the door. 'I'll put the kettle on,' she offered. 'Unless you want something stronger.'

'I do,' Lissa said.

'Coffee for me?' Tony whispered.

Pauline busied herself. 'Why have you got nowhere else to go?'

'We were on a caravan site,' Lissa explained. 'Had to leave in a hurry.'

'I see,' Pauline said, giving Lissa a whisky.

Lissa gulped it down. 'And that's not all. They've kidnapped my dad, haven't they?'

Pauline sighed and shook her head.

'Sorry Pauline,' Tony offered.

'For fuck's sake, stop apologising, Tony,' Lissa ordered. Tony looked at her. 'It's all you do when she's around.'

'Do I? Er Sor,' he was about to say sorry but stopped himself in time. He grinned ruefully, then frowned. 'Were you on your way out?'

'Hexham, to post a card,' she said. 'I thought it might be the police again.'

Lissa bristled. 'Why? What do they want?'

'Jonathan died yesterday. I found him,' Pauline struggled, her voice breaking with emotion. Tony put his arm around her, but she got herself under control.

'Come on, Pauline, sit down,' Lissa said gently, her anger vanishing.

'How did he die?' Tony asked.

'Heart attack. I told the police he'd been murdered, but they didn't believe me.'

'You talked to the cops?' Lissa asked.

'I called the ambulance,' Pauline replied. 'The police came with them.'

Tony was upset. 'Why, though? Why kill the vicar?'

'What is it you're not telling us, Pauline?' Lissa said quietly.

Pauline sighed. 'Does the name Buchan mean anything to you?'

Tony paled and muttered, 'Christ!'

'You know him?'

'Oh, yes.' He sat up. 'How do you know him?'

'A couple of days after I went with Mary in the air ambulance, I was arrested.'

'Why?' Tony asked.

'I don't know. I'd tried to publish the dossier on a university computer in the library, but their firewall rejected the information.'

Lissa nodded. 'It figures.'

'Leaving Mary in the hospital was awful. After everything, I felt deranged.'

'What happened?'

'A couple of days later. I went to Hexham to do some shopping. I dropped the flash drive down a drain. Then I was arrested.'

'Why?' Tony asked.

Pauline shrugged. 'I don't know. I was abducted on the street and thrown into the back of a white van. They mentioned the Prevention of Terrorism Act and took me to a disused swimming pool. They left me for a couple of days, then they interrogated me.'

'Police?' Lissa asked.

'I never saw a uniform.'

'What did they ask about?' Tony said.

'You mainly? They wanted to know where you were.'

'What else?'

'They thought I was working for someone.'

Lissa nodded. 'They would.'

'They began to fill the pool. I thought I was going to die.'

Tony stood up and put his arm around Pauline. 'What else did Buchan say?'

'He said you were evil. I said I was no Judas, he said he wasn't asking me to betray Jesus.'

Tony smiled thinly. 'He wanted Barrabas.'

'What?'

'He used to use that line with the Provos he was trying to turn back in the day. Buchan, Jesus.'

'So, who is he?' Lissa asked

'Colonel Alistair Buchan, formally of the Cold Stream Guards. He ran a hush-hush unit in Northern Ireland during the troubles. Force Seven, as it was called, was notionally intelligence gathering, but they did a lot of very dirty stuff.'

'What kind of stuff?' Lissa asked.

'Murders. Some straightforward assassinations, but usually, they'd get some loyalist paramilitary maniacs to do it.' He looked at Lissa. 'Did Matt ever mention him to you?'

Lissa snorted. 'I was a teenager with attitude. He couldn't even tell me it was a nice day without me flying off the handle. Besides, Force Seven is ancient history now.'

Tony nodded. 'It was all arm's length, deniable. Force Seven used some regular army, but they also recruited ex-cons, low-lifes and nutters.'

'You worked for Buchan?' Pauline asked.

Tony shook his head. 'Not directly. I was in an army unit directed by his lot. We'd do the observation and then he'd send in the nut-jobs to finish the action.'

'Christ,' Pauline said quietly.

'That's when I left the army.'

'But Matt didn't?' Pauline asked.

'No. He was recruited while we were in Ulster. He's Belfast born and bred, he had a girl there then.'

'My mother,' Lissa snapped.

'But now you and Matt work together?'

Tony nodded. 'In the private sector.'

'What happened to Force Seven?'

'Disbanded after the peace process; too many potential miscarriages of justice.'

'And Buchan?'

'Promoted to Colonel and transferred to another shady operation.'

'So how is he involved with this?'

Tony shook his head. 'Dunno and why was he so interested in me?' He swayed on his feet and grabbed the table edge.

'Tony?' Pauline stood up and put her arm around him. His eyes opened and he smiled lightly. Lissa came over too.

'Think I may have overdone things,' he muttered.

'You'd better lie down,' Pauline suggested. Tony nodded and Lissa helped him upstairs. She came back down a couple of minutes later.

'Take him a cup of tea in an hour, then give him some breakfast.'

'Where are you going?' Pauline asked.

'I need to lose the bike, don't I?' And with that, Lissa was gone.

Pauline pottered about the kitchen and worried about not sending her letter to Lavinia. The last thing she wanted was for Lavinia to think she didn't care. Nevertheless, staying away from her would keep her out of danger. It would just have to wait.

She'd tried to escape from the black hole, but, at least, Lissa and Tony understood. Before Jonathan's death, she had been able to persuade herself that she was just visiting their world, but now she'd been given leave to remain indefinitely. At least she wasn't alone.

She took him a cup of tea and watched him drink it.

'Thanks for this,' he said, holding the cup tightly with both hands.

'Feeling better?'

He grinned. 'Well, I'm knackered, but the sleep and the antibiotics seem to be working. Lissa downstairs?'

Pauline shook her head. ' She wanted to get rid of the bike and check a couple of things. She'll be back later. She told me to make you some breakfast.'

'Sit on the bed for a moment?' Pauline sat and he reached out and touched her face tenderly, then pulled her towards him.

'What're you doing?'

'Carrying on where we left off,' he whispered, kissing her. 'The mistletoe?' She began to say something, then they were lost.

Afterwards, they lay in each other's arms.

'You definitely are getting better,' Pauline whispered. 'You said you were knackered.'

'Not totally,' he grinned. 'I was just thinking.'

'What?'

'You're the oldest woman I've ever been to bed with,' he grinned.

She hit him playfully. 'Well, you're the oldest man I've ever had.'

He laughed. 'I thought it would feel different being older,

but it's just the same. Don't you think?' He began to kiss her again, then stopped, a strange look on his face.

'What?'

He pulled the knife from under the pillow. 'Is that a knife under your pillow, or are you just pleased to see me?'

'Oh, I that,' she blustered. 'I forgot I'd put it there.' She kissed him again and then got out of bed. 'I need a shower,' she explained. She was almost out of the door when he spoke.

'Why didn't you tell me you'd been arrested?'

She looked at the man she'd just made love to and lied through her teeth.

'I was scared. I thought they were going to drown me.' Tony's eyes became hooded; a look of regret crossed his face like a windblown cloud.

'I'm sorry.'

'Don't let Lissa hear you say that,' Pauline grinned.

Tony smiled back. 'Why are you on your own?'

'I could say the same to you,' Pauline replied. 'Besides, how do you know I haven't got someone hidden away?'

'Lissa told me,' Tony answered. 'I just wondered why.'

Pauline sat down on the bed again. 'I got out of the habit. I've had dalliances, but none of them stuck.'

'Why not?'

'The men were either dull and reliable or superficially exciting with a chaotic hinterland.'

'Which category am I in?' Tony asked.

'The second, definitely,' she grinned. Tony grabbed her hand and pulled her into his arms.

'That's what I've missed,' she whispered. Tony frowned, puzzled. 'Being held. I'd forgotten how it felt to be in someone's arms.' He squeezed her tightly and she luxuriated in the sensation.

As she showered, Pauline pondered her situation. She and Tony had made love and it had been delightful, but it was also unsettling. She wasn't sure she wanted to fall in love, but even though she told herself that it was no big deal, she knew that it was just that. Was that why she'd lied for him in the church? No; she'd helped him because he'd asked her and because his pursuers radiated a kind of threat. Yes, there was chemistry, but Tony was wrong about it being the same as when they were young. Age brings baggage—the vast hidden history we all carry inside against which we weigh every new experience. The past is a country of secrets and some of them we want to bury in a lead-lined box deep under the Antarctic ice cap. Pauline hadn't told him everything because she refused to jeopardise Lavinia and the girls. Romance would have to take its chances.

36. Lambeth Walk

Matt had been in the shadows for the best part of his adult life; still being around after thirty-five years was no accident; he'd planned for it. The ones who survived always had a secret escape plan that they never, ever told anyone about. Most agents had an official fallback position and that was good, but what Matt had learned was that you needed some private insurance on top of the company policy because one day your number would definitely come up. What was the phrase that Buchan used back in the day - 'a cost of doing business.'

His first thought was to throw the mobiles he'd taken from Buchan and the other two into the river, but then thought better of it. If he did that, the mobiles would all disappear from the system at the same time and trigger an alert. He was wondering what to do when a dustbin truck lumbered up the street, the lads emptying the bins with practised efficiency. Matt placed the phones in one of the bins still to be collected. With luck, if anyone were tracking them, they would see the three phones were travelling together. At the very least, it should give him more time before the batteries ran out and time was something he desperately needed.

Like the hidden gun and the heavy bedroom door, the tiny one-bedroom ex-council flat in a tower block off Salmon Lane was known only to Matt. Registered under a fake identity, nobody, not even Tony or Lissa, knew about it. It was rented because he hadn't wanted to provide detailed proof of identity. He'd had the place for twenty years, ever since he started working at Wharefedale Systems. He'd never lived there; the bills were paid out of an account he'd set up for an operation that had never happened. He had clothes, food, money and a weapon stashed. He visited twice a year, once just before Christmas when London was mega-busy with shoppers and once in mid-summer when there were loads of tourists. He avoided CCTV, which meant not using tube, bus, or cab and was content to take the three hours to walk the ten miles downriver. That way, he had time to spot if anyone was following.

It was a one-time-only solution, but having been beaten and grilled for twenty-four hours, this was the time. It was still dark; an east wind blew icy gusts into his face, slowing his progress. His bag was light, but it was still awkward to carry. His knee was acting up after his New Year manoeuvres and, after going without sleep and being interrogated, he was limping badly. It was just after seven, another hour until sunrise, but the elation of his escape was gradually supplanted by exhaustion and the fear that he might not make it. Hilary was dead; Tony was still in the frame and although publishing the dossier had stirred up some dust, they didn't know anymore and now he was a fugitive. He'd run out of ideas, so he fell back on agent procedure and hoped to God something broke.

It took him an hour and forty minutes to get to Westminster Bridge. He stopped and checked again for signs of a tail, but found none. He took a phone from his bag, inserted a SIM card and texted, 'Let not light see my black, dark desires.' After checking that the message had gone, he switched off the phone, extracted the SIM card, and threw it in the river.

37. The Cottage

Tony was resting on the couch when Lissa burst in the back door, slamming it behind her. She was out of breath from running and collapsed over the table, heaving.

'What's happened?' Pauline asked.

Lissa shook her head and gestured for them to go outside. It was bitterly cold again and they stood shivering in the lee of the outhouse.

'I've heard from Matt,' Lissa said.

'What did he say?' Tony asked.

Lissa shook her head. 'He texted me, didn't he?'

'And?' Tony asked.

'It was the second part of the security check, but he left out a word.' Tony pursed his lips.

'What does it mean?' Pauline asked.

'He's burned,' Tony muttered. Pauline frowned, not following.

'The second part of the security check means everything's fine,' Lissa explained.

'But he left out a word?'

Lissa nodded. 'The text was supposed to say, 'Let not light see my black and dark desires', but he left out 'and'.'

'Macbeth,' Pauline smiled in recognition.

'It's not funny, Pauline!' Lissa shouted. 'He's on his own.'

'Easy, tiger,' Tony said gently to Lissa before turning to Pauline. 'Omitting a word is an SOS. He needs immediate help.'

'Is he alright?' Pauline asked.

Lissa shrugged angrily. 'Christ knows what state he's in. He was over twenty-four hours late sending.'

'He must have escaped and now he's in the wind,' Tony surmised.

Lissa nodded. 'Yeah.'

'So what's the plan?' Pauline asked.

Lissa scowled and looked at Pauline. 'Was it you?'

'Was what me?' Pauline asked.

'You knew he was going south. You could have told them, couldn't you? Is that what you did?' Lissa put her face close to Pauline's. Pauline took a step back; Lissa followed.

'You did, didn't you? You shopped him!'

The memory of Jonathan lying gasping on the floor of St. Leonard's seemed to fill Pauline's mind; something snapped. She hit Lissa across the side of her face with such force that it knocked her to the ground.

'Don't you dare!' Pauline was shaking with rage.

Lissa felt her face and got to her feet. This time, the gun was in her hand.

'For god's sake, put that away, Lissa,' Tony barked, but Lissa only had eyes for Pauline.

'Dad reckoned you were a pro.'

'They killed Jonathan yesterday, or have you forgotten?' Pauline spat.

'Put the gun down, Lissa,' Tony said evenly, but Lissa was still focused on Pauline.

'Good cover again; that's what Dad would say.'

Pauline went to hit Lissa again. Tony caught hold of her wrist and stood between her and Lissa. 'Cool it, both of you.'

'Tony, can I have a bleeding word in private?' Lissa demanded.

'Give me the gun,' Tony held his hand out expectantly. Lissa shook her head.

Tony let go of Pauline's wrist and shouted, 'Give me the gun!' The volume surprised Lissa for an instant, but it was long enough for Tony to snatch the weapon from her.

'Bastard,' she hissed, but she didn't try and get it back.

Tony leaned into her. 'Lissa, if they're onto us, it's not because Pauline or anyone else is talking to them; it's because Buchan's involved and has been for a long time. Buchan knows Matt and me from the old days. He knows how we work; he'll know Matt's security habits.'

Lissa shook her head, but she wouldn't meet his gaze.

'Come on, Lissa! It has to be Buchan.'

Lissa nodded moodily and shrugged. Tony checked the magazine in the automatic and looked up.

'There's only one round left.'

Lissa nodded. 'That's why I need more ammo, don't I?' Then she had a thought. 'Shit. What time is it?'

'Ten to ten,' Pauline said, looking at her watch.

'What's that in new money?' Pauline didn't understand. Tony answered. 'Nine-fifty.'

Lissa inserted a SIM card into her mobile and turned it on.

'Protocol says to check every hour at a specific time,' Tony explained to Pauline.

Lissa looked at the phone screen. 'Fifty-two, that was the time he texted before. Here's hoping he texts again.'

At nine fifty-two, a single bell toll signalled the arrival of a text. Lissa read it, then switched off the phone and removed the SIM.

'Well?' Tony asked. 'Is he alright?'

Lissa nodded. 'For now. He's in a flat in Limehouse; he wants me to go and get him.'

'How?' Tony asked.

'Bike.'

'I thought you'd got rid of it?' Tony frowned.

'Too good for that. I hid it in some woods about a mile away.'

Tony shook his head. 'I thought the same about my Merc, but it was a mistake.'

Lissa shook her head. 'No alternative. I've got another set of plates.' She paused and looked at Pauline. 'Sorry about before. I was worried about Dad.' Pauline nodded without softening. Lissa became exasperated. 'This is where you're supposed to say sorry for hitting me.'

'I'm not,' Pauline said.

Lissa felt her cheek. 'It was a great blow. You sure you're not a pro?' Pauline remained poker-faced.

'What about the campsite?' Tony asked. 'What if Phil calls the cops?'

'He won't,' Lissa insisted. 'If the insurance company finds out he's been renting out of season, it'll invalidate any claim he makes. Besides, the bike is brilliant in traffic and with a helmet on, nobody's going to see Dad.'

Tony nodded. 'What about us?'

'Oh yeah; he wants you to go and brace Evans in Bedford.'

'Bobby Evans? I didn't know he was still in touch with him,' Tony muttered.

'Evans took Dad's place at the hospital appointment, the one he set up for his alibi. Dad thinks someone must have got to Evans,' Lissa explained. 'I'll collect Dad and meet you there.' Lissa wrote down an address.

'How am I supposed to get there?' Tony asked. 'I'm on the run. You want me to steal a car, here?'

Lissa swore. 'For Pete's sake, Pauline can drive you.'

'You've changed your tune. A minute ago, you were going to shoot me,' Pauline snapped.

'I've said I'm sorry, haven't I?'

'We can't use Pauline's car,' Tony said. 'They could be tracking it?'

Lissa nodded. 'Alright, hire a fucking car in fucking Hexham, then drive to fucking Bedford. Is that clear enough?'

'Crystal,' Pauline replied. Lissa grinned.

Tony nodded. 'What time do you want to meet up?'

Lissa shrugged. 'Five hours to get to Matt's place, another two to get back to Bedford. I wouldn't mind stopping off for some more ammo and a bigger gun. A bit of leeway, say between six and seven tonight?'

Tony nodded. 'What can possibly go wrong?'

38. Eagle House

By the time Matt reached Salmon Lane, it was almost ten-fifteen and the rush hour was subsiding. He had made good time, hobbling through the peak of the morning commute. For the umpteenth time, Matt did his security ballet. Dropping to one knee, he retied a shoelace, then stopped to look in a shop window, all the while checking vehicle number plates to see if he recognised any. He had texted Lissa twice and received a reply, which meant there was a good chance she would come and collect him. When he'd been interrogated, it had crossed his mind that he might not make it. After all, he was getting on, who knew what state his insides were in? There was a chance that something might break and he would be gone. Lissa was his regret. She was all he had; there was so much of Julie in her—the fiery temper, the sense of humour, the fearlessness. Whatever happened, this was his last job. If he survived, he would get a place in a village in North Yorkshire or Somerset, perhaps, and spend his days doing bits of DIY and gardening. But that only made sense if Lissa was able to come and visit.

When he was near enough to Eagle House, he waited for a Docklands Light Railway train to rattle past to hurry up an alleyway and make the rear entrance. His flat was on the thirteenth floor and, despite his exhaustion, he followed protocol, avoiding the lift and climbing the stairs. In common with other tenants in the tower block, he had installed a wrought iron gate in front of his front door as extra security. The padlock was intact, as was the lock on the front door. Nonetheless, he entered cautiously, fearful of being surprised again, but he needn't have worried. Apart from a patina of dust, the flat was untouched. The living room had a small balcony with a brilliant view of the river and Canary Wharf to the south-west. Matt checked the flat, then locked the padlock and double-locked the reinforced front door. There was just one way in and nobody was getting in without Matt knowing. But if he was cornered, there was no way out, apart from jumping.

Matt checked his supplies in the kitchen. He emptied a tin of mixed beans into a bowl and put it in the microwave with some instant rice. He had plenty of tins plus rice and pasta, so he could survive undetected for several days, if not weeks, if he needed to. The trouble was, he didn't have several days. He was knackered, he needed a plan. At least he'd managed to send the two messages. If all went well, Lissa would arrive to collect him. In the meantime, he needed food and sleep. The microwave pinged. Matt mixed the beans and the rice and ate quickly. Throwing off his shoes, he lay down and tried to sleep. He smiled at the thought of Buchan and the other two struggling with the radiator in his bedroom.

Back in the day, when Matt and the others had been handcuffed to the radiator in the Provo's flat, he'd been scared. The Provo had told them he was going to come back with his pals and do to them what they had done to him with a few extras. Knowing they were under sentence of death added urgency to their efforts. It had taken a while for them to work together, but finally, they attacked the radiator and managed to dislodge it from the floor. With water spurting everywhere, they used it to break the window and attract attention. Force Seven alerted the loyalist gang's mates, who sent a squad. Of course, when the Provo's mutilated body was found, they realised they shouldn't have worried, but the feeling of terror had stayed with Matt. It wasn't something you forgot.

Matt thought Buchan and his friends would still be attached because he had chosen a bulky, industrial cast-iron radiator and anchored it securely to the reinforced concrete under the wooden floor. He didn't think they'd be going anywhere soon but alarms would trigger when their mobiles weren't answered and they didn't show. If he could brace Evans before they got to him, he might be able to do something. He fell asleep before he could decide what that might be.

39. Road Trip

Three hours later, Pauline and Tony were in a shiny Fiesta hire car driving south on the A1. They carried on past Scotch Corner and Wetherby, south towards the M18. They didn't say much; both were lost in thought. Tony was wondering what the endgame was going to be; he didn't have a good feeling about it. Driving a strange car in mist and drizzle on a gloomy January day was some way from Pauline's idea of a good time. Then she recalled the image of Jonathan gasping his last on the ancient slabs of St. Leonard's.

'Is it worth it?' She snapped.

He looked at her. 'What?'

'The risks, the deaths, chasing about like this?'

'It wasn't supposed to be like this,' he murmured. Pauline snorted with derision. 'Look, there are some bad people who want to do bad things. I think it's important to stop them.'

'What kind of bad things?' Pauline asked. 'So they can sell a deadly toxin for a king's ransom, but, in the end, does it matter? History's full of self-obsessed despots and their flunkeys who'll do anything to stay on top.'

'It's about justice,' Tony replied. 'We have to try and stop the forces of darkness from taking over, even if it is difficult and dangerous.'

'You can't tell where the light ends and the darkness begins.'

'We have to try.'

'But why should I care if the Argentina gang plans to poison a high-value target?' Pauline asked.

Tony looked at her. 'Because they're ruthless and will kill anyone who gets in their way? Because they killed Jonathan?'

Pauline drove for a while without speaking.

'Lissa said something about a molecular trigger?' Pauline said.

Tony nodded. 'That's right, but we don't know how it works. One of Matt's pet boffins reckoned they could be using an MRNA viral fragment.'

'So, what happens? You get infected?' Pauline asked.

Tony shrugged. 'Probably.'

'What did they do to you?'

'I was stripped, placed in a paper suit, clamped to a gurney and anaesthetised.'

'I'm no wiser.'

'Before I passed out, I got a look at the room. It was all high-tech, with a fancy air filtration system. Up above, almost out of sight, was this glass inspection chamber with gauntlets attached to access the inside.'

'To what end?' Pauline asked.

'Inside the chamber was a cage with wires and tubes all over the place.'

'And?'

'The cage was about the same size as one we had for a parrot when I was a kid.'

'You think they did something to the birds?'

Tony nodded. 'Yes, the peregrines and other rare falcons; they're all protected by law. That's why they've got all that security. We used to think that they smuggled something in the transport cages because they were fast-tracked through customs. But I don't think that's it.'

Pauline looked at him. 'What are you getting at?'

'What if the birds themselves are the transmission mechanism?'

'How?'

'Suppose the viral fragment is injected into the bloodstream of a bird and then extracted at the other end?'

'Then what?' Pauline asked.

'They inject the fragment into the human emissary.'

'Who then approaches the target?'

Tony nodded. 'It would explain why they were so paranoid.'

212

Pauline thought for a moment. 'If that's what they do, how did they kill Charlton and Jonathan?'

Tony shrugged. 'They must be able to inject something more general, or at least get the victim to ingest it somehow.'

Pauline nodded. 'I suppose so.'

'I still don't get why they let me go,' Tony muttered. 'They don't know what insurance I've set up in the event of my disappearance. If they've got something big planned, they wouldn't want anything to stir things up and encourage the press to examine the dossier that you managed to post.'

Pauline changed the subject. 'What happens to the birds?'

Tony shrugged. 'Don't know.'

'I mean, they've got this viral fragment in their blood?'

'I've never really thought about it.'

'Does the fragment decay, mutate, or what?'

Tony pursed his lips and shook his head. 'Beats me.'

They drove on down the A1 for a few miles. The mist obscured the horizon; the muted winter landscape appeared brown, sodden, and forlorn. Shredded plastic bag fragments, weathered into a dingy colourless grey, caught on tree branches and fences and flapped in the wind. Below, the verges were covered in discarded cans and plastic cups. Tony kept looking at his watch, which irritated Pauline.

'Any chance of going a bit faster?'

She ignored him, but when they passed a signpost to Nottingham, her frustration over Lavinia boiled over. She banged the steering wheel and began to shout.

'I never wanted to be involved! I've been arrested and threatened, a friend of mine has been killed. All because I stupidly took pity on you in a church.' She paused as if the tirade had exhausted her, but it hadn't. 'And now, I'm driving you to a meeting with someone I've never met because you and Lissa and Matt have run out of ideas?'

After the tirade, all that could be heard in the car was the swish of the tyres and the deep hum of the engine. After a moment, Tony nodded in agreement.

'That's about the size of it, yes, Pauline.'

A large SUV cut into their lane without signalling. The driver was shaven-headed and overweight. Pauline was forced to swerve and brake sharply. She honked the horn violently and yelled.

'Fuck off, you fucking fat fuck!'

There was silence for a moment until Tony tried unsuccessfully to stifle a giggle. Pauline saw the funny side and, after a moment, they were roaring with laughter.

'Is that how you talked to your students?' Tony smirked and they started laughing again.

'You never told me your story,' Pauline asked after they'd stopped laughing. 'Kate?'

Tony shifted in his seat and sighed. 'I messed up. We were together for ten years, we were going to be married, kids, the whole thing.'

'What happened?'

'I was working as a freelance journalist, getting bits of work, but it was hand-to-mouth.' He paused, remembering. 'Matt head-hunted me.'

'Doing what?'

'Security Analyst at Wharfedale Systems, which, according to him, was just journalism but with decent money.'

'And?'

'It was a spook job. I spent my time trawling through archives, looking for specific stories, but it was secret.'

'Kate didn't like it?'

Tony nodded. 'No. She had no time for the cloak and dagger stuff, I would disappear without warning, the fact it was dangerous. But, most of all, she hated the secrets.'

'Mmm,' Pauline nodded.

'It was like an affair—something I kept secret from her and always returned to.'

Pauline peered at the road ahead; the rain was getting heavier. It was after four p.m. and the gloomy half-light had morphed into a winter night. It was Friday, the first of the New Year, everybody was bad-tempered and in a hurry. Nobody wanted to be on the road and it was everybody else's fault.

'So?'

'We split up for a while but stayed in touch. Then we tried again, got back together; it worked OK, but I still had the job. She walked out.'

'Really?'

'I came back from an operation and she'd gone. She told me not to try and find her.'

'Did you look for her?'

He shook his head. 'I heard later that she was in Scotland.'

'You weren't tempted to go and see her?'

'Yes.' He looked away, his eyes distant with memory. 'After a couple of years, I got a letter. She'd met someone, they were engaged. She's got two kids now.'

Pauline considered telling him about Lavinia but decided against it. The letter was safe in her pocket; whatever happened, she would post it tomorrow.

40. Argentina Farm

Snow fell silently onto the foothills of the Cheviots, coating the frosted tussocks of tough, moorland 'spart' grass with icing-sugar filigree while the ancient rocks and soil turned to white iron. In the abandoned compound of the stone farmhouse, there was movement. Two of the ridgebacks prowled back and forth in front of a wire mesh, occasionally hurling themselves at it, growling and snarling. Forgotten, they had been left and they were ravenous. Steam rose from their sweating flanks, their barks created small clouds of vapour. Along with several alsatians, they had been let out to chase down an intruder on the night of the explosions, but these two had returned late and found the compound deserted. Because of the haste with which the farm had been shut down, several items had been left. In the aviary, a peregrine was still attached to a perch by a leash. In the snowy darkness, it had flown up to the roof of the flying area and been missed. Now it too was hungry and bad-tempered. Outside the mesh of the aviary, the ridgebacks ran back and forth, eyeing the bird and licking their lips, but no matter how much they tried, they could not get in.

Below ground, it was the same story. Access to the lift had been blocked, but the damage was superficial and the shaft had been left intact. They had left Brian in charge of the shut-down, but he'd been unwilling to destroy the high-tech equipment that had functioned so brilliantly. He had been retained when the facility had been sold to the hedge fund, but, despite his expertise and loyalty, he had been left behind like the dogs and the peregrine. They'd sent an email stating that his contract had been terminated immediately. There was a list of tasks to complete and a bonus for that work, but that was it. Tina might not have noticed him, but facilities like Argentina didn't run themselves. They'd thought that everything ran smoothly and it did, but that was because he anticipated problems and fixed them before they happened. It was their loss and when the 'fuss' died down, he planned to pose as an anonymous buyer and re-open the place as an independent bio-research facility with him in charge. After six months, who would care? He'd sent an anonymous tip-off to the authorities, Argentina Farm and Tina's goose would be cooked. The rest of the site had been emptied. Plans, equipment, results, computers; all were removed and sent to new locations. The place had been electronically stripped but Brian hadn't destroyed the clean rooms as ordered and much of the equipment remained, together with a few samples.

His headlights lit up the road as he drove towards the compound. He was engaged in something illicit and it excited him. They'd thought of him as unthinking and obedient, someone who didn't ask questions, but he noticed things and made deductions. The owners had tried to keep him in the dark, but Brian knew where the light switch was. Despite promising himself that he wouldn't come back for several months, here he was driving back to examine his treasure and make sure it was still intact. No one would know. He needed to check a few things if he was to make plans.

41. Eagle House

Matt came to with a jerk. For a moment, he had no idea where he was and began to hyperventilate. Then he remembered. He was in the lifeboat, the ex-council flat that he had walked to after getting away from Buchan. He flexed his arms and legs to see how they were. He was sore, his back hurt like hell but he appeared to be in one piece. It was dark. He checked his watch and found that it was after four. He rolled out of bed and tried standing, but his right knee clicked and almost gave way. He leaned against the wall and took the weight off it. He wasn't going to be running anywhere anytime soon. He found his phone, fitted a new SIM and waited for it to register. Then he sent a five-word text: 'Dinner is on the table.' He sat down and waited for an answer. Half an hour later, Lissa called.

'Where are you?' he asked.

'On my way,' she answered, breathing heavily. The sound was muffled but behind her breathing, he could hear traffic noise.

'You on your bike?' Matt asked

'Yes, you should have been a detective.'

'In London yet?'

'An hour.'

'Make for Limehouse. I'll text something.'

'You OK, Dad?'

Matt frowned. She was breaking protocol. 'Fine.'

He switched the phone off and wondered about his next move. He decided on a shower and a bowl of porridge and honey, which he followed with strong black coffee. The thing he kept asking himself was, how they knew? Obviously, they knew about his flat, where they'd ambushed him, but how did they know about the rest? Ever since Bobby Evans revealed he had a dodgy heart, Matt had been queasy. He wondered if he was any further forward than he had been before his interrogation in Wandsworth. Well, Hilary's suspicions that the outsourcing of the NSDD was a very high-level treachery had been correct. And he knew that Buchan was involved, but he still didn't know about the poison or the target. They must have missed something, but what? Maybe seeing Bobby Evans would jog something; otherwise, they were all in deep shit.

At four forty-seven, he texted Lissa's mobile with a map reference. It was a code that she knew and anyone listening wouldn't. It was easy to break, but not quickly. Twenty minutes after that, the entry phone chimed. Matt looked at the screen and glimpsed a slight character wearing a crash helmet and leathers. He buzzed the entrance door, unlocked his front door and the wrought iron drawbridge and waited by the lift. When she appeared, he directed her into the flat. After a look down the stairwell, he went back into the flat, locking the iron gate and the door behind him. He went to the balcony and looked down to the base of the building, craning his neck.

'See anyone?' He asked, scanning below. Lissa shook her head. 'Sure?'

'Course I'm sure,' she said as she removed her helmet and ruffled her hair which was damp with sweat. 'Got anything to eat?'

'Porridge?'

'Jesus.'

'I haven't had time to go to Harrods. There's honey with it.'

'Go on then, porridge and honey it is.' Matt poured some into a bowl. As she ate, he told her what had happened.

'How bad was it?'

'Bad enough.'

Lissa considered this. Although she cared about Matt, she hated showing affection to his face.

'Buchan mentioned you, Lissa.'

'How?'

219

'He said you were like a bull in a china shop.'

'Twat. Did he say anything about you being my dad?'

'No.'

Lissa shrugged. 'They killed Jonathan.'

Matt frowned. 'Who?'

'The vicar in Bridgford, Pauline's mate. Heart attack. She found him in the church. She told the local plods that he'd been murdered with an untraceable poison.'

'Did they believe her?'

'No.'

Matt took a walk around the living room, then turned back. 'That's nasty. How is she?'

'Pissed off,' Lissa replied, but he heard the doubt in her voice.

'What?'

Lissa shook her head. 'I don't know. I think she's hiding something.'

'When did it happen?'

'Yesterday morning.'

Matt nodded. 'How's Tony?'

'Pissed off too.'

Matt nodded. 'He's had a rough time.'

'Haven't we all? So what's the plan?'

Matt shrugged. 'What I said. Pay Bobby Evans a visit.'

Lissa nodded. 'Right. Tony's meeting us there; Pauline's driving him.'

Matt frowned, straightened his back and groaned.

Lissa looked critically. 'You going to be able to manage?'

'I'm getting too old for all this malarky.'

'Mmm. I never thought I'd be looking after three geriatrics.'

Matt regarded her and sighed. He knew that his daughter cared about him, but the anger over her mother's death and his absenteeism were never far away. He attempted levity, which he immediately regretted. 'I didn't know you cared.'

Lissa faced him. 'I don't want to have to worry about you if it kicks off.'

Matt looked at his watch. 'We need to get going.'

'Got any warm clothes?' A questioning look appeared on

Matt's face. 'It's cold on the bike at this time of year.'
'Oh yeah. I'll have a look and see what I can find.'

Fifteen minutes later, Lissa led Matt to her motorbike. She gave him a helmet and then headed north onto Mile End Road.

42. Bedford

Situated some forty miles north of London, Bedford is an ancient market town and for those who look, the mediaeval street plan is still discernible. John Bunyan began writing 'The Pilgrim's Progress', while imprisoned in Bedford Gaol; three hundred years later, the A6 murderer, James Hanratty, was hanged there. For those who lift their eyes from the new shops in Bedford's centre, the glass and steel extensions of the modern gaol rise above the surrounding roofs, allowing the inmates a glimpse of the modern town.

In mid-summer, the Victorian embankment of the River Great Ouse, with its wide, grassy verges, stunning flower beds and magnificent horse chestnuts engenders tranquility. People of all kinds are drawn to meander and muse as they stroll between the bridges. In mid-winter, when freezing winds blow in from the fens and the North Sea, the only people to brave the river are rowers, runners, dog walkers and druggies.

Freezing drizzle was spotting the Fiesta windscreen as Pauline and Tony drove into the city. Festive decorations hung careworn and listless as if they, like everyone, had had enough of partying. It was the back end of Christmas, January yawned like a crevasse. A lot of people were drinking.

Bobby Evans' pad was a two-bedroom bungalow in Goldington, an ex-council estate on the east of the town. From five o'clock onwards, Fridays were spent in his local, 'The British Flag'. 'Every Premiership Game here' was scrawled on an A-frame blackboard on the pavement underneath the Union Jack pub sign. Inside, it was noisy, crowded; television screens on mute showed the endless replays of goals against the backdrop of a tinny jukebox. The clientele was mostly male, mostly white, mostly middle-aged, mostly cockney and mostly legless. It was the end of the week—time for letting go, time for a laugh, for forgetting all the shit—and when Tony and Pauline pushed into the bar, it sounded as if everyone was yelling at the same time.

After the spat, the journey to Bedford had been relatively straightforward; they made the outskirts just after six. Pauline hated being at the mercy of events she had no control over but she didn't have much choice. She was still pissed off about not seeing Lavinia but keeping her secret was the right decision. She had decided to go along with Tony until the situation was resolved, one way or another.

Tony was apprehensive. Since his meeting with Matt at Porlock Lodge, everything that could go wrong had done. Meeting Evans was the kind of 'hit and hope' longshot that he hated because they never worked out. The argument with Pauline hadn't helped. He understood her anger all too well; she was dead right. If she hadn't helped him in St. Leonard's, she wouldn't be in this mess and her friend, Jonathan, wouldn't be lying on a mortuary gurney in Hexham but there was no way to rewind events. And there was something else: there was chemistry between them. Any other time, they could have behaved like ordinary people, going to restaurants and having drinks but events had shot that possibility in the back.

In a quiet street of rectangular, sixties bungalows and small gardens, Evans' house was a low, ugly blockhouse shrouded in darkness.

'That must be it,' Tony said as they nosed down the street.

'Doesn't look like he's in,' Pauline said, peering through the rain.

Tony nodded. 'He'll be in the pub. Just wanted to check it out first.'

Pauline looked at him with a questioning frown. 'Why?'

'Old habits,' Tony replied. 'Back in the day, you always scoped the fallback position before you faced a target. If he does a runner, this is where he'll come.'

223

'You think he will run?'

'He might.'

'When was the last time you saw him?'

'Not since the army.'

'What if you don't recognise him?'

Tony grinned. 'Better hope I do, then. Come on; let's go and find the pub.'

The plan was painfully simple. Find Evans, front him up and hope that something shook loose.

Tony spotted him at the bar. He was in a group of four and laughing at a joke. His face had puckered with age, but Tony knew him. Bobby Evans, the moaner with anal warts, had not worn well. Short and stocky, he had acquired a substantial beergut; his nose was a battlefield of burst capillaries and his fingers and grey hair were stained a tawny orange by nicotine. His fashion choices were in keeping with the rest of the pub: grey tracksuit bottoms, trainers, a hoodie, which, in his case, had once been blue. Unlike his skin, which was flaccid and tired, his eyes were alert, darting back and forth like a feeding bird as he scoped the room. Was he expecting them? Was he uneasy because he'd been 'got at' or was this him? Tony thought he knew. Even now, after thirty years, the security habits learned in Belfast were hard to shake. You never talked about politics in public; you always ordered a cab from the end of the street and you never took anyone home. Every door was reinforced and even though you didn't do it, you still had the urge to check under your car. Evans saw Tony and immediately looked away but Tony caught the flash of recognition and the glance at Pauline before the emotion shut down.

'A few Brexit slogans,' Pauline said, looking around. On the wall, there were UKIP posters and a signed photo of a smiling Nigel Farage. 'Want me to go to the bar?'

Tony nodded. 'Get me a pint of IPA, please.'

Pauline eased through the men at the bar. They gave her the once-over, but no one made any 'remarks'. She supposed it was because age had transported her into grey invisibility.

'Can I squeeze in?' She asked a builder, whose overalls were covered in plaster dust.

'Yeah, darlin',' he grinned. 'With a pound of margarine, you can go anywhere.' He winked and she laughed as she caught the meaning. She brought the drinks and they found a corner to observe the bar.

'Has he seen you?' She asked. Tony nodded and sipped his pint. 'So, what now?'

'We wait.'

Forty minutes later, Evans came across and gestured to go outside. They followed him out into the rain and the dark. Tony tensed, wondering what was happening, but Evans produced an e-cigarette from his pocket and began puffing away. He led them to a plastic bus shelter in the car park at the back.

'Bugger me, Tony. Didn't expect to see you in the Flag.'

Tony had forgotten Evans' cockney accent, which had become more exaggerated with age. Tony nodded but didn't speak. Evans shook his head.

'Well, you haven't changed, have you? Still the quiet, thoughtful bleeder you always were.'

'Nice of you to say so,' Tony replied.

Evans looked at Pauline. 'This your lady? Aren't you going to introduce me?'

'I'm Pauline,' Pauline said, holding out her hand.

Evans shook it and grinned. 'Classy. I heard you'd given up the fairer sex, Tony.'

Tony shrugged. 'Is there somewhere we can talk, Bobby?'

'What's wrong with here?' Evans said, blowing smoke into Tony's face and making him cough violently.

'Matt's worried,' he replied, coughing violently.

'What? You've heard from him?' Evans' eyes widened for a second before he recovered himself. Tony missed it because of his coughing fit.

'As I said, he's concerned,' Tony said, getting his breath.

'Don't I bleeding know it?' Evans swore. 'Look, I went to the hospital, I did the business. How was I to know I had a dicky heart? Last time I had a check-up, I was fine.'

'When was that?' Pauline asked.

'Dunno, six months ago; eight months tops.' Evans puffed his e-cigarette repeatedly.

Tony sipped his pint. 'Look, Bobby, why don't we go back to your gaff and chat?'

'I had to change my name, you know? I'm Bobby Stevens now.'

'Stevens?'

Evans nodded. 'Change as little as possible, easier all round.'

'You chose here?'

Evans nodded and looked around furtively. 'Know what's special about Bedford?

Tony shrugged. 'No.'

'Fuck all. It's anonymous. I feel safe here.' Evans looked around, then continued. 'I wanted somewhere...' he paused, searching for the right word, 'somewhere uncontroversial to start over. I landed here. Yeah, I'm drinking too much with a few tossers but they're my mates now and I don't think I'll get slotted in the Flag.'

'You think you might at home?' Tony asked.

Evans' energetic puffing was starting to mist up the smoking shelter in the cold night air. He leaned into Tony. 'Anyone from the Emerald bleeding Isle comes in here; well, they wouldn't last long. So, I don't have to worry and I can get drunk. Then, if they do me, I'll die happy.'

'Are you worried?' Tony asked quietly.

'I know the score, don't I? I must have been pissed when Matt asked me, because just a moment's consideration would have told me it was dangerous. And now, I've put my head above the bleeding parapet, haven't I? I'm back in the crosshairs.'

Tony was about to ask a question when the side door of the pub opened and a bald head above a thick, tattooed neck appeared.

'Alright, Bobby?' The words were unthreatening, but the tone and the stance were hostile. The pub was his territory, Evans was his mate, strangers weren't welcome.

'No worries, Frankie,' Evans replied with a grin. 'Just having a chinwag with some old mates. Back in a mo.'

'You'll be wanting another then?' Frankie said deadpan.

'Too right!' Evans shouted, Frankie grinned. A roar of laughter erupted from inside the pub. Frankie nodded and ducked back into the bar.

Evans scratched his backside vigorously and turned back to Tony and Pauline. 'Can't stay long.'

'Still giving you gip?' Tony frowned, nodding down at Evans' behind.

'Don't mention the bleeding war. Never been right since the army. Tried everything, but nothing gets rid of the boomerangs.'

'Boomerangs?' Tony asked.

Evans grinned and nodded. 'Because they always come fucking back.'

Pauline frowned, wondering what he was on about. Tony smiled sympathetically. 'Anyone been in touch?'

Evans peered up at the plastic rain hood as if deciding whether to come clean. He sighed and gave in. 'Yeah. Billy Zed turned up just before New Year, out of the blue.'

'Billy Zed?' Tony frowned.

'SAS Billy?'

Tony was momentarily confused, then he got it. 'From the OP?' Evans nodded.

'Why would he come and see you?'

Evans shrugged. 'I knew him back in the day, we've kept in touch.'

'What did he want?'

'Nothing. Said he was in the area on business. We had a meal and a few drinks. Talked about the old days, you know?'

'Not really.'

'Remember the OP explosion? Six legs and five livers?' Tony remembered. That's what started him off in the first place at Wharfedale Systems. 'Well, Billy reckoned that Force Seven had this idea of infecting the Provos with hepatitis.'

'How did Billy know Force Seven?'

'He worked for them at the same time as me. His SAS

squadron were Colonel Buchan's personal bum chums. Did his dirty work.'

'I didn't know you worked for Force Seven?'

Evans nodded. 'After the army, Matt recruited me. A red operation went belly-up. I had to get out quickly. Matt helped with my severance.'

'I see,' Tony answered, but he didn't see at all.

'Would have had to give it up anyway, because of the boomerangs. That's how I got so out of shape,' he patted his gut. 'Can't train when your arse is on fire.'

Tony nodded. 'If Buchan wanted to infect the Provos with hepatitis, how come it was the Provos who were looking after the livers?'

Evans sneered. 'That's Buchan for you; slipperier than a lorryload of cum. He fed the Provos a line about wanting to get rid of the UFF and the Red Hand Commandos so the British Government and the Provos could do business without interference and the Provos only went and bought it.'

There it was: the mystery that had begun Tony's descent into darkness explained in a throw-away line. Tony looked to the side and then back at Evans.

'Billy Zed? Did he say anything else?'

Evans shook his head, then stopped. 'Yes, he did. He told me to avoid grapefruit juice.'

'What?'

'I swear to God, that's what he said,' Evans whispered. 'Look, I'm going back in. And don't come round my house, right?'

Tony nodded. 'Billy Zed? Is that his name?'

Evans shook his head. 'It's Zuchowski. His mates call him Billy Zed.' The rain was hammering down on the plastic roof now. Evans got ready to run.

'I'd like to say it's been nice meeting you and your squeeze, but let's face it, it's been utter shit,' Evans coughed and ran across the car-park and back into the pub.

Pauline looked at Tony. 'Did he just call me your 'squeeze'?'

Tony sighed. 'Yeah.'

'Nice friends you have.'

'He's not a friend; he's someone I spent time with a long time ago.'

Back in the car, they sat staring at the windscreen as the rain puddled, obscuring the view.

'Well?' Pauline asked. 'Did you learn anything important?'

'Don't know.'

'We've come all this way for nothing?'

'Maybe, maybe not.'

'Nobody knows anything.' Tony looked at her, frowning. 'That's what you said in that cafe.' Pauline snapped.

'What're you driving at?'

'You, Matt, Lissa, Buchan; you're all just banging about in the dark hoping to find a way through.'

'It's not as bad as bad as that,' Tony said quietly.

'Enlighten me then. What have we found out apart from the fact that Bobby Evans scratches his backside and has let himself go?'

Tony looked at her. 'There's something he's not telling.'

'How d'you know?'

'He's scared for one thing and then there's Billy's visit. It can't be a coincidence.'

'What's a red operation?' Pauline asked.

Tony sighed. 'It was a prefix Force Seven used during the troubles.'

'And?'

'It denoted liquidation.'

'Murder?'

Tony nodded, then banged the steering wheel. 'Is that it?'

'What?'

'R7 Securities, the shell company that's part of Tweedsmuir Holdings.'

'Tweedsmuir Holdings?'

'The hedge fund that controls Argentina Farm Is that why they were worried about the bloody dossier?'

'You've lost me.'

'Buchan's speciality was the red operations by Force Seven.'

229

'R7?' Pauline said. 'Isn't that a bit obvious?'

Tony shrugged. 'Anyway, what's it got to do with Tweedsmuir?'

Pauline frowned and shook her head. 'No.'

What?'

'John Buchan, the writer? The Thirty-nine Steps?'

Tony shrugged. 'So what. Our Buchan's first name is Alistair.'

'John Buchan's other name was Baron Tweedsmuir.'

Tony started at her. 'Really?'

'Yes.' She shook her head. 'But would he really be so obvious?'

'He's a lifelong spook, clever, devious but he can't ever tell anyone. Maybe it's his way of thumbing his nose?'

'Tweedsmuir and R7; they could be a direct link back to him. Is that why he had me shut down?' He shook his head. 'It could still be a coincidence.'

Pauline put a hand up to her face and touched it. Her head felt tight and hot, as if it had been plunged into very hot water. Was it the casual talk of murder and assassination that had detonated something, or just the accumulation of experiences because she wasn't the person she had been before all this began? And here, now, in this godless place, on a filthy night at the end of a very long, wild goose chase, she felt empty and lost. Tony reached his hand across to touch her shoulder and comfort her.

'What is it?' He asked gently.

'That man,' she shuddered as she remembered Bobby Evans and his mates.

Tony sighed. 'Sorry.'

They were damp after the rain, the car windows were starting to mist up. Tony fiddled with his mobile as Pauline turned the engine on and set the heater on high.

'What're you doing?' She queried.

'Sending a text,' he replied, switching off the device and removing the SIM again. 'To Matt and Lissa.'

'Saying what?'

'Telling them to meet us outside Evans' bungalow.'

'What if he comes back from the pub?'

Tony shrugged. '

It was just after ten past seven.

43. Suburbia

Bobby Evans returned to his mates at the bar. He drank his pint and laughed at the banter, but the joy had gone out of it. His sanctuary had been breached and he couldn't settle. Tony Brooks in the 'Flag' asking him questions was total bollocks. If Tony could track him down, anyone could, he didn't like that. He'd changed his name and had himself deleted from various lists as part of his leaving package from Force Seven. His red operation had been the assassination of a big name Provo, which had been successful, but Evans' jacket had been covered in whitewash during the action; he'd been identified getting out of a police vehicle later. Consequently, there was a price on his head—forever. Bobby Evans had worked hard to shed his past life; he didn't like it coming back to haunt him.

Despite having described Bedford as anonymous, he had to admit that the town had grown on him. It was a Goldilocks place, not too small and not too big and it had the advantage of being in striking distance of London. He didn't want to have to relocate again. He thought about the upheaval and the expense involved in finding somewhere else to start over and rejected the idea. Standing there in the bar on a raucous Friday evening, he felt like a visitor in his own bleeding life. Tony Brooks fronting him up in his own boozer was bloody upsetting; the unscheduled meeting had given him indigestion. Frankie noticed his friend had stopped having fun.

'Alright, Bobby?' He asked.

Evans forced a grin and rubbed the top of his gut. 'Fine Frankie. I think I might have eaten something that didn't agree with me.'

Frankie smiled sympathetically. 'That geezer in the car park bovver you, did he?'

Evans shook his head. 'Don't worry about it.'

Frankie took a large drink from his pint. 'If you don't want me poking my nose in, tell me to piss off Bobby.' Evans said nothing. 'Thing is, him coming here on a Friday night; it's not on.'

Evans nodded. 'Too right.'

'So, we could go out and look for the tosser, give him a bit of advice.'

'Yeah.' Evans replied, but an idea was forming. 'No point in wasting good drinking time, though.'

'Tell you what, Bobby, when we've finished here, I'll come back to your gaff and make sure the coast is clear?'

Evans nodded. He couldn't deny that the idea of going back to the bungalow mob-handed was appealing. It would be the first time he'd invited his pub mates back to his gaff. He had the persona of Mr. Normal to maintain with the neighbours, but the couple on one side had to force themselves to say hello to him while the widow on the other side had never acknowledged him. Well, bollocks to them.

'Good idea, Frankie. We'll get a carry-out and invite some of the lads back. Order in a curry. Make a night of it.'

Frankie looked delighted that his suggestion had been taken seriously.

Three hours later, Bobby had gathered a posse of five happily inebriated mates to take back to the bungalow. Eric, Leroy and Graham bailed out at the pub door.

'Sod that for a game of soldiers,' Leroy said, peering into the gloom. 'It's like the fucking monsoon out there.' Eric and Graham agreed. Bobby tried calling a cab, but there weren't any because of the rain. Frankie tried to encourage them.

'It's just a bit of rain. Bobby's gaff ain't far.'

But the three were adamant, so Bobby and Frankie, together with Frankie's monosyllabic mate, Melvin, staggered into the driving rain to walk the half-mile to Bobby's bungalow. Frankie and Melvin got into an argument about the relative merits of Chelsea's Eden Hazard and Tottenham's Harry Kane. Frankie thought Kane was better.

'He's an 'ard-working, stand-up Englishman, honest and brave. Hazard's just another sly foreigner.'

'He's a genius,' Melvin slurred. He was known for not saying much, but he was a Chelsea fan and Hazard was their best player.

'Piss off, Melvin,' Frankie roared. 'Hazard's a bleeding Belgium, isn't he?'

Bobby was joining in, offering an occasional opinion, but only half his mind was engaged; the other half was calculating. He'd envisaged a gang of them coming from the Flag, but him and two others would have to do. As they turned into his street, Bobby missed the final exchange between Frankie and Melvin. He was busy scanning the road for anything out of the ordinary the first he knew something was awry was when he saw Melvin disappearing down a side street.

'Where's he going?'

'Spat his dummy out,' Frankie replied.

'Mel!' Evans called after him. 'What happened?'

'Reckons Hazard is a better player than Kane.'

Bobby sighed. This wasn't turning out the way he'd planned. If anyone was waiting for him, instead of a group of lads, all he had with him was Frankie, who was seriously pissed. They approached the bungalow, still in darkness. A peculiarity of the design was that the two bedrooms faced the front garden. The front door was at the side and the back door was round the back, reached via a wooden gate. Bobby led the way noisily, making no attempt to disguise their presence. As he passed the garage, he bent down and retrieved a key from under a plant pot, opened the back door and gestured to Frankie to go in first. Frankie staggered in, laughing; Bobby followed and put the light on. Frankie had never been in Bobby's gaff before and he was surprised by the neatness and quality of the kitchen.

'Blimey, Bobby. Bloody smart, that is. Very nice.'

Frankie worked as a labourer for a local builder on a zero-hours contract. It suited Frankie; he was always broke, his personal life was a disaster and his home was the high-rise flat he'd shared with his Ma until she died of cancer. Secretly, Frankie was impressed by Bobby because he always had money and was generous with it. Bobby ushered Frankie into the living room and turned the light on. Frankie stepped onto the carpet and collapsed with a moan. Tony stood holding a cut-glass vase that he'd used to cosh Frankie. Bobby stepped back and took something from the pocket of an ancient donkey jacket hanging in the small hallway. Tony saw that Bobby was holding a revolver and smirking.

'Thought I told you not to come round here,' Bobby sneered. He was pleased with himself. He'd seen this coming and he'd got the drop on them.

'Always did think you were better than me, didn't you?' Tony shrugged. 'See, I leave this insurance in the donkey-jacket 'cause you never know what's around the corner. Smart eh?' Bobby bragged.

'It's very smart, for you,' Tony smiled which irritated Bobby. He took a step forward and waved the gun around.

'The question is, what the fuck am I going to do with you?'

'No, that's not the question, Bobby, so it isn't.'

Bobby Evans stiffened as he recognised Matt's accent and felt something hard in his lower back. 'That's right, Bobby, and it's pointed at your vital organs,' Matt said. 'Tony, take his gun and check for others. Better check Bobby's low-life mate while you're at it.'

Tony took Bobby's weapon and pocketed it. He searched him carefully before turning to Frankie, who was starting to come around.

'What're you doing, you bastard?' Frankie demanded, starting to fight. Tony shoved Bobby's gun in Frankie's face, the bravado evaporated. Confused and fearful, he looked up at his friend.

'Do as they say, Frankie. It's all a misunderstanding,' Bobby whispered.

Frankie struggled to his feet.

'Blindfold him, tie his hands behind his back,' Matt ordered. Pauline blindfolded Frankie while Tony tied his hands with plastic restraining ties.

'Lassie, take this creep into the bedroom. If he causes you any bother, shoot him.' Lissa took hold of Frankie's wrists and guided him into the bedroom at the front.

'Pauline. Go and keep her company, will you?'

'No. I'm staying.' Pauline had had her fill of being excluded from critical decisions.

Matt looked at Tony, who nodded. Evans quivered as Lissa and Frankie left. Matt watched, then closed the door. 'Well now, Bobby, just the three of us plus Pauline. Almost like old times, so it is apart from Terry, poor sod. You heard what happened to him?'

Evans nodded. 'Cancer?'

'That's what it said on the death certificate, but they can be manipulated.'

'Terry was the fourth member of our brick. In the army,' Tony explained to Pauline.

'Sit yourself down, Bobby,' Matt said.

Bobby rubbed his brow. 'I'm not feeling great, Matt.'

'Don't give me that shite.'

Matt pulled a dining chair from a table and offered it to Bobby Evans. The chair was a modern, oak block design with an inset cream leather cushion; it looked unused. Bobby sat down and mopped his brow. 'I don't know anything, Matt. Swear to God.'

Matt grinned. 'Whenever a suspect said that, we knew they were lying, so we did. We used to laugh about it, remember?'

Bobby nodded, defeated. 'Why do I have all the bad luck?'

'Hasn't changed, has he, Tony?' Tony shrugged. 'Terry was fun, but you always were a moaner.'

'I haven't done anything, Matt. I did what you asked. I didn't know my heart was dicky.'

Matt nodded. 'No, I don't think you did, but you talked to someone?'

Evans shook his head. 'No! I swear.'

'We've just had all that, Bobby.'

Evans looked at them both and shook his head. 'I don't feel great.'

Pauline spoke next. 'In the pub, when Tony said that Matt was concerned, remember what you said?'

Evans shook his head. 'I said, I understood.'

'No. You were surprised.' Pauline insisted. Evans shook his head. 'You said, 'What? You've heard from him?' As if you didn't expect to hear from him again.'

Matt smiled. 'Is that right, Bobby? Did you think I was out of the picture? Or worse?'

'No.'

'That would make sense because I think you told someone about the hospital visit.'

'I didn't. I wouldn't, honest, Matt.'

'Honest. Another very dangerous word.

'I didn't tell anyone.' Evans was sweating a lot and starting to breathe quickly.

'I think you told your old CO, Colonel Buchan, didn't you?'

Evans shook his head. 'No.'

Matt sighed. 'We'll come back to that. Tell me about Billy Zed. Came to visit you?'

Evans nodded. 'I told Tony. It was out of the blue between Christmas and New Year. He brought me some Christmas cake.'

'Why, though, Bobby?'

'Said he wanted to look me up, for old times' sake.'

"And you believed him?' Matt sneered.

'Why not?'

'Why would anyone come and visit a sad old tosser like you?'

Evans shook his head. 'It struck me as odd at the time.'

'And that's it?' Matt probed.

Evans looked around as if hoping for a way out. 'After a few drinks together, Billy told me he was pissed off with Buchan ordering him about.'

'And?' Tony asked.

Evans paused, uneasy about saying more. Matt grabbed him by the scruff of the neck and shook him.

'Spit it out.'

'He said Buchan had a job to do in February.'

'How the fuck did Billy Zed know that?' Matt hissed.

'The last time Billy Zed saw Buchan, Buchan had had a phone call about something going down in the hills.'

'Anything else?' Matt asked.

'He heard a name.'

'What name?' Tony asked.

Evans looked around anxiously before muttering. 'Sandra. '

'Fucking Sandra in the fucking hills?' Matt roared, incredulous. 'Sounds like bollocks to me.'

'It's the truth, I swear it,' Evans said, wiping his brow with the back of his hand. Pauline stared open-mouthed. Sandra was the name Jane Percival had mentioned. Pauline was about to say something until she remembered Lavinia.

'So why do you think Billy Zed visited you, Bobby?' Tony asked.

Evans looked at the three of them, wide-eyed. 'I don't know. Really. Maybe he just wanted to see me?'

'Did you eat the cake?' Tony asked.

Bobby nodded. 'Soon as he left. It was nice.'

Matt shifted on his feet. 'Tony, tell him your theory.'

Tony moved to the back window and looked at the dark garden, where the rain was coming down in ropes.

'Buchan's got a new poison, something to do with viral fragments and messenger RNA. It's untraceable because it's a virus that disappears after it's infected the target. The emissary delivers the viral fragment; if they know the target's genome beforehand, Bob's your uncle.'

'D'you see Bobby?' Matt asked. 'D'you see what we're getting at here?'

Evans nodded. 'A poison?'

Matt nodded. 'Tell him how it works, Tony.'

'The target dies of a heart attack.' Evans looked up, wide-eyed with understanding.

Matt nodded at him. 'Exactly, Bobby. So why did Billy Zed look you up two days before your hospital visit?'

'To give me the cake?'

Matt nodded. 'And?'

'To infect me?' Bobby answered. clutching at his chest,

Matt nodded. 'It's a definite possibility. How else could you have a dicky heart at the check-up?'

'You said yourself that you were A1 six months ago,' Tony added.

'That can't be why SAS Billy visited,' Bobby muttered.

'Can't it?' Matt said, looking at him.

'I did wonder about it at the time,' Evans said. He fished a tissue out of his jeans and mopped his face. His breathing was becoming more laboured.

'Think carefully before you answer this, Bobby? Did Billy Zed visit you after you told Buchan about me, or before?'

'After.' The word was out of Evans' mouth before he realised he'd been snared. There it was, laid out. Evans told Buchan about Matt asking him to double for him at the hospital. Buchan sensed an opportunity and sent Billy Zed to make a call. Evans went to the hospital and hey presto, Matt's got a dicky heart.

'They were waiting for me. I wondered how they knew,' Matt said quietly.

Evans put his head in his hands. 'He had me over a barrel. Said if I didn't keep him informed, he'd publish my whereabouts.'

Matt nodded. 'Well, you always were second-rate, Bobby.'

Evans didn't look good. He was sweating heavily, his skin was waxy and pale. 'I don't feel so good.'

'Don't try that old trick,' Matt replied, but even as he spoke, Bobby Evans clutched his chest, moaned and fell forward onto the carpet. Pauline bent down and turned him onto his side.

'What are you doing?' Matt asked.

'Putting him into the recovery position,' Pauline replied; she examined his eyes and his skin. 'I think he's dying,' she gasped.

'He'd better not,' Matt hissed.

'He looks like Jonathan did.'

Matt knelt and whispered in Evans' ear. 'Don't you die on me, you scumbag.'

As if on cue, Bobby Evans gasped and breathed his last. The moment was impossible to miss. Pauline began doing CPR compressions on his chest.

'For Christ's sake!' Tony swore. Pauline continued her two-handed compressions.

'Don't think there's much point in that,' Matt said. 'If the poison works, they aren't going to want a target recovering after a bit of vigorous first aid.'

Pauline carried on with the CPR because of Jonathan.

'What do you think about what he said?' Tony asked.

Matt shrugged. 'Sandra? Dunno.'

'We need to talk to Billy Zed,' Tony mused, distracted. Something about Evans was bothering him.

'We need to deal with this first,' Matt replied.

Pauline stopped CPR and leant back, breathing hard; Evans wasn't coming back.

'That's why they didn't kill me,' Tony cried.

'What do you mean?' Matt asked.

'When they had me in Argentina, I wondered why they moved me to that second cleanroom and put me in pyjamas. They did something while I was unconscious.'

Pauline looked at Tony. 'What are you saying?'

'They infected me,' Tony said. 'I must have triggered Evans' heart attack.'

'I don't follow,' she responded. 'They couldn't have known you'd be seeing Evans?'

Matt went walkabout in the small living room. He turned back. 'That's right. Buchan didn't want Evans dead; he had him in his pocket. He could then extract favours whenever he wanted and have him eliminated anytime.'

'So, Tony meeting Evans was a coincidence?' Pauline asked.

Matt nodded. 'The reason they didn't kill Tony when they kidnapped him is that they had him down as the trigger for this big hit in the hills that Buchan and his cronies have sold.'

'Sandra?' Tony murmured.

'Tony meeting Bobby tonight was Bobby's bad luck and theirs.'

'I hope it's not mine,' Tony added.

Pauline looked at him, concerned. 'Why?'

'What happens to the carrier afterwards?'

'How do you mean?' Matt asked.

'Mayflies after mating?'

'Dear God,' Pauline said, suddenly aware that she didn't want to lose him. After everything they had done together, she wanted some time with him. A sharp headache materialised;

her legs felt unsteady and the room began to sway. Tony came to her side and kissed her. She clung to him with a desperation that surprised even her. Matt allowed the two a moment before interrupting.

'We need an exit plan, Tony.'

Tony pulled away from Pauline. 'Why didn't you tell me that Evans worked for Force Seven with you?'

Matt regarded him for a moment. 'I knew it would upset you.' Tony began to protest, but Matt overrode him. 'You're a brilliant analyst, but you were vulnerable after Katie dumped you. I had to shield you from the unpleasantness, so I did.'

'I'm not shielded now, am I?' Tony snapped.

Matt sighed. 'No.'

'You mentioned an exit plan?' Pauline asked. They both looked at her. 'A man is dead on the floor?'

Matt nodded and came to a decision.

'Sorry, Squaddie, but I think it's time you and I handed ourselves into the authorities. We'll call the police to report a death. We're old friends having a reunion, talking about the old days.'

'But Tony's wanted, isn't he?' Pauline asked, concerned.

Matt nodded. 'There will be some argy-bargy, but the bottom line is that he hasn't done anything wrong.'

'Apart from taking the dossier.'

'Deny it. They can't prove anything.'

Tony nodded. 'OK. We need to get rid of the artillery.'

Matt agreed. 'And the mobiles. Lissa! Get in here!'

Lissa appeared in the doorway and saw Evans lying on the floor. 'Is he?'

Tony nodded. 'Heart attack.'

Lissa swore to herself as she absorbed the implications. Matt gave her the two guns and two mobile phones.

'Take these,' he ordered.

'What do you want me to do with them?'

'Lose them. Take Pauline on your bike and get as far away as possible now, tonight.' Lissa nodded.

'What about the hire car?' Tony asked.

'Pauline can come back for it when the fuss has died down. Right, where's the slaphead?'

Lissa brought Frankie from the bedroom. He was still blindfolded and manacled. Matt spoke to him quietly, exaggerating his Belfast accent.

'We're going to send you on your way, but only if you promise to keep your gob shut?'

Frankie attempted bravado. 'That depends,' he said with a swagger.

'Ever heard of the Shankill Butchers?' Frankie shook his head. 'Back in the day, if they didn't like you cause you were a Seamus or a Sean, they'd slit your throat from ear to ear and your front from throat to gizzard, like that?' Matt made two blood thirsty gurgling noises as if slitting someone open. 'Are you receiving me? Over?'

'Yeah.' Frankie wasn't acting brave now.

'Because if you don't keep your trap shut, I will come back and give you the treatment personally, so I will. Alright?'

'Yeah.'

Matt switched off the hall light, opened the front door and removed Frankie's blindfold. Outside, the rain was still bucketing down. Frankie began to look around, but Matt gave him a hard slap on his head.

'Ah, ah, ah! No, you don't. Don't look back or...' He made the gurgling noise again and gave Frankie a shove, propelling him into the night. His still-manacled hands gave his gait an odd robotic quality. Matt watched for a moment as he headed off into the rain, then closed the door.

'Right, Lissa. Take Pauline to a place of safety and rest up. In a couple of days, come back for the car. Got that?'

Lissa nodded. 'Course I have.'

'And don't forget to lose the guns and the phones,' Tony added.

'Christ! Getting ordered about by wrinklies.' She shook her head. 'Come on then, Pauline.'

Pauline hugged Tony tightly, then turned and went quickly from the bungalow. Lissa blew a kiss to Matt. 'Be seeing you,' she said and followed Pauline.

Matt rechecked Evans' pulse and looked at Tony. 'Know the story?' Tony nodded. Matt picked up the receiver and dialled 999.

Lissa headed north-east and joined the A423 heading towards St. Neots and Cambridge. The driving rain sluiced everything liquid black, but the traffic was light and Lissa was able to open the throttle. Pauline was wearing a quilted winter coat, which afforded some protection from the deluge, but her jeans were soaked through in seconds. Lissa was stressed and rode too quickly for the conditions. They'd run out of options and she didn't like not having a fallback position. The bike would be on CCTV footage in London and Bedford. She planned to get out of Bedfordshire and into the jurisdiction of another constabulary. She knew from her time in uniform that messages took longer to surface if they had to cross boundaries. The plan was to make the A1 and speed up the road into Cambridgeshire or, better yet, Lincolnshire.

At the Black Cat roundabout, she attempted to overtake an articulated lorry, realised too late that she'd overcooked it and began to brake just as she was starting to make the left turn onto the A1. At that point, the rear tyre grip lost out to centrifugal force, the bike slipped onto its side and slid along the black, wet tarmac at sixty miles an hour, corkscrewing towards the back wheels of a coach. Maybe it was the crash helmet, but the noise of the bike clattering and scraping along the floor was muted; sparks flew past her visor, reminding Pauline of being on the dodgems when she was a girl. A distant voice was screaming; Pauline wondered if it was Lissa before realising that it was her yelling at the top of her voice. Time slowed as they careered towards the coach; Pauline wondered if she were going to die and decided that she probably was. She suddenly remembered the letter to Lavinia in her pocket; if it got too wet, she'd have to write another. She caught sight of the misty windows of the passenger compartment, illuminated from inside. The passengers stared down in horror, frozen in the moment, as the motorbike hurtled towards them, closer and closer. And then, blackness.

February 2019

North Pennines

44. Long Hills

At forty-six, Alessandra Bianchi was a renowned Italian eco-journalist who worked for 'La Respiration', a Parisian political magazine that focused on environmental issues. Famous for reporting from lawless, war-torn cockpits, outspoken in her criticism of the world's 'strong men' and heedless of her own safety, 'Sandra's' eloquent witness and articulate reporting had changed policies around the globe as well as irritating more than a few powerful people. She ignored the threats she received and refused all offers of protection. It wasn't that the threats didn't scare her, but she simply couldn't countenance the idea of anyone, especially a man, sharing her space and disturbing her equilibrium.

An intensely private person, Sandra owned a small flat in the sixth arrondissement but she was rarely there. Her abiding restlessness was legendary; she loved being in constant motion without time to think when after a story. She claimed that her passion for the environment was common sense; if we didn't fix the problems that we had created, there would be nothing left for our children and their offspring. An imposing ashblonde who stood just under six feet tall, Sandra was famous for speaking truth to power and not suffering fools gladly. Her air of aloof self-possession attracted men and women alike, but she rejected all emotional advances and refused point-blank to discuss her personal history. Born in the Czech Republic, Alessandra Bianchi's family fled to Italy in 1967 to escape the Russian invasion. Sandra had grown up in the Dolomites and took a degree in modern languages before turning to journalism but she never forgot her childhood fear of the Soviet invasion and her family's escape. It fueled her investigations and she was never shy about naming those responsible for the environmental catastrophes. Across the globe, environmental activists, many of whom were friends, had a habit of being imprisoned or killed but each new injustice only made Alessandra more determined. Dictators with corrupt legal systems were a favourite target and, perhaps because of her childhood flight from Prague, she reserved her greatest ferocity for Putin's Russia.

Despite her public profile, little was known about her. There were rumours that she had been a model, but despite the brilliance of her own journalism, details of her early existence were sparse and difficult to excavate. The truth was that she'd suffered a profound breakdown in her twenties after a miscarriage and the collapse of her marriage. Recovery had been glacially slow until she discovered yoga and meditation as a way of controlling the anguish. The ability to place order on the emotional chaos of life had freed her, but not without cost. On the rare occasions that she was in Paris, she rose at six and did an hour's yoga before embarking on the tasks at hand. Before bed, she meditated for at least an hour while her diary governed the hours in between. She hated surprises of any kind and shunned all festive occasions. She didn't 'do' Christmas, avoided 'holidays' and never went to parties or weddings. Apart from anything else, she loathed dressing up. Despite her evident elegance and grace, she made no effort with her appearance, avoiding make-up and choosing functional clothing over fashion. It had become a trade mark; her lissome, long-striding sophistication clad in combat fatigues against the backdrop of some war-torn eco-disaster was a familiar trope. Despite shunning holidays, Sandra made one exception. The third week of February was reserved for a week's yoga and meditation with her good friend Annie in a remote valley in the North Pennines.

Forty miles south of the Cheviot Hills, the valley of the West Allen is at once beguiling and inviting. Seen from the A686, the main Newcastle-Alston road, the dale is wide and verdant at first, before narrowing and climbing to a distant, misty confluence of hills shrouded in mystery and possibility. Settlements are small and infrequent and, until the advent of cheap imports in the nineteenth century, prosperity derived from lead mining rather than subsistence farming on the weathered fells. Old spoil heaps adorn the lower slopes, along with warning signs guarding dark, barred entrances to abandoned workings. In midsummer, when the sun is warm and the meadows full of wildflowers and the exotic calls of curlew and lapwing, a few enthusiastic visitors explore. In winter, when the early dark and icy grip turn the higher fells into a forgotten wilderness, few venture forth unbidden. The quiet, enfolding isolation was what attracted Sandra after a skiing accident left her with a swollen left knee and an article to write. It was her editor, Max, who had offered her the cottage—a bequest from a distant cousin who'd escaped Germany in the thirties.

The first time Sandra saw the long, worn hills with their dusting of snow, she felt as if she'd come home. She'd visited every continent and seen all kinds of weather, but something about this small corner of the North Pennines spoke to her. The light was gentler than the bright Italian sun of her childhood, which she still loved, but she was captivated by the boundless shades of green darkened by low clouds as they hustled over the fells on the nagging breeze. With a panoramic view, the isolated cottage stood guard on a small promontory. As Sandra had explained to Max, she needed inner calm for the external turmoil; the cottage was perfect.

And it was here that Sandra had met Annie Morgan, a divorced, freelance yoga teacher who'd come to the cottage and coaxed Sandra back to fitness. Despite being polar opposites, the two women had hit it off. Where Sandra was willowy and austere, Annie was dumpy, garrulous, and fun-loving, but it worked. When they weren't doing yoga, Sandra loved to walk in the woods next to the river, where the ground was covered with the muted colours of decay, the browns and yellows of oak, beech, birch, and chestnut leaves lying on a carpet of pine needles. In the process, the two women had become friends. Annie lived in Hexham and spent a lot of time rushing up and down the local roads in her ageing Nissan Micra, teaching yoga and providing for her disaffected teenage daughter, Ziggy, who yearned for big city lights. Annie enjoyed her job because she could earn money while doing something she loved. She was her own boss, worked when she wanted and she'd had plenty of clients until the advent of online courses eroded her client base and left her struggling to make ends meet.

February was usually a quiet time for Sandra's magazine and the third week suited Annie. Sandra paid well and demanded little, apart from privacy, but, this year, Annie was under financial pressure. Now, with a month to go, a new client was offering a substantial amount of money for Annie's services for six straight weeks, which would solve her financial problems for the year. The trouble was that they wanted to start in the same week as Sandra. Annie had tried to re-negotiate the timing of the new offer, but the answer had been clear: take it or leave it. For the first time since becoming a yoga teacher, Annie didn't have a solution.

And Sandra had her own problems; she was behind with a story given to her by Max about illegal construction in a Russian nature reserve and the deadline couldn't be changed. There was a European Council meeting about climate change at the beginning of March, to which a Russian delegation had been invited. Max's aim was to publish the article in the February edition, allowing three weeks for the material to be circulated and absorbed. But something must have leaked because some strange things had started to happen at Sandra's Parisian flat.

She had come home one day to find her phone off the hook and her bedroom window wide open. The flat was on the third floor and the Louis Quinze window opened outwards with no guardrail. She thought she must have had a brainstorm, but the next day, her hair brush was missing, her spice pots had been reorganised and a running shoe was in the freezer. Then, as she was scrolling through a draft of her article, a disembodied voice spoke from the laptop.

'Zapovednik.'

One word, clear and loud like a pistol shot - 'Zapovednik' - and simultaneously, a red circle with a diagonal red line appeared on the screen over the text. 'Zapovednik' was the Russian name for one of their protected nature reserves. She took a deep breath, closed and re-opened the file but the disembodied voice and the symbol did not re-appear. She read the draft article through again and it appeared to be intact, but the experience unravelled her. She checked all the windows and the locks on the front door and rearranged her spice rack.

If she complained, she would sound neurotic. Despite her instinctive resistance to intimidation, it was hard to escape the sense of insecurity. The trouble was that the intimidation felt like an overreaction. Toxic dumping that damaged the population was bad and the fact that the authorities had attempted to cover it up was a scandal but it wasn't the first time it had happened, so why the extreme reaction? Whatever the reason for the intrusions, Sandra refused to be swayed; the article would be published or it wouldn't, but she wasn't going to miss her week of yoga with Annie in Northumberland.

45. Hospital

Pauline closed her eyes, put her fingers in her ears and tried to imagine being in her own bed in Bridgford, but no matter how hard she tried, there was no escaping the memory of careering towards the coach on the pillion of Lissa's motorbike. If she tried breathing really slowly, the panic of that memory was supplanted by the overpowering smell. Disinfectant and food dominated the aroma landscape, but underlying them were bleach, floor polish, body odour and plastic. Two days earlier, they'd changed the disinfectant to something stronger or, more likely, cheaper. When she'd been in ICU, she'd become intimately acquainted with the tube in her mouth. Now, the plastic cutlery that came with the hospital grub reminded her of the ICU tube and made her gag. Food was the other dominant smell, but there was always a taint of plastic and metal, like the tube.

She had her own room, but it was hot and she was constantly drowsy. The articulated hospital bed was never completely flat. She had been in suspended animation for a long time, never wholly asleep and never fully awake. The distant thrum of machinery created slight but discernible vibrations. By night, the blinking monitor attached to her arm seemed to connect with the faint light under the door, while outside, people moved back and forth on arcane tasks to a descant of distant alarms and occasional screams. By day, the corridor was busy with nursing staff and doctors hurrying past, head down. Cleaners and orderlies wandered in and out of her room while other functionaries brought books and the unappetising food.

She had made friends with Roberta, the tiny, craggy-faced Filipino cleaner in her sixties who trailed the scent of patchouli oil in her wake. Over the last week or so, the two women discovered they both had grandchildren. Relentlessly cheerful, Roberta worked hard to feed her single-parent daughter and her two boys. Pauline told her about Lavinia and the girls and next day, Roberta brought in some birthday cake from the youngest grandson's fifth birthday. Roberta was worried about being able to stay in Britain. Although she had lived in Bedford for many years, she had never bothered to complete the citizenship process. Pauline helped her write a letter to the Home Office; if the answer was no, she might be deported back to Manila.

Despite the gravity of Roberta's situation, the ordinary, human contact buoyed Pauline. It was Roberta who told her she had been in Bedford Royal Infirmary for three weeks. She had been in ICU for the first four days, unconscious and then heavily sedated. Then she had been moved into this room on the eleventh floor. Apart from the medical staff, Pauline had seen very few people and had no news. She'd had no visitors and only vaguely remembered the events leading up to the accident. In the last few days, she had begun to feel better and decided to try and build her stamina. Despite feeling safe and cocooned in the hospital, she wanted to go home to Bridgford. There was a light knock and Roberta appeared, mop in hand and smiling.

'How are we feeling today?'

'The same, thanks.'

'You've got a visitor.'

'Who?' Pauline asked warily.

Roberta grinned. 'You sound like you've got something to hide. Have you?'

'It's not the police again?'

An older, uniformed traffic cop had interviewed her about ten days before. He knew her name and address from the stuff in her pockets and asked what she could remember about the accident. Pauline feigned forgetfulness and said she could only recall fragments. No, she didn't know how she came to be on a motorcycle or who she was with. Overweight and tired, the policeman wrote it all down and nodded, but the look on his face said it all. He'd been around the track and he knew when something didn't add up. He gave her his card and told her to call him if anything came to her. Afterwards, Pauline had been exhausted.

Roberta opened the door wide and Oliver Campion walked in carrying a carrier bag. He was dressed in the thirty-something uniform of jeans, heavy boots and a 'puffa' jacket over a white tee shirt.

'I'll come back later,' Roberta smiled, closing the door behind her.

'Oliver?' Pauline sat up in the bed, smoothing her hair as he came over.

'You've been in the wars, Pauline?'

'How did you know I was here?'

He smiled. 'Someone rang me.'

'Who?'

Oliver shook his head. 'Didn't give her name.'

Pauline was confused. 'Why, though?'

'My solicitor has been trying to trace you.'

'Me?'

'Mum left you something in her will. I'm in a bit of a hurry and I wanted to give it to you in person.'

'Give me what?' Pauline frowned. Oliver pulled a small jiffy bag from the carrier and handed it to her. Pauline upended the bag, tipping something black, plastic and ugly onto the bed.

'A mobile phone?'

'Not just any mobile. Mum's state-of-the-art, top-of-the-range, super-duper mobile; it's fully charged.'

Pauline examined the device gingerly as if it were covered in acid. 'I hate mobiles.'

Oliver was grinning. 'It's Mum's joke, Pauline. She knew how you felt about them.'

Pauline nodded. 'Oh.'

'It does work. The passcode is Shakespeare's birthday.'

'What?' Pauline felt herself reddening.

'April 1564. 041564, Shakespeare's birthday. Mum couldn't remember passwords and shit, so I suggested one she wouldn't forget, as an English teacher. You'll need a new SIM and your own contract eventually, but this one's still got a couple of months to run.'

'Funny sense of humour, your mother,' Pauline muttered.

He laughed. 'I know.'

'You could have posted it.'

'I need a signature.' He produced a form, which Pauline signed. 'Besides, you looked after Mum. If you hadn't happened along, she would have died alone in that bloody house.' Pauline remembered arriving in the snow with Tony. It felt like a very long time ago.

'I wanted to say goodbye. It's not really out of my way.'

'Isn't it?'

'I'm off back to Thailand tonight.'

'For good?'

He nodded. 'I'm settled there.'

'What about Greenside?'

'I've instructed the solicitor to handle the sale. I've put the precious stuff in storage.' He paused. 'Didn't like being there without Mum.'

Pauline wondered if he'd come because she had a connection to Mary. Then another thought sent a pulse of fear into her guts. Had he been sent? Oliver shook himself.

'I would have given it to you after the funeral, but you didn't come back.'

'No,' Pauline remembered. 'The service upset me more than I expected.'

Oliver nodded and sighed. 'I wish I'd spent more time with her after Dad died, but my business in Thailand has been doing well this last year.'

'Everyone feels guilty when a parent dies. It's part of the process,' Pauline offered. Oliver wasn't persuaded.

'I've met someone, a Thai girl.'

'I see,' Pauline said, but she didn't.

'She's pregnant. I should have told Mum.'

'Why didn't you?' Pauline asked.

'She was dying. There was never a good time.'

Pauline sighed. 'Don't be too hard on yourself, Oliver. You

came back; you were there at the end.'

That seemed to help. 'I suppose you're right.' They said nothing for a moment, then something occurred to him.

'You heard about Jonathan?'

Pauline nodded. 'I was the one who found him.'

'Bad heart apparently?' Pauline nodded. 'Must be something in the air.'

'What?'

'Mum, then Jonathan, now you.'

'I'm not dead,' Pauline smiled.

'You should be; a high-speed collision with a coach.' Pauline said nothing. Oliver leaned closer. 'What were you doing on a motorbike at your age?'

She bristled. 'What's age got to do with it?'

He put his hands up in mock surrender. 'Alright, point taken. How are you anyway?'

'Fine.'

He looked dubious. 'Come on.'

'They tell me I've been lucky. I had a head injury, a serious concussion and lots of bruising down my left side, but all the tests for something dire have come back negative. No broken bones; I'm going home next week.'

It was true. The consultant had said that she could leave as long as there was someone to look after her. Pauline had told him that Lavinia would be staying which satisfied him. In an attempt to exercise and improve her stamina, she had taken to walking up and down the long corridor past all the side bays and nursing stations. She forced herself to eat the hospital grub and fantasised about going back to Bridgford. How many times had she yearned to get her life back? After everything that had happened, she was determined to try.

Oliver accepted her explanation. 'That's great, Pauline.' He picked up the carrier bag and handed it to her. 'There's erm, some grapes and chocolate and stuff.'

'That's very sweet of you.'

He shrugged and looked at his phone. 'Right, I must be going.' He stood up, leant over and kissed her on the cheek.

'Thanks for everything.'

She smiled and found herself crying. Was it because Oliver was a link to her old life of pilates and university gossip? Oliver put his arm around her. After a moment, she pushed him away.

'I'll be alright, honestly.'

Oliver smiled. 'If you're sure?'

She nodded and he left. Afterwards, she put Mary's mobile in the drawer in her bedside table with a shake of her head. Two days later, she had another visitor.

She was on one of her peregrinations, exploring the ward on the other side of the lifts, when a young, underfed staff nurse challenged her. Pauline was wearing a flimsy dressing gown over the awful lime-green hospital nightie and she still had a wrist band with her name on it.

'Where do you think you're going?' The staff nurse peered imperiously through smudged reading glasses perched on the end of her nose.

Pauline smiled. 'I'm sorry. Have I wandered into a restricted area?'

'This isn't your ward.'

'No, I'm from the head injury unit,' Pauline smiled.

The nurse waved her hand airily. 'You must go back.'

Pauline understood that the staff were under pressure, but being a patient didn't make her a fool. She smiled. 'Why?'

'Do you want me to report you?' The nurse threatened.

'Go on then,' Pauline grinned. After all, what could they do? It was petty but Pauline was bored and self-important officialdom had always irritated her. The nurse grimaced, then gave it up and walked away leaving Pauline smiling. It was at the precise moment of her little victory that she glimpsed Alistair Buchan exiting the lift. Her mouth dried and her heart began to pound. What was he doing here? Pauline followed him as he made his way to her room. He was wearing an expensive worsted suit, an open-neck blue shirt and looking at the view when she entered. He turned and regarded her.

'Ah. You are here? And up and about. Excellent.'

Pauline stood by the door. 'What do you want?'

'To see you. Find out how you are.' Pauline didn't reply. He took a step towards her.

'I'll call security,' she threatened.

Buchan regarded her and took a deep breath. 'Why don't you sit down?' Pauline didn't move. 'Close the door then. I've got something to say.' She did as he asked and leaned back against it, suddenly tired.

'Don't you want to know how everyone is?' He asked smoothly. Despite being keen to find out, she kept silent.

'Matt's fine,' Buchan said. 'He had some questions to answer, there's some work to do at his flat but he's back at work. He's being watched, of course.' Buchan took a hike around the room. 'Tony, on the other hand, hasn't been too good. He's in Belmarsh Prison, sharing facilities with the most disgusting child molesters, violent criminals and assorted serial killers.'

Despite her efforts, Pauline couldn't disguise the alarm in her eyes.

'That's where they put you when you're charged under the Prevention of Terrorism Act.' He smiled grimly. 'That's not strictly true. That's where they put you when they want to unsettle you. Anyway, he's been in intensive care in London; trouble with his heart, apparently.'

Pauline felt her anger rising. Buchan hadn't finished yet.

'I told you that, one day, I would want you to do something.' He paused for effect. 'Well, this is the day.'

He turned away and surveyed the view over Bedford.

'How close are you and Tony?' She still said nothing, and he turned back. 'What I mean is, have you two been intimate with each other?'

Avoiding his gaze, she stared at the end of the hospital bed.

'Because if you have had 'relations', as the tabloids so delicately put it, then you're already inoculated.'

Pauline thought back to the last time she'd seen Tony, standing over Bobby Evans' body.

Buchan hadn't finished. 'You're going to take Tony's place. Being a woman, it's a much better fit.'

'I won't,' Pauline replied. Buchan looked at her, put his head on one side flexing his jaw as if considering what to do. At that moment, there was a knock and Roberta entered, mop in hand.

'Sorry, I'll come back later,' she grinned and made to leave, then stopped and whispered to Pauline. 'By the way, I've heard from the Home Office. They're reviewing my case. My solicitor is delighted; they're giving me leave to remain.' She reached up and kissed Pauline. 'I'll tell you everything later.'

'Just a moment,' Buchan said, smiling. 'Will you come over to the window, please? Pauline and I have been arguing about something. I wonder if you could help settle the issue?'

Roberta smiled at Pauline and raised her eyebrows. She crossed the floor, surveyed the panorama and asked, 'What is your question?'

Buchan opened the window wider and stood behind Roberta. He looked at Pauline, his eyebrows raised, and mimed, pushing the tiny woman out of the window with a cupped hand.

'It's alright, Roberta,' Pauline forced. 'Can you come back later? We're in the middle of something.'

Roberta turned and frowned, looking at Buchan. 'Of course.'

Pauline smiled as Roberta picked up her mop and bucket and left the room. 'You would have killed her?'

Buchan looked out of the window and nodded. 'Eleven floors up. Unlikely to survive.'

'But why?'

'To demonstrate the seriousness of my intent. I would have thought the vicar would have been sufficient encouragement.'

'Jonathan?' Pauline gasped. 'You killed him because of me?"

'Sit in the wheelchair!' Buchan hissed and produced a gun from his coat pocket. 'I'm prepared to use it. Sit in the damn chair.'

Suddenly aware of how vulnerable she felt in the flimsy hospital attire, she had the presence of mind to grab her bag from the bedside cupboard before she sat in the chair. Buchan opened the door and peered out. Then he pushed her quickly down the corridor to the lift. It was weird because the ward floor was calm and normal; everyone preoccupied with their own stuff. Roberta had disappeared. On the ground floor, Pauline considered yelling to the staff and patients, hurrying back and forth, but nobody took any notice. Buchan wheeled Pauline down a long corridor to a rear exit overlooking the staff car park. He pushed her towards a looming, black SUV with tinted windows and propelled her into the back seat. He got into the front passenger seat, The woman from the church was behind the wheel. Tina glanced at Pauline, then stared at Buchan, her face a mixture of surprise and anger. Despite the fear and shock she was feeling, Pauline noticed that Tina was wearing the same coat and earrings she'd worn in St. Leonard's before Christmas.

'Drive,' Buchan ordered. Tina let out the clutch and reversed carefully out of the parking bay.

46. Manor House

Pauline came awake with a gasp. It was pitch dark; she was lying in a small cot beneath a sloping roof. Moonlight shone through a skylight illuminating a small attic room but it was bitterly cold. Pauline shivered, she was still in her hospital gown. They were south or south-east of London. They had driven around the M25 and turned down the M2 before turning off and stopping. The athletic-looking man called Milo, was waiting for them in a cavernous, low-ceilinged kitchen that reeked of mildew and damp. Milo's left arm was in a sling and there was an angry sneer across his face. Despite her near-catatonic state, Pauline realised that he was in pain; Tina was concerned but Buchan didn't appear to notice. Apparently, Milo had been told to prepare a meal, but all he'd produced was three ham sandwiches in white sliced bread. He protested that his arm made cooking impossible. Tina smiled encouragingly at Milo and took a bite of her sandwich, but Buchan swept his sandwich off the table and ordered Milo to search Pauline's bag. Tina went forward.

'I'll help him,' she said quietly.

'He can manage!' Buchan snapped.

Feeling sorry for himself and distracted by his arm, Milo's search was cursory and superficial; he didn't bother to search Pauline herself.

Pauline was taken to the attic room and locked in. Besides the skylight, there was an ensuite shower room and loo, but without heating, it was colder than the nave of St. Leonard's. Shivering, she climbed into bed and tried to sleep, but she was too wired to relax. Images of Charlton, Jonathan, Mary and

Evans replayed on a loop, pulsing adrenaline back into her system. She must have dozed off eventually because she woke up needing to pee.

She sat on the loo and checked her watch—four thirty. They must have been desperate to abduct her. If only for Lavinia's sake, Pauline had to try and take control of herself. She stood undressed and took a long, hot shower. Warmer, she dressed in her own clothes for the first time since the accident. The left leg of her jeans had been shredded in the accident, but someone had patched it. She wondered who could have done it, but the small kindness created a squall of sobs that caught in her throat. She was trying to put her boots on when she encountered an obstruction. She held the boot upside down and Mary's mobile phone fell out onto the cot. Pauline stared at it, then picked it up.

Ten minutes of swearing later, she'd succeeded in turning the damn thing on, but her mind refused to help when it demanded a passcode. Pauline checked her pockets and found the business card that Jane Percival had given her. Jane had said to call her at any time. Pauline wanted to find out if she meant it but she would have to recall the passcode first.

Pauline hadn't been concentrating when Oliver had explained the mnemonic. When confronted with digital technology, she tended to panic and glaze over, but she forced herself to relive Oliver's hospital visit. He'd said something about Shakespeare, then it came to her: Shakespeare's birthday. The bard had been born in April 1564, so the passcode was 041564. Pauline entered the number, and the phone icons appeared with a cheerful jingle.

'For fuck's sake!' Pauline muttered under her breath. She returned to the ensuite bathroom and turned the shower back on. Pauline pressed the phone icon and dialled the number for Jane Percival. It rang for a long time, but nobody answered. She was about to give up when she heard a voice.

'Who is this?' Jane Percival asked warily.

'Me, Pauline,' Pauline hissed.

'Who?'

'Pauline Atkinson.'

'Whose phone are you using?'

'Never mind that. Buchan has kidnapped me.'

'Ah, yes.' Pauline heard Jane yawning. 'Sorry, that must be rather unpleasant.'

'It's terrifying.'

'What do you want?'

'To be rescued, of course.'

'Why has Buchan kidnapped you?'

'He wants me to do the job that Tony was set up for.'

'Where are you?'

'A biggish house south of London, in the country somewhere.'

'Sounds like the Buchan family pile. What's the state of the place?'

'Untidy, unwashed pans and crockery.'

'No home help then?'

'Doesn't look like it.'

'Using his own home as a bolthole; must be his end game.'

'He threatened to kill a hospital cleaner yesterday.' Pauline rasped. 'He would have done it if I hadn't agreed to go with him.'

'He's betting everything on this operation.'

'How long will you be?' Pauline whispered.

'How long?' Jane queried.

'Coming to get me?'

'I can't possibly do that.'

'What?' Pauline asked.

Jane sighed. 'I haven't got any power. Besides, it's too good an opportunity to catch Colonel Buchan red-handed. We need to know who his paymasters are.'

'What about me?'

'Just do as he says.'

'I was in hospital when he came for me. I've only just got out of intensive care.'

'I'm sorry about that. How are you?'

Realising Jane wasn't going to come and get her, Pauline felt her strength ebb and she collapsed onto the cot. 'They were letting me go home next week. That's what I want to do: go home.'

'Can you imagine what would happen if this 'natural poison' was available on the open market?'

'The viral fragments?' Pauline asked.

'Yes, except they're not really fragments as such. They're two different MRNA strands that are harmless until they combine.'

'There must be someone else who can help?' Pauline protested.

'We won't get another chance like this, don't you see?'

'Not really.' Pauline was beginning to feel light-headed.

'Whose mobile are you using?'

'My friend Mary's, Mary Campion. She left it to me in her will.'

Pauline heard a chuckle. 'You really are a natural, my dear.'

'What?'

'Using someone else's phone, brilliant. But don't call me again. If you want to communicate, use text.'

'I'm not sure I can do this.'

'Yes, you can. Remember, Buchan is desperate. You're his last chance; you can exploit that.'

'How?'

'Needle him. Make him lose his temper.'

'Isn't that dangerous?'

'He can't afford to lose you.'

'I'm not sure I want to put that to the test.'

'You won't be alone, but now that you're on board, you must carry on. Turn the phone off and hide it. If you need to communicate, text on the hour, then switch off immediately. If you text at any other time, I'll assume it's under duress.'

'Right,' Pauline replied, wondering if any of that would be possible.

'They might have some kind of scanner with them. You'd better hang up.'

Pauline sighed. 'If I go along with this, I want a quid pro quo.'

'What sort of thing?' Jane asked. Pauline began to explain what she had in mind.

47. La Respiration

Environmental journalist, Sandra Bianchi, was having a bad day. Max knew she was booked on the Eurostar to London that afternoon, but he had ordered her into the magazine office. She hated surprises at any time but he'd insisted. She hurried to the small suite of offices on the third floor of the building near the Boulevard St. Michel, where 'La Respiration's' office was based, and found Max on his knees gathering files and bits of paper and putting them together.

'A break-in,' he explained unnecessarily; the magazine offices had been ransacked and turned upside down.

'What are you doing?' She asked, mystified.

'Tidying up,' Max grunted. Sixty something, greying at the temples and corpulent, he was persistent but patient as an editor. Max Gompper had grown up in East Germany and made his name with an expose about the Stasi, the East German Secret Police. He'd moved to Paris in the mid-nineties. Sandra watched for a moment, puzzled.

'Isn't everything on the computers?' She asked, wondering why a junior wasn't on their knees, cleaning up.

Max shrugged. 'It was.'

'What happened?'

'The system was hacked, the files wiped.'

'What?'

He nodded. 'We had a phone call yesterday.'

'Saying what?'

'Not to publish your story.'

'Why didn't you tell me?' she asked.

'It's not the first time. We've had a few calls recently.' He sighed and looked at the wrecked office.

A good story always upset someone in high places, but Sandra hadn't anticipated that this story about illegal construction in a Russian nature reserve or zapovednik would elicit such an extreme reaction. The nature reserves were a valuable resource; there were over a hundred of them all over Russia, some small and some very large, but the main identifying characteristic was that, other than designated rangers, no one was allowed in. The story had been dropped in Max's lap by a ranger called Gennady Koralev, an old friend from their days of military service. Max spoke Russian and had been seconded to Gennady's unit in Dresden as a liaison officer. They'd got along with each other, had some wild times, and after they were demobbed and the Soviet Union had disintegrated, they'd stayed in touch for a while. Inevitably, contact had faded over the years, so the recent phone message had been a shock. For the last thirty years, Gennady had been a zapovednik ranger in the Russian Far East, near the Amur River. He'd sent a file about illicit construction on the zapovednik to Max by the hand of his son son, Vlady, who, with his shock of black, tufty hair, had the look of his father. Max had wanted to chat, but Vlady had been twitchy and keen to deposit a floppy disc and a dog-eared notebook and get away. Gennady was totally committed to his 'reserve' on the edge of Siberia, which predated the revolution; he'd grown to love the vast forest of larch and alder and the animals that thrived there. He'd been warned off, but Gennady was passionate. There were maps, drawings, notes and on the CD-ROM, photographs of a Russian general greeting an unknown male civilian.

Alessandra had cross-checked the facts as far as she could and written up the story almost verbatim. They'd managed to identify the general as a high-up in the GRU, the Russian military security service, but they hadn't been able to identify the civilian. That news of the article stirred up some dust wasn't a surprise; powerful organisations were always upset if their plans were revealed, especially if they were illicit. Even so, breaking into the magazine office felt over the top. 'La Respiration' survived by selling stories to larger outlets worldwide. So, even if they broke into the office, the story was likely to be everywhere already.

'I've got a copy of the article at the flat,' she said pointedly.

'Have you?' Max looked at her over his owlish spectacles.

Sandra pointed to her head. 'If they've hacked my laptop, it's still in here.'

'Go home and check,' Max replied. He was sympathetic to her fiercely guarded privacy because she always delivered. Nevertheless, there was an inference in his remark, which took a moment for her to decode. If she'd been hacked, he wanted her to rewrite the story.

'I'm going away tomorrow,' she said sharply.

Sandra was beginning to fret; she hated having her schedule disrupted.

'Have you got a flash drive copy?'

'Let me go home and look?'

'Or copy it to a CD,' Max added. 'Or print it out and post it.'

Sandra distrusted electronic storage of any kind because she'd once lost a whole bunch of research when a flash drive ceased to function without warning. Since then, she had trusted her photographic memory and used the laptop as a backup.

Max came over and looked around furtively before asking. 'Has anything else happened?'

'What kind of thing?'

'Something out of the ordinary?'

'Why?'

Max sighed. 'Gennady has disappeared.'

'Are you sure?'

Max nodded. 'Vlady called from Helsinki.'

'Helsinki?'

'He's in hiding. He's not going back to Russia.' Max looked at the chaos of his office. 'So Sandra, has anything strange happened to you?'

She sighed. 'Someone may have been in my flat.'

'Tell me,' Max commanded. She sighed and related the story of the rearranged spice pots, the disappearing hairbrush, the open window and the trainer. He removed his spectacles and wiped them carefully, shaking his head.

'What?' She asked, annoyed.

'Corrosion; the Stasi called it.'

'The Stasi?'

Max nodded. 'In the early days in East Germany, anyone who expressed opposition to the regime was taken out and beaten to a pulp. After detente, they needed to present a reasonable face to the outside world. So, they came up with 'corrosion'.'

'What is it?'

Max dipped his head. 'A technique designed to 'switch off' political opponents by undermining their self-confidence until they became nervous and uncertain. They couldn't complain to the police or the press because, individually, the events appeared trivial and unimportant. The whole point was to make the target feel insecure all the time.'

'The Stasi are long gone.'

'The FSB aren't,' Max muttered, putting his glasses back on.

'The FSB?' The FSB were the Russian Secret Police, the successors to the KGB. 'Here, in Paris?'

Max nodded. 'Or the GRU. Both are enthusiastic adopters of Stasi techniques.' He touched her arm. 'Perhaps we should reconsider?'

'Gennady's story!?' She couldn't believe it.

Max shrugged. 'We've touched a nerve. These people are ruthless.'

Sandra snorted with derision. 'Death threats come with the territory, Max.'

'True, but they've never broken into the office before.' He paused and lowered his voice. 'Someone told Vlady you would not survive publication.'

Sandra and Max had known each other for twenty years; he had given her her first job when he'd set up his environmental magazine. It wasn't like him to react to threats. 'There must be something more in the file,' he whispered.

'What though?'

'The facility they're building must be important to go to all this trouble.'

Sandra found herself getting irritated. 'Come on, Max, we've reported stories like this before. In essence, it's the same old story.'

'Then we wouldn't lose anything by withdrawing publication,' he said quietly.

'Are you so worried about losing the magazine, Max?'

'I'm worried about losing you.'

The two old friends stared at one another. After a moment, Max sighed and went back to tidying up the office.

Sandra let herself back into her flat cautiously and stood, listening for intruders. She opened her laptop and checked that the story file was intact. Knowing she hadn't been hacked, she breathed a sigh of relief and went back to packing her stuff. On a whim, she copied the story onto a flash drive, just in case. She'd decided to take a copy with her to the North Pennines. She opened the story file on the laptop just to check that it was all there; it was.

She downloaded a copy of the story onto a new flash drive and sent another copy to Max via Dropbox. Then, she collected her things for the trip to Northern England, but as she left, she couldn't shake the feeling that she was being watched.

48. Prison Walls

After Matt called the police in Bedford, he and Tony had been taken into custody. But where Matt's questioning had been relatively light, Tony had been subjected to hard interrogation by Special Branch. There was a warrant out for him under the Prevention of Terrorism Act but he'd stuck to his story. The meeting with Evans was an annual event that the three old comrades never missed. As far as Tony was concerned, he knew nothing about being wanted; he'd been working hard and taken a late break in Northumberland to write up some notes and have a rest. So far, so predictable, until the chest pains started. At first, he'd thought it was indigestion, but when he experienced shooting pains in both arms, he'd told his interrogators. Not surprisingly, they'd been sceptical until he collapsed. Fortunately, a doctor had been on hand and she'd had Tony rushed to hospital and placed in intensive care, where he remained for forty-eight hours. After a week, he'd been transferred to Belmarsh and solitary confinement. Meals were eaten in his cell, exercise was was an hour a day with a screw watching. Apart from that, he'd had no contact with the outside world. As the days slipped by, he'd felt himself being absorbed into the world of half-light, steel and concrete, his pallor fading to match the grey of his remand tracksuit. He hadn't heard from Matt or anyone else and he'd been denied news access in any form.

Like the Tower of London, Belmarsh is close to the river and its ceaseless surge of swirling currents and eddies. In February, mist seeps around the prison like a wraith, blurring perception and lowering spirits. Damp penetrates walls, clothing and bones causing inmates and screws alike to shiver involuntarily and stamp their feet. It is a state-of-the art, modern prison built in steel and concrete with high-tech security, but the pervading stench of cabbage, stale sweat and urine, together with nightly screams, were the usual signature of humans devoid of hope.

Denied books and reading matter, Tony remembered his training and attempted to keep his mind sharp with elaborate exercises. One of his favourites was remembering the trek across the moor in the blizzard with Pauline in minute detail. He wondered how she was and what she was doing, but, as one day merged into another, he'd felt himself sinking. Belmarsh is escape-proof, most prisoners blank out their ruined lives with a mixture of legal and illegal forms of anti-depressant. Thus far, Tony had refused all offers, but his resolve was weakening.

They came for him in the small hours. The screw shook him awake, then pointed to his clothes, indicating that he dress. He was escorted through the silent prison, waiting patiently as gate after gate was unlocked. Finally, he was directed across a freezing yard to the outer wall, all without a word being spoken. As he waited, another screw unlocked a heavy reinforced steel door, pulled it open and pushed him through into the outer darkness. The door banged shut behind him, leaving him alone in the freezing, damp dark of a winter night. A familiar voice spoke.

'Don't just stand there, Squaddie. You're a free man now,' the skirl of Matt's Ulster accent stronger than ever.

'What's going on?'

'Come on,' Matt said, clicking a key and causing the lights on a nearby SUV to light up. 'You've been sprung, so you have.'

Tony sat in the warmth of the vehicle and stared dreamily at the monochrome nightscape of the instrument panel and headlight shadows as they drove away. Matt indicated a thermos and some warmer clothes.

'Put those on and get some decent coffee inside you.' Tony did as he was told. Eventually, he looked at his old friend.

'Why?'

Matt raised his eyebrows. 'There's a job for us.'

Tony sighed. 'Don't tell me; we're on our own?'

'Not quite, old son. I couldn't have got you out of there without help.'

'Then, who?' Tony asked.

'All in good time. How're you feeling? '

'I've felt better.'

Tony had had a heart attack, but they'd got it early and there was little underlying disease. The quiet prison routine hadn't been great for his morale, but it had given his body a chance to heal.

'I was worried about you,' Matt said, consulting the Satnav on his phone.

'Why didn't you contact me?'

'I was being watched so I was.'

'Special Branch?'

Matt nodded. 'Something like that. They let me go after my interrogation but I was in the cross-hairs.'

Tony nodded. 'Did you manage talk to Billy Zed?'

Matt shook his head. 'I tried but he's in the wind. Soon as news about Evans got out, he got a flight to Morocco.'

They were out of the city, driving past hedgerows and fields. 'Where are we going anyway?' Tony asked.

'About twenty miles south, near Biggin Hill.'

'As in the Battle of Britain?'

'Aye son, we're the last of the fucking few, so we are.'

Tony got it. 'We're doing the job now?'

'That's the idea, bonny lad.' Matt grinned and gunned the engine.

Matt laid out the plan, such as it was. When he had finished, Tony shook his head. Matt grinned.

'Cheer up. It's better than being in Belmarsh.'

Tony sighed. 'What are you going to do, Matt, after?'

'Let's get this out of the way first, shall we?'

Tony shook his head. 'I want out.'

'To do what?'

'Something that doesn't involve people dying.

271

'You'd miss the buzz, so you would.'

'I don't think so.'

Matt regarded his friend with a look of concern. 'You're tired. Get some rest. I'll wake you nearer the time.'

The gentle motion of the vehicle, coupled with the warmth and comfort of the cockpit, caused Tony to first doze and then to sleep. He'd meant to ask after Pauline and Lissa, but he was asleep before he had the chance.

49. Up and Away

It was still dark when Milo and Tina came to get her. Pauline was dressed; she felt better wearing her own gear but, more importantly, she needed to keep Margaret's mobile hidden.

During the hours before dawn, she'd thought about Jonathan and his certainty about 'doing the right thing', how he'd been liquidated to encourage her. She remembered finding Fred Charlton and watching Bobby Evans expire on the carpet in his bungalow.

Tina and Milo grabbed an arm each and walked her down three flights of stone stairs to a damp cellar, where they sat her in an antique chair. Moss glistened in a corner and a metronomic plink of water dripping somewhere reminded Pauline of the disused swimming pool. Pauline didn't bother trying to struggle; she assumed that what Buchan had said was correct and that they needed her. Compared with the night before, the mood was warmer. Milo was moving his arm more freely and he and Tina chuckled and joked together. Tina peeled back Pauline's sleeve, inserted a hypodermic and carefully extracted a quantity of blood. When she was satisfied with the sample, Tina took it into an antechamber while Milo escorted Pauline upstairs to the kitchen where a fire crackled in the hearth. The Napoleon clock over the inglenook said it was six-fifteen; it was still dark outside. A few minutes later, Buchan entered carrying a sheet of A4 and looked around cheerfully.

'Alright?' He smiled and held up the sheet of paper triumphantly. 'Good news all round.'

'What?' Pauline asked.

'The viral fragment; it's already incubated. You slept with Tony; you're good to go!'

'When?'

'Now, this morning,' he smiled again. 'Sleep alright?'

Pauline shook her head. 'Not really.'

Buchan looked concerned. 'The bed's not bad.'

'It wasn't the bed that kept me awake,' Pauline hissed. 'I kept thinking of all the people you've murdered.' Buchan said nothing but his face hardened. 'How does it happen?' Pauline continued. 'How do you end up so empty and twisted that you don't understand what you've done? That you can just ignore it?' Again, Buchan didn't respond. Remembering Jane's advice, Pauline carried on. 'Once upon a time, you must have been young and idealistic. What happened?'

'I got old,' he snapped. 'I've been around too long. I know where the bodies are.'

'You buried most of them.'

'Seven grammes of lead,' Buchan smirked.

'What?'

'Stalin's maxim, the solution to every problem: lose the man, lose the problem.'

Pauline grimaced her distaste. 'Jonathan wasn't a problem that needed solving.'

Buchan shrugged. 'You were. The powerful have always paid to get rid of irritants.'

'Is that what Jonathan was? An irritant?' He grunted. 'They'll catch you, you know?'

'I doubt it,' he replied smoothly.

'They'll see you wheeling me away in the hospital on the CCTV.'

Buchan leaned down and put his face close to hers. His breath was stale, and he looked tired.

'This is my big bonanza. After this, I disappear.' He turned back and marched around the kitchen. It was working; she had nettled him.

'That's just a pipe dream.'

'I'll let you know,' Buchan muttered, checking his watch.

'You can go to the ends of the earth, where nobody knows anything about you but there's someone you can never outrun.'

'Who's that?' Buchan asked, looking at her sharply.

'You,' Pauline replied.

Buchan grinned, then cocked an ear. 'Did you hear something?' Everyone listened, but apart from the crackle of the burning logs in the grate, there was nothing. Buchan looked at Pauline.

'You were saying?'

Pauline nodded. 'This world of smoke and mirrors; you'd be lost without it.'

Just for a moment, a quizzical look appeared in Buchan's expression until a missile came through the kitchen window. It rolled across the stone floor, cracking and fizzing, before exploding with an ear-splitting roar. Simultaneously, the door was kicked open, and two hooded figures rushed in, carrying automatic weapons and shouting.

Buchan threw himself to the floor but Pauline was deafened by the explosion which muted the scene to a silent movie. She stood, turning slowly, bewildered and lost. In slow motion, she saw Milo fire an automatic pistol before he catapulted backwards against the kitchen wall and slumped to the floor. Pauline struggled to stay in control, but her legs gave way and she blacked out.

She was only unconscious for a moment, but when she came to, she found herself cradled in Matt's arms. He had removed his balaclava and was looking away from her. She followed his gaze to see Buchan holding Tony from behind with a kitchen knife at his throat. Tony's balaclava was also missing.

'Mexican stand-off,' Matt said. 'What now?'

'Swap,' Buchan snapped. 'Sleeping Beauty for Tony?'

'I don't think so,' Matt replied. 'I've got the gun.'

'I've got Tony,' Buchan responded, pressing the blade into the pulse of his jugular.

'Tony?' Pauline whispered.

Tony smiled. 'You OK?'

She nodded. 'What are you doing here?'

'We came to get you,' Tony grinned. He'd lost weight and looked vulnerable somehow.

'That's nice,' Pauline said, suddenly confused. 'Did I fall over?'

'You fainted, lassie,' Matt rasped.

'And gave me a chance,' Buchan grinned, pressing the blade deeper into the soft skin of Tony's neck.

Tony was pissed off. Right from the get-go, the plan had been shit: two old men, one recovering from a heart attack, with some ancient equipment on a wing and a prayer. The whole operation had been half-arsed, sanctioned but not officially, supported but not completely. And here they were, more Dad's Army than James Bond. And having gone to all this trouble, it had gone pear-shaped because Pauline had fainted.

'His life for hers,' Buchan repeated.

'Piss off,' Matt said.

'That's what you're going to do,' Buchan replied evenly, 'when I get her.'

Tony shook his head. 'Take Pauline and go, Matt.'

Matt shook his head. 'I'm not leaving anyone behind.'

Tony stared at him and shook his head again.

Buchan grinned. 'Think you might have to this time, Matt. By the way, that trick at your flat was impressive. Took us a while to get out.'

Matt grimaced. 'We haven't got all fucking day.'

There was a brief hiatus before Pauline broke the moment.

'Let Tony go,' she said, struggling to her feet. 'I'll stay here.'

'No!' Tony yelled.

She peered at him. 'He won't hurt me while I'm useful, Tony.'

'She's right,' Buchan muttered.

'This is fucked up,' Matt hissed. 'I've got automatic weapons; all he's got is a bleeding kitchen knife.'

'A razor-sharp kitchen knife,' Buchan replied.

Matt looked at Pauline. 'We came for you, Lassie. If we leave, you're on your own.'

Pauline grinned mirthlessly. 'I've been on my own from the start.'

In three short steps, she crossed the divide and stood next to Buchan. He grabbed her from behind and transferred the knife to her neck, shoving Tony away at the same time.

'Come on, Squaddie, time to go,' Matt ordered, but Tony didn't move.

'No,' he said, unmoving.

The last thing Pauline wanted was to see Matt and Tony leave. But, more than that, she didn't want anyone else to be hurt because of her.

'Go with Matt. Feed the cat till I get back,' she smiled.

Matt grabbed Tony and began to drag him back towards the door. Tony allowed himself to be pulled but he kept his eyes on Pauline until Matt checked the back door and pulled him outside.

Buchan held the knife blade against her flesh until they heard a car drive away. Then he relaxed, but not before cutting into the soft skin of her throat and drawing blood. Then he pushed her aside and checked the door before checking Milo's pulse.

'Is he alive?' Pauline asked.

Buchan ignored her. 'Did you know they were coming?'

Pauline frowned. 'No!'

'That distraction routine was clever.'

'What?'

'I was off-balance because of you.'

'For heaven's sake, this time yesterday, I was in hospital recovering from a major concussion. How could I have known? I didn't know where we were going.'

Buchan nodded. 'Maybe. But if you were a pro and you had distracted me, then maybe your fainting routine was another charade?'

'That's ridiculous!' Pauline protested. The cellar door opened and Tina appeared, an automatic pistol in her hand.

'It's alright, they've gone,' Buchan said.

Tina caught sight of Milo and ran to him. She put the gun on the floor and cradled his head before checking his pulse. Buchan went over and talked quietly. He put his arm around her but she shook him away and fussed over Milo. Pauline braced herself as Buchan crossed the kitchen back to her.

'What happens now?' Pauline asked.

Buchan stepped behind her, she felt a stinging sensation in her neck. She put her hand up to the pain as Buchan moved into view and she glimpsed the hypodermic in his hand.

'You're going to sleep for real this time,' he said. Once again, she felt her legs buckle as she fell into a deep, black pit.

50. Off the Rails

Sandra loved travelling by train because it reminded her of childhood. The endless muted browns and grey-greens of the winter landscape slipping by soothed her. With her phone turned off, nobody bothered her; she was in suspended animation and that was just what she needed or it should have been. The trouble was that she couldn't stop thinking about the break-in at the magazine and the vandalism at her flat. Despite her confident response to the attacks, Max hadn't backed her up. There was nothing new in the story; why was it so important? At St. Pancras, as she walked the short distance to Kings Cross Station, she reached into her bag and checked her phone. There were six calls from Max and a text telling her to call the office immediately. Sandra paused near the station entrance and punched in Max's number.

What's wrong?' she asked quietly.

'It's not there.'

'What?'

'The article.'

'Open the file. I sent you the link,' she shouted.

'The file's empty,' Max repeated.

Sandra was confused. 'I saw it last night before I sent it to you.'

'Did you check all of it?' Max asked.

'Yes. Well, I scrolled through.' She omitted to tell him that her laptop had said 'Zapovednik' aloud and posted a warning symbol over the text. 'What are we going to do?'

'Rewrite it.'

'I'm in London. I haven't got my computer with me.'

'Buy one,' Max ordered.

'I haven't got my notes,' she replied weakly, remembering the flash drive in her pocket.

'You said it was all in your head.'

'What about my holiday? I've paid for a week of intensive yoga.'

'Write it in your spare time. Get it to me by Wednesday. I'll fill in any gaps. I've got some background notes.'

'I thought you wanted to walk away?'

'Look, you were right about not backing down. La Respiration is our magazine in Paris. The dirty tricks are confirmation that we're doing our jobs.'

'I see,' Sandra replied. She was annoyed but Max was right about not giving in to pressure. And he had laid down a challenge, asking her to write the article from memory. She didn't know if she could, but she wasn't going to betray her doubts to him.

'Alright, Max.'

'Good,' he replied, sounding more like his old self.

'While I'm away, can you get my laptop from my apartment and take it to a computer technician? See what's happened to it; maybe retrieve the original.'

'Will do,' Max replied.

'I'll phone the concierge; tell her to let you in,' Sandra said, ending the call.

As she scanned the departure boards for her train, she felt better. She had a plan, and the challenge of rewriting the article while doing the yoga sessions with Annie was invigorating.

Normally, the second three-hour journey usually functioned like a slow-motion airlock, as the pressures of Paris were supplanted by the promise of the ancient northern hills. This time, there was no relaxing. Sandra retrieved a notebook and pen and began sketching out the article structure.

51. Low Winter Sun

Colonel Alistair Sebastian Buchan, MC, CBE, was not a happy bunny. Ever since Tony Brooks and Wharfedale Solutions started sniffing around Argentina Farm, the operation had been compromised. Matt and Tony turning up at the house; how had that happened? How come Tony Brooks wasn't locked up? How did they know where to find him? He had dealt with the situation but at the cost of Tina, who insisted on remaining with Milo at the house. It was annoying. Tina had been integral to this part of his scheme but battle plans rarely survive contact with the enemy. Tina had agreed to follow him north and meet up later. He was still on course to deliver and achieve his payday.

Unconscious in the passenger seat, Pauline slumbered on as Buchan drove through the midland lowlands on towards the north. They stopped at a lock-up outside Durham, where Buchan exchanged the black SUV for a metallic blue BMW. The difficult part was moving Pauline to the beamer on his own. It was first light and he didn't want any witnesses. She'd started to come round and he'd had to give her a second shot but at least he'd found the bloody mobile. It had fallen to the floor as he'd tipped her into the BMW's front passenger seat. Where the hell had she got that from? Another loose end. That must be how Matt and Tony knew where to come.

He shook his head. Not searching her after the hospital was a basic error. Giving her a second shot was another 'no-no' but he had no choice. She'd done well for an amateur and that nagged him. A few hours later, Pauline began to moan and wriggle in her seat. She was coming round.

It was like rising out of a swamp. She could see lighter patches above, and she tried to point towards the glow, but it kept changing position. At the same time, she became aware of a low hum accompanied by a familiar, mild vibration and opened her eyes. Low winter sun flared into her eyes out of a pale blue sky. They passed a road sign for Hexham; Buchan looked across and grunted.

'You're back with us? How do you feel?'

'Groggy.'

'It'll wear off.'

'Where are we going?'

'An Air B&B in Hexham for evenings, then Allendale during the day for your yoga session.' Buchan explained.

'Why?'

'That's where the target's going.'

'It's years since I did any yoga.'

'You've done pilates; same difference.'

'Won't they smell a rat when I don't know what I'm doing?' Pauline asked.

Buchan grinned. 'You'll probably only do one session before she gets ill.'

'Was Tony going to join in the yoga?'

Buchan shrugged. 'We would have engineered a meeting.'

Pauline absorbed this and looked around the car. 'And afterwards?'

Buchan grinned. 'Haven't got that far.'

Pauline nodded. 'Where's Tina?'

'She stayed behind to look after Milo.'

'On her own?'

'Yes,' Buchan said quietly, staring at the road ahead.

'How is he?'

'Should be OK. The bullet went straight through and didn't hit any bones or organs. I left plenty of medical supplies. He's young, fit.'

'You're not worried?'

Buchan shrugged. 'Milo's been well-paid.'

'Is Tina a doctor?

Buchan nodded. 'Not the kind you mean, but she's a clever woman.'

'Really?'

'Learnt English and Italian from watching TV in Bucharest. She migrated to Italy when she was ten years old. Studied hard and got a PhD in biochemistry.'

'How did you meet her?'

'She was working on viral immunity in a research institute when she chanced upon a pathogen that caused cardiac arrest. She understood its implications immediately and brought it to us.'

'Really?'

Buchan nodded. 'Foreign national with a brilliant mind, she was on our radar.'

'I see.'

'She perfected the viral fragment delivery method. It's really very neat.'

'If you know the genome of the target, you only need one fragment?'

'Something like that. Apparently, it's a matter of protein manipulation—complicated but much simpler once the technique is perfected.'

'Surely you didn't know Jonathan's genome or Charlton's?' Pauline asked.

Buchan shook his head. 'No. They got an injection of the full virus with a mini hypodermic which leaves a tiny puncture wound. The recipient dies of a heart attack and the virus dissipates.'

'Right,' Pauline said, watching long, bleak hills flash by. 'Are Milo and Tina an item?'

Buchan laughed. 'Milo's a second cousin. Tina feels responsible to the family. Very clannish, Romanians.'

Pauline nodded. 'What happens to Tina afterwards? Is she an irritant?'

Buchan grinned. 'I'll pay her what she's owed and she'll head off into the sunset with or without her cousin.'

'Like you?'

Buchan nodded. 'Yes.'

'What if the target genome is incorrect?'

'It isn't. It's been checked recently,' Buchan smiled.

'Who is it then?' Pauline said after a moment. 'Who's the target?'

Buchan shrugged. 'A French journalist called Alessandra Bianchi, a longtime irritant, but her latest story has annoyed the hell out of a foreign government.'

'What's the story about?'

'A top-secret facility in a Siberian nature reserve.'

'Russian then, the irritated foreign government?' Buchan nodded. 'Don't they do their own killing?'

'Yes, but in a modern 21st-century way. They've been thinking about outsourcing their 'wet work' for some time. The trouble is, in this brave new digital world, anyone with a laptop can find incriminating camera footage as we saw with the Skripals.'

'Wet work?'

'Assassination, elimination, killing. Shooting people is so last century but if an irritant dies of natural causes, it's sad, but that's it. That's the beauty of this new technique.'

'Which you're selling to them?'

Buchan nodded. 'When Alessandra's passing is announced in the press, I'll receive the first installment. Then, when I'm far away, I'll send them the instruction manual.'

'That's disgusting.'

Buchan shrugged. 'Depends on your point of view. This technique is the first step on a new continent of possibilities. It'll give them a head start for a year or two until the others catch up. '

'Others?'

'The rest of the world. Poisoning has been a global arms' race since before the Romans.'

'Is that what the new facility in the Siberian reserve is for?'

Buchan nodded. 'They're obsessed with secrecy.'

'Charming.'

'Stop being so bloody protestant about it. All you have to do,

Pauline, is enjoy some yoga sessions in a mountain retreat.'

'What if I don't want to?' She asked, but she already knew the answer.

'Lavinia,' he smiled. 'After a difficult start, she's done well for herself. Qualified as a teaching assistant in her spare time plus she's an excellent mother. Be a shame to mess that up.'

Pauline feigned indifference and looked out of the car window, but Buchan wasn't finished.

'I found the phone.'

Despite herself, Pauline looked at him wide-eyed.

'I didn't see that coming. I thought you were a technophobe.'

'What did you do with it?'

He looked at her and drummed his fingers on the leather steering wheel. With his small, sharp teeth, there was something ratlike about the activity.

'No more tricks, Pauline.' He turned back to the road. Pauline felt her hope dissolve.

52. Hexham

Annie Morgan looked at her watch for the umpteenth time as she waited outside Hexham railway station. A traffic warden was checking parked cars and giving them tickets. Annie was on edge, worried about the lack of space on the back seat which was stuffed with yoga mats and other exercise equipment and nervous about telling Sandra that she'd double-booked herself. She'd rehearsed different versions of the speech in the bathroom mirror a few times, but it never came out right. Annie was looking the other way when the passenger door opened and Sandra got in, tossing a small rucksack onto the yoga mats in the back. Annie smiled a welcome, but Sandra was uncharacteristically brusque.

'Take me to a shop,' she ordered.

'It's alright. I've got everything we need at the house,' Annie smiled, but Sandra shook her head impatiently.

'I need a new laptop.'

'What?'

'I've got to rewrite an article while I'm here.'

Annie thought for a moment and nodded. 'I think there's somewhere nearby.'

'Let's go there.'

Annie smiled and started her ageing Micra. 'Is everything OK?'

Sandra nodded. 'Why?'

'You've never written anything during our sessions before.'

'It's a rewrite.' Annie looked at her. 'It shouldn't take long.'

Annie took a deep breath. 'Sandra, there may be another client at our yoga sessions this week.' Sandra looked at Annie sharply, her brow furrowed. 'They offered a six-week booking at the same time. I couldn't afford to turn it down.'

'You need money?'

Annie nodded. 'I've been losing clients to the internet and Ziggi is off to college in September.'

Sandra dipped her head to one side. 'Who is this other client?'

Annie shrugged. 'No idea. They've booked and paid a deposit but I haven't heard from them recently. I was expecting an email confirming everything.'

Sandra absorbed this. 'Six weeks is a very long booking.'

Annie nodded. 'I know.'

'Staying in the house with us?'

Annie shook her head. 'Of course not. She's got her own place. We can still explore and go to cafes.'

Sandra grinned. She had left Paris uncertain and worried but the wet northern market town was a world away from La Respiration. Whatever happened, she would rewrite the article and enjoy the yoga.

53. Salute the Sun

The evening before the first yoga session, Buchan ordered a takeaway curry. Buchan devoured his portion while Pauline picked at her food.

'You need to eat,' he said as he drank some beer. 'We don't want you falling ill before the job's completed.'

'What if it doesn't work? What if Alessandra doesn't get ill?'

'That would be a shame,' Buchan smiled.

'Why?'

'I've lodged a letter with a solicitor detailing your daughter's earlier transgressions. If I don't get in touch, that letter will be forwarded to the appropriate authorities. At the very least, she'll lose her teaching position.' Pauline watched as Buchan spooned more curry onto his plate.

Next morning, Buchan drove Pauline to the lonely cottage on the ridge in the valley of the West Allen. The BMW drove off in a cloud of dust, leaving Pauline standing alone. She didn't want to be there, didn't want to do yoga and didn't want to be the angel of death for someone she had never met. She didn't want to but she had no choice.

Pauline hung back like a kid at a new school but Annie welcomed her with an exuberant hug, admiring her leggings and top. Pauline tried to pull away but the bubbly Geordie just held her more tightly. Because it was an unusually warm and sunny morning, Annie decided that they would work outside on the terrace overlooking the valley. Pauline was relieved; the virus didn't transmit as well outside. Three yoga mats were laid out on the apron, each with a bottle of water. Pauline chose the one furthest away from the others and surveyed the view.

Below the cottage, the steep hillside fell away towards the fields in the valley bottom. Sheep dotted the lower pastures, as did an occasional cow. Lapwings swooped and tumbled in the warm air accompanied by the occasional bubbling call of a curlew. Across the valley, the opposite fell-side was green and lush. 'Infectious, isn't it?' Annie smiled.

'What?'

'The view, the sunshine, feels as if spring is on its way.'

Pauline nodded and wondered where the 'target' was'. Just before ten o'clock, Annie checked her phone and ducked her head towards Pauline.

'Sandra isn't coming.'

Pauline smiled, relieved but curious. 'Why?'

'She's got some work to do.' Pauline looked blank. 'So, it's just us.'

Pauline nodded. 'Right.'

A grandfather clock in the entrance hall struck ten o'clock, Annie stood at the end of her mat. Pauline followed suit and the session began. Annie explained in a few words that the approach was about identifying tension and reducing stress. Lying on her back, Pauline did her best but the idea of letting go of all the stress she was feeling was ridiculous. Nevertheless, she got through the morning session and had to admit she did feel more relaxed. Sandra appeared as they were eating a sandwich. Annie was delighted and fussed over the willowy newcomer; Pauline kept her distance. Sandra nodded but made no effort at small talk. After a few minutes, the sun disappeared behind a cloud and the temperature plummeted. The three women moved inside the conservatory and the yoga got serious. Annie abandoned her explanations; Pauline was left trying to follow the others who seemed to have a telepathic rapport. With minimal indication, Sandra and Annie spent long periods in difficult, painful postures. Pauline attempted to copy them and was grateful for the morning session she'd had on her own. Towards the end of the session, she began to feel pain in her left side. She was still struggling to stand when Sandra nodded to her and walked away. In the distance, the sound of a motorbike as it downshifted and climbed out of the valley briefly dominated before fading.

'Well, how did it go?' Buchan asked as they drove back towards Hexham.

'She wasn't there this morning,' Pauline replied. 'Sandra.'

'Why the hell not?'

Pauline shrugged. 'She had work to do—something urgent.'

'Bollocks!' Buchan roared, almost colliding with a tractor.

'She turned up for the afternoon session,' Pauline offered when they were driving more sedately.

Buchan thought about it. 'Well, the afternoon should be enough to infect her.'

By evening, Buchan was much more cheerful. The pain in Pauline's side intensified and began to throb. The yoga had awakened muscle and bone memories that the hospital hadn't detected. Pauline tried to tell Buchan but he insisted on taking her to a hotel near the Roman Wall to celebrate. He ordered steak and chips for both of them and an expensive bottle of red. Preoccupied with her aches and pains, Pauline ate without pleasure.

Next day, the weather mirrored the first day; clear skies and warm sunshine in the morning and no Sandra until after lunch when they ventured indoors. Buchan was annoyed when he heard that Sandra had been unaffected by illness.

'Are you sure she was alright?' Buchan asked as they drove back to the villa.

'We did another hard two-hour session; she seemed fine.'

'Why is she still walking around? Bobby Evans was dead in three hours.'

'Jonathan didn't get three minutes.'

Back at the villa, Buchan pushed Pauline into her bedroom. 'Strip!' He shouted.

'What?'

'Undress. Get your bloody clothes off!'

Pauline did as she was ordered. 'Is this really necessary?'

'After the mobile phone bollocks, I should have checked daily.'

When he was satisfied that there was nothing to find, he looked at Pauline's body and nodded.

'Kept yourself in shape?'

Pauline hated being naked in front of him, putting her arms over her breasts and crossing her legs, but he wasn't interested. He told her to dress before extracting some blood from her arm. He produced a small probe attached to a transformer, which he plugged into the mains. The other end was dipped into the blood sample.

'What are you doing?' Pauline asked.

'Just checking that you have enough of the virus. Very clever this detector. Could make someone a fortune.'

Pauline wasn't interested. 'Have I?'

'What?'

'Got the virus?'

'Plenty.'

With that, he left, locking the door behind him.

Over breakfast, he quizzed Pauline about the yoga, making her draw a diagram of their positions in the conservatory. Pauline did so, and he shouted with fury.

'You didn't get close enough!' She shook her head and began to protest but he overrode her. 'Today, hug her!' Pauline frowned. 'I'll be watching with binoculars. Grab her and give her the continental greeting, a kiss on both cheeks and a bear hug.' Pauline stared. 'Got it?'

'Yes.'

Next day, Sandra appeared for the morning session, which they did outside on the new stone terrace. Again, she appeared aloof, paying little attention to Pauline. The session was strenuous and had them all giggling when Annie farted while attempting a headstand. The moment broke the ice and Sandra relaxed. Pauline couldn't join in and enjoy the session. At the conclusion, Sandra came over and hugged her. Pauline was horrified and tried to pull away, but Sandra held her and whispered in her ear.

'Do not worry.'

Pauline pulled away and looked at Sandra, confused. They

moved inside for the afternoon session but Pauline couldn't engage with the exercises.

Unlike the previous evening, Buchan was cock-a-hoop. 'You did it! I saw you.'

'What happens now?' Pauline asked.

'We'll confirm that she's had a cardiac arrest tomorrow, then we can go.' Pauline nodded but wondered what Sandra had meant by her inscrutable whisper.

Dinner at a local pizzeria was subdued. Pauline assumed that she would soon be surplus to requirements. So much had happened to her since helping Tony in the church that she didn't bother to consider the future. She drank heavily and slept fitfully, waking with a thick head.

Thursday's drive up to the isolated cottage was tense; neither of them spoke as they pondered what was to come.

Only two mats were laid out on the terrace, facing down the valley. Sandra appeared and smiled.

'How are you?' Pauline asked, confused.

'Tres bien, merci.' Sandra looked fine.

Pauline went up to her and whispered. 'Go inside and lock the doors and windows.'

'No, it is such a beautiful morning, we have yoga to do.'

'Is Annie alright?'

Sandra nodded. 'I gave her the day off.'

Pauline grabbed Sandra's wrist and whispered. 'They want you dead.'

Sandra nodded and smiled. 'You and I are going to do yoga together. Shall we begin?' Sandra went and laid down on her mat. Pauline did the same and they began their warm-up. Pauline was still stretching when she realised Sandra had stopped. Tilting her head, Pauline looked back and saw Buchan standing at the edge of the stone terrace, a gun in his hand. Pauline slowly got to her feet and faced him. His face was red and he was breathing noisily through his nose; he took a step towards them. Pauline and Sandra both took a step backwards.

'Why aren't you ill?' Buchan spat at Sandra. Sandra shrugged.

'It hasn't worked,' Pauline hissed at Buchan.

'I'll shoot her then.'

'But that won't get you the big payday, will it? The big money was selling them the method. It hasn't worked.'

Buchan was like a boiler without a safety valve. He jerked this way and that, shaking his head, waving the gun and muttering. 'It should have worked. It should have bloody-well worked.'

'You are not Russian?' Sandra asked.

'You don't miss much,' Buchan sneered. 'What did you do, Pauline?' Pauline was about to reply, but another voice answered first.

'She do nothing. You are the one who do something.'

The figure of Tina stood at the side of the house, pointing a shotgun. Buchan shook his head, but Tina wasn't finished. 'You kill Milo.'

'It was a flesh wound. You had enough medicine. Something must have gone wrong.'

'You poison him!'

Buchan shook his head again. 'Why on earth would I do that?'

'Because he is loose-end, like me.'

'It's not true, Tina. He must have died from the gunshot.'

'I develop the poison. I know symptoms. You kill him.'

Buchan opened his hands. 'Milo was a hothead, a loose cannon. He wouldn't have been able to keep his mouth shut.'

'He was my cousin,' Tina hissed.

Buchan grinned. 'Is that why you care about him so much?'

Tina's eyes were bulging; she was swaying from side to side. Buchan took a risk and fired from the hip. He got lucky and hit her in the chest.

Tina swore in Romanian and collapsed to the terrace; the shotgun clattered across the concrete. Buchan was distracted and not fully in control. Pauline took a step towards him; Sandra joined her.

'Get back. I'll shoot both of you!' Buchan shouted.

'You just shot Tina. She was your friend.'

'No friends in this business!' Buchan hissed.

'You've nowhere else to go.' Pauline said evenly. 'No fall-back position.'

Tina lay on her back, her right hand fluttering like a wounded bird, and muttering to herself. Buchan looked from her to Pauline and Sandra; he'd run out of options. That had never happened to him before. He, Colonel Buchan, MC CBE, Coldstream Guards, was about to lose and he didn't like it.

'Why aren't you infected?' Buchan spat.

Sandra smiled but said nothing. Buchan looked at Pauline. 'Was it you?'

Sandra smiled again. 'Not her.'

'Too bad for you then,' he said, checking his gun and aiming it at Sandra. It was clear he intended to get rid of all of them but Pauline had other ideas. As Buchan half-turned to Sandra, Pauline aimed a kick at his crotch with all her strength and connected spectacularly, causing him to double up and drop his gun. Pauline snatched the weapon up. Sandra nodded to Pauline appreciatively. 'Thank you.'

Pauline nodded back and sighed. Grimacing with pain, Buchan slowly straightened and faced Pauline. 'So, what now?'

A pulse began throbbing in Pauline's temple. Despite the morning sun, a cold breeze had sprung up, ruffling the trees nearby. In the distance, the motorbike changing gear could be heard again as it careered along the valley road. Was it only three months since she'd taken pity on a dishevelled stranger in St. Leonard's church? It might as well have been three millennia. Pauline had changed; night had entered her soul. She remembered Jonathan's bobbing diffidence as she'd railed against his certainties. Buchan interrupted her train of thought.

'You sure you're not a pro, Pauline?' Pauline said nothing. Buchan shook his head. 'You won't shoot me.'

'No?' Pauline asked and aimed the automatic at Buchan's heart.

'You haven't got the stomach,' he said ruefully. 'Why don't you give me the guns?'

'Go to hell,' Pauline hissed.

'Pity, I could use someone like you.'

'Like you used Tina?'

'She'd become expendable, like her hotheaded cousin.'

Buchan took a half-step towards them. He smiled, then stopped. A puzzled look appeared on his face as his left eye exploded. His body went slack and he crumpled to the terrace. Tina was half sitting and holding another gun, her face a rictus of effort and rage. Seeing Buchan's collapse, she gasped and fell back.

Pauline felt light-headed; the air around her seemed to shimmer and she was convinced she was going to faint, but it was Sandra who sank to the ground. As Tina's blood drained slowly across the terrace to mingle with Buchan's, the prone figures were outlined in the late winter sun, but it was Pauline, still standing, who cast the longest shadow.

54. Nightfall

It was bitterly cold in the abandoned quarry above the cottage; a heavy frost was already forming on the upland tussock grass. Despite being sheltered by the south-facing hill, a harsh wind buffeted the trees. The three women couldn't risk using a flash light but the new moon gave them enough brightness to work. The silvery gleam cast gigantic shadows illuminating their ethereal breath as they hauled the bodies of Tina and Buchan into the abandoned mine shaft. Rock formations protruded from the hillside like the bones of the earth, so that their exertions felt like an intrusion.

After the shooting, Pauline checked Tina's pulse and then helped Sandra to her feet.

'Is she dead?' Sandra asked. Pauline nodded and sighed as a motorbike skidded to a halt on the stone terrace. The rider took off her helmet, assembled a collapsible crutch, and hobbled towards them. It was Lissa.

'You?' Pauline gasped.

'Someone had to rescue the wrinklies,' Lissa grinned. 'Where do you think Sandra got her anti-virals?'

'Anti-virals?' Pauline frowned.

'So what are we going to do about them?' Sandra asked, nodding to the bodies of Buchan and Tina.

'If you're gonna call the cops, me and Pauline will have to go,' Lissa said, looking around furtively.

'Both of you?' Sandra asked.

Lissa nodded. 'It all makes more sense if it's just you.'

'Does it?' Sandra asked. Lissa and Pauline explained the

details of Buchan's mission and the real reason the Russians wanted to kill her.

'Then, I will need to rewrite the story,' she said. 'But I would rather not call the police.'

'What do we do then?' Pauline asked.

'Bury them,' Lissa whispered.

Pauline looked around. 'The ground's too rocky.'

Lissa nodded. 'There's an abandoned mine shaft in the quarry up there,' she said, pointing to the hillside behind the cottage. 'You can't see it from the road.'

Sandra shook her head. 'Will that work?'

'Buchan wasn't supposed to be here. He's off the radar, false papers, the works.'

'And Tina?' Pauline asked.

'She's the same,' Lissa insisted, then frowned and indicated her crutch. 'You two will have to do the donkey work.'

Pauline looked at Sandra, who nodded; it was decided. The three women went into the cottage and waited for darkness.

Before they began, they wrapped each body in an old blanket, which they soaked in creosote to disguise the smell. For Sandra, the night-time exertion was oddly cathartic, reminiscent of her childhood in the Dolomites. As she dragged and sweated the dead weights up the fellside, she realised that she wanted a garden to go back to, somewhere to grow and nurture new life when she returned from her trips. And while Pauline and Sandra struggled with the wheelbarrow that carried the two bodies the hundred metres or so uphill, Lissa checked the tunnel. She unscrewed the metal gate and then insisted that Pauline and Sandra deposit the bodies thirty metres inside the hill. The ceiling was low, and the going was difficult in places.

'So far from the entrance?' Sandra gasped.

'Just keep pushing the wheelbarrow, will you?' Lissa had a phone flashlight, which she aimed at the floor to help them as they struggled into the hill.

Finally, the three women were half standing, half crouching over the cadavers wrapped in their blankets. Pauline and Sandra were breathing heavily and covered in sweat. They stood for a moment.

'Should we say something?' Sandra asked.

'He was a bastard. Let him rot,' Lissa muttered.

There was a pause while they absorbed this. Pauline was the first to respond.

'Tina wasn't much better, but I'm sorry she's dead.'

Sandra nodded, but Lissa shook her head. 'It was her choice. Come on; let's go back down to the cottage.'

'We're leaving them here?' Pauline asked.

'They'll be alright until I get some explosives. I'll come back in a couple of days.'

'Explosive?' Sandra asked.

'Just enough to bring the roof down so it looks like a rock fall. Then I'll put the railings back in place across the entrance.'

They retraced their steps back down the tunnel. At the entrance, Pauline stopped.

'There's a letter,' she whispered. The other two looked at her. 'If Buchan doesn't report in, a letter about Lavinia will be sent to the authorities.'

'Could he be bluffing?' Sandra asked. Pauline shrugged.

'I'll sort it,' Lissa said.

'How?'

'I know someone who will. Now come on, Let's go back to the cottage.'

Next morning, the three women embraced one another before Lissa climbed onto her motorbike and Pauline drove Buchan's BMW back down the valley. After dumping the car near Alston, Lissa carried Pauline back to Bridgford on her pillion. As Pauline dismounted, Lissa gave her a hug.

'What was that for?' Pauline asked.

'I thought you needed it,' Lissa replied.

Pauline sighed. 'Thanks.'

'Why did you do it?' Lissa asked.'

'It seemed like the right thing to do.'

Lissa absorbed this. 'Bloody brave, Pauline.'

Pauline stared at the familiar landscape around her cottage. She couldn't think of anything to say so she shrugged and walked awkwardly towards her front door. She got the front door key in the door but found that she couldn't open it. Then, everything went black.

November 2019
Northumberland

55. The Cottage

It was a wet, northern November day, persistent rain falling from brooding clouds in a darkening sky. Terrible weather but great cover, Pauline noted as she scanned the woods and the skyline beyond. She switched her focus to the garden, where Luna and Miriam chased each other around, screaming with laughter. Luna was five and Miriam seven, but, despite the inevitable disputes, they played happily with each other most of the time. Luna had pink wellies and a matching waterproof, while Miriam's colour was mauve. They had accepted the idea of Pauline being their grandmother easily.

'They're getting soaked,' Pauline said as Lavinia joined her at the back door.

Lavinia grinned. 'They've got anoraks and wellies. They'll be fine.'

'They're amazing.'

'They're young, Pauline. They don't see the weather.'

'No shade, no shine, no butterflies, no bees. No fruits, no flowers, no leaves, no birds November.'

'What's that?' Lavinia asked.

'Some poetry from school, seems appropriate,' Pauline replied.

'Yes.'

The two women stood for a moment before turning back into the kitchen. They had agreed to call each other by their Christian names, but they were still awkward.

'About your suggestion?' Lavinia began. 'Last night?'

Pauline looked at her daughter apprehensively and braced herself. After they'd put the girls to bed, mother and daughter chatted over a bottle of wine. Despite telling herself to take things steadily, the wine had gone to Pauline's head and she'd blurted out an invitation for Lavinia and the girls to come for Christmas. Instead of saying yes immediately, Lavinia had become quiet before saying that she wanted to sleep on it. As a consequence, Pauline had slept fitfully, worrying that she had overdone it.

'You've made a decision?'

Lavinia's reply was cut off by a loud banging on the front door. Pauline frowned.

'Expecting someone?' Lavinia asked.

Pauline shook her head and fought to keep the apprehension from her face. She wasn't expecting anyone, certainly not the figure of Jane Percival standing under a large umbrella.

'Jane? What are you doing here?'

'I was in the vicinity. I thought I'd drop by. Mind if I come in out of the rain?'

Pauline moved aside as Jane collapsed the umbrella and bustled past. Pauline did mind; it was bloody inconvenient. It was Lavinia and the girls' first visit to the cottage; Pauline didn't want it messed up. The sound of the girls shrieking in the back garden percolated through the tiny vestibule. Jane looked at Pauline.

'I'm sorry. You have visitors?'

'You could have phoned,' Pauline said as she opened the door to the living room. Lavinia appeared from the kitchen.

'Oh, hello, my name's Jane Percival,' Jane said, putting her hand out to Lavinia. Pauline had a momentary panic as she wondered how to introduce Lavinia.

'Hi, I'm Lavinia, Pauline's daughter,' Lavinia replied and shook Jane's hand. Sometimes, the most significant events pass as an anti-climax. Pauline found herself welling up; it was the first time that Lavinia acknowledged her as her mother.

They had finally met face-to-face at on the last Saturday in April. Lavinia had suggested a cafe in the Lace Market in Nottingham but the place was standing-room noisy and they ended up moving to a tiny pub. Pauline was amazed by her daughter; she was beautiful with an oval face and her father's dark eyes. Lavinia listened to Pauline's story about her pregnancy and her regret and heartache over Lavinia's adoption. When she explained that Lavinia's father had done a runner when he'd found out that she was pregnant, Lavinia nodded in recognition. She too had been abandoned and had had a hard time as a single parent. It was a good meeting but both women were wary. Pauline booked into a city centre hotel for a week; she and Lavinia met three more times and began to warm to one another. Lavinia wanted to know more about her half-brother, Robert and Pauline was keen to find out about Lavinia's childhood and teenage years. Lavinia had had a tough time and wasn't about to welcome Pauline with open arms, unlike her daughters, who accepted their new grandmother enthusiastically as if it happened every day. Whatever the reason, Pauline was grateful for their uncritical acceptance.

The main difficulty between Pauline and Lavinia was that there were things that Pauline couldn't explain, such as why it had taken three months to meet after the first contact. She said she'd been ill but Lavinia knew there was more to it than that. Pauline hated not telling her but ignorance was the best protection for her and the girls. As a reassuring counterweight, she'd told Lavinia that she had no other living relatives. Lavinia had nodded and that's how it had been left. They were still feeling each other out.

Jane Percival smiled at Lavinia. 'Do you mind if I have a few minutes with your mother?'

Lavinia grinned. 'Of course not. Can I get you anything? Coffee, tea?'

Jane shook her head. 'No, thank you; I won't be here long enough. Is there somewhere we can talk, Pauline?'

Pauline led Jane upstairs to the cramped spare bedroom and faced her.

'What do you want, Jane?'

'To see you, my dear, see how you're getting on.'

Pauline looked at Jane and snorted. 'Don't talk bollocks. Say what you want to say.'

Jane thought about this for a moment, then dipped her head in acceptance. 'We want you to come and work for us.'

'Who's we?'

'Oh very well, me. I want you to come back.'

'I don't want to,' Pauline began, but Jane cut her off.

'It wouldn't be full-time, just now and then. You'll be well paid for your time and obviously, we will continue to keep an eye on Lavinia and the girls.'

Pauline sighed. She was happy, happier than she would have thought possible a year ago, but now there was always a 'but'. Before she had made contact with Lavinia and met the girls, Pauline had only had herself but her new extended family brought a boatload of fear. And now there was Jane.

'You are so very good at it, my dear,' Jane smiled. 'But that's not really surprising, is it?' She paused. 'Considering?'

'Considering what?'

'Environmental Activism.'

Pauline looked at Jane and let out a long sigh. 'I see.'

'We did some digging. You're a pro, or you were.'

Pauline sighed. 'I was twenty-two when the French blew up 'Rainbow Warrior' in Auckland Harbour. After losing Lavinia, I was angry. I wanted to do something, a lot of us did. I went to New Zealand and joined a local group. It was all rather amateurish.'

Jane looked at her. 'You were trained?'

Pauline nodded. 'Short courses: fieldcraft, spotting tails, basic security.'

'Firearms?' Jane asked. 'I hear you're a crack shot?'

Pauline smiled and shook her head. 'No, I worked as a courier.'

'Why did you stop?'

'I fell in love with my instructor, Ralph. Then, I fell pregnant.'

'Ralph? He was your husband?'

Pauline nodded. 'Until our son was killed.'

Jane nodded and sighed sympathetically.

305

'Why now, Jane? After six months?'

'I wanted to wait until you were your old self.'

'You've got something you want me to do?'

'No, but it helps to have one's ducks in a row, in case?'

'The shit hits the fan?' Pauline offered. 'You've got the formula now, haven't you?' Jane took a deep breath but said nothing. 'Have you used it? Are you going to?'

Jane emitted a posh chuckle. 'Of course not. We're the ones in the white hats. Besides, I think you owe it to us, don't you?'

'Because of Buchan?'

Jane pursed her lips. 'No.'

Pauline remembered the mine-working and sighed. She looked at Jane. 'Is it a problem?'

'Not unless he comes back. The last thing the government wants is a story about an honoured British colonel selling state secrets to the Russians going viral. And now that their plan has gone south, it's the last thing the Russians want too.'

Pauline absorbed that. 'Right.'

'Don't look so glum, Pauline; I'll make sure Lissa's in your corner.'

'You sent her to Allendale?'

When Lissa had appeared on the noisy motorbike and banged on the door of the cottage, Sandra had been wary of the foul-mouthed, tattooed English urchin who claimed to be a fan and urged her to take some unmarked tablets. But when Lissa cited every article Sandra had written for La Respiration and even critiqued them, Sandra called Max. He'd heard whispers about a new poison and, given the strange events in Paris before Sandra's trip, he urged Sandra to take the tablets, which she did. And when Pauline and then Buchan appeared at the cottage, Sandra had been prepared.

Sandra's rewritten article about illicit construction in a Russian nature reserve with its scoop about the top-secret poison facility had gone global, securing the magazine's future and Sandra's name. It also put pressure on the Putin regime to sign up for a European environmental agreement.

After the shootings, Pauline had collapsed at her cottage and been taken to the RVI in Newcastle. She hadn't fully recovered from the motorbike accident and the hospital had kept her in for another five weeks. Lissa had visited on crutches.

'How're you doing?' She'd asked gently and kissed her cheek.

'Better now, thanks,' Pauline replied.

Lissa dragged a chair to the bedside and collapsed onto it. She looked at Pauline and grinned. 'Who's the fucking dark horse, then?'

Pauline frowned. 'What are you on about?'

'Karate kick to the balls?'

'That was just luck.'

'What about the top-of-the range mobile that you phoned Jane with?'

'You know Jane?'

'Who do you think gave me the anti-virals for Alessandra?'

'Right.'

'She'd been working on an antidote cocktail. She asked me to come and help you.'

Pauline nodded. 'What happened after the crash in Bedford?'

'I was hurt, a hairline fracture of my left femur, but I could still walk, just,' Lissa winced at the memory. 'Sorry about leaving you; I didn't like that.'

'You had no choice,' Pauline lay back on the pillow. Then something occurred to her. 'Did you tell Oliver Campion where I was?'

Lissa nodded. 'It was Jane's idea.'

Nothing was ever quite what it seemed. 'Any news of the others?'

Lissa grinned. 'I've brought someone to see you.'

Lissa hopped away as Tony appeared in the doorway, grinning sheepishly.

'Pauline?' He asked hesitantly.

'Come here,' Pauline beckoned, her arms wide. They hugged and held the pose for a long time.

'I'll go and get some diet coke,' Lissa whispered and slipped away. After a while, Tony pulled away and looked at Pauline tenderly.

'How are you?'

'Better than the last time I saw you,' she said, remembering when he and Matt tried to rescue her.

'Really though, how are you now?'

'Much, much better,' she smiled, but her experiences had left an indelible mark. And Tony had suffered too. Something had been taken from both of them.

A couple of months after Pauline left the RVI, he stayed at the cottage for a long weekend. They talked, walked, and slept together; it was lovely but without the pressure of the chase, there was something vaguely unreal about their coupling. They both had secrets that they couldn't or wouldn't divulge. Tony was a career spook and so used to keeping secrets that the ability to be open had atrophied. And Pauline, too, had grown used to keeping her own counsel. She told Tony about Allendale but omitted any mention of Jane Percival. When she'd called Jane from Buchan's manor house, Pauline had agreed to continue on condition that Lavinia and the girls were placed under some kind of protection. Jane had agreed.

After their weekend together, Pauline and Tony stayed in touch, and he'd visited a few times. It was lovely, and they worked well together. Despite their secrets, their emotional rigidities had begun to slacken. They began to imagine a future with one another and the cat was pleased to see him. Tony hadn't met Lavinia and the girls yet, but that was next on Pauline's agenda. A new start living an ordinary, open life with Pauline's daughter, grand-daughters, Tony and the cat.

And yet, here she was, in her spare bedroom with Jane Percival, making secrets again. 'It seems I don't have much choice,' Pauline said quietly.

'That's the ticket,' Jane said briskly. 'Now, I'd better let you get on with your weekend.'

Pauline nodded. 'Were you really in the vicinity, or was that another lie?'

'I'm not that devious; well, maybe I am. I had to come up

here; a problem at Argentina Farm.'

'I thought it had been shut down?'

Jane pursed her lips. 'A misguided former employee thought he'd restart it. We had to correct his misapprehension.'

Pauline shuddered at the memory. 'So it's sorted now?'

Jane shrugged. 'Hopefully.'

'What does that mean?'

'A bird may have been sent to China,' Jane replied. 'A lab in a place called Wuhan.'

'Really?' Pauline asked, wide-eyed.

'Don't worry, he had no time to prepare. If the creature ever had any active virus, it's almost certainly decayed by now.' Jane patted Pauline on the arm. 'Rest assured, the culprit is under lock and key.'

Pauline sighed and followed Jane down the stairs. Lavinia heard them and came to say goodbye.

'I hope you didn't mind me butting in, my dear,' Jane said as she put her coat on.

'Not at all. Come anytime.'

'Cherish your mother, Lavinia. She's brave and honourable, rather rare qualities these days. Now, I really must be off.' And with that, Jane Percival bustled out. Pauline followed her out into the rain, and the two women had a brief, intense exchange.

Lavinia watched from the shelter of the front door. As Jane drove away, Pauline hustled back into the cottage; she was soaked. 'It's hammering down out there. Do you want to call the girls in?'

Lavinia didn't move. 'What was that about?'

Pauline sighed. 'It's a long story, Lavinia.'

'I've never met anyone that posh before.' Pauline nodded. 'Who is she?'

'A friend,' Pauline replied.

'Important?' Lavinia asked.

Pauline nodded and called the girls in from the back door.

Luna and Miriam ran in, scattering wet clothes and muddy boots in their wake. Pauline checked outside, then locked and bolted the back door before going and doing the same to the front door.

'Is that really necessary?' Lavinia asked.

Pauline sighed apologetically as the girls crowded into the small kitchen. 'Now, who wants homemade soup for lunch?' Pauline asked.

Miriam put her hand up. 'I don't like that green one.'

'Neither do I,' chimed Luna.

'You'll have what Grandma gives you if you want to come here for Christmas?' Lavinia interjected, smiling. Both girls jumped up and down and yelled that they did.

Pauline looked at Lavinia in surprise. 'You've decided?' Lavinia nodded. 'I thought you wanted to think it over?'

'I have.'

'Soup it is then,' Pauline announced, turning up the heat under a pan. In the corner of her eye, a sudden movement outside the kitchen window created a pulse of alarm but it was just the cat. Pauline sighed with relief, hoping against hope that she wouldn't have to see Jane again. Outside, the darkness was coming.

END